Stephanie Butland is the author of the beloved bookshop tale *Lost For Words*, *The Heart of Ailsa Rae* and *The Woman in the Photograph*. Her first two books were memoirs of her dance with cancer.

Praise for Lost For Words

'Quirky, clever and unputdownable'   **Katie Fforde**

'Beautifully written and atmospheric. Loveday is an endearing heroine, full of attitude and fragility. The haunting story of her past is brilliantly revealed'   **Tracy Rees**

'Loveday is a marvellous character and she captured my heart from the very first page . . . her bookshop is the book-shop of readers' dreams'   **Julie Cohen**

'Loveday is so spiky and likeable. I so loved Archie, Nathan and the book shop and the unfolding mystery' **Carys Bray**

'An exquisite story'   **Liz Fenwick**

'Intriguing and touching'   *Sunday Express*

'An appealing character with a fascinating hinterland'
                Daily Mail

'A beautiful book'   *Prima*

By Stephanie Butland

Found in a Bookshop
Nobody's Perfect
The Woman in the Photograph
The Curious Heart of Ailsa Rae
Lost For Words
The Other Half of My Heart
Letters To My Husband

Non-fiction

Thrive: The Bah! Guide to Wellness After cancer
How I Said Bah! to cancer

FOUND
IN A
BOOKSHOP

STEPHANIE BUTLAND

REVIEW

First published in Great Britain in 2023 by
HEADLINE REVIEW
An imprint of HEADLINE PUBLISHING GROUP

8

Cataloguing in Publication Data is available from the British Library

ISBN 978 1 4722 9181 3

Typeset in Baskerville by CC Book Production

Printed and bound in Great Britain by
Clays Ltd, Elcograf S.p.A.

Headline's policy is to use papers that are natural, renewable and recyclable
products and made from wood grown in well-managed forests and other
controlled sources. The logging and manufacturing processes are expected
to conform to the environmental regulations of the country of origin.

HEADLINE PUBLISHING GROUP
An Hachette UK Company
Carmelite House
50 Victoria Embankment
London EC4Y 0DZ

www.headline.co.uk
www.hachette.co.uk

for Eli

Before

/

'Welcome to the best bookshop there is,' Kelly says, although she's not sure you can welcome anyone to somewhere that's actually closed.

Craig puts his arms round her waist, tucks his head on to her shoulder. 'Hello, bookshop.'

It's ten o'clock on a Thursday evening in December and Kelly and Craig are somewhere between tipsy and giddy. Kelly isn't sure whether it's the mulled cider or the fact that, over dinner, they exchanged their first 'I love you's. York is full of pre-Christmas parties, but the cobbled street that is home to the Lost For Words bookshop is quiet.

Kelly loves working here. She gets to be herself; she gets to be an expert; she gets to meet people who care about books as much as she does.

Craig starts to sway her back and forth, and Kelly turns in his arms and rests her hands on his shoulders. They keep swaying. Their movement is not quite a dance, but it's harmony. Craig isn't usually one for public displays of affection – he says he's too old, though he's only thirty-seven – so

1

Kelly leans in. Enjoys. This is what it is to be a couple. This is what it is to be loved. And to love.

At the end of the street, a group carouses past. Craig pulls away. 'Your place?' he asks, and she nods. Maybe tonight he'll stay.

1

To a book lover, a bookshop is not a place in the world, but a world in itself.

You know.

You know what it is to open a door, and for the bell above it to chime, low and summoning.

You know how the smell of pages is in the air like smoke; you know how the sense of homecoming descends on you, whether you have ever truly had a home or not.

You know that somewhere in this place is a book that can give you what you are craving.

You know that books are safety and escape and wisdom and peace and the things that get you through. Whether they are showing you the best way to prepare mushroom soup, or breaking your heart with someone else's loss so you can better bear your own, or making you laugh when there is nothing funny in your life, or making you afraid so that real life seems less fearful.

You understand.

And so you understand, too, or can imagine, the strangeness

of an empty bookshop. It's been a sudden world, this one, where people can no longer pass a book from hand to hand and say, I think this could be just the thing you're looking for. Where booksellers – even the ones who like books more than people – cannot help but long for someone to come and interfere with their perfectly alphabetised shelves.

And where even the most beloved of bookshops might begin to struggle. Being filled with second-hand treasures of all kinds, books loved and passed along, is useless when there is no one to open the door, and inhale, and ask a question of the bookshop.

My mother wants to re-read something she remembers from school, but she doesn't know the title any more.

I've just finished my exams and I want to read a book that has nothing at all to do with wars or history.

I can't sleep. So I read. Where are the books that will make me feel surrounded, befriended, rather than as though I am the only person awake in the whole dark world?

It is easy to ask these questions, silently, when you're in a bookshop; easy to walk around the shelves, to touch spines and turn pages and think, are you the book I need?

It's sometimes straightforward to talk to a bookseller, to say, I want something light, or, I'm looking for a recommendation; and the bookseller will hear, beneath your words, I cannot bear how long the afternoons are, or, I don't know what my life is about any more.

But not if the bookshop door is closed.

Not if you are trying to explain, over the phone, what it is you need when what you need is for the bookshop to invite you in and let you know it's okay to wander, to touch, to mull.

Not if you don't know what you need, especially when the ache for a new book feels both trivial and privileged: when, if what to read is your only worry, then you shouldn't be worried at all.

Not if it seems that the whole world is lost for words.

2

Rosemary, 2020, Whitby

There is pain in the joints of Rosemary's fingers, but she can't seem to loosen her grip on the handle of her bag. Today has brought a sense of looming calamity that she fears might wash her away, a great invisible wave rending their cottage to rubble, ripping their plants from the ground, tipping them and every part of their long-joined life into the cold North Sea.

She closes her eyes, tight.

She just needs a minute. Just one.

She tells herself that nothing has actually happened. The doctor asked George a lot of questions and a nurse took some blood. That's all. Nothing to be concerned about.

Beside her, George fumbles the front door key into the lock. Rosemary notices her husband's shoulders sag in the second after the key slides home. She knows what that sag means. She has, after all, been next to George for all these years, since they first met in 1964. They have barely been apart since they retired from teaching in 2005, and never not together since the pandemic began. That shoulder sag means that her husband has just achieved something he thought was close to impossible. She remembers it from when they reached the summit of Scafell Pike, in the rain, shortly after they were engaged; when the school orchestra got through the whole of Tchaikovsky's March of the Nutcracker at the Christmas concert without disaster, the players within a bar of each other; the year they realised they'd finally dug all the Japanese knotweed out of the garden of their beloved Whitby cottage that overlooks the sea.

And now, George is so worn out he can barely open their own front door.

'Cup of tea in the garden, my girl?' he asks, once they are inside.

'I'll make it. You go on. Maybe have a look at the snap-dragons on the way.'

'Wilco.' George smiles at his wife the way he always has, and for a moment Rosemary wonders whether all could be well. Lots of people lose weight. All old men get up to go to the loo in the night, don't they?

The water boils, and Rosemary takes their old brown teapot from the shelf above the kettle; but then she puts it back, and goes instead to the cupboard where they keep their special-occasion crockery and glasses. She brings out the bone china teapot, painted with sweet peas, delicate and beautiful. They bought it as a fortieth anniversary present for themselves, at a craft fair in the grounds of Whitby Abbey in 2009. It usually comes out at Christmas and on birthdays. But they should use it more often. People are always saying that life is short; and Rosemary knows, in her heart, that they can no longer ignore the slow changes in George, or write them off as tiredness or the everyday sort of old age

7

that makes Rosemary lose her reading glasses every five minutes. That's why they went to see the doctor.

From the window, Rosemary watches George making his way down the garden. He's stopping to inspect their plants and beds as he goes. He seems slow; but then again, so is she. They will both be seventy-eight when autumn comes, she in May and he in August.

Rosemary pours the tea from the teapot into the flask, and tucks their tin mugs and the screw-top jar of milk into the basket that's easier than a tray. She knows that by the time she joins him, he will not only have checked the snapdragons for rust, but noticed other jobs: a prune here, some water there, a place where they need to lay down used tealeaves to keep the slugs away from tender growth.

She's right. When she sits down next to him on the old, warm wood of their bench, he says, 'I need to get that honeysuckle cut back, or the jasmine will never get through.' It's as though this is any sunny, late spring afternoon since they retired.

Rosemary pours their tea. She hands him the mug and notices how his fingers are cold to the touch.

'I forgot the blanket,' she says, 'silly old brain.'

'No matter,' George answers. And then, as though he's commenting on a story in the newspaper: 'All this time we've kept ourselves safe from Covid, and we were looking the wrong way.'

Rosemary wants to say that nothing is certain yet: the doctor only said he needed to do some tests, maybe refer them to the hospital, depending. But she finds she can't speak. George is right. They've worried about whether their shopping delivery would have everything they needed in it, because they haven't been going to the shops, and there's no one across the fence to ask for help. The rest of this little row of houses are holiday cottages now, their old neighbours all having sold up and moved on years ago, and this last year has been so very quiet, without new holidaymakers week in, week out. The only places George and Rosemary really venture to are the doctor's surgery or the pharmacy, where Rosemary makes sure the young man sanitises his hands before passing their bag of prescription medicines across.

She looks out over the sea.

George proposed to her, more than five decades ago, as they walked along the promenade at Whitby. Being able to sit here and watch the wind move across the same water is part of what helps Rosemary to know that, for all of the ageing and the aching, they still belong in this, their precious world. They have always said it's hard to imagine anything better than sitting here. She takes a breath, pulls it down deep. Come on, Rosemary. Don't get soft now. You've no need to feel sorry for yourself. You've already had more than some people will ever get.

The clouds are slow, the sun steady, the wind slight. It's almost impossible to think that the world is in crisis, and that they, George and Rosemary Athey, married since 1969 and all each other has, could be starting to fail.

Here, on this bench, which has been in this garden for as long as they have lived here, their life is what it has been for the thirty-three years since they bought this little old cottage with its long strip of garden. Over the decades they've restored their home, mended it, made it beautiful, kept it going; and now, like them, it's declining. The back window blows open in the night and the radiators bang and rattle like nobody's business. They haven't bothered with the greenhouse for the last couple of years, buying tomatoes and lettuce from the market instead, something that would have been unthinkable when they first moved in. Then, they had started turning over the soil ready to plant potatoes before they'd even made their bed.

But when they're sitting on the bench, gazing across the water, their overgrowing garden and the tired paint on the back door are behind them. Nothing has been able to worry them, here. Not even on their worst days. This old bench is where they have come to be content, to rest, to make peace.

'You'll be all right, my girl,' George says.

'What do you mean?'

He takes her hand, but he's looking out to sea. 'When I'm gone. You'll be all right.'

A great sob breaks from her, surprising them both. Rosemary has never been a crier.

'I won't,' she says, and she knows she sounds like one of any of the thousands of petulant children she encountered in her long teaching career. George says nothing, but his fingers squeeze hers. 'And anyway, you're going to be fine.'

He nods, and she feels relieved. But then he says, quietly, 'Not for ever, though, eh?'

Bedtime. George is reading a history book that he borrowed from the library before lockdown; it smells of someone else's pipe smoke. Rosemary cannot manage non-fiction before sleep, so she's on an Agatha Christie. She's sure she's read

10

it before, but it doesn't matter. She just needs three pages before she drops off. Most nights, anyway.

'I was thinking,' George says, a few minutes later, closing his book.

'Be careful you don't hurt yourself,' Rosemary answers. It's an old joke. He smiles.

'All those books we gave away. When we thought we were old.'

Rosemary laughs. 'Yes.' It was when they turned seventy, eight years ago. They had decided to donate their small, beloved home library to the school where Rosemary had begun her teaching career and George had become Head of Maths. They had wanted to be sure that, when they died, their carefully kept books would be well looked after. And schools don't have much money for books any more.

'Do you remember how we used to read to each other?'

Rosemary, propped against her pillows, sits very still. Suddenly she's warm, all the way through. Once, they had bought books one at a time, and read aloud so they would experience the pleasure of the pages, the first time, together. She's not sure when they stopped. When they got too busy, she supposes. Or when owning a book became less of a luxury.

'I remember,' she says.

She thinks of the second-hand bookshop they used to visit when they went on day trips to York, and wonders if it's still there.

3

George, 1964

The first day at school as a teacher seems to be just as awful as the first day at school as a pupil. George is well prepared for his lessons: he's spent the summer going over his training notes, making lesson plans, and trying not to fret himself to insanity when he thinks about whether he can really be a teacher, at the age of twenty-two. He has no idea how he will find the authority to teach children not much younger than he is. He tells himself he's qualified: he knows that, when it comes to it, it will work, the way it did when he did his teaching practice. But approaching the shining new secondary modern school in Harrogate in the autumn of 1964, he feels like a nervous boy. And entering the staffroom, which is smoke-filled and bursting with the chatter of people who already know each other, doesn't make him any more comfortable.

He puts his bag down next to a chair that seems unoccupied and hopes no one will notice him. He isn't sure his voice will work if he tries to speak. Not a good start to his teaching career.

And then Rosemary walks in.

George is so nervous – only fifteen minutes to the first bell, now – that the fact he falls instantly and fully in love with her almost passes him by.

There is just something about her. He's never seen anyone so precisely themselves. In that first instant, with her looking around the staffroom and him spooning coffee into a mug, it's as though he sees all of her. Her kindness, her seriousness, and the fact that she will understand him. George is a mathematician. He doesn't think like this. And yet. He smiles and gives a wave; everyone else is too busy catching up with their old colleagues to spot the new ones. Rosemary notices George's wave, as though this is the signal she has been waiting for, and makes her way across the room to him.

'George Athey,' he says as he holds out a hand. 'New starter.'

'Rosemary Bell,' she replies, shaking his hand. 'Me too.'

Before they can get any further, they are swept up by their respective department heads and taken to their classrooms.

They don't exactly decide to sit together every lunchtime, but it happens. George is quiet to begin with, because he cannot balance small talk with the overwhelming feeling of rightness that comes over him when Rosemary is there. So he asks her how her morning has been, and he listens to her excitement about being a real teacher, in a real classroom, with real pupils of her own, at last.

And they make the chairs near the door in the staffroom theirs, as though they have chosen them; as though the other teachers have not deliberately sat further into the room, where they are not vulnerable to answering the knocks of pupils sent with messages, tales, or reports of wrongdoing. But George and Rosemary are happy there. Most days, George brings a sandwich, and sometimes an apple. Rosemary soon starts to bring a second piece of cake with her lunch. After they eat it, she carefully flattens, folds, and saves the greaseproof paper it comes in, to reuse. Something in him knows that she will do this always. And their life together will prove him right.

4

Kelly

Kelly's walk to work is beautiful, the perfect commute: her route takes her along the River Ouse and over the Lendal Bridge into the old city of York.

It's become the best part of her day.

She has noticed that she's no longer full of excitement at the thought of being in the bookshop, which is no longer a busy, lively place, where time rushes along. Kelly worked in a pub to finance her first degree and as a care assistant to get her through her Masters. Working at Lost For Words was supposed to be the thing that kept her going through her PhD, but rapidly became the place she goes to escape it. She took the job almost four years ago, and until the pandemic hit she had never been happier working anywhere.

Now things don't feel so good. The money through the till – from internet orders, customers phoning in, and the occasional passer-by stopping at their improvised book-buying hatch, a table across the recessed doorway to the shop – has amounted to less than Kelly's part-time salary. Loveday, her boss, can't be taking a wage, and heaven only knows how she is covering the other shop costs. Kelly is aware that Loveday inherited the bookshop, and her home, from the previous owner of Lost For Words, but it doesn't automatically follow that she can underwrite the shop costs for ever. Or would want to, come to that.

Every day now Kelly takes her beautiful walk to work while wondering if this is going to be the day Loveday lets her go. And then she would be all alone, in her little flat that her dad helps her pay the mortgage on even though she's thirty. All day, every day, it will be just her and her stalled PhD on writer-wives, writer-mothers, writer-sisters and writer-mistresses, lost in the shadow of the lauded men they sacrificed their own talents for. And she supposes she'll have to find a way to count herself lucky so long as she and Dad stay well. At least she has her funny, sweet, loving Craig, even if she hasn't seen him in the two long months since lockdown began.

When Kelly gets to the bridge, she leans over the cold metal railing and watches the water flow. York is so quiet that she can hear its rushing wetness that makes the soles of her feet prickle with longing to walk in the Whitby sea.

Her phone buzzes in her pocket. It will be Craig, checking in as he does every morning. Her relationship with him is something else the pandemic has sucked the joy from, although to complain seems wrong, given the state of the world. They met the previous October, via a dating app, and had seen each other a couple of times a week since. From the beginning, Craig was funny and caring, and didn't mind a bit that she wanted to take things slowly – not even when she told him she was going to Whitby to be with her father for two weeks over Christmas and New Year. But despite

Kelly's caution, Craig had edged his way into her heart. She cannot remember when she began to love him, though she often thinks of the evening she first said so. When he texted her at midnight on New Year's Eve with the words, Happy New Year. I want you to spend every moment of this year knowing that I love you, she had felt a deep sense of rightness. Something in her had relaxed. She knew he was the one.

When lockdown loomed, they had talked about moving in together. Kelly had spent a long time getting used to living alone, but could never quite love it, despite the pleasure of being able to read, uninterrupted, for a whole weekend, or sleep on the sofa when the day working on her PhD in bed meant that her duvet was swamped by carefully sorted piles of research that she didn't want to have to move. She had told him she thought they should try living together, even if it meant they were moving a little faster than they might in a non-pandemic world. Craig said he felt the same way, but then, just when Kelly had made space in the wardrobe, he changed his mind. It wasn't that he didn't love her, he'd said, his voice down the phone sounding muffled with emotion. It was that he was afraid of ruining a good thing. She was too precious to him to risk. Of course, she couldn't be angry, especially as she knew that rushing into commitment after an accidental pregnancy had done for a previous relationship of his.

Morning, says the message in her WhatsApp, followed by a heart.

She sends a heart back, then adds, Talk?

CRAIG:
Gimme 5, I'll call you. Early meeting just ending.

17

Kelly leans against the bridge; she tips her head back and looks at the May-blue sky. The river seems even more present when she can only hear it. Now that the Lost For Words bookshop isn't open to the public, Loveday is even less concerned than before about Kelly's timekeeping. She'd told her at her interview that she had no intention of interfering with Kelly's running of the shop and, though it had sounded almost like a threat or a warning, it was bliss to Kelly. If she stood here and talked to Craig for half an hour, she's pretty sure Loveday wouldn't mind.

'Hey,' she says when he calls back, five minutes later. He's always true to his word.

'Hey. Is everything okay?'

She can hear his footsteps, slapping along a pavement. It's so long since he last ran up the stairs to her flat, kissed her nose, felt her bum. 'Where are you?'

'Just nipping out to get some shopping. I've got calls all day and I'm nearly out of coffee. Danger zone.'

Her phone pings with an image: a piece of paper that reads 'coffee, pears, newspaper', and Craig's blunt thumb and clean, flat-clipped fingernail in the bottom corner. Kelly wants to kiss it.

'You wrote a shopping list for three things?'

'I know, right?' She loves how he laughs at the end of sentences. Loves pretty much everything about him, really. 'So, what's up?'

'I don't know,' she says, and suddenly she couldn't care less about the river or the sky or the silence, 'I'm just – I'm on my way to work and I just wish I knew what was going to happen.'

There's the sound of a pedestrian crossing beeping

permission, and then Craig says, 'Why don't you ask? Your boss with the funny name, why not ask her what's going on?'

'She'd tell me if she knew, wouldn't she? And nobody knows what's going to happen.'

'You're not asking her to predict the course of a global pandemic, love. You want to know if you're still going to have a job.'

Oh, that 'love'. She would put it in her pocket if she could. It's hard to remember how life was, before Craig.

'I know. But I don't want to be extra pressure. You know? She's got a lot on her plate. I don't want to be a problem.'

'But you're worried. That matters.'

'I know.'

'You don't sound convinced.'

Kelly laughs. 'I'm not.'

'If you know what you want, you can ask for it.'

'I want to know if my job's safe. I want to go and see my dad. And I want you to come round with a takeaway, and stay the night,' she says.

5

Jenny

The women, when they first arrive at the shelter, all have expressions that are 50 percent cannot-believe-they-have-got-away gladness and 50 percent cannot-believe-they-have-got-away terrified. This woman, Jenny, is no different. She cradles her child, a three-year-old called Milo. He's still subdued, as the children often are. It's only been a few hours since they entered a place where they are not yet certain they are safe.

Carmen is the volunteer showing Jenny round. The shelter staff have done the paperwork and settled her into her room. It was the room that Carmen was given when she got away from her marriage, almost five years ago, and she remembers the feeling of lying in bed that first night and daring to think that she might be safe. It's a white-painted room on the third floor, with heavy grey velvet curtains, donated by a hotel and altered to fit by volunteers. They are perfect for deadening the night sounds that can make some women start awake. There's a painting of flowers on the wall, yellow cushions on the bed, and the child's bed has bright yellow bedding. Carmen was the one who put the welcome pack together while Jenny talked to the staff, and another volunteer entertained Milo within Jenny's line of sight.

In the walk-in donations cupboard, Carmen had gathered the usual things: a three-pack of knickers still in the packet, a bar of chocolate, toothbrush and toothpaste, a full-sized bottle of shower gel and another of shampoo. Hotels often donate miniature toiletries, but Carmen thinks it's better to give the big bottles. She doesn't want any woman who comes here to think she is safe only for as long as a two-shower bottle of body wash lasts. Then she took clean towels and pyjamas from the drawers. They're not new, but they're something, and once Jenny has got settled then one of the other volunteers will help her with clothes from their wardrobe room. It's something Carmen would like to be able to do one day, but she needs to go on the training first. Many of the women who have come to them from an abusive relationship have lost their sense of what they are, or haven't been allowed to choose their own clothes. They simply do not know how they want to look, and it takes both gentleness and expertise to help them. For Milo, Carmen took a colouring book and pack of crayons. Jenny will be able to choose what he needs from their children's storeroom; but most mothers arrive with the things that their children need to be comfortable, even if they themselves have nothing.

Carmen has made sure to deliver the things she has collected to Jenny's room while Jenny is still in the office. The fewer unexpected knocks at the door while someone new is settling in, the better. Then she goes to meet Jenny and show her around.

'This is your home for as long as you need it to be,' she says, and Jenny nods. Carmen makes sure to look at her with utter neutrality; she has been trained in this, so she keeps her eyes away from the bruises at the clavicle and throat, the steri-strips stretched across the cut skin on Jenny's bruised and swollen cheekbone. Instead she keeps intermittent eye contact, and talks quietly. A slammed door can be enough to trigger panic in any of the women who come here; and panic can be enough, too, to send them home, however terrible home might be. In a frightened state, familiarity can matter more than safety.

Carmen walks Jenny from room to room. Every step seems to take an unrepeatable, unsustainable amount of effort. Jenny is carrying Milo, asleep now as though he is a little leopard and his mother a tree. His dangling limbs sway when Jenny moves. Carmen knows better than to offer to carry him.

She shows Jenny the way the security works. Here's a camera that overlooks the gate and another that covers the main doorway, monitored twenty-four hours a day and filmed, the recordings all kept and stored securely off-site. She talks her through the panic button locations, and makes sure Jenny remembers the safe word she has chosen to use at any time if she doesn't feel comfortable. Carmen takes her to the visitors' room and Jenny shakes her head, as if to say, there's no one who I will want to see.

'If you come through here,' Carmen says, 'you'll find the living room.' It's the room she liked best when she first came here. It feels a bit less institutional than the rest of the place; it's big enough for the locks, operated from inside, and the posters about safety and benefits, to be diffused

22

by the everydayness of worn sofas and overflowing toy boxes.

Leanna, who has been here for two weeks, is flicking through a magazine, sitting in a bean bag which faces the door. She flinches when the door lock unclicks, but there's no longer a terrified look on her face.

'Leanna, this is Jenny. She's just arrived,' Carmen says. Leanna says hello, and when Jenny doesn't respond, she nods and goes back to her reading. Carmen knows from experience that most of the women here are patient with each other, and can find it easier to be kind to others than to themselves.

The living room is a long space, with a window at both ends, making it light and bright, though reassuringly high walls are visible to anyone who looks out. There's a playmat for the tinies, a box of cars, another of Lego, another of cuddly toys and dolls. Board games are stacked on a shelf. Although nothing is new, everything is cared for; the women who come here keep it clean and tidy, and Carmen hopes it's because they feel at home, and not because they fear retribution if they leave a mug out of place.

'At the moment,' Carmen says, 'because of Covid, we ask you to book a session. The rules mean we can only allow two women or families at a time, and we ask that you keep your distance. When your session ends, you can put everything you've used in the box by the door so we can either clean it or quarantine it for three days before we put it back into circulation. When things get a bit more normal we'll be able to have yoga and meditation classes in here again.'

But she can see that Jenny has stopped listening. She's looking beyond the sofas and the coffee table to the bookcase next to the TV. It's well stocked, thanks to Sarah-Jane, one of their volunteers, who also runs cookery classes, and whose daughter has a bookshop. There are classic novels, books about nature and travel, history books, great fat beach reads, mysteries and science fiction. No crime, or at least nothing grittier than an Agatha Christie.

Jenny shifts Milo in her arms, looks Carmen fully in the face for the first time, and starts to cry. 'I didn't think there would be books here,' she says.

('Something I would like us to think about,' the therapist Jenny sees at the refuge will insist, gently, at one of her counselling sessions, 'is that you were not to blame. It was not your job to understand what David was and run away. It was David's job not to trap you and not to hurt you.'

And, after a lot of talking, Jenny will agree that none of this was her fault. Her mind will have understood it, by then; but her gut will remain a breeding ground for the reasons why she made it happen, for years to come. Perhaps for ever.)

6

Loveday

Loveday used to love the reading refuge she had made,
upstairs at the Lost For Words bookshop, after the fire that
almost put an end to it, and led to the death of her beloved
old boss, Archie. When she had learned he had left both
the business and his home to her, she'd been overwhelmed;
and then the work began. She knew she would never be
able to make a bookshop that was better than the one that
had gone before, because that could never be.

Instead Loveday had, with the help of her boyfriend
Nathan and her mother, created something that she hoped
was just as good, in a different way. Part of that was the
reading refuge, designed to be a place where anyone who
needed peace could come. They could read, or sleep, or talk
about nothing, or talk about everything. Loveday's mother,
Sarah-Jane, who used to volunteer in a women's shelter
before the pandemic, had a good instinct for who could
do with a leaflet about what help was available to them, or
a calm and quiet shoulder to cry on. There was a mobile
phone there for anyone who needed to make a call when

their own phone might be being monitored or tracked. After some experimenting with providing tea and coffee, Loveday had set up a tab with the cafe next door, and she or Sarah-Jane would go and fetch drinks for anyone who wanted to stay for a while.

Although Loveday had made it her business not to get involved with anyone who came – she isn't the good listener that her mother is – she has taken quiet pride in a place that she hopes teenagers like the one she was would find. Archie had folded her into his world with grace and kindness, but those things came naturally to him. Loveday's resources are buried deep and feel as though they could run out at any second. So her way of caring is the reading refuge. Whenever her mother has told her, without ever naming names, that a woman she spoke to here made a call to a helpline and got herself to a shelter, or even called the police, Loveday knows she is doing the right things.

But now the reading refuge has the coldness that spaces without purpose develop even when the air is warm. Loveday forces herself to work up there when Kelly is downstairs, to try to keep an appropriate distance. She loves it when Nathan comes in to help with something, and they fill the refuge with real live talking as they work, and he makes Kelly laugh as he talks to her downstairs.

But here's what's really bothering Loveday: an unused refuge, coupled with a bookshop down on its luck even before the pandemic began, might not survive for much longer.

When Kelly arrives, Nathan goes next door for coffee and cinnamon buns. Richard Morris took over the cafe two years ago and turned it into something far superior to the chintzy, cutesy place it was before. Loveday sometimes misses the possibility of being able to order only tea or coffee, without the infinite variations now available. But if she finds herself tempted to be churlish she thinks of the cinnamon buns. Fresh and, if you're lucky, warm. The perfect balance of sweet and salt, softness and crunch. And just that little bit too big: no point in leaving a tiny bit.

The three of them settle into the reading refuge, at safe distances: Kelly in the armchair, Loveday at the furthest end of the sofa from her, Nathan on the floor, his head against her knees.

Now so many taken-for-granted small pleasures have vanished – a film at the cinema, a haircut, a drive to the coast on Sunday afternoon, chips on the seafront and choosing a pebble from the beach to take home – the buns have taken on a significance they could never have had before.

Loveday, who fears she might be full before she gets to the best, most cinnamon-ish bit in the middle, chomps through from one side to the other. Nathan eats so fast that it's hard to imagine he isn't just swallowing the bun whole. Kelly has a technique for the buns – peeling away the outside of the swirl and eating the slowly unfurling ribbon of dough. But today, she has picked off an edge and is holding it between her fingers, looking at it as though it's a button she has found on the floor.

'Kelly, are you okay?' Nathan asks.

Kelly glances up, hesitation on her face. She shrugs and says, 'Just trying not to get fatter.'

'We're all getting fatter,' Nathan says. 'If that's the worst thing that happens to us in a pandemic then it's good with me.'

If Loveday had said that, it would have sounded like an insult or a dig, but Kelly gives half a laugh and says, 'Fair point.' She still doesn't start to eat.

Loveday takes a breath. 'We need to talk about how the bookshop is doing,' she says.

Kelly puts down her bun. 'I've been worrying about my job.' She says it as though it's a reply, which of course it is.

'I should have talked to you about it before. I've just been – there's been a lot.' She thinks about how Nathan says there's no such thing as too much information. Loveday doesn't agree, of course, except when it comes to old encyclopaedias, which she would establish a separate bookshop for if she could. But she can see it helps when it comes to things that directly impact you. 'I suppose I've been hoping for things to get better.'

At the beginning, it had seemed as though there might be a hiatus on normality for maybe a month or so, and then a burst of book-starved spending when doors could open. She and Nathan and Kelly had agreed on the inevitability of it. They had tidied and reordered and taken stock in readiness. But it soon became clear that selling two or three books a day might be their new normal in the pandemic world's new normal. Kelly sent a press release to the local newspapers about the bookshop doors being closed but the booksellers being ready to post or deliver to the doorstep. It hadn't made a lot of difference.

'Are you going to have to sack me?'

'No!' Loveday's stomach lurches at the thought of it; but also at the knowledge that it might come to that. She adds, more calmly, 'I didn't want to talk about letting you go, Kelly. I wanted to talk about how we get through this.

You know.' She finds herself gesturing, as though scooping inspiration out of the air towards her. 'Ideas.'

'I was thinking,' Nathan says, 'about a poetry competition. Run by the bookshop. Either with a theme or just – how you're feeling.'

Loveday smiles. She doesn't much bother with poetry now. There was a time when writing poetry had felt as though it saved her; and saying the worst things about her life, out loud, at the poetry night Nathan runs, had been the moment when she had, at last, been able to make a kind of peace with her past. Now, she loves to read poetry, or listen to it, but she's said all she needs to say. Nathan, though, can work it into anything. 'Online?'

Nathan grimaces. 'I think people are starting to get fed up of online? I mean, it's great, but you can see from people's faces when you log on to things – even good things – that they're sick of looking at a screen. And so many people just keep their cameras off, so you don't know if they're even listening. They could email their poems to us, or send them in.'

Kelly sighs, and puts her half-drunk coffee in the bin. Loveday knows that Nathan will take the cup out, wash it up and recycle it. 'How would it make money?'

Nathan laughs. 'Fair point.' It looks as though he's about to come up with something else, but he just tears open the bag his bun came in and runs his finger across the inside, collecting the caramelised sugar into a pile before tipping it into his mouth. He and his sister, Vanessa, who moved in with them for lockdown, have dedicated themselves to entertaining the people in the streets nearby, teaching juggling from the pavements and bellowing jokes through a couple of megaphones they found in the shed and painted bright

29

yellow. Vanessa is a hairdresser, usually working in film, so she has very little to do until the industry starts up again. Loveday imagines that, in Vanessa's position, she would have been afraid of losing her livelihood; but Vanessa has settled in to wait for things to change. She and Nathan seem genetically incapable of anxiety. Loveday tries very hard not to envy them, and the way they can find joy for themselves and others so lightly. The two of them share an easy-going brightness of spirit, an ability to find good in everything. It's a knack Loveday knows she will never acquire. But being close to them, it's a little infectious. (Vanessa has offered to cut Loveday's hair, but Loveday feels as though that would be cheating, somehow, when hairdressers are closed; so she cuts her hair the way she always does, putting it in a ponytail and taking off the bottom inch with the kitchen scissors.)

'We can't close,' Loveday says, in a way that makes both Kelly and Nathan look at her, and Nathan put his hand on her knee and squeeze. 'Archie left me this shop. I can't fail.'

'We can't fail,' says Kelly, then adds, 'I could take a pay cut.'

'No, you couldn't.' Loveday shakes her head, instantly dismissing the possibility, and a glance at Kelly tells her that she is both reassured and afraid. 'I mean, I'm not going to let you work for nothing, but the shop can't do without you.'

'Are you sure?'

'I'm sure,' Loveday says, but then adds, 'as I can be.' Because if she needs to close the shop altogether there'll be no job for Kelly. But she can't say that, not yet. Partly for Kelly's peace of mind. Mostly for herself.

Nathan squeezes her knee again. 'Even Archie wouldn't have predicted a global pandemic,' he says, 'though he would probably turn out to have known the people who discover the vaccine, when they do.'

Loveday smiles. Not so much at the idea of a vaccine – why hope before you have to – as at the thought of Archie. He was the best-connected bookseller in the land, or the one with the best stories. It doesn't matter which, as far as Loveday is concerned. She just misses him.

'Archie would have found a way to make money.'

Nathan reaches for Loveday and pulls a chocolate coin from behind her ear. Loveday laughs. Nathan flicks another chocolate coin through the air to Kelly. 'Sorry I can't get close enough to magic it,' he says.

'I'll take it,' Kelly says.

'Archie would have put money in,' Nathan says, his tone gentle. 'That's not the same as making it.'

'I suppose so.' Archie was rich-rich, or at least always had money in the bank. Loveday, now that she owns his house, is asset-rich. But she used to rely on her wage, when she took one; she and Nathan live like any other couple, budgeting and talking about what they'll do when they have money to spare. They live in a lovely big house, but it comes with big bills to match.

'I've been thinking of what we can do,' Kelly says, 'and talking about it with Craig. Apart from a better website, there wasn't a lot we could come up with. Social media.' She pulls a face, to show Loveday that she knows it's an idea that her boss will be less than enthusiastic about.

Loveday nods. 'You're right. But it's not really us, is it? And I don't know where we'd start, with getting everything online.' Lost For Words has always been a pop-in, give-us-a-call bookshop. Their website has first editions, rare finds, and the kinds of things collectors might be looking for. Loveday set it up, a long time ago, and she knows what a lot of work went into it. To catalogue and list everything they have in the shop on the website would be both impossible and impractical.

Kelly says, 'I suppose we just keep being good to the customers we have, and hope this doesn't go on for too much longer.'

Nathan takes Loveday's cup from her, and retrieves Kelly's from the bin. 'I thought I might take a look at the bit out the back. Maybe we can do something with it.'

The unloved yard is the least of Loveday's worries. When the bookshop was rebuilt after the fire, the ramshackle staffroom at the rear became smaller and better organised, the fire escape obvious and always clear, and the area outside less of a hotch-potch of added-on walls and leftover crates and broken shelves. So it's better than it was, she supposes. She has no more energy for it than this.

Kelly gets up, sighs and stretches. Loveday knows she should say something extra, something reassuring, but all she can manage is, 'Thanks, Kelly.'

'I'm going to get on,' Kelly says. Loveday almost asks what with, but she realises that she never asks in a non-pandemic scenario, so she should let her manager be.

'What are you thinking? About the yard?' Loveday asks Nathan.

He shrugs. 'Well, if it's tidy, you could sit outside for your lunch breaks.'

Fresh Air And Sunlight is a frequent theme of conversations in their home. Nathan and Vanessa were brought up to be dyed-in-the-wool outdoor enthusiasts, always ready for a bike ride or a picnic. Loveday's mother, Sarah-Jane, has her own reasons for loving being outdoors, and was making the garden at home her lockdown project, before long Covid made even half an hour of pruning or weeding too much. Loveday isn't really keen on outdoors for outdoors' sake. She is happy to ride her bike in order to get somewhere, and she's all for a day of walking around a beloved place, or somewhere that has a point. A point being history, or a view, or a connection with a book. When this is over, Nathan has promised her, they will go to Stoneleigh, Jane Austen's inspiration for Sotherton in *Mansfield Park*, and get up to no good in the ha-ha. They both have the same quote from *Mansfield Park* tattooed around their left wrists: 'Every moment has its pleasures and its hope.' Nathan's tattoo is in Loveday's handwriting, Loveday's in Nathan's.

And when frivolity is allowed again, and her mother is better, Loveday cannot wait for them to visit Whitby together. Ah, their beloved sea.

But outside for the sake of it, you can keep. Except that if clearing the area outside makes Nathan happy, Loveday's all for it.

At the beginning, the pandemic had seemed distant, as though it was in a book Loveday was reading – scary when you gave it your attention, but easy to put aside and leave alone for a while.

Then it all became real: first Loveday's mother came down with Covid, then Kelly's father was told to shield because of his emphysema. The bookshop's financial problems were amplified by the absence of passing trade and regulars coming in for a chat. That's small beer compared to their own losses – and to all of the other deaths, grief almost tangible in the 5 p.m. air sometimes, in the minutes after the latest figures are announced. But the days when a customer-free shop was a pleasure belong to a long-gone world.

Nathan often says there's no point in worrying about things you can't control, and of course he's right. But Loveday thinks, often, of the women she doesn't know the names of, who used to come upstairs and sit in the reading refuge. She doesn't know where they are, or what they are dealing with. She looks at Jane Austen's words inked on her wrist, and hopes that they are safe. Hope doesn't feel like enough but she doesn't know what else she can do.

7

Kelly

Kelly arrives early the next morning. She and Craig were up late, talking over WhatsApp, but instead of it making her tired it had make her feel happy, excited, alive.

He'd asked her about her research. She tried to brush the conversation away: but when she said, 'It's too boring, you don't want to hear about that', Craig had laughed and said she was never boring, and anyway, he had just about got to the end of Netflix, so she was now his best bet for entertainment. 'I've asked you about it before', he'd said, 'and you always try to tell me that I won't be interested. You must know by now that I'm interested in absolutely everything about you.' Sometimes when he talks like this, he sounds as though he might cry, and Kelly's throat aches with the happiness of being so completely seen. She has never really been able to be all of herself with a man before; even her clever boyfriends at university had needed to be cleverer than her. But Craig isn't like that. He just – well, he loves her. This is what it's like.

So, she had begun to explain. And before Kelly had

known it, it was after 1 a.m., three hours later than she usually stayed up, because she hates the feeling of being alone in the night. But she hadn't minded the lateness as she tucked into bed, Craig's voice still clinging to her skin. And she had slept, deeply, and woken before her alarm, to a message from Craig saying simply, I don't know how much longer I can manage without seeing you.

Me neither, she'd replied.

She steps through the door of Lost For Words. She's the first one here, Nathan and Loveday having taken a morning off. Nathan runs a weekly open mic poetry night, which moved online with the pandemic; he's told Kelly that he makes Loveday breakfast in bed the morning after, for old times' sake, something that Kelly thinks might be too much information, but who can tell, in a lockdown?

There's a letter on the mat. The envelope is crisp and blue. It's addressed to the shop, not to Loveday, or even Archie – who still regularly receives postcards and parcels from all over the world. So Kelly opens it, and she reads:

Dear Lost For Words,
Once upon a time we were regular customers of yours. When we were seventy, we stopped buying books and donated the ones we had, and we started using the library more. Now we are trying to stay at home, and our library is closed.

I am enclosing a cheque for £100 and I hope that you will use it to send us some books. I thought perhaps you could send one every ten days or so? We like to read aloud, and our eyes are getting old, so if you have large-print or hardbacked books they would be best.

I suppose I ought to send you a list of books we would like

to read, but it's hard to know. I have one request: *Persuasion*, by Jane Austen, my favourite book of all time.

Please send us books that we might think are wonderful. (Is that unfair? I think it may be.) We love nature, and things that make us laugh, and old-fashioned romances. We believe in good food and fresh air and the smell of the sea. We spent our careers as teachers and we don't have any family of our own. We do crosswords in the evening and our garden is our pride and joy.

I'm not sure how far £100 will go, but I'm hoping it will keep us in books for a few weeks. Please let me know when it's running out.

Kind regards,

Rosemary Athey (Mrs)

Enc. Cheque

8

We know the power of a book. Let's not forget the power of a letter. It's doing the same thing as our beloved books, only in a more specific way. It is taking feelings, knowledge, requests and hopes, and transferring them to paper. And then that paper conveys the feelings, knowledge, requests and hopes, and unfolds them in front of someone else. No wonder people who love books also love letters.

Look at Kelly, standing in the doorway of her beloved bookshop.

All she has in her hand is a pale blue sheet of writing paper, but from that, she is conjuring a world. She sees a woman who looks like her own grandmother; she smells scones, or maybe fresh bread. Kelly is imagining a garden that is tumbling with flowers, a trug on the garden step. She sees a bird-bath, raspberries growing up canes, a lean-to with a wheelbarrow outside it. A distant man, in her imagination, is whistling as he digs.

All this, from a letter.

And more.

Kelly imagines packing up her library and taking it to a school. She can see how kids like her, the studious kids, will get excited, and the kids who consider reading a punishment and learning a chore will use the library as a cover for flirting and joking and picking on the studious kids. It could be worse.

And Kelly, without noticing she is doing it, presses the letter to her body and closes her eyes. She'll find the copy of *Persuasion* with the largest, clearest type, and pack it up ready to go to the post office this afternoon. And then she'll call her dad, even though it's not one of their days for talking.

9

Jenny

Jenny has been back through the history of her marriage time and again, and wondered when she should have realised what David was. Or maybe – and it will take her a long time to see beyond this – what she did that made David into what he was.

Like all relationships, it started well. David was the manager in the estate agency that handled the purchase of Jenny's flat. He always chatted to her when she came in, and called to check that all was well a week after she had got the keys. It had begun as a formal conversation, but Jenny – not lonely, exactly, but unused to being alone after years in student halls and, later, flat-shares – had relaxed into talking about her wider life. She'd told him about her job as a primary school teacher, and her plans for the flat. When, at the end of the call, David had said, slightly hesitantly, 'I've really enjoyed talking to you and I wonder if you'd like to meet for a coffee sometime', he had sounded unsure, vulnerable, and she had remembered how they always smiled at each other in the estate agency office, and said she would like that very much.

But maybe he hadn't been what he became, then. It had seemed natural.

And David, the outside-work-David she met for a coffee that weekend, was a relaxed version of his work self. He was attentive and funny, considerate and kind. He spent more time listening than talking and he didn't forget anything she told him; whenever they met, after that first coffee, he would start by picking up a strand of their last conversation and asking her about it. (How did the parents' evening go? Had she got to the bottom of the odd noise in the kitchen?) So their weekend coffees became more like one long conversation.

Then he asked if she would have dinner with him, 'like a proper date', and she'd said yes with some relief, because she was starting to wonder whether what they were doing was becoming friends, and she had misunderstood his intent when he asked her out the first time. At the end of that evening – a pub, cosy in the rain, cider and chicken pies and sticky toffee pudding with two spoons – he called a cab for her on his Uber account and she was a little bit sorry that he hadn't wanted to walk her home. The next day he sent her flowers. They were a blaze of hope and colour in the drab living room she couldn't afford to decorate.

But now, she wonders, was it odd that he used her address without checking it was okay with her first? Of course, he knew where she lived, and it would have been ridiculous to pretend otherwise. But she wasn't sure he would know the addresses and postcodes of every property around York he'd had a hand in selling.

She had no idea, back then, of how these things worked. She thought that controlling men, violent men, happened to women who were, in some way, pre-broken. Not that it was the women's fault. But Jenny thought that there had to be something about them. Maybe they were poor – not in the first-few-months-of-a-mortgage way that she was, but properly, anxiously, anything-for-a-meal poor. Or they'd had their hearts broken, recently, and it was as though the flesh of their sad, rejected bodies gave off a signal that attracted men who liked their women temporarily weakened. Or in their past there was a vicious father or an abusive stepfather or a mother who thought that a woman's value was only in being loved by a man, and it didn't matter much which man or what he did once you'd got him.

Jenny had not been any of these things. She was a teacher. She was self-sufficient. Her parents, living and in good health and devoted to each other, had always let her know that she was loved and special and that she could always rely on them. They'd bailed her out, once or twice, the usual teenage scrapes of being drunk and stranded and needing a lift home at 3 a.m., some first-year-at-uni credit card debt, a place to stay when she split up with her uni boyfriend and all of her plans fell through as a consequence. She got on well with her older sister. She was not, she thought, vulnerable.

So when did she begin to suspect that she was in trouble – the frightening kind of trouble, not the I-can't-stop-thinking-of-you variety – with David?

Was it when she slipped, on their third or fourth date, and laddered her tights, and once he was sure she wasn't hurt he walked her to the nearest Tesco so she could buy a new pair? It had seemed chivalrous, this desire to help her fix something that had broken, but afterwards whenever they met he would joke, do you have a spare pair of tights just in case, and before long she always did?

Was it when he took her out for a half-year-anniversary dinner, six months after their first official date, to a restaurant she could never have afforded on her salary, and insisted that they have the tasting menu with the matched wine, even though she said she wasn't keen on some of the dishes and she didn't like to drink a lot because it wiped her out the next day?

Was it when she went away with her mother on a cruise, something her father paid for because he knew it was what her mother wanted, but couldn't do himself because he only had to look at moving water to be ill? Jenny remembers feeling anxious about telling David about it, and being pleasantly surprised that he didn't object, although she hadn't known exactly why she thought he would. Instead he had driven them to the airport so they could fly to Southampton, and when they got back Jenny found that he'd had her flat repainted. It was all done beautifully, and she could never have afforded to pay someone to do it. Yes, she had definitely been uneasy then. But, she had rationalised. She had told him that she planned to paint it; that she wanted it to be lighter. It had seemed churlish to say she wouldn't have chosen the peaches and cream colourway; and she had learned to live with it soon enough.

Shortly after that, she had noticed that he referred to the men at the estate agency where he worked by name, but had nicknames for the women: the housewife, the lard-arse,

43

the nightmare. Or was it later that she realised he did that? It must have been. She would have ended it immediately, if it had been when they first met. Wouldn't she?

Was it when her father died? David came to the funeral, and embraced her mother and sister and said all the right things, and kept his hand at the small of Jenny's back, all the time. But afterwards, whenever she said she needed to go to see her mother to help sort her father's things, or just to be with her, David said, it's too much for you. Or maybe, she has to learn to manage. Or, your sister can do it, she's closer.

Yes, it was then.

She knew for sure then that David wasn't a good idea. She heard the bewilderment in her mother's voice at the end of the phone, and she tried to text her sister explanations for her absence but found that there weren't really any explanations at all.

But somehow, when she was with David she couldn't quite see why she didn't want to be. They were almost always together, at that point, almost two years into their relationship. It made sense. His place was bigger, and closer to her work, and had a garden which was a suntrap, perfect for reading in the evenings, although he would rather that they talked or watched TV together than have her read. It's like you're cutting yourself off from me, he'd said.

And then she was pregnant, and so very, very sick. She was so sick that she was signed off work and she barely left their bedroom and didn't leave the house for three months. He didn't imprison her: there was simply no physical way she could have got as far as the front gate. She had slept and vomited and slept again, and he had taken care of her. Such good care. He coaxed soup into her – sometimes not even that, sometimes only water – from a spoon. He massaged her hands and feet. He told her how well she was doing, how the child she was growing would be strong and healthy and it was she, Jenny, who was making it so. He made it bearable for her.

When the scan showed that their child was a boy, David said, well done.

By the time she was better – when she was five months gone and a stone lighter than she had been before – the summer holidays came. They went, together, to see her mother that summer, and David was his charming self, and Jenny's mother had shown them the blanket she was knitting, the same pattern as the one she had knitted when she was expecting Jenny and her sister and her twins who had been born too soon and died within a day. David had rubbed it between his fingers and said, such fine stitches, and Jenny had known from the way the edge of his mouth didn't quite join in with his smile that the blanket would never be allowed anywhere near the baby. He wouldn't want anything home-made, anything from her family, or anything he hadn't chosen or been consulted on. She'd resolved then to leave him. But she hadn't.

Well, that's not quite true. She had tried. Not the day after, but the next, she had said, David, I don't think this is working. She was braced for fury, even though he didn't often lose his temper; and so when he said, why don't I make us some tea and we'll talk, she'd agreed, instead of packing a bag and taking a cab to her mother's house as she later, and so often, wished she had.

David had brought peppermint tea for them both. He had suggested they give up caffeine for the sake of the baby, and because he was doing it too, Jenny couldn't object, although hot, strong tea with sugar stirred in to the point of not-quite-dissolving, gritty at the bottom of the mug, was the only thing she really wanted. He'd sat at one end of the sofa, tucked her legs over his knees, and a blanket over her legs even though it was a warm August day, and said, tell me what all this is about.

She had said, I'm just not sure we're right for each other. The pregnancy has moved us on too far too fast. I feel a bit scared of how quickly things are moving. Maybe we should—

Yes, he'd said, his gaze on her face. So calm. I'm listening.

Maybe I should move back into my place. Just for a while. And we can—

We can do whatever you want, he'd said. His hands felt heavy through the blanket, where they lay on the top of her feet. But I don't understand. What have I done wrong? I thought our baby was a bit of amazing luck. It felt like confirmation we should be together.

It feels like rushing, she had said.

You must feel so overwhelmed, he'd said. All that sickness. And worry about your mother. I know you've been fretting about work.

Yes, she'd said, yes. He was right. She had been overwhelmed. Everything was difficult. Except the man who made her peppermint tea, who cared about every aspect of her life, who was, even now, trying to understand why she was unhappy, even though the thought of it made him unhappy.

By the end of that day they had agreed that she would move in permanently. They would get married; they would sell her flat. Jenny had thought perhaps she should keep it, rent it out, but David – who, after all, knew much more about this than she did – said it was a great time to sell and added, in a slightly wounded tone, that it felt as though she was keeping her options open. Of course I'm not, she had said. It's my hormones. You're quite right.

They married in the next few weeks. David arranged it all. It was the kind of August day that shimmers your vision and makes everything feel like too much. David had bought her a pale silk dress to wear. She wouldn't have chosen it for herself: it was an odd shade of creamy yellow that didn't really suit her. But she could see that it was beautiful, and expensive, and as far as she could judge, given her unfamiliar body, it looked nice enough. David wore his work suit, and they asked two passers-by to be witnesses, in the best romantic tradition, David said. Jenny thought it was romantic, too. Her mother and sister didn't agree. David shook his head when he saw their disappointed, chiding text messages. They can't see that it wouldn't have been good for you to have a fancy wedding, he'd said. Especially given how hard this pregnancy has been on you.

He was right. Jenny was more tired than she thought it was possible to be. The sickness faded, but never left. She took iron tablets and slept and watched her belly and breasts grow round and her chin and knees and wrists sharpen. David rubbed her back and bathed her feet and said, it makes no sense for you to go back to work. So she resigned. And it felt as though she slept the remainder of her pregnancy away.

In the hospital, bright with pride, David declared that his squalling son looked like a Milo. Jenny, who was being stitched up at the time, was too tired to remind him they had agreed that their child would be Joseph, Joe for short, after her father. One of the midwives asked her if all was well at home. She said yes. Even as she did it, she didn't know why, except that to say no would, surely, make things worse.

And once Milo came along, doubts and worries and thoughts of leaving became irrelevant in the sticky-sweet newborn struggle of the first weeks. It was November and the days felt too short to achieve anything in. David went back to work after a week. He had no taste for the reality of a baby, however proud he was to be a father. He loved Milo when he was clean and content, and he loved Jenny when she was, as he said, 'like her old self'.

The physical violence hadn't started until after Milo was born; but of course, Jenny hadn't really refused David anything until then. The first time he forced himself on her was three weeks after the birth, and she put it down to her being too tired, too hormonal, to be clear with him that she was sore. She had cried throughout, but she was crying almost all the time then, with hormones and sleep-lessness and the burning of her breasts every time Milo wanted to feed.

The second time she woke from a milk-sodden sleep to find him already on top of her.

After that she tried to anticipate; even to seduce. It seemed easier. Milo picked up on her moods and if she was scared or hurt he was restless and hard to please. And if Milo grizzled, David complained – not by complaining, exactly, but by wondering if she needed more help, or mentioning the women with babies younger than Milo who were moving house or returning to work at the agency ('the milch cow').

Milo was a year old the first time David hit her. Across the back of the legs, as she was bending to pick up something from the floor. She hadn't been sure, at first, whether this was going to be his new sex game – he had become increasingly keen to bite, to slap, and to constrain of late. But no. He hit her and he walked away.

David had the only set of car keys. He monitored her phone – by then he had stopped pretending it was a kindness, to protect her sleep or help her to relax. She still could have called her sister, who David considered below his notice, but by then – when Jenny's family had seen the baby only once, in a strained hour-long visit after Christmas – relations were not exactly cordial. (Later, when the restraining order was in place and Jenny and Milo moved in with Jenny's sister, she would say, of course you should have called me, I was just waiting for the call to come. I never dared text you because I knew by then he might hurt you if I did.)

So Jenny stayed. And stayed. After the first few times, David didn't much care where he hit her: either he trusted her to hide the bruises, or he didn't mind about them being seen. Afterwards he would never apologise, but he would be gentle with her: the day after he would text from work and say, I thought I'd bring home a takeaway, or, I'll do Milo's bedtime so you can have a bath, as though he was nursing her through a flu. Usually, he didn't break things, though once he stamped on her foot so hard that she heard

49

a bone in her toe crack. He took her to the hospital and, on the way in the car, reminded her how heavy their Le Creuset frying pan was. She took the hint. By then she was too afraid to do anything else.

As Milo grew they started to go to playgroups, though Jenny kept herself apart. She didn't want to have to answer questions about her life, or hear about others who had partners who were kind or jobs where they were valued or – oh, what bliss – were single. One day, taking a longer route home through town, so that Milo could walk along the pedestrianised streets, they passed a second-hand bookshop. The next time they walked that way, they went in. The time after, Milo lay down on the floor and declared he was 'too tired for the day', so the woman sorting through cookery books suggested Milo could nap in the reading refuge upstairs. Jenny sat down in a great, overstuffed armchair, and her boy curled up in her arms. A woman sitting on a sofa, crocheting a striped blanket, said hello and introduced herself as Sarah-Jane. She went to fetch Jenny a mug of tea, and passed it to Jenny when it had cooled. Milo slept; the women talked. And though nothing more significant than the weather, and books, and how fast babies grow, was discussed, Jenny felt calm – really calm – for the first time in weeks. Months, perhaps.

The next time they went to the bookshop, Sarah-Jane said, as Jenny was leaving, I'm not going to give you a leaflet in case it endangers you, but there are safe places. Come here and we can help you.

The day before the lockdown was announced, David spent the afternoon ill-temperedly moving the things he would need to work from home from the main office in

York to their spare room. The night before, during sex, he had tried to strangle Jenny in a way that suggested he really meant it. Usually, when he did something like that in bed, he kept his eyes open, his gaze flicking at her face for signs of pleasure (he would stop) or pain (he would continue). But that night, he had closed his eyes, as though concentrating his effort, and Jenny had felt a cracking in her throat. She had had a vision of herself, paralysed by a broken neck-bone and trapped in more than just the way she was now. Terrified for herself and for Milo, for once she had struggled and kicked rather than waiting for it to be over. She was still gagging for breath when David hit her across the face with something. She didn't see what, but it was cold and hard and she felt blood warm on her cheekbone.

She spent the night on the sofa, not sleeping, but curled in a ball, a cold flannel pressed against her cheek, trying not to cry for fear of the sting of salt in the cut and the fury of David, who did not like to have his rest disturbed by wife or child. Her tongue poked at a rattling, damaged tooth. Her throat throbbed. Her face ached, cheekbone and eye socket, but nothing seemed broken. So she lay in the dark and she started to try to untangle her memories, to find the place where she stepped off the track of happy, confident teacher who had just bought her own flat and had instead headed off in the direction of friendless, frightened woman with a fractured face. But instead of her mind running backwards, it insisted on rushing on, to what might happen next, to her. And to Milo.

David left for his final morning at the office the next day. As soon as he did, Jenny gathered some of Milo's clothes and his favourite rabbit. Not much. If David saw her from the car it needed to look as though she was walking to the shops.

And she made her way to Lost For Words, and asked for Sarah-Jane.

10

Kelly

Kelly cannot stop thinking about the letter from Rosemary. She doesn't know why. Maybe it was because it was a letter. Not a phone call, not an email. Or maybe it was because when she saw the return address, she imagined she smelled the sea.

She keeps the letter in her handbag. It nestles in the bottom, with her keys and mask and hand sanitiser and the purse she hardly ever seems to open any more, and the paper placemat-menu she has kept from the last time she saw Craig. They had dinner in a pizza restaurant and he doodled a heart on her placemat while they talked about the virus and how it was spreading and how it couldn't possibly get this far and disrupt their lives. It was the night they talked about moving in together. Little did they know. When she went to the loo he added their initials, and an arrow, and underneath he wrote, 'Kelly is the woman for me.' She folded the placemat into careful quarters, and she carries it with her like a charm.

The letter is a second charm. Kelly opens the envelope,

sometimes, in the morning, before she goes to work, and reads Rosemary's words. It seems to galvanise her in readiness for walking along the river, across the bridge, through the city, trying not to feel herself as vanishingly small.

This is only one of the ways in which Kelly thinks the pandemic is making her ridiculous. It is also making her obsess about Craig in a way she used to obsess about getting her footnotes right.

She cannot decide if she is becoming less of a person, or more. Has the Covid world made her stupid, blunted her, so that she has become one of the girls at school she both scorned and envied, the ones who only cared about boys? Or has it helped her to see beyond her endless intellectual goal-chasing and consider that she could complete a PhD in overlooked women and also find a deep, human connection with a man who loves her? Is it possible that the two are not mutually exclusive after all? Trying to work out the answer to this question makes the skin across the bridge of her nose pinch.

Loveday comes down the stairs from the refuge. Their latest press release, which basically says, use us or lose us, has done a little bit to improve business. The phone calls and emails that were frequent in the first days of lockdown have started up again, and people sometimes come and knock at the bookshop door, having made the trip deliberately, rather than passing by on their daily walk and thinking that maybe a book will be the thing that makes today different to all the other days. Not even the book itself, perhaps, but the conversation. The fact that they can go home with something that's the closest they are going to get to an anecdote: you know that second-hand bookshop near the city walls? Well, I stopped there today . . .

But Loveday and Kelly both know that this little surge of interest is not enough.

'I think you're right about setting up social media,' Loveday says, as though she's about to have dental surgery.

'Shall I do it?' Kelly is on Facebook a lot in the evenings, watching friends apparently delighted by their family online fancy-dress competitions, or 'finally getting around' to everything from repointing their brickwork to learning Spanish. She always thinks social media will make her feel better. It never does. So she might as well be doing something useful on there, as she can't seem to give it up. Without it there would only be waiting for Craig to call, or feeling defeated by her thesis.

And it might make her less dispensable.

'Do you mind?' Loveday looks beyond relieved. She doesn't often give a lot away, and Kelly has always spent at least half of every working week convinced that her boss dislikes her, and the other half watching her with customers and coming to the conclusion that Loveday, in fact, dislikes everyone. Craig has suggested that she might just have RBF, which Kelly thought, at first, might be a disease. Google told her that it meant 'resting bitch face'; an odd term for a thirty-seven-year-old man to use, it had seemed. But then, when Nathan or Sarah-Jane, Loveday's mother, come to the shop, Loveday becomes someone with a light inside her. Kelly has concluded that Loveday is just not a people person. Well, not most people.

'Of course I don't mind. Facebook, Instagram, Twitter?'

'Yes please,' Loveday sighs. 'I don't have the heart for it. I know I shouldn't complain.'

And she looks so defeated that Kelly feels her own

seriousness and worry drop from her, and laughs. 'We could, though. There's no one here except us. Shall we complain?'

Loveday looks perplexed, and for a moment seems as though she hasn't understood. Then she looks at her watch, looks up at Kelly and smiles, in exactly the way that Kelly has always imagined Bobbie from *The Railway Children* would smile: quiet, impish, surprising. 'Okay. Five minutes. You start.'

'I'm sick of not having any sex with another human,' Kelly says, before she's had a chance to filter what was going to come out of her mouth.

Loveday nods and the look in her eyes is a startled delight. 'Bold start. I miss seeing the sea.'

'Me too.'

'No, you can't have mine. Think of your own.'

'Okay, I wish my meals were sometimes a surprise.'

'I wish my meals were sometimes beans on toast. When everyone takes turns to cook, everyone does their best to make something nice and that always seems to mean complicated.'

Kelly nods. Though she had beans on toast twice last week because she was too tired to think. 'I'm sick to the back teeth of my sodding PhD and I don't think I'm ever going to finish it. And if I do, no one will read it. And I have no idea what I would do then.' Kelly had once seen her future in academia, coaxing brilliance from students and making breakthroughs by deciphering marginalia that have been missed by generations of academics before her. Now all she wants to do is curl up in bed and read, while Craig rubs her feet and tells her she's amazing.

There's a pause; Loveday has the slightly hunted look of a woman going through her pockets to find her house keys, while being increasingly certain that those keys are in her other coat. Then she says, 'I'm failing and I don't know how to stop it.'

Kelly closes her eyes. 'We all feel like we're failing.'

'Yes.'

Loveday is turning away and Kelly wants to stop her, because the complaining should have made everything feel better, not worse.

There's one thing that will always get Loveday's attention, and that's a question about books.

So Kelly asks, 'What books would you recommend to someone who was – who felt as though they had lost their purpose?'

Loveday looks up at the ceiling, every part of her concentrating. She closes her eyes. Then she opens them and starts to move around the shelves, pulling out volumes so rapidly that it looks as though the bookshop is, in fact, pushing them into her hands. Despite all the ways that Kelly feels safe with Craig, there's no feeling to match watching a bookshop at work.

Loveday puts four books into Kelly's hands. *Small Pleasures* by Clare Chambers, *Dear Life* by Alice Munro, *Are You There, God? It's Me, Margaret* by Judy Blume, and *The Heart Is A Lonely Hunter* by Carson McCullers. 'See how you get on with those,' Loveday says.

Kelly nods. She could cry. She already feels less alone.

'What do you need?' she asks Loveday.

'Me?' Loveday has got her usual closed-off look again,

but Kelly remembers what she said. Loveday feels as though she's failing.

'Wait here.' Kelly moves from shelf to shelf, travel to fiction to poetry, and hands four books to Loveday. *The Bell Jar* by Sylvia Plath, the poetry of Elizabeth Barratt Browning, *Wild* by Cheryl Strayed, and *All my Friends Are Superheroes* by Andrew Kaufman.

Loveday nods. 'Thank you,' she says, then, with an effort: 'I think I'm starting to forget what books can be.'

11

A bookshop needs to be used. It's as simple as that.

The money keeps the doors open, but it's the people, the conversations, that keep it alive.

If you've ever bought a book in a place-where-books-are-sold, a supermarket or the gift shop at a stately home, you know precisely what I mean.

The book is the same wherever it comes from. That is to say, the basics of the book are the same. The cover, the paper, the carefully selected words in the worried-over order the author has chosen for them. The typesetting, the proofreading, the thinking and planning: these are the same for every copy, wherever it is sold from, whether it ends up treasured, loved and re-read, remaindered, or something in between. It's the state of mind and heart of the person reading it that will make the book grow into something greater than the words printed in it.

But the book bought from the Lost For Words bookshop feels different. Partly because it's already been through another set of hands, which have softened its edges, made it relax because it has been understood once already. And partly because the bookshop's years of experience in giving the right book to the right person means that you can be sure that the volume that ends up with you, is for you.

12

Hozan

Professor Azad's home study is not the silent sanctum it once was. It used to house his one desk; the rug he brought from his father's house lay before it, and when he was trying to work something out, to formulate a thought or to think of the best way to challenge or inspire a student, he would pace back and forth on it, in the same way his own father had once paced. Though his father, a member of the Kurdish armed forces known as the Peshmerga, had had different issues on his mind. When Hozan Azad was growing up, his father was more often what his mother used to say was 'away'. 'Away' meant fighting in the Kurdish Uprising. Later, when Hozan had left Kurdistan to study abroad, his father and uncles were hiding in caves in the Kurdish mountains, pushing back Saddam Hussain's troops who would raid villages in the night. They did nothing so obvious as slaughtering the people. Those troops poured cement into the water supply and left the village, animals and then people to die a slow, fading death. The smallest first.

The Professor first came to study here in York more than

thirty years ago. He and his family have often returned to Kurdistan, when they could, and his children have both spent time living and studying there. But England is where they live. As the world watched Covid awake, the Professor's family all made their way home. His daughter Vaheen and son-in-law Gohdar returned from their educational work with girls in Afghanistan to their tiny flat in Harrogate; it had not occurred to the Professor then that he would not be able to see them. And his son Shwan and daughter-in-law Sazan, along with his precious, precious grandchildren Yad and Lana, have moved in with the Professor and his wife. It feels good that at least some of his family can be here together.

Sometimes, little Yad will come and sprawl on the floor in front of Hozan's desk and draw, tractors and dragons and butterflies all lined up as though they are equal – and equal sized – parts of the same world. A world which, strangely, he does not seem to find at all terrifying. Little Lana is more likely to spend her days in the garden or the kitchen, fingers sticky with earth or food, but when the Professor goes downstairs when his work is done, she is on his lap with a book within seconds. They are reading something called *Paddington*, which the Professor's daughter-in-law Sazan assures him is an essential part of a British childhood. A Peruvian talking bear in a coat and hat seems odd to the Professor, but he likes the vocabulary. Lana cannot get the hang of the word 'marmalade', often saying 'marmade' or getting too many syllables in, 'marmamalade'. The Professor felt as though he performed a minor miracle when he bought a jar at the corner shop and brought it home for her. Now she eats it every morning, and has confided in her grandmother that she would like to be a bear when she grows up.

They have never gone much beyond politeness with their neighbour, Lorraine. She is out most days; the Professor assumed that she was going to work but his wife Zhilwan assures him that no, she would be looking after her grandson while her daughter went to work herself. Lorraine lives alone and her daughter and the child live alone and the Professor will never, as long as he lives, get used to this strange way of separating families from each other. Perhaps this is why so many people look so sad. And why so many others have such terrible lives. When the Professor's first wife died, so unexpectedly and so suddenly, he had been alone in the house in Erbil that they had planned to fill with children. A French colleague from the university had – thoughtlessly, perhaps, or even deliberately, if alcohol was his way of managing – left a bottle of whisky when he came to visit. The Professor had never drunk alcohol, but he took the lid from the bottle and inhaled.

And then he looked around his silent house.

And then he called his mother.

She sent his brother, and his brother brought him home.

For a while, the Professor lived – existed, rather – in the tight and watchful embrace of his family. When his father returned from war the two of them sat, silent and sleepless, in the night.

And then he was offered the chance to study abroad, and he took it. He didn't know exactly what drew him to this cold and cramped city, where he knew no one. But he came, and he studied, and he made one friend, and then another, fellow students who were as serious and quiet as he was.

And then Eid came, and he was invited to his friend Khaled's home, and he met Khaled's sister, Zhilwan. She was so full of colour and shine that she seemed almost impossible to look at, in her gold-and-green jli Kurdi that caught the light, with her bright smile and her brighter laugh. She was as different to his quiet, devout first wife as it was possible to be. But just as perfect for him, as it happened. He will never not be grateful for her. And he will never forget those bleak times of his widowerhood.

And this is why, when he sees Lorraine, he recognises loneliness.

Lorraine has a chair by her back door, and in the morning she sits there and smokes.

The morning is also the time when the Professor's daughter-in-law, Sazan, likes to work on her PhD, tapping away at her keyboard at the extra desk they have squeezed into his office. She is a great one for coloured pens and Post-its, notebooks and coffee cups. The Professor is proud to have such a bright and ambitious daughter-in-law – he jokes to his son Shwan sometimes that he had better hope his wife never finds out that he lives only for football and everything else is show – but he thinks it best that they both have some time on their own to work. (Once a week, he walks to the town centre and stands on his favourite of York's bridges, the Lendal Bridge, designed by his favourite civil engineer, Thomas Page, who also designed Westminster Bridge. His family tease him about having a favourite, but the Professor doesn't mind. He feels inspired every time he stands there, or walks beneath it, to admire the span of the arch. And Sazan, no doubt, finds inspiration in having some time to herself to work.)

One morning, when Zhilwan chases the Professor from the kitchen so she can get on with breadmaking, and Shwan is working on his laptop in the living room while Yad and Lana watch cartoons, the Professor takes his second coffee outside. The smell of cigarette smoke reminds him of his grandfather. 'Hello,' he says.

Lorraine nods. 'Morning.'

'How are you?'

She sighs. 'Not so bad. I suppose.' She looks at him as though he's an idiot for even asking.

'I meant,' he says, carefully, 'I suppose I meant, how are you, considering everything?'

She gets up, drops her cigarette end, stands on it, and exhales. Meets his eyes, for just a second. 'I don't know.'

The next day, she smiles and nods but doesn't speak. The day after, she is in her dressing gown, and pulls it more tightly around her when he speaks to her, though she answers cordially enough.

The day after, he has an early Zoom meeting, and the day after that is Saturday so he builds Lego towers with Lana and discusses dinosaurs with Yad. On Sunday, he and Zhilwan walk to the Museum gardens with the children and let Sazan and Shwan have the house to themselves for an hour. Unexpectedly, there's a coffee van at the entrance to the gardens; walking along the grass with warm cups in their hands, watching the children scamper and chase, feels like a holiday.

'I thought you'd abandoned me,' Lorraine says the next morning, and the Professor is about to leap to his own defence when he recognises the famous British sense of humour. His colleagues often use it too. He has to remind himself it isn't rudeness.

'Grandparenting duties,' he says with a smile, and then realises he's said exactly the wrong thing, because Lorraine sucks hard on her cigarette and looks away.

'Lucky you,' she says.

'I know,' he says, 'it's not the same on the computer, is it?' They talk to Zhilwan's sisters, one in Scarborough and one in Silemani, on Zoom every week and more often than not Zhilwan is sadder and lonelier afterwards than she was before.

'I don't have a computer,' Lorraine says, 'never needed one. If I had anything needed doing my daughter used to do it for me. I've got my phone and I can't get the hang of anything fiddly on there.'

'So how are you keeping in touch with your family?'

Lorraine shrugs. 'Phone calls. The grandbairn's too little, though, really. Sometimes he cries when he hears me. My Claire says he can't understand why I've stopped coming to see him.'

The Professor has the sense to look away as he says, 'That must be hard. For all of you.'

'Everything's hard for everyone, isn't it? Except for them that's rich enough to bend the rules.' Lorraine gets up, goes into the house and slams the door behind her. For a moment the Professor thinks she has accused him of – he's not sure what. Wealth, or rule-breaking? Then he realises she's talking about the government.

The next morning, the Professor says, 'If you wouldn't mind wrapping up and coming to sit in our garden, we've found a laptop and we can show you how to talk to your grandchild.'

Lorraine looks at him out of half-closed eyes, as though they're playing poker. 'I didn't ask you for a laptop.'

'I know,' the Professor says, 'but I thought –' he laughs, 'my wife tells me I am a busybody. Always interfering. My colleagues too.'

Unexpectedly, Lorraine laughs. 'I'll see how I'm fixed, later on,' she says.

Shwan is a great charmer: none of the aunties will ever hear a word against him, even when his mother complains of his laziness. So when Lorraine comes through the gate that afternoon, looking anxiously at the house as though it might eat her, the Professor brings his son into the garden. They sit at a distance on wooden chairs that the Professor needs to get around to sanding and revarnishing. Shwan gets Lorraine to log in to her Facebook account, and talks her through making a Messenger video call to her daughter. There's a horrible moment when the panic in Lorraine's daughter's voice is evident – how careful one must be now, the Professor thinks, to not worry people with even an unexpected call – but Lorraine explains that 'the people next door I told you about' have loaned her a laptop. 'The foreign ones?' Lorraine's daughter asks, and Lorraine replies, apparently without shame, 'Yes, them ones.' Shwan rolls his eyes at his father as if to say, I don't know why you bother, and they leave Lorraine to talk. Half an hour later, when Yad and Lana are ready to run off some energy, the Professor checks to see that Lorraine has finished her call before he opens the door and lets them tumble into the garden.

Lorraine looks up as he approaches. 'Little Arthur's grown like I wouldn't have believed,' she says. 'Two months since I've seen him. I mean, Claire sends photos, but I haven't seen him talking. She sends videos but I can't play them on my phone.' The Professor is about to offer Shwan's help, when Lorraine gets up, and shakes her head. 'He's gone from being a toddler to a little lad.'

'Please,' the Professor says, 'take the laptop. Borrow it for as long as you need.'

She shakes her head and walks away, waiting until the gate has closed behind her before she lights up a cigarette.

'She probably doesn't have the internet,' Zhilwan says later, as they drink fresh mint tea from istikan, the curved glass cups that make them both think of Kurdistan. Sazan and Shwan are washing up. The sounds of Yad's snuffling snores and Lana's deep sleep-breathing come through the baby monitor.

'We didn't know,' the Professor says, 'that the happiness of having our children would never stop. Did we?'

Zhilwan puts down her tea and takes his hand. 'We didn't know anything. We still don't. And so it will continue, insh'allah.'

'Insh'allah,' he echoes, automatically.

'You could ask her if she wants to make a support bubble with us,' Zhilwan says. 'If you see her tomorrow. Then she can come and use the internet whenever she likes. And Yad and Lana might cheer her up.'

'What about Vaheen and Gohdar?' It is impossible, not being able to see his beloved daughter, even though she is only twenty miles away.

'They need to care for his parents, you know that.'

'I'll think about it,' the Professor says, and next to him, his wife smiles.

It's Lorraine who starts the conversation the next morning.

'Claire asked me what your names were yesterday, and I realised I don't know. I just call you the Prof. I know Jilly's name, o'course. But not the others.'

Sazan has introduced her father-in-law to the concept of the micro-aggression. One of them is to be 'unable' to pronounce names that are considered 'foreign'.

'Jilly isn't my wife's name. It's Zhilwan.' He exaggerates the beginning 'zh' sound, 'Like the "s" is pronounced in Persia.'

'Persia,' Lorraine says, then, carefully, 'Zhilwan.'

'Yes, Zhilwan.' She is close enough.

'It sounds lovely when you say it,' Lorraine says, then asks, 'What about you? Your name? Am I allowed to ask?'

'Hozan,' he says.

'Hozan,' she repeats. 'Funny, how I never knew.'

The Professor almost points out that she has never asked. He's tempted to remind her that, when they first moved in, she had made a point of sniffing the air when she was in her garden when Zhilwan was cooking. She had always brought a Christmas card, but delivered it to their door while saying things like 'I'm not sure what you believe, but in England everyone has a proper Christmas.'

Instead he takes a deep breath, and nods. 'Hozan and Zhilwan,' he says. 'We have lived here for a long time now.'

Lorraine laughs, a little uncertainly. 'What about the others?' she asks. 'Your son and his family?'

She finds 'Sazan' easy; 'Shwan' she cannot immediately seem to find an anglicised reference for, so she repeats and repeats until she thinks she has it. The Professor's coffee is long drunk and his hands are cold. No good deed goes unpunished. 'What about your grandkids?' she asks.

'Yad and Lana,' he says. He cannot even say their names without feeling a swell of love and pride.

'Yad!' She laughs. 'That's a proper little boy's name, isn't it? Yad. I like that. And Lana. That's pretty.'

'What, Poppa? What?' Lana, who has come into the garden to search for a toy abandoned outside yesterday, has the hearing of a bat.

The Professor hands his granddaughter his empty cup and lifts her up so she can see over the fence. She's getting heavy but he doesn't mind. 'I was just telling the lady who lives next door your name.'

'Lana.' She pokes herself in the chest. 'It means I am safe in a little nest.'

'Does it, now? Well,' Lorraine says, with a smile. She looks much happier, the Professor notices, now that there's a child here.

'What is your name and does it mean a thing?' Lana asks.

'Lorraine. It's the name of a place in France where my mum and dad went on a holiday. When they had just got married.' Then, to the Professor, though he's not sure what to do with the information, 'It was their only time abroad. They said they didn't really like it.'

'Rain?' Lana asks. 'Like from in the sky?'

The Professor squeezes his granddaughter a little tighter and smiles at her, as Lorraine repeats her name, more slowly.

'Zhilwan and I were wondering,' he says, 'if it would make sense for you to become part of our family bubble? Then you can come and use the laptop whenever you like, to talk to Claire and Arthur, and you can be indoors when it gets colder.'

* * *

If the Professor is honest – and he is, with himself, and he doesn't need to be, with his wife, because she can read him like a book – he had half-hoped Lorraine would decline their invitation. Surely she would make a bubble with her daughter, if she hadn't already? Or someone – well, someone that she liked more than she seemed to like them? But she knocks on the door that afternoon, with a plate of jam tarts, something that makes her immediately beloved by Yad and Lana. The Professor has an online seminar about to start, so he apologises and leaves Shwan to set up the laptop.

When he closes the meeting window an hour later, he's tired. So much more tired than when he's teaching in person, when it feels as though there is an effortlessness in the flow: his expertise, his questions to the students, their responses, their questions, and so a busy, buzzing seminar would often overrun. Online, it's different. Some of the students don't turn on their cameras. Others don't say a word for the entire, dragging hour. They seem more dimmed, online; there's no sparkle to their observations, very little laughter. Talking over the top of each other, in a seminar room, is an expression of brains at work and ideas coming through. Online, it feels like a mistake; requires an unsnarling. And screen-sharing and annotating is a marvel, really it is, but there's nothing quite like a whiteboard for an old engineer like him. The Professor knows that when he looks at his university email inbox there will be at least one student who has contacted him from a place of struggle and hardship: illness or anxiety or family circumstances that mean pressure and stress. He will be accommodating, comforting, kind. And he will feel helpless.

To delay the helplessness, he goes down to the kitchen,

71

where he expects to find Zhilwan preparing food, or sitting at the kitchen island with a magazine and some chai. He is half right; she's there, with her chai. And with Lorraine, who has a full istikan of chai in front of her too. They don't stop talking, though Zhilwan flashes him a smile, and a look that says, you probably won't enjoy this conversation much. Yet she is almost breathless with anticipation as she leans towards Lorraine and says, 'So someone shot him and everyone thought he had died in the canal but he came back – how many years later?'

'Fourteen!' Lorraine says, with a raised eyebrow. Then she looks around and says, 'Hello, Hozan. This working from home must be nice for you.'

The Professor stops himself from telling Lorraine just how trying he finds it all. He knows she used to work in one of the tourist shops in York when she wasn't looking after her grandson. He's the lucky one here. 'It is,' he says.

'Lorraine has invited the children to go and make corn-flake cakes and –' Zhilwan looks uncertain – 'thumb cookies?'

'Thumbprint,' Lorraine says, making a surprisingly violent twisting motion on the worktop with her thumb. 'You make a dent and put jam in.'

'Ah,' the Professor says, although the idea seems a little unhygienic to him, 'I'm sure they will enjoy that.'

'And Lorraine is going to come and eat with us, next time I make my mother's dolma recipe,' Zhilwan adds.

Although it's Zhilwan's mother's recipe, she has made the dish her own; the bottom of the pot lined with butterbeans to absorb the juices from the cooking, and then layers of onions, aubergines and courgettes, stuffed with lamb, spices and herbs. The Professor closes his eyes at the thought of it. It has been easier to eat less-fuss meals, with the children to care for. 'You are in for a treat, Lorraine.'

She nods, with, the Professor thinks, about the same level of conviction as he did at the mention of thumbprint cookies. 'I can't for the life of me imagine stuffing an onion,' she says.

'And I am going to start watching *EastEnders*,' Zhilwan says. 'Then Lorraine will have someone to talk to about it.'

'I miss my girls at work,' Lorraine says. 'We used to be desperate to get in if something good had happened. Just to see what everyone else thought.'

And the Professor realises that this is what he misses, too. No matter how often he and Zhilwan count their blessings. No matter that Sazan says – and she is right – that the children will grow strong bonds from this time they spent living with their grandparents, instead of seeing them for a day every three weeks or so. No matter that he can talk to his colleagues on the internet, and he can pray with his family in their dining room. He cannot spend two minutes with Mo at the security desk at the university, talking about the news from Iraq; or with Katya who cleans the offices giving him an update about how her nursing training is going. He misses telling his colleagues about a documentary he watched, or hearing about their training for triathlons, and their hangovers, and their newborn godchildren. Although he has much to be grateful for with his family and his work, the foundations of his life intact, the realisation comes to him, standing in the kitchen, that it is the small things that are missing. Without them, nothing is wrong. But everything is . . . flat. Without texture. A little bleaker than it should be.

That evening, Lana climbs into the Professor's lap with her

book, smelling of synthetic strawberries, her curls still damp from her bath.

'The weather-name lady says the little boy she talks to on the screen has not read *Paddington*.' She looks at him, big-eyed, expecting him to be as shocked as she obviously was.

'Her grandson? Well,' the Professor says mildly, 'some people like different books.'

Lana nods vigorous agreement. 'Her boy on the screen likes a cartoon about farms,' she says. 'And the weather-name lady says she has got no books in her house except one with her – biscuit plans – in.'

'Recipes.' The Professor smiles. And he begins to read. Paddington is getting to grips with the neighbourhood and making friends; he's taking his bear/child point of view out into the world, and changing the world as he does so. No wonder Lana likes him.

'Lana says Lorraine doesn't have any books,' the Professor says to Zhilwan over their tea that evening.

It's been a fractious couple of hours; Sazan has hit a wall on her dissertation and all Shwan could think of to say by way of support was to tell her that it wouldn't matter if she doesn't finish it. The Professor knows his son means well. But he is no help to his bright, ambitious wife that way. Zhilwan talked to Shwan as she is much better with him than the Professor is. Sazan and the Professor sat in his office – their office – while Sazan explained what she thought the problem was. The Professor thought of what he would say to his students and finds that, although Sazan is a sociologist and he's a civil engineer, the advice still holds. If you're stuck, and you weren't before, it might be that there's a recent mis-step. Check your last piece of work. Go back to your hypothesis. Maybe even take a break. Sazan had listened to everything he had to say, with her head in her hands, but when he stopped talking she looked at him and said, 'Thank you. I should have known you would understand,' which made him feel that he is not such a trial of a father-in-law after all.

Now Sazan and Shwan are in their room, and after some tears it's gone quiet. It's not the first time Zhilwan has instructed her son in how to be a good and supportive husband. Hopefully this time her words will have got through. Vaheen seems to be doing much better with Gohdar, who has always treated his relationship with their daughter as something to be nurtured.

Zhilwan laughs a little, and says, as though explaining something to Yad, 'Some people don't have books, my sweet. Lorraine is one of them.'

'I know,' the Professor replies. 'But –' he thinks of Yad, when he and Zhilwan collected him from his home in a village on the outskirts of Leeds and took him to see a film in the city, not long after Lana was born. Driving through the suburbs shortly after 3 p.m., they'd stopped for a lollipop man, and Yad had pointed at him and exclaimed, 'I didn't think they were real! I thought they were only in storybooks!'

'But nothing,' Zhilwan says, firmly. 'Lorraine is allowed to not read. She's joined our bubble, not invited us to improve her.' She twitches her fingers around the word 'improve' as she says it. Zhilwan has worked in a nursery since their children grew up, and has seen a much greater range of people than the Professor has, he knows. He spends his days with university colleagues and staff, with students, with his family and the people at the mosque. Zhilwan has spent time in the real world. She is used to being snubbed and ignored in shops, assumed to be less by some of the parents who bring their children to nursery, because she is brown and covers her hair. She is the one who, twenty years ago, went to school again and again to repeat the names her children had been called in the playground, and insist that the insults be dealt with as serious racist issues, rather than 'high spirits' and 'children just repeating what they've heard'. The Professor knows she knows more about the world. But he can't quite let it go.

'What does she do all day?'

Zhilwan shrugs. 'Watches TV. Makes jam tarts. She used to be busy and now she isn't. She's not wilfully choosing not to read. It's probably never been part of her life.'

'I suppose,' the Professor says. He decides to call his friends at Lost For Words tomorrow. They have always been able to hunt down academic books and research texts for him. Finding something for Lorraine should be something they can do too.

13

George, Now

It's been a busy afternoon in the garden. The cutting bed is starting to run riot, and this year, there's no one to give their flowers away to. Rosemary has talked about filling jam jars and putting them by the gate for passers-by, but they don't seem to have got around to it yet. The passers-by aren't really passing, anyway. The jasmine is coming through the honeysuckle as happily as ever, and the lilac, which doesn't bloom every year, has chosen this one to fill the air with scent and bring butterflies in something close to clouds. George had found himself transfixed by them, yesterday, unable to move. Rosemary had worried at him, coming down from where she was pruning her namesake-plant, which grew in a pot at the kitchen door, to see that he wasn't in trouble. He had told her that he was watching the butterflies. Which he was. He was also trying to – well, it's hard to describe. He wasn't exactly trying to commit them to memory, but to remember the whole feeling of it: the air, the scent, the feeling of busy-ness and total absorption that the bustling insects gave off.

He doesn't think he will see another summer. He didn't mention that part to Rosemary. She is wise enough – they are old enough – for her not to try to jolly him out of the certainty of his coming death. But if he tries to talk about it her face turns to shadows and he cannot bear to be the one that clouds out her sun.

He has chronic kidney disease, and is not just an old man who needs to pee a lot, as Rosemary had so fervently insisted he was. 'The thing about kidney disease', the consultant had said at their appointment, 'is that it is symptomless in the early stages. So by the time you do have symptoms – the frequent urination, the weight loss, the insomnia, the short-ness of breath – it's . . .' George hadn't needed to look at Rosemary to know that she was bracing herself in the same way that he was. The news they didn't want was coming and there was nothing they could do about it. The consultant had looked directly at George. 'When we see symptoms like yours, George, we know the treatment is more difficult, because the disease is more advanced.'

George had understood what the consultant was saying. There's not really anything to be done. He'd gone for an ultrasound scan, and a biopsy, and then they had come home. They'll be back at the hospital next week, for the official diagnosis. Until then, there is each other's company, and the garden, and reading.

He opens to the page of *Persuasion* where the bookmark waits. They are both sticklers for proper bookmarks: none of this pages-turned-over for them. Years of handing out textbooks that are dog-eared, foxed, and have inappro-priate doodles in the margins, have taught them that paper remembers how it's treated. And even if he was so disposed, Rosemary looks after books so well that you would think it was the eleventh commandment. Thou shalt not fold down the corners.

They're nearly at the end of Anne Elliot's story. It's taken them a while to get through *Persuasion*, because every chapter has made them remember something-or-other from their own time in Lyme Regis, on their honeymoon, all those years ago.

Rosemary arrives with the tea-basket: flask, tin cups, milk in a screw-top jar. A tea-towel for spills and a packet of chocolate biscuits. George has noticed that since the visit to the hospital they don't have the plain ones any more. He has always liked Rich Tea biscuits, but he can see that Rosemary needs to give him the best of everything between now and the end. He'd asked for a baked potato and beans last night, and when he'd dug down into it he'd realised there was proper butter under the topping. He can't bear that he's going to leave her.

'Here you go, love,' she says, and he takes the mug and biscuit. There's a cheerful pattern to their usual tea-time chatting: the colour of the sea today, whether the traffic is getting up again, how their old colleagues are managing with doing everything on the computer instead of in the classroom. But George can't find a way to start on it. He's too full of things that will upset his wife. She doesn't want to talk of death. Not his, anyway. They make a point of listening to the daily announcements of the mounting numbers of those who have died of Covid, heads bowed, as though they are standing at a war memorial on Remembrance Sunday. And afterwards they speak of all the families who must be devastated, and the few that they know of amongst their small circle. But Rosemary brushes away any talk of George's possible death, as though mentioning it will bring it closer.

'The air's warm,' Rosemary says, closing her eyes and raising her face. He must have seen her make that gesture thousands of times.

He puts down his mug. 'How about I read a couple of pages while the tea cools?'

'Lovely,' she says, without opening her eyes. If she noticed the tremble in his voice she doesn't show it.

To begin with, George's voice is unsure, the words blurring, these faraway fictitious characters a nuisance when he has so many more important things to think about. It's been harder to put the fear of what's to come aside, today. But gradually, Jane Austen's words find a rhythm in him. The smell of the North Sea at Whitby becomes the smell of the English Channel at Lyme Regis; the sound of waves lapping against Whitby harbour's walls merges with water slapping up against the bricks of the Cobb. Beside him, Rosemary's breath steadies the way it does when she is reading, or sleeping.

Between the leaves of the book, Frederick has written his letter, and Anne is reading it. 'I am half agony, half hope,' Frederick writes, and George reads.

Rosemary puts her arm on his. 'Don't forget your tea,' she says. There's a catch in her voice.

He puts down the book and picks up his mug. 'You old softie,' he says.

'Not so much of the old.' Normally they'd laugh, but the air around them goes silent. George drinks his tea, and eats the biscuit afterwards. Chocolate ones don't dunk so well.

Rosemary packs the mugs away. 'I thought I'd make a mince and onion pie,' she says.

'Lovely.' He hasn't much of an appetite – he's not sure if it's illness, or his old body knowing it's time to take up a bit less space, but when Rosemary puts a plate down in front of him he can usually manage something. She cooks, he washes up, and she hasn't tried to stop him, though he can see her watching him as she potters about, in case standing at the sink is too much. It could annoy him, except that when she broke her arm falling off her bicycle when they were touring the Dales in '84 he was just the same, hovering and watching and wishing she would just let him take over.

'Are you coming in?'

'I might just sit here for a bit longer.'

She nods, put the back of her hand against his cheek. 'Don't get cold.'

'I won't. I've got my thick socks on.'

George listens to Rosemary as she makes her way through the garden. He can tell, without looking, where she is when her footsteps pause, and what she's doing. Looking up into the apple tree to see if she can spot the greenfinches that nest there. A few more steps and then taking a strand of clematis and wrapping it round the willow stakes they train it up. Almost at the back door, and a pause to pick the slugs off the lupins. And then the wooden thunk of the back door opening.

George watches the sea. He's aware that he's saving it up, this constant water, inside him, in case he ends up in hospital and can't hear it or see it or smell it any more. And it seems, well, just better to be out here.

The birdsong has seemed louder since Covid came. Of

course it won't be – it's just that background noise has diminished so they can hear it more clearly, and there aren't so many folk about to bother the birds into flight, to spook them to silence. George can't untangle the sounds into individual birds, but that doesn't matter. What matters is that, for now, he's here.

Half agony, half hope.

14

Rosemary, 1969

Rosemary and George are not really ones for being the centre of attention, and so their wedding is modest, held in her father's church, and causing a ripple of delighted scandal as Rosemary's mother walks her down the aisle so that her father can conduct the ceremony. What Rosemary will mostly remember from that day is the smell of the lavender and rosemary of her bouquet, picked from the vicarage garden that morning; that, and George's face, alight with happiness, more tearful than she was as they spent a few quiet moments in the vestry together before walking to the church hall for their reception.

The next day, they set out for their honeymoon. George drives their brand-new, dark green Ford Cortina, and it takes them a long and winding day to get to the south coast and Lyme Regis. Rosemary looks out of the window, reads the map, and dozes. She's tired, and part of her is curled up in shyness at the thought of what they did, last night: how strange it was, how different to what she had expected and yet how – nice. George says they will get better, with practice.

Rosemary watches the countryside to her left, and then looks at her husband, to her right, and wonders how many miles they will drive in their life, and whether she will ever come to take his profile for granted. The silence between them is warm and full of smiles and soft noises, as they shift in their seats and look across at each other, for reassurance, maybe: yes, we did get married, yes, I am happy about it, yes, this is our life now. Rosemary feels grown-up, awake, alive at last with the ache in her thighs. The swinging sixties might have been and gone in the bigger cities, but in 1969, the village where Rosemary grew up was still much as it had been in the 1950s. And cultural revolutions were certainly not permitted into the grounds of the vicarage.

'Shall I read to you?' Rosemary asks.

'I'd like that,' George says.

And Rosemary pulls *Persuasion* from her bag.

In Lyme Regis, they stay in a funny little hotel that is supposed to have a sea view, but that would only be the case, George says with a laugh, if you stood on the chimney pot. They peer from the window on tiptoes, and then Rosemary, learning to dare, twists sideways and kisses her husband's neck, just behind his ear, and feels him exhale in a way that's almost a growl. She has decided that she likes sex, very much indeed, and that it doesn't need to be the endurance test that her mother gave her the impression it would be.

On their last day, they get dressed – their new married-life clothes have relaxed, too – and make their way along the Cobb for the final time. Rosemary, unsentimental in most things, practical in everything, nonetheless insists on walking down the perilous steps where Louisa Musgrove fell in Austen's novel. George waits to catch her, and she jumps, with a cry; being in the air, his arms outstretched and waiting to catch her, felt adventurous, even though she only jumped the last three steps. Maybe, she thinks as they walk back towards the town, this is how marriage will be for us: George breaking my falls, me making him laugh. That will do, very nicely, until the children come along.

On the way back to the hotel, they buy a watercolour of the Cobb as a souvenir. They have no camera, yet.

Back in their hotel room, Rosemary unwraps the painting and props it on the windowsill; she lies on the bed and looks at it and cries, although she can't say why. George takes the print of flowers in a vase from the wall, and hangs their new painting there instead, and then he sits next to her and holds her hand.

That picture of the Cobb has hung in their living room for as long as they have lived in their cottage.

15

Two things we did not know about pandemics, before one arrived. First, if you are one of the lucky ones – not unwell, not specifically afraid for anyone else, enduring only the new-normal level of fear that everyone feels – pandemics are dull. This is not what we might have imagined. If we are lucky, we might look back at the pandemic as months of staring-at-a-screen or working-at-a-distance-behind-a-mask, with a bit of solitary cupboard-cleaning at the weekends when we could not bear to watch another episode of the thing everyone is watching, no matter how good it really is. Of being cheerful when talking to distant relatives and being systematic when shopping so you don't mess up the one-way system. Living through capital-H history can, it seems, be deeply uninteresting.

And secondly, pandemics are lonely. Time usually spent in clothes-shop browsing or talking to a neighbour when you meet in the stairwell, in going to the cinema or mooching round a market, in playing netball or doing a 5k on a Saturday morning or tidying the house because a friend is coming round – those little pockets of time yawn, empty, and wait to be filled.

Books will fill them, naturally. Reading will pack them full of words different to the ones in your head, and before you know it, it will be as though those time-yawns were never there, as forgotten as a glove on a wall by a bus stop.

So long as it's the right book, of course.

And so long as the pandemic has not robbed you of your ability to concentrate, to focus, or to give any portion of your mind to someone else's story. If that is the case: I'm sorry. Don't worry. Books will always wait for you.

16

Kelly

When there's a tap at the door, Kelly is deep in Instagram conversations. She's set up the Lost For Words account and asked people what they are reading, and she's surprised by how many responses she's getting. She thinks of when she asked Nathan how a poetry competition would make money, and hopes social media makes a difference. There have been no website visits, sales or enquiries yet, but she only has thirty-nine followers so far, and Twitter is much the same. If social media is going to save them, they should have started with it a long time before they needed saving.

The ringing phone sounds like a lifeline.

'Lost For Words Bookshop. Kelly speaking.'

'Ah, hello,' says a woman's voice, soft and rounded and slightly formal, 'my name is Rosemary Athey. I wrote to you a little while ago and you sent me—'

'*Persuasion*!' Kelly says. 'I've been wondering how you were getting on with it.' She thinks this is less peculiar than 'I have been carrying your letter around with me as though it will keep me safe.'

'Oh! Marvellously. We read it years ago, you know – well, I read it as a girl, and then I read it aloud to George when we were first married. We went to Lyme Regis on our honeymoon.'

'I'm so glad.' Kelly's imagination conflates the world of the novel with that of Rosemary and George, and imagines a young Rosemary in a Regency dress looking serenely from a window while a hopeful George stands nearby, the book open, 'I am half agony, half hope'. 'How can I help you today?'

'Oh, there's nothing I want, dear,' Rosemary says, 'except to say thank you. George and I take all sorts of tablets between us.' Kelly thinks she hears a catch in Rosemary's voice, but she can't be sure. 'But I really think this is the best medicine we've had in a long time.'

'That's so lovely to hear. I put something else in the post to you yesterday. To appeal to your silly side. I'd love to know what you think.'

Rosemary sounds surprised. 'It's nice of you to want to hear from a daft old woman like me.'

Ah, this is one of Kelly's bugbears. The pandemic hasn't changed that. 'Nothing you've written or said to us makes me imagine you're daft,' she says.

There's a sigh down the line. 'You're right, of course. I used to be in charge of a school. But when your brain gets old you make mistakes. And bits of your body start to ache and go wrong and it's hard not to feel that you're not what you were.'

It's Kelly's turn to sigh. She's taking care of her brain, with Sudokus and the weekend cryptic crossword, and her research when she can find the energy for it. But she must start running again. She might not enjoy it now, but when she's old she'll be glad of her good, dense bones. 'Do you have someone to help you? Family?'

'Oh, we've always managed. If you ever find yourself in Whitby, you're welcome to come and say hello and see for yourself.'

'My dad's in Whitby,' Kelly starts, but has to stop as her heart seems to fill her throat at the thought of him.

'Well, there you are, then,' Rosemary says. 'Goodbye, dear.'

There's a click and buzz that tells Kelly Rosemary has hung up. Back to social media it is.

Twenty minutes later, and Kelly is so busy scrolling that she jumps at the sound of a tap on the window; jumps again when she sees Craig there, waving and smiling. She opens the shop door, and oh, how she wants to touch him; but she clenches her fists at her side and makes her feet stay inside the doorway, feeling her longing curl across the space between them to meet his, coming back towards her. Her mouth is moist; her palms itch to reach for him. It's been two months since they've laid eyes on each other in person. The rules don't yet allow them to see each other. They've been holding out for the prospect of a socially distanced walk for weeks now.

And here he is.

'It's good to see you,' he says. He looks paler than she remembers – though now she thinks of it they may never have seen each other in daylight, their dates having all been wintry and after-work, and Craig never staying over.

'You too.' Then panic replaces longing. 'Are you – has

anything happened?' Though if he is standing there, in front of her, and he is well, and she is well, nothing much can be wrong. In their world, anyway.

'Yes, I'm okay. More than okay.' He lifts an arm, as though to touch her, remembers, jams his hand into his pocket. 'Nothing has happened.' That smile. 'Work has mandated an hour away from screens from one to two so we can all un-square our eyes and get some air. And walking along here seemed like the best possible use of that time.'

'Didn't you have to drive into York though?'

Craig laughs. 'Yes. I'd say it was a necessary journey.'

Kelly really doesn't agree. If everyone bends the rules a little then everyone will suffer. But oh, she has missed Craig so much. His smile. His herby shampoo smell. The way he looks at her. She cannot help but smile. No, grin. 'It's so good to see you.'

'It's so good to see you too.'

They look some more. Grin some more.

Then Craig looks at his shoes – he's wearing proper shoes, and a navy suit she has seen before. He would often be in it when they used to meet after work, have a meal, walk back to her place along the river. That tie is one she has hunted for on the chaos of her bedroom floor where their clothes have been abandoned. Desire cramps her lower belly, claws at her thighs. It has been too long. Craig looks up, and to the side of her face, as though her earring is the most interesting thing he has ever seen. 'The thing is, Kelly, I just can't stop thinking about you. And – say if this is a terrible idea – well, I wondered—'

She knows what he's going to say, just a fraction of a second before he says it. He's going to suggest they move in together. She's never even been to his place. It's too far out of town for it to have ever made sense. But with the roads quiet—

'I wondered if I could move in with you. I just – we're both miserable, aren't we? From not being together, I mean. So I thought it would make sense. And I didn't want to ask you over FaceTime. It didn't seem right.'

'We have done a lot over FaceTime,' she says, with a laugh.

He laughs back, maybe even blushes. 'Believe me, you and FaceTime have kept me sane. But this – I wanted to be able to look at you and see if you were sure.'

She loves him for this decency. It's the kind of thing her father would appreciate, too. She and Dad speak at least twice a week over Zoom, but as he often says, it's just not the same. Kelly has noticed that they rarely talk of her mother on these calls, though if they were sitting in his kitchen, eating cheese on toast and doing a crossword together as they used to, one of them would have mentioned her as a matter of course. She would have been in the room, somehow. In the air. The world might be digital, but humans have a way to go.

Perhaps he mistakes her silence for unwillingness, or doubt. 'That night we stood here and said we loved each other. I'll never forget it. And I wish we'd moved in when this whole lockdown started. I –' he looks away, then back, 'I suppose I thought if we were together all the time you would go off me.'

She reaches out a hand. Craig takes it and holds, tight. It's almost overwhelming, to touch, to be touched. 'Why would I go off you?'

Craig doesn't say anything. He looks at her hand in his, strokes his thumb along her skin.

'My flat's tiny.'

Craig smiles. 'It's cosy. And you can get food delivered – no one comes out to my place.'

'Won't we get on top of each other?' And then she laughs. 'Also, of course, that's what I want.'

Craig looks at his shoes again. 'I'm just a bit embarrassed by my place. It's a tip and it needs decorating, and there's mould in the kitchen and the bathroom. It doesn't feel like a place for you.'

She remembers him telling her all this, on one of their first dates. She had never laughed so much, she had thought afterwards, when talking about damp courses and cavity wall insulation. The builders were supposed to be starting in February, but Covid came, and lockdown came, and it all seems to be on indefinite hold. 'I don't want to pressurise you,' he says. 'But would you think about it?'

'I've thought,' Kelly says.

Of course they can manage at her place.

Craig kisses her forehead, tells her he loves her, and says he'll see her at seven. Kelly watches him go. She almost goes upstairs to tell Loveday her news, but the temptation to keep it hugged all to herself wins.

So she gets stuck into social media, and watches the clock. Once she finishes work at 4 p.m. she has time to get home, take the greyest of her knickers and bras off the radiators where they have been drying, clean the bathroom, and clear some wardrobe space for Craig. Maybe she'll have time to go to the supermarket and buy – buy what? What do couples eat? Camembert? Tiramisu? Things with fresh herbs snipped over the top? She's working on a shopping list, Instagram and Twitter forgotten, when the phone rings. It's Professor Azad, one of her favourite customers.

'Kelly, my dear,' he says, 'I hope you are well.'

'I am,' she says, and for once it feels as though she's giving a truthful answer to this most ubiquitous of questions. 'And how are you? And your family?'

'We are –' He laughs, such a kind laugh. 'Most of the time we are very grateful to be together. And our grandchildren make us young.'

Kelly glances at the clock. 'What can I do for you?' Professor Azad teaches at the university and his area of specialism is civil engineering. He's always interested in books about bridges; and he always wants to hear about any Kurdish history, or politics, or geology books that come into the shop. Loveday, who loves this kind of ongoing challenge, regularly comes across something that Professor Azad is delighted by. Or used to be. Given the way things are going, she might be looking for more profitable requests.

'Well, this is not my usual field,' the Professor says. 'I would like you to help me with something for my neighbour.'

17

Trixie

Trix's house-share mates bolted for home when they saw lockdown coming, and she can't blame them – Philippe's parents live on a farm in the south of France and Izzy's family is loaded, so they'll both be a lot more comfortable there than here. Izzy had asked Trix if she wanted to come: 'I'm going to live in the granny annexe so you could have my bedroom in the main house.' But at the time, lockdown had looked like six weeks, and six weeks had seemed both too long to live with a family Trix didn't know very well, and too short a time to worry about. And Trix is an adult. She likes her own company, her own space.

That's what she thought then.

After all, she had coped admirably, if she says so herself, when Caz took the job in Wales. Cardiff hadn't seemed far, then, and Trix didn't want to leave her job and start again. They weren't even living together, not really.

Managing a restaurant might not look like the height of achievement, but Trix had worked her way up from waitressing when she was doing her A-levels, supervising while she resat them, and taking the job as the assistant manager as a temporary stopgap while she decided what to do when she still didn't get the grades she needed to study veterinary medicine at uni. In the five years since then, she's become confident and capable, good with customers and better with staff. She's considered a rising star in the company; she's the youngest manager in the country. And she hardly ever thinks, now, about the fact that what she really wanted to do was be a vet.

Trix met Caz when she started to come in for late lunch on her own. Caz favoured a 2.30 p.m. time slot, so the restaurant was quiet, and she and Trix started to look, and then to talk, and then Caz left her card on the table one day when she paid her bill and said, I don't know what the ethics of manager–customer relations are, but it would be nice to see you away from here sometime.

That was two years ago. Things progressed quickly; Trix felt as though Caz was the first grown-up she'd ever dated, and that made her more of a grown-up herself. They liked the same food, the same films, the same music. Caz always wore black and it made her brown eyes shine dark from her face; when Trix watched her getting dressed in the morning, she felt as though she was watching her naked, pale beloved transform into another woman she loved, just as dearly but more discreetly. When they went to gigs, Caz always bought Trix a T-shirt, and Trix would wear it to sleep in that night. When they went to see films, Trix liked an aisle seat, so she went for popcorn and coffees once they had found their places. Even though both Trix and Caz were in their mid-twenties when they met in 2017, their idea of a high old time was a day out at Fountains Abbey, where they would eat scones outside the cafe that looked out over the water, and improvise dialogue between the ducks and swans. (Caz is the only person her age Trix has ever met who also has a National Trust membership.)

Soon, nights apart were the exception. Trix met Caz's family – a welcoming, ramshackle coalition of cousins, in-laws, and courtesy aunts and uncles – at Caz's brother's wedding. Caz put in her most discreet eyebrow and nose studs to visit Trix's grandmother, who now lives in a care home. Caz had been out for, as she tells it, all of her life, and Trix was welcomed into her family without so much as a flicker. Trix's grandmother had little grip on reality any more. Trix had told her, when she was sixteen, that she was gay. Her grandmother had made a hmmm-hmmm noise and the topic was never mentioned again, but at least no more 'nice boys from church' were mentioned.

And then Caz was offered the job in Cardiff.

Well, let's be accurate: Caz applied for a job in Cardiff. She didn't tell Trix, but she said that was because she didn't think she'd get it – wasn't serious about it, really. And then she went for the interview. She told Trix she was going to see a friend in Cardiff, which was not untrue: she stayed with the friend the night before the interview she'd failed to mention to Trix. To the woman whose bed she shared, whose body she adored, five nights a week.

Somehow, in the argument and the making-up that came when Caz was offered the job, neither of them mentioned that Trix might move. Trix liked to think that this was a respectful position. They both understood that Trix's job was important to her. They weren't some hetero couple where the bigger earner dictated the life path of their partner.

They hired a van and drove to Cardiff, to the flat-share Caz was moving into until she worked out how the land lay. It was only on that night, when Trix stayed over before driving the van back to York, that Caz cried, and told Trix that she couldn't bear to lose her. And so Trix left with certainty in her heart. And the certainty stayed. She and Caz kept up a non-stop WhatsApp chat as Caz got to know her new job and city. Caz didn't work weekends so she came to York every other Friday. Trix had to work Christmas Day, but when she got back after her shift Caz was waiting for her, having driven up for a surprise visit after their early-morning Merry Christmas call.

The pandemic didn't seem anything much, to begin with. A hypothetical. An over-there occurrence. Caz got anxious first, because the company she worked for had offices in China, and she was hearing things. To Trix, recovering from the usual busy December, and using January for stocktaking and deep cleaning and trying not to worry about how every other week saw a new restaurant opening in York, Covid was a mildly interesting news story.

And then.

There was a stretch of time – a week, maybe – when Caz could have decided to come back to York, or Trix could have gone to Cardiff. The wind was blowing very firmly in a very clear direction. The restaurant was running down stocks of perishable goods as best they could: no one seemed to feel like eating out. Trix made a daily run to the food banks with the things she knew they wouldn't use in time. Caz was doing complicated analyses of supply chains and spending a lot of time talking to concerned managers from offices all over the globe.

They talked about the possibility of moving in together, late one Friday night. Caz was a little drunk, and Trix was punch-drunk tired. They agreed that some sort of a lockdown was coming. They knew that they wanted to be together: that they missed each other. 'You could come down,' Caz said. 'The restaurant will have to close, won't it?'

'Yes.' The managers' weekly dial-in conference call had become less of a chore, of late, as they all waited for news of strategy and contingency. 'But I might still have to be around. You could come here. You said everyone's getting kit for working from home for a bit.'

'I could,' Caz agreed, and Trix's belly did a little happy rumble at the thought of Caz being within reach, all day, every day, if the whole world had to stay indoors for a while. 'But my flat here is nicer than your place there. And Philippe hates me.'

'Philippe's going back to France,' Trix said.

There was a moment of quiet. All that was needed was for one of them to say, let's do it, or, I'll come to you, or, I really think I'll feel better if I stay here, but I really want to find a way.

And then Caz said, 'Well, it sounds as though you need to get some sleep,' and somehow, they never talked about it again.

Trix thought, afterwards, that if neither of them was sure then of course it was best that they didn't. Caz said something similar during the first week of lockdown, as they compared notes on their shopping, and Trix offered to put some of her sachets of instant yeast in the post.

If they had known, then, that it would be months, not weeks, would they have done it differently? They both agree that they would have.

18

Medicine. We understand medicine as something ingested that will heal the body: something to fix a particular malaise. Take paracetamol for your headache; take antidepressants to make life more bearable, or to make everything less – well, just less. Explain your problem to someone who is qualified, and let them hmmmm and ah and poke and press. Give them a little blood, be cheerful while you lie, vulnerable, under a bleeping machine in a paper gown and feign bravery. When the results are in, ask an acceptable number of questions and take your medicine. Be glad you are alive. Especially now. It could be worse. Especially now.

Medicine is not the only thing we use to heal.

Or perhaps, there is more to healing than medicine.

There is the osmosis of love, one to another, through embrace if you are able, and smiles and looks if you are not. There is closing the door and disinfecting our hands and knowing we have made ourselves the safest we can be. There is the magic of shared experience: what relief, to know that there is something impersonal in this suffering, that there is hope of coming to the end of it!

And there are books. Readers know that, when their heart hurts with loss or absence, then a book that they have read before can lessen the ache. Readers, faced with a new experience, find a book to help them navigate: a travel guide to a new city, say, but also a novel set there.

Readers give books to other readers, telling them, this will make you laugh, or, read this, please, so we can talk about it. Here you are, readers say, I don't know why but this made me think of you.

But what about when the pain is too generalised, or too acute, or too strange for us to self-diagnose? What happens when the new pain cannot be cured with the old medicine? Or when the problem seems too trivial to mention – we are not dying, we are not even coughing, we have no right to claim we are suffering – or too great to fix?

What if reading itself feels like a chore, or someone who has always found solace in books suddenly cannot find the energy or the empathy to so much as pick up a favourite paperback?

That's when a bookseller can help you.

19

Loveday

When Loveday comes down the stairs, Kelly is saying goodbye and putting down the phone. She looks up. 'Professor Azad sends his best wishes. He wants us to think of something for his neighbour who doesn't read. And a couple of other things.' Kelly is frowning at the piece of paper in her hand, as though she doesn't quite believe what she's written there. 'I said we could drop them off by the end of the week.'

'Sure.' Loveday loves cycling through York's almost-car-free streets, although it feels as though she shouldn't be enjoying a side-effect of the lockdown. And Professor Azad is one of the few customers Loveday genuinely misses. It would be good to talk to him, even a quick hello from the pavement. 'Have you got time to talk? I've had an idea.'

'Sure. Always here for ideas.'

'I was thinking about you asking me about books, earlier. And I think – I think I see why we aren't making sales.'

Kelly waits. Loveday likes this about her. She always gives Loveday time to formulate what she needs to say. Kelly had applied for the post as shop manager shortly after the

103

post-fire reopening of the Lost For Words bookshop. The interview had been a lot of silences. The other candidates talked into them. Kelly waited.

Loveday says, 'When people ask us for books. When they could come to the shop, I mean. A lot of the time they're not saying, "Have you got any Charlotte Perkins Gilman?" They're saying, "I've read all of Virginia Woolf and I don't know where to go next."' She waits, to see if Kelly gets it. For as long as Loveday had worked at Lost For Words – since she was a teenager, working off the debt of a shoplifted copy of *Possession* by A. S. Byatt – she had noticed that for every customer with a list or a request, there was one who was browsing, not knowing exactly what they needed, looking for an answer to something; these were the people a book-seller could really help. This is the part of the shop being open that she really misses.

Before she says anything else, Kelly sits up very straight. She points at Loveday with both hands, an 'I see what you mean' gesture: 'Yes. You're right. Rosemary said *Persuasion* was better than medicine. Professor Azad wants something to help his neighbour. This is what we used to do.'

Loveday nods. She's not being ridiculous after all. 'We used to – prescribe books. As though they were medicine. We used to talk to the person, diagnose the ailment, and find something that could fix it.' Archie, with his Victorian ringmaster energy and enough friendship for everyone and anyone, seemed to be able to find the right book for anyone just by looking at the way they walked through the door. Loveday wishes, as she does every day, that he was here. He would have known what to do with a pandemic.

But he would also expect her to do things for herself.

For the shop. For readers. For this strange and suffering world. He wouldn't expect her to invent a vaccine or lead a march on parliament. But he would expect her to know how to turn Lost For Words into a place that was a force for good in the world.

'So I think what we need to do,' Loveday says, 'is to open a book pharmacy.'

20

Hozan, Now

It's Loveday who delivers the package, as the Professor had quietly hoped it would be. There's something about this young woman that makes him think of the many orphans he has met back home in Kurdistan, their fathers Peshmerga who fell foul of Hussein's regime, their mothers lost to disease or worse. Loveday doesn't smile much and she has a kind of diligence to her that suggests she is always, always trying to hold on to her place in the world, convinced it will not be hers for ever.

She stands at the gate, having placed the package on the ground and stepped back. She's picked up her bike and leans the saddle against her hip, holds the handles. Everyone is ready for a quick getaway now.

'Not your usual, Professor,' she says.

He laughs as he opens the package. He had asked for something for his wife to help her with keeping track of everyone in the wretched *EastEnders* that now dominates their lives – the Professor only watches it to keep Zhilwan company – and, despite his wife's warnings about judging and interfering, a book for Lorraine. Perhaps all she has lacked in her life is someone to put a book into her hand. And he also requested a copy of *Paddington*.

In a move he really tries not to mind, Lana has transferred the privilege of reading her favourite book to Lorraine. And the two of them have started reading it on FaceTime with Claire and Arthur. 'Lorraine is more good at voices, but you are more good at carrying me,' Lana had said, when the Professor had offered to start on the next book in their Paddington boxed set with her. Sazan had laughed and, for once, not corrected her daughter's grammar. Perhaps they are all learning.

Aside from *Paddington*, the package contains an *EastEnders* encyclopaedia for Zhilwan, and a book called *From the Year Dot*, an autobiography of someone named June Brown. When the Professor returns to campus he looks forward to discussing all of this with Tim from Media Studies. 'Thank you,' he says.

Loveday nods. 'I'll keep an eye out for anything interesting on civil engineering too, when people can start to bring books in again. There will be plenty of lofts being cleared out.'

'Treasure to be had,' the Professor smiles.

'You never know.'

'How are you, my dear? How is your mother? And your magician?'

Loveday shakes her head. 'My mother hasn't really got over Covid. She had it right at the beginning. None of the rest of us did. She didn't seem too ill with it, apart from the cough, but she's still exhausted all the time.' He sees how she looks at her hands, which are gripping the bicycle's

107

handlebars. 'The doctor says this is all unknown and we have to wait and see.'

'Zhilwan's mother used to say, "Wait and see" about everything.' The Professor laughs at the memory.

'And Nathan is fine. He's clearing out the yard at the back of the shop, just for something to do. There's not been a lot of call for close-up magic.'

'Was there before?'

Loveday laughs, and Yad comes over to peek across the threshold at the woman his Poppa is talking to. 'There was. It always amazed me. Corporate events and parties. Nathan could make more in an evening than the shop made in a week,' all laughter falls from her features, 'a month, probably, now.'

'Patience is the key to contentment,' the Professor says, and then imagines how Zhilwan would tease him if she heard him say such a thing when she so often counsels him to have patience himself. He shakes his head. 'Forgive me. I should say, I hope that all will be well for you, Loveday.'

Loveday looks at her hands. 'So do I. We've had an idea, but if it doesn't work I'm not sure what I'll do.'

And before the Professor can say another word, Loveday has mounted her bicycle and ridden away.

21

York Herald

**FAVOURITE LOCAL BOOKSHOP 'LOST FOR WORDS'
HAS OPENED YORK'S FIRST BOOK PHARMACY**

Lost For Words, one of York's longstanding cultural institutions, has found a way to help those struggling through the pandemic.

The second-hand bookshop in central York is now offering a 'book prescription service'. Owner Loveday Cardew explains: 'When the bookshop was open, many customers wouldn't come in looking for a specific book. Rather, they were looking for the solution to a problem, or some reading that would make them feel better. As we aren't allowing customers in at the moment, we have found another way that we hope will fill this need.'

Anyone who visits the Lost For Words website will find some 'general prescriptions': books for boredom, books for anxiety, books for people who are missing their families, etc. These are not self-help books, though there is a self-help section. 'It's easy to find the self-help book you need,' Loveday explains, 'but it can be harder to locate the novel or non-fiction that might change your mood or help you think differently. That's where our book pharmacy can help.' And it doesn't end there – there's also a more bespoke service. 'If anyone has a specific need they would like a book to help them with,' Loveday adds, 'they are very welcome to contact us via the website, or give us a call. We don't charge for prescribing books, and we can provide doorstep delivery or shop collection within York, or put book prescriptions in the post. We really want to help.'

22

Casey

Dear Lost For Words

Casey can't remember the last time she slept. As in, spark-out, dreamless, waking feeling ready for another day, or night, or whatever shift she was on. She can't believe that was ever even really something she has been capable of doing.

But she could sleep, once. In the early days of the pandemic she would stagger from work to the shower in the utility room. Her parents had originally installed it for her father, who would wash before coming into the house after a particularly filthy day at work: he had spent thirty years clearing hazardous waste for a building company. Later, when he retired early with back problems, the shower was handy for sluicing the worst of the mud off the dogs after winter walks.

None of them ever imagined that Casey would use it, especially as she had her own en suite. But once the pandemic got a grip, she would wash herself in water two degrees hotter than she could bear, put on the clean

111

pyjamas she had left on the utility room sink on her way out to the hospital, get her scrubs into the washing machine, wash her hands again, and only then go through the door into the main house. Depending on her shifts her parents might be awake, or they might not; they might be in, or they might be out. Casey soon got to prefer it when they weren't there to greet her, because she had no way to respond to their 'how was your day'. She couldn't find words; and even if she had been able to, she didn't want them to know.

In those early days she would eat the food her mother had left for her, say hello to the dogs, and get into bed. She'd put her headphones in, choose a sleep meditation, snuggle her head almost completely under the covers, and be out like a light until the alarm went off. She could sleep for ten hours at a go, then. In those days her body didn't know how to keep going after a long shift, and she had only her own needs to think about. She had moved back in with her parents after her marriage broke up, in 2019; they talked about it being temporary, but soon found the rhythm of how their family life had been before Casey married Josh.

Apart from her time in halls and house shares when she was training, Casey had lived at home until she got married. And she found she liked living at home again, during her divorce; her family was the same happy triangle it has always been. And she likes being able to focus on her work, which has always been the best and most satisfying thing in her life. Which Josh said was part of their problem. And not, in any way, his gambling. Still, that was behind her. She bought a new car on the day the decree absolute came through, a sporty little BMW, and sometimes when she finished her shift in the middle of the afternoon or the early morning, she drove away from the city and up and over the moors, fast, with her music on loud.

23

Kelly

Dear Rosemary,

This doesn't exactly fit what you asked for, but it's such a beautiful edition, and somehow, when I saw it, I thought of you.

I can't remember when I first read *Alice*, or more likely had it read to me. I remember my first time reading a lot of things – even as far back as my first Malory Towers! – but this must have been with me almost since I was born. It wasn't until I read it as an adult that I realised how very odd it is. But life's odd, I suppose, or at least not what we think it is going to be. I have had a nice surprise, for a change, and I'm just trying to enjoy it rather than over-thinking.

I hope you and your husband are well. (Or perhaps I should say, as well as can be expected.)

With love from the Lost For Words bookshop,

Kelly x

PS Loveday, the owner, and I were talking about Whitby and how we miss seeing the sea.

Craig has started to make Kelly a packed lunch. He prepares his own lunch at the same time, busy in the kitchen while Kelly showers and dresses. His first meeting is usually online at 9.30, so she makes sure she leaves the house by then, kissing him on the top of the head as he sets up his laptop.

If Kelly had had time to think about Craig moving in, she might have been worried about the things she would lose: time to work on her PhD, time spent soaking in the bath, her habit of preparing all the elements of her meal in advance and putting them in little bowls, something an ex-boyfriend teased her about and that she's been embarrassed by ever since. But if anything, Craig has given her more time. Sometimes when she gets home he's still working, so she spends an hour at her desk, rather than flopping in front of the TV or reading Agatha Christie until she's hungry enough to cook, as she would have done if she was on her own. Craig washes up after dinner so if Kelly wants to take a bath she does; and sometimes, he will come and join her when the dishes are done. He's even a fan of her prepare-the-vegetables-first methodology.

So this morning, she kisses him goodbye and takes her lunch, and sets off along the river path to work. Her toes itch with the urge to skip. It feels wrong, to be so happy. But then again, why add to the burden of sadness in the world by pretending?

When Kelly gets to work, Loveday is at the laptop. 'It's working,' she says, as Kelly comes through the door. 'We've had fifteen prescription requests overnight.'

'Fantastic.' For Kelly, this is another sign that her life is going in the right direction. She isn't going to need to find a new job after all.

'It really is,' Loveday says. 'I've printed the emails off so we can put our ideas against them.'

Kelly nods. 'Right.' Then, because she can't say nothing, she blurts, 'I've never been in love when it's been so easy.'

Loveday looks at her and Kelly remembers, too late, the things she knows about Loveday's family, her past. But Loveday smiles and says, 'I know.'

24

Mo

Dear Lost For Words,

When lockdown began, I thought I would be okay. I'm used to living on my own, I can work from home, I'm not in any of the vulnerable groups. My only relative, my brother, lives in London with his family and we're used to not seeing each other for a long time.

I was fine at first. But now my flat is redecorated and I've done a couch to 5k. I've watched everything that's supposed to be brilliant on TV, and I've read all the books I have here that I meant to read and never got around to. My inbox is at zero at the end of every working day.

I've never had a problem being single (people say I'm selfish, but I think it's more selfish to half-commit to a relationship for the sake of the bits you like). But I've realised that I miss all the small inconsequential interactions that I used to have. Talking to people at the gym. Work chat. Everything that would be nice/mildly interesting to talk about in person sounds trivial over Zoom. And selfish, when seven other people have to listen to it.

I suppose what I'm saying is: there's nothing wrong with me, and I have nothing to complain about. But if you have any books that could help me, I'd be grateful.

Yours,

Mo

Dear Mo,

Ah yes. We are alive so we can't complain. I know just what you mean. Until recently I was in a very similar position to you. I thought I would love all of my extra time and finally get things done. It sounds as though you did better than me on the getting things done front, but I can certainly relate.

I'm suggesting five books here. I suspect you are pretty well-read, so I won't be offended if you've read them all and I need to send another list! You'll find a mix of classics and more modern novels. Let me know which ones speak to you and I'll get them sent out as soon as possible. Depending on where you live we'll either post or do a doorstep delivery by bike.

Yours,

Kelly

Middlemarch by George Eliot. A novel about community and all of the small and strong ways the people of the town are bound to each other. Like the best novels (I think), it focusses on the everyday but is about things that are so much bigger.

A Piece of the World by Christina Baker Kline. About a woman who is bound to her home by illness, and her relationship with life and art.

118

The Adventures of Tom Sawyer. I re-read this recently and loved it. It's such a great evocation of a child's world, and I ended up totally absorbed in things like how to find a lost marble.

A Man Called Ove by Fredrik Backman. Stay with this one. It's about a man you might dislike to begin with, but I hope it will speak to you.

The List of my Desires by Grégoire Delacourt. A dressmaker in a small French town wins the lottery, but she's not sure if she wants her life to change.

25

Readers can hold complex thoughts, contradictions and moral oppositions in their minds, quite comfortably. It's one of the skills that we learn from words on a page. You can root for Emma Bovary while at the same time seeing that she is selfish and unkind. And you probably shouted 'no!' at the novel in your hands when she does . . . (no spoilers) quite a few of the things she does. You can feel wistful for both Henry Crawford and Edmund Bertram as you read *Mansfield Park*. Katniss Everdeen might annoy you but you would sharpen her arrows for her if you could.

So here is a contradiction for you: you can love books, and you can also decide not to finish a book.

Yes you can.

Books don't judge you.

Books can contain, and invoke, every feeling that there is. Books can bring you to rage or tears or happiness or all three, in quick succession. Books can have such a profound effect on your emotions that they can change the course of your life. How many lawyers have been made by *To Kill a*

Mockingbird, how many vets by the James Herriot books, how many teachers by Roald Dahl's *Matilda*?

This is how books work. They take what's in them, and add what's in you, and the interface, more often than not, leads to picking up that book every chance you get. Sometimes the power is so great that you're up all night; sometimes you have to (and yes, I do mean have to) cancel a coffee date so you can get to the end.

And sometimes, there's a missing part of the chemistry. Or something in the book that just doesn't work for you. Maybe the supposed romantic hero has the same name as the ex you will never quite recover from. It could be that the setting doesn't appeal or there's something in the way the characters relate to each other that doesn't fit into the receptor that you need it to fit into.

Sometimes, you do not care enough to want to read on.

This is something that books understand. That writers understand. That other readers understand. It's a fact of life. All foodies do not love bananas.

So if you haven't understood this yourself yet . . . take a moment. Take a breath. The next time you are fifty pages into something and rather than pick it up, you're scrolling through your phone . . . you can stop reading that particular story. You can donate or pass on that book, and you can start something else.

Reading should be a pleasure and a joy, an education and a promise, a release and an escape. The books you choose for yourself should never, ever feel like a punishment or a chore.

26

George, 1980

George and Rosemary plan to start a family after their fifth wedding anniversary, in 1974. Rosemary stops her birth control and – though it's hard to look back and imagine it was ever true – they assume that babies will come along.

That's not how it works out.

Rosemary's fifth miscarriage coincides with the beginning of the school summer holidays in 1980. George collects her from the hospital. He tucks her into the car seat, half-expecting her to tell him off for fussing. But she closes her eyes and lets him fasten the seat belt, put a blanket over her knees, even though it's a warm day in July. It's all he can think of to do.

When they get home, she walks slowly upstairs to their bedroom, gets into bed in her clothes, and falls deeply asleep. George watches over her. When she wakes he offers her every food he can think of, but she looks at him and says, 'George, I don't want anything, except my baby.' Her face folds in around the sadness of her mouth, her eyes closed tight. 'Just one of them.'

George has never felt so helpless in his life.

After the first four miscarriages (one that was closer to a late period, the others at between nine and twelve weeks) Rosemary had turned quiet, inside and out. And then they had talked, just a little, about their losses, and then they had agreed that it wasn't easy for some people but that was just how it was. And it would be worth the effort when they had their child.

George had said things like, it's up to you, and, I can't bear to see you go through this. Their doctor had referred them for tests, and they had put up with indignities, together and separately. But there was nothing wrong. Keep trying, was the advice, and they did. Their sex life, once loving and happy, was no longer pleasure for itself but a means to an end. As soon as it was over, instead of cuddling into George's chest, Rosemary would turn herself around, put her hips on her pillow and her legs against the wall, and close her eyes. George would reach for her hand, and sometimes she would take it.

This fifth loss, at fifteen weeks, and after they have told their wider family and friends, rather than just their parents, feels unbearable. It's unbearable for George, and he isn't the one who has been sick, has felt his body change in readiness and welcome for a child. Rosemary's mother had said, that baby's got a good strong hold of you, and Rosemary had beamed and nodded and said that she knew. They had started to plan, and to hope. On the outside, especially at school, George had watched as Rosemary had tried to be her usual self. He – perhaps he alone – had known that inside, his wife was fizzing with a mix of tiredness and excitement. In the evenings, over dinner, she talked about what was happening inside her body, those blood vessels in her uterus reaching out to the ones in her placenta, the nutrients in her body crossing into the baby, letting him or her begin to assemble their joints, their organs, their brain. She confessed to him that in classes she set reading tasks, and discuss with your partner tasks, so she could write lists of baby names on pieces of paper.

'Flower names,' he had said. 'Rose. Lily. Zinnia?'

Rosemary had laughed. 'Zinnia? Do you think we're brave enough? Zinnia Athey. She sounds very special.'

'She does.' George had thought of how, despite the sickness and the tiredness, it was a long time since he had heard his wife laugh so much. She laughed even more, when he suggested Basil for a boy, and she thought he was joking. George didn't mind. He was sure they were having a daughter, and anyway, after what Rosemary had been through, she could call their baby anything she pleased. When the pains started she had abandoned any attempt at the stoicism she had found through the previous miscarriages, and wept throughout the long night and day that followed.

More superstitious with each pregnancy, they had not bought baby clothes that time. But Rosemary had bought books. And of course, one of them was by Lewis Carroll.

27

Rosemary

When Rosemary opens the package from Lost For Words and sees that it is *Alice's Adventures in Wonderland*, in an edition illustrated by Helen Oxenbury, her impulse is to put it straight in the charity bag and pretend to George that the knock from the postman had been someone checking that they were okay. But she has never – almost never – hidden things from him, and today does not feel like a good day for a lie.

She walks down to the bench to join him. There's a nip in the wind, so she brings a blanket, as well as the book. He's been quiet since yesterday, and he's quiet now. Of course he is. It was not the hospital visit they had hoped for.

It had started well enough. They had been walking down the broad corridor towards the outpatient clinics, when they had bumped into a nurse who remembered them from school – in fact, she had called out Rosemary's maiden name, after them, down the corridor. It had been difficult to make out who she was at first, with the mask covering all of the bottom of her face, and the strip of the visor across her forehead. But she repeated, 'Miss Bell?' and added, 'It's Carol, Carol Johnson, you used to teach me English?' And Rosemary was back in her first classroom, finding her voice and her way, abandoning reading-round-the-class in favour of acting out the opening scene of *Romeo and Juliet*.

'Carol!' Rosemary said. 'How good to see you!' They hadn't chatted; Carol was obviously in a rush to get somewhere. But she said, 'I hope you're both well,' in a way that conveyed the certainty that they weren't. They all knew that they wouldn't have been invited to come through the hospital doors otherwise.

'We haven't been in hospital this much since –' George had said, as they sat in the waiting room, beneath the white-board that read, 'This clinic is running 35 minutes late'.

'I know,' Rosemary said. Her hand found his. It was hard to believe that hospitals still smelled the same as they did then, but the smell was unmistakeable. Bleach and boiled sweets, and bodily fluids beneath.

The kind-eyed consultant might have had her words muffled by her visor, but the diagnosis was unequivocal. The words 'conservative care', Rosemary had realised, meant there was nothing to be done to reverse George's condition, or to fix him. George had reached for Rosemary's fingers, clasped them, and Rosemary had clasped back. Someone had said, 'I'm sorry.' Not someone. Rosemary. She had been crying. George's face had been still.

'I'm not ready.' Her words had sounded desperate, pleading, and she had made herself stop talking. This was not about her. It was about George, strong, steadfast George, who deserved better than this.

'Well, that's good, because neither am I,' he had said.

126

And now, here they are, twenty-four hours later, and everything is still quiet. They have barely said a word. It's just like when they lost the last of their babies. (Lost. Why do people say 'lose'?)

Rosemary pours the tea, and hands George his. It's on the tip of her tongue to ask him how he is, but she must have asked him four times an hour today, and he just nods, as if to say, I'm here and that's all I know.

'We had another book from Lost For Words,' she says, instead.

'Oh?'

She passes it over and he turns the pages, slowly. 'They're not the illustrations I remember,' he says.

'No,' she says, 'it's a newer version. We had the Tenniel illustrations.' Rosemary remembers how, sick and sorry with grief, she had stuffed their baby's library into a bin bag and sneaked it into the dustbin, after dark. She has never thrown books away, before or since. 'I threw the baby's books away. I never told you.'

'I realised. One day they were then the next they had gone.'

Rosemary almost laughs. She's kept this secret for years and of course, it was never a secret at all. 'I'm sorry,' she says.

'You've nothing to be sorry for. I'm sorry we couldn't be parents,' George says, closing the book and taking her hand. 'I don't know whether I said so, at the time.'

'It doesn't matter now.'

It does, though. They should have talked about it. Now, they would be given counselling. Then, they were handed a leaflet about adoption. Rosemary had thrown that away too.

Something had died in Rosemary after that last

miscarriage, and perhaps, if she had let George help her, something else would have grown.

Rosemary watches her husband as he looks out over the sea. Perhaps it's her turn to bear witness, as he bore witness to her pain. She can't tell what he's thinking. Then he turns to her and stretches an arm along the back of the bench. She sees him wince as his body flexes. 'If we're going to read this,' he says, 'you're going to have to come closer so we can both look at the pictures.'

28

Loveday

Those fifteen prescription requests on the first day were only the beginning. The Lost For Words Book Pharmacy is probably the closest it's possible to get to an overnight success in a world where everything is slowed by illness and social distance. The online form is filled in at least thirty times a day, and people come to the door, too, looking for escapism, help with boredom, or just 'anything to stop me watching the news'. The more personal questions come online. Well, Loveday can relate to that; she wouldn't want to stand in the street, telling a stranger that she's starting to hate her own mother or that she's convinced that everyone she loves is going to die. She wouldn't even want to fill a form in and email it off saying those things, but a lot of people do. Not everyone, she reminds herself, thinking of her mother safe at home and Nathan within touching distance, not everyone is as lucky as I am. (Succeeding feels indiscreet, somehow, but Loveday is glad of it all the same. She would never have forgiven herself if the business she inherited from one of the best humans she had ever known had failed within six years of his death.)

The story in the local press made it to a feature on the BBC News website about community. Feelgood stories seemed to be few and far between, and so news of their book prescriptions has travelled.

The Bookseller called for an interview, which Kelly was delighted by, though Loveday couldn't really see that giving their idea away to every other bookseller in the land was helpful. It would have been churlish to say so, so she didn't.

The main thing is, they are busy. It's such a relief to have a way to spend the day that doesn't feel like marking time – no matter how much you love poetry, there's only so tidy a poetry section can ever be – or wasting it. Enjoying things feels wrong when there is so much amiss in the world. But work feels good. The book prescriptions ready for collection sit in paper bags to the left of the door; the ones waiting to go to the post office are in sacks and will be collected. The days of Loveday nipping to the post office with her panniers full are over. She still likes to deliver local parcels by bike, though.

'Craig says he can come in and give us a hand on Saturday if you like,' Kelly says from the other side of the shop where she's parcelling recipe books in brown paper, for someone who is sick of their own cooking and doesn't know where to start with something new.

Loveday makes a noncommittal noise. She has, for no good reason, taken a dislike to Craig. Which is ridiculous, because she hasn't even met him. Nathan says it's her default position – dislike someone until they prove they're worth the effort – and he's not wrong.

Kelly adds, 'It's so nice to be with someone who really cares about me.'

Unexpectedly, Loveday hears herself saying, 'I know.'

Kelly smiles. 'And he says what he feels, and he doesn't seem to think anything is complicated or difficult as long as we're together. He says, the world's outside the door and it can stay there.'

'I'm glad you're happy.' And she is.

Loveday thinks of the previous evening, on the sofa, legs tangled with Nathan's, both of them reading. Vanessa had been washing up to the sound of her 'Domestic Drudgery Playlist'. Vanessa and Nathan had been running lines over dinner, in preparation for some sort of cycling-joke-marathon they are planning to take round the local streets. Loveday isn't sure how the two of them have managed to bag Fun Pandemic, but they're good at it. Better than she would be.

Loveday had worried, when Vanessa moved in, that they would get on each other's nerves; they had never spent longer than a family lunch together. But Vanessa is as easy-going as Nathan, and Loveday soon found that she actively likes her, rather than having to make an effort. Sarah-Jane says the two of them are like the Dashwood sisters from *Sense and Sensibility*; and Loveday realised she'd feared their relationship would be closer to that of Elizabeth Bennet and Caroline Bingley in *Pride and Prejudice*.

The newspapers were full of gloomy tales of the rise in online searches for 'quickie divorce', and every other radio programme seemed to contain a joke about how your partner must be driving you insane after all this time. And yet Loveday, with her boyfriend and her book, and her face sore from laughing at Nathan and Vanessa's jokes, was so very content. Or would be, if her mother was more like her pre-Covid self. She was able to isolate properly in her room, which has an en-suite, and did so from the second she started to run a temperature. So no one else in the house had caught it, or if they had, they hadn't known; there were no tests, then. Loveday remembers how relieved she was. And yes, her mother wasn't hospitalised, isn't dead; but this skulking malaise is still a hard thing for Sarah-Jane to endure and Loveday to witness.

Loveday had glanced up from her reading and seen Sarah-Jane turning the pages of a magazine, listless and pale, although she had seemed to enjoy her meal this evening, rather than glumly pushing food around her plate and saying, 'I'm sure it's lovely, it's just that I cannot taste a blessed thing.'

'Mum? Are you okay?' she had asked.

Sarah-Jane had looked up and said, 'I can't complain.'

And Loveday had known what she meant. Loveday's father had been – not at first, of course – a violent man, and when he had found out his wife was planning to leave him, the resultant fight had ended in his death. Sarah-Jane went to prison, Loveday went into the care system, and it was years before the mother and daughter were able to reunite, to forgive each other's long years of silence, to build their relationship into something meaningful once more. So of course Sarah-Jane feels she cannot complain. She is safe and comfortable, and in the same room as her daughter. Lockdown is still freedom for her.

'You can, though, Mum.' Loveday had put down her book and gone to sit at her mother's feet. She knew that if she leaned back, her mother would stroke her head, and Sarah-Jane did, the dry skin on her fingertips catching at Loveday's hair. 'You're allowed to feel ill. And to say so.'

Sarah-Jane had nodded. 'I know. I know. But even if I have to rest halfway up the stairs every time, this is still the best my life has ever been.'

In the shop, Loveday's phone pings with a message from Nathan. Be there in ten minutes, it reads, will do some more on the yard if that's okay? Love you x

Loveday loves that he keeps on telling her he loves her. Every text message, every night, every morning. It's the sort of thing she would have assumed she would find annoying, before it became part of her everyday life. She might have wondered, too, whether 'I love you' needed restating. Surely if you know, you know, and once it's said, it's on record? But that has turned out not to be true, either. Telling Nathan she loves him – sometimes, she is even the one to begin it – is like reading a favourite page, over and over.

29

Bryony

To: Lost For Words
From: Bryony

Help! I saw the article about your pharmacy in the York Herald.
I need something completely escapist. I've always loved crime,
of all sorts. True crime, police procedurals, anything with a
serial killer. Now I'm in lockdown on my own and I can't sleep.
Lone women being murdered in their beds doesn't seem to be
the pleasure it used to be. I'm not convinced psychopaths and
murderers are likely to be Covid safe?! Although you never know.
My budget is £20 and I can collect from the shop.

To: Bryony
From: Kelly at Lost For Words

Dear Bryony,
Everything is upside-down, isn't it? I thought lockdown would

mean I would finally get around to Dostoevsky. Instead I have hardly any time for reading. Life is never what you think.

I've had a look through our £4 fiction section – they are all paperbacks in good condition. I'm listing six books, below – if you can let me know which you like the sound of (if any) I'll put them aside for you. You can collect at the door. We're only accepting card payments at the moment.

Stay well,

Kelly

Books for a sleepless crime fan:

The Daughter of Time by Josephine Tey. A recuperating police officer with a broken leg becomes fascinated by the idea of whether Richard III was so terrible after all.

Dissolution by C. J. Sansom. The first of a detective series set in Tudor times. Crime, but not the sort that is going to keep you awake at night.

The Prime of Miss Jean Brodie by Muriel Spark. A teacher exerts a lot of influence at a girls' school between the wars. This is funny and chilling and I envy anyone who hasn't read it yet.

Birdcage Walk by Helen Dunmore. Hard to describe this one – it's a sort of historical murder mystery/psychological thriller, and I loved it.

The Woman in White by Wilkie Collins. Wilkie Collins pretty much invented detective fiction. This is twisty and absorbing without being terrifying!

Gone Girl by Gillian Flynn. This might mean you can't sleep for a different reason – I couldn't stop reading once I started. A woman disappears, her husband is suspected . . . but nothing is as it seems.

30

Loveday

An hour later, and Loveday goes out to the yard to see how Nathan is doing. He looks to have taken all of the dust, weeds and rubbish that was lying around and rubbed them through his hair. She loves him for this confidence he has, to launch himself into something.

He smiles when he sees her. He always smiles when he sees her. 'Hey,' he says.

'Hey.'

He rubs at his head. 'I'd say sit down, but I don't think there's anywhere safe. Or clean.'

Loveday shrugs and sits herself on the ground, where she can put her back against the wall. 'These jeans are going in the wash anyway.'

He sits down next to her. 'This space could be really nice, you know.'

Loveday looks around. The old shed didn't survive the fire, five years ago. There's paving, and a couple of bins, and even though the cafe next door has been mostly closed since lockdown began, and is now only doing takeaway hot drinks and cakes sold from the doorway, the air has retained the memory of sour milk and chip fat. Or it could be that the drains need flushing. Or whatever you do with drains.

'Nice for rats?'

Nathan laughs and bumps his shoulder against hers. 'No. For bookworms. We could build some sort of trellis over there to screen off the alley.' He gestures, his conjurer's hands making shapes in the air, 'And we could have some seating, so people can sit outside and read. If we paint the wall a good colour it'll feel like a room. And we could have waterproof patio furniture, and if we get a storage box we could keep cushions in it . . .' He glances at Loveday. 'No?'

Loveday sighs. She doesn't really like being the one who says no, but it tends to be her job, as Nathan is so used to making things happen, through a combination of enthusiasm and a general expectation that the world will say yes. He has taught her that more things are possible. And if there's something that Loveday wants to do, she's learned that the best way to achieve it is to mention it to Nathan, and then let his positivity power her through her own doubts.

Plus, sometimes he's right.

But not this time. 'We haven't got time. Well, I haven't. I don't like leaving Mum as much as I do as it is. And I don't think we should be spending money at the moment. Not until –' Loveday's gestures aren't as fluid as Nathan's, but she still manages to convey: until we are making more money, or we know for sure the book pharmacy is more than a novelty and the shop will survive the pandemic, or the pandemic is over. Or I have the energy to think about something over and above this new, unchosen everyday.

'But you don't mind if I keep at it out here? Make it nice for your lunch breaks?'

'Of course not.' Loveday wants to say, I cannot think of a single thing you would do that I would mind. But then she thinks of the poetry competition that she couldn't find enthusiasm for. Running a business – even a beloved bookshop – is hard. There's a lot to it. Not least, deciding where to put your effort, because there's never enough time for all the things you want to do; and never knowing whether you've made the right call.

Instead of saying anything at all, she squeezes his hand and bumps her shoulder to his, in what he calls her penguin move. Loveday closes her eyes and, next to her, Nathan exhales. 'I love you,' she says.

There's a banging on the shop door: or, if not a bang, something more assertive than a knock.

Loveday feels the old shock, even though there's nothing to fear now. No one who comes here can hurt her or frighten her. The worst that can happen, now, is a customer with a complaint about a book. Nathan takes her hand, squeezes, 'Do you want me to go?'

'No.' She gets to her feet. 'But thanks.'

Loveday walks through to the front door of the shop. There's a child, waiting at the other side, peering through the glass. Well, a teenager. Ironed-flat hair and attempted cat-eye mascara and her teeth still a little too big for her face.

'Hey,' Loveday says when she opens the door. She suspects, from the kid's unsmiling face, that she's not the sort who wants people to look pleased to see them, so she doesn't. 'What can I do for you?'

'I saw your thing.'

139

'The book pharmacy?' Loveday asks.

'Stupid name,' she replies.

Loveday doesn't say anything. She props the door open and starts going through the slips on the desk that tell her which books are still to be collected, and the approximate times the buyers might arrive. Not that they hold people to anything – and they're not going to turn anyone who misses their slot away – but she doesn't want to risk a queue at the door. If she's responsible for a bloom of disease, she will never forgive herself.

Loveday glances over then looks away. She has an instinct for kids like these. 'I'm called Loveday. I like stupid names.'

The girl laughs, and when she does she looks like someone else: a happy goblin. 'I'm Madison,' she says. 'People say that's stupid.'

Loveday shrugs, a what-do-they-know gesture. 'I think it's a cool name,' she says, before realising that cool probably doesn't mean cool any more. 'Do you need a book?'

Madison glares at her for a moment, and then says, 'A book's not going to solve anything.'

'It's not going to solve everything,' Loveday almost-agrees.

'I don't really like reading. But my mum, she used to get magazines from work. She says she's sick of the sight of the telly and she's given up reading the paper because she's got enough problems of her own.'

'Sensible woman. What sort of books does she like?'

Madison looks away, 'She doesn't usually read. We don't. Her or me.'

Loveday is not given to affectionate gestures with strangers. She rather likes the way social distancing means that people you barely know can no longer lunge into a

140

hug with you. But right now she wants to take Madison by the shoulders and give her a big old squeeze. What courage it takes, to be fourteen or fifteen and stand at a bookshop door and try to buy a book for your mother, even though neither of you reads. Loveday has no idea what she would be without reading, but she knows she wouldn't have survived her childhood.

'Okay. What does your mum watch?'

Madison pulls a face. 'She can watch what she likes now my dad's gone. Stupid stuff. *Emmerdale. Casualty.* And she likes anything with,' she gestures at Loveday's head, with her hair in its lockdown topknot, 'hats.'

'Hats?'

Madison puts her hand on her own (hatless) head, flat, then moves it upwards. 'Tall hats. And big dresses. Horses.'

'Oh!' Loveday gets it. She immediately wants to rename the historical fiction section 'Tall Hats, Big Dresses and Horses'. 'Period drama? Like *Downton Abbey*? Or *Bridgerton*?'

'Yes.' Madison rolls her eyes, and Loveday rolls hers back. It seems she's not the only person who could live happily without ever seeing another visiting card on a silver tray.

'Hold on.'

She comes back to the door with *Riders* by Jilly Cooper and *The Grand Sophy* by Georgette Heyer. 'This,' she holds up the Cooper, 'is basically posh Emmerdale with horses.' The Heyer is an old Pan mass market edition, pleasingly scuffed at the corners, with Sophy depicted leaning on an ornate fireplace in a cream satin dress, dangling a fan and resolutely ignoring a leering man in peach breeches. 'And this is about a woman who has to sort a whole family out.'

Madison takes both, then hesitates.

'You can have them for nothing,' Loveday says. And – hang on—' She nips into the YA corridor of shelves and pulls out *Solitaire* by Alice Oseman. 'Here's one for you.'

'I don't really like reading.' She's looking at the cover with something approaching interest, though. That bold strip of red, only knife-shaped if you concentrate. 'What's it about?'

Loveday shrugs. 'Read the first page to see if you like it.'

Madison shoves the books into her bag as Loveday tries not to wince. Still she stands. Eventually she says, 'Who else works here?'

Loveday says, 'Me, and my shop manager. And a couple of volunteers.' Inspiration strikes. 'Are you looking for a job?'

Madison looks at her with scathing patience. 'I'm fifteen? I have school?'

'I'm looking for someone to help out on Saturdays. Packing books, sorting out, that sort of thing.'

Madison hesitates, then shrugs. 'Okay. I can't start till twelve. I have to get the bus in. And do my hair.'

'See you Saturday, then,' Loveday says, and Madison slings her bag over her shoulder and walks off.

'Nice work,' Nathan says, coming through the door that leads, via the staffroom, to the yard.

Loveday laughs. 'How long have you been listening?'

'I was just coming in and I heard from "I have school". Teenage sarcasm carries a long way.'

'Kelly and I were just saying we were going to need some help,' Loveday says. Nathan grins and kisses her head.

142

31

Casey

Dear Lost For Words,
I'm not much of a reader but

It was about two months into the pandemic that the dreams started; Casey assumed exhaustion was giving way to anxiety. She knew a lot of her colleagues were experiencing the same thing.

The dreams were not precisely dreams. They were more like jumbles of memories, out of order and out of sync. Casey dreamed of watching patients being intubated while she stood in a circle of applauding medics. She dreamed of taking a patient in a wheelchair to the morgue instead of the main entrance to the hospital where their family was waiting to take them home. She dreamed of taking blood that curdled into something living, something with spikes and eyes, in the ampule. A rasping sound that turned out to be her own breathing. She dreamed that she was unqualified, and no one realised, not even her, until she was standing at the entrance to her ward and everyone was waiting for her to tell them what to do. She dreamed of admitting her father, of her mother unconscious with her oxygen levels plummeting like a boulder from a cliff.

The worst of all: she dreamed of trying to intubate herself because there was no one left to do it.

32

Zoe

To: Lost For Words
From: Zoe
Re: Book prescription

Hello,

I saw your book prescriptions online and I wonder if you can help. I have a four-year-old son and a three-week-old baby. My husband is a key worker (paramedic) and we have decided it's best for him to live away from us for now, in case of infection.

My mum was supposed to come and stay with us to help when the baby was born, but my dad is unwell and she can't travel.

I'm telling you this because I don't want you to think I'm being feeble. I know lots of people have it much worse than we do. I'm just a bit – I don't have anyone to ask about things, or help me with things. (I'm not feeling sorry for myself.)

I wondered if you could find some books for my little boy? To help him feel brave? He's only four, he has a new sister, he's missing his dad, he can't go to nursery or see his friends. I'm doing my best but I'm quite tired – the baby is more of a napper than a sleeper, and I haven't had more than three hours in one go since she was born. I'm using the TV as a babysitter a lot for Tommy, even though I know I shouldn't.

We have a few books at home, but we used to use the library – we don't have a lot of money and our flat is tiny.

Would you believe it has taken me two days to write this email in between feeds and everything else?! We went to the park yesterday but I got a bit freaked out by all the other people so we came straight home. Tommy cried a lot. But I think if he can't see his dad in case we all catch Covid, I don't want him on a slide straight after a load of kids who might not have washed their hands. I should have thought of that before I took him out. I can't manage him on his scooter when I've got the buggy with Ellie in, and he's not got as much control as he thinks he has!

Thank you,

Zoe

PS I don't know how much books are but what could I get for £20? And what do you do to make your books safe before you send them?

As soon as Zoe presses 'send' she wishes she could get the email back. All she had to do was say, 'Please send some books suitable for a four-year-old, to a value of £20'. At least they don't know who she is, at the bookshop, and if she walks past she doesn't have to identify herself. Central York is actually quite nice for a walk, now there's not so much traffic. When she has the energy she and Tommy play a game called 'see interesting things'. They take it in turns to pick things out and the other gives them a score out of five. From this, she has learned the things Tommy finds most interesting are: dog poo on a double yellow line, a discarded mask hanging on a tree 'like a fruit, Mummy!', a banana skin. Literal rubbish. He scores her highest on: a rainbow poster stuck in a second-floor window, that she has to lift him up to see, and a cat on a wall, flicking its tail back and forth in watchful annoyance. How Zoe wishes she were a child.

Right now, at 4 p.m. on a grey Thursday that feels too wet for June, both children are asleep. Zoe knows she will regret this later, when she is on her knees with tiredness, and Tommy is still bouncing around, getting out the doll's house or the box of cars, when all she wants is to lie in the dark and let some low-impact TV wash over her. If she closes her eyes then, she will imagine herself to be in the company of adults. Ellie's 'grizzle zone', as Will calls it, is reliably 7 p.m.–10 p.m. The one time Zoe ventured online to ask a bit of advice from other mothers, she wished she hadn't. Most of the mums in Zoe's antenatal classes were on their first pregnancy, and it showed: lots of talk about 'looking forward' to the birth and wondering whether they could take their hair straighteners into hospital. Still, their WhatsApp group is the only place where there is guaranteed to be someone online. So she'd asked the question, and the answers hadn't helped a bit.

SCARLET:
Sweetheart, have you considered that if you're expecting Ellie to be tense, she might become tense? Don't underestimate your bond!

BEX:
Is this after bathtime? Could the water be too hot, or too cold? Are you changing her into sleepsuits that might have been washed in non-organics?

JUDE:
What do you have for lunch? Maybe it's coming through in your milk. I'm so glad we went to clean eating when we found out about the pregnancy!

There was only one response that was actually useful to Zoe. She is, as far as she can tell, equally tense at all times; she uses the same washing powder all the time, for all of their clothes, and cannot afford to even think about organics; she considers it a food luxury if she manages to butter the bread for her lunchtime crisp sandwich.

LOUISE:
Only three hours of grizzling? I'll swap Ellie for Cate. She's doing it the other 21 hours. Leave Ellie on the step and I'll be round in 10 minutes.

Zoe had laughed. It was a good sound. Tommy looked round at it. 'Do you know a joke?' he asked.

'No, it's just that baby Cate's mum thinks we should swap Ellie for her baby because Cate cries a lot more than Ellie does.'

Tommy had glanced at the bouncing chair where Ellie was contorting her face as though holding a silent argument (although, more likely, preparing to shoot shit up the back of her nappy and vest and into her filament-fine yellow-brown hair). 'I don't think we should do that if baby Cate cries more than Ellie,' Tommy had said, and the sheer, world-weary, four-year-old pragmatism in his voice had made Zoe laugh again.

Zoe knows she ought to try to sleep too, even if it is the

148

middle of the afternoon. But she can't let herself close her eyes for more than a blink's breath. Quiet time is her only time to really miss Will. To really think about him, properly, rather than low-level worrying about him all the time, in case an anti-masker has spat on him or a patient has died on him. Her husband holds himself responsible for each and every death in his care, regardless of the odds. She looks forward to the chance to immerse herself in thoughts of him. She saw him last when he kissed the top of Ellie's head, then the top of hers, and then backed out of the delivery room, tears in his eyes. They had agreed that he would go to stay with his colleague for as long as they felt it was necessary. Some people they know – nurses, doctors, fellow paramedics – have rigged up showers in the garden so they can wash before they enter the house, or have made utility room no-go zones for the family, washing, changing and disinfecting before they resume their home lives. Will and Zoe don't have the space in the flat, and anyway, there's a shared hallway downstairs. So they made a wise and sensible choice, and they made it for the greater good of their family, and their community. And oh, it hurts. Zoe has friends who treat their husbands or partners as encumbrances, annoyances, or extra children. She and Will aren't like that. They never have been.

It's as though she conjures him up. Her phone screen leaps to life. 'Hey, Zo,' his face, his darling face, 'can you talk?' FaceTime is a wonder but oh, he looks tired. And she cannot get used to him without his big, beautiful beard, that had soft-scratched at her for as long as they have been together. It had to go, so that the PPE could form a proper seal around his face. She had cried when he had shaved it

149

off, and then felt feeble. She has nothing to cry about. Not really.

'Always,' she half-whispers, though that's not true. The last twenty-four hours have been all missed calls and texts as they have tried to snatch five minutes. 'They're both asleep. Have been for half an hour.'

He glances at his watch, and she knows that he's doing the same calculation she is: peace now, versus sleeplessness later. 'I don't care,' she says. 'I think I'm just going to ignore time from now on. And look.' She reverses the camera, and points her phone down at her chest, where Ellie is sprawled, a milk-drunk expression on her face, her cheek and nose still squished against Ellie's breast. Tommy is next to her on the sofa sleeping neatly, as he always has: on his side, knees together, fists clenched under his chin like little paws. They had to make the effort to stop calling him 'Mouse', when he turned a year old, for fear it would become his name.

Zoe turns the camera back to her. Will is pink-eyed and she wonders, suddenly, if this helps. She has always assumed keeping in touch was a good thing. But maybe if they were out of sight, they'd be out of mind, and that way they could both get on with what they had to do, and stop tearing at each other's hearts like this. Politicians talk about the pandemic as though it's a war. If she couldn't talk to Will it would feel like one. And maybe in a war she would be braver.

He's scrutinising her and she suddenly wishes that she looked – better. Though she doesn't know what better is. The last time she planned to put make-up on, the Christmas before last, her mascara had been dried shut, and her lip

150

gloss had separated into a thick dark goo and a watery slime. She laughs at herself.

'What's funny?'

She shakes her head. 'I was just thinking, I wish I looked nice for you.'

'You and the kids are the best things I've ever seen, Zoe. Don't forget.'

And although she wasn't fishing, she can't help but look forward to what he'll say next. You always look nice to me, or, you couldn't look bad if you tried, or you and the kids are the nicest things I could ever see. But he doesn't say any of those things. Instead, he says, 'Zoe, I've got something to tell you. You're not going to like it.'

The worst has happened at last.

Instead of dreading Covid coming to her family, living with a hunched gut and a sense of shadows looming, Zoe can face it. Well, sort of. At least she and Will now know that they were right in separating themselves from each other, despite what his mother had had to say about drama, and his father's tutting in the background of the Zoom call when they held brand-new Ellie up to greet her grandparents, and explained that, no, no one would be visiting, and in fact, Will would be living with another one of the ambulance crew when Zoe went home with Ellie. Tommy had stayed with their downstairs neighbour and bubble-mate, 'Auntie' Julia, and though it wasn't ideal it had felt like a triumph. As had Ellie's birth coming at 1 p.m., with no epidural, so Zoe could be home, exhausted but just about upright, for Tommy's bedtime.

Will has promised to call her whenever he wants to, or if

things change, and not worry about whether he might be disturbing her. And that he'll be honest with her: no saving her feelings, no protecting her from the worst. In turn he made Zoe promise to stay away from Google and the news.

His 5 a.m. text reports that he's been coughing all night but there's no sign of a fever. His temporary flatmate Barney has gone on shift, and left cereal, milk, a flask of tea and a packet of biscuits at Will's bedroom door. Will is going only between the bathroom and bedroom, and sterilising everything he has touched when he has left his room. Zoe puts her arm across the space at Will's side of the bed. Tommy hasn't bounced in with her yet, and Ellie is asleep in her Moses basket, arms flung above her head, close enough for Zoe to hear the softness of her breathing. Zoe has never imagined a situation where one of her family was ill, and she couldn't be the one to take care of them.

So. If he's being honest, there's nothing to do but get on with the day. She gets up and takes photos of Ellie and Tommy, curled up and snoring still – it's almost eight, but it was gone midnight when he went to sleep last night – and WhatsApps them to Will. He isn't online. She hopes he's asleep. The not-knowing pulls at her guts.

33

George, 1983

George was never sure when they decided that they weren't going to have a family. Or rather, he doesn't think they ever discussed it. It was just clear, one day, about six months after the fifth and final miscarriage, that it was just them, and it was always going to be. They had become A Childless Couple.

George's desire to be a father is tiny in comparison to his need to ensure that Rosemary never, ever suffers again the way she suffered after the last miscarriage. So he's okay. He's sorry that they haven't talked about it. But, as his mother says about almost everything, least said, soonest mended.

And they have mended, as far as George can tell. They sleep well, and they eat as though they are hungry, and they feel – well, it is, George imagines, the way it might be if the business you have been trying to keep afloat for years finally goes under. Rosemary didn't really talk about it, except once, to say she felt as though she had taken off shoes that had been blistering her feet day-in, day-out for all of a long, cold winter.

Rosemary repaints the living room in primrose yellow, rather than the previous dull green. George re-grouts the tiles in the kitchen. They talk about having a new bathroom. Rosemary had chosen their original suite, which included a pale peach shell sink, and George had imagined he would learn to live with it. He hadn't, and thought of his shaving time every morning as being akin to Orwell's Two Minutes Hate in *1984*.

George tells Rosemary this, one Sunday, as they stand in the kitchen waiting for carrots and peas to be done. It's the date their baby was due to be born; Rosemary hasn't mentioned it, but she's quiet, and George is desperate to distract her from the pain she must be in.

Rosemary looks at first as though she might cry, and George curses himself for rocking their barely-afloat boat. But instead she laughs, holding her sides and leaning against the kitchen worktop, gasping out, 'I'm so sorry' and shaking her head as though she has no idea why this is so funny. George laughs, too. It's a moment that allows the possibility of happiness.

Re-doing the bathroom gives them something to talk about. They look at catalogues, but in the end they don't do anything about it. Autumn deepens and the garden needs to be put to bed; and by winter, the sink is too much of a joke for them to feel anything but affection for it.

Still, the year after the final miscarriage passes slowly. At the end of it, the work they have done on their house, and the time they have spent together, reminds them they can be happy. During that first winter, while Rosemary is out visiting her ailing father, George takes the things they had put in a drawer for their various babies and moves them to a cardboard box in the loft. If Rosemary notices, she doesn't say anything. George doesn't ask her. He doesn't mention the missing children's books, either. George pretends that this thing between him and his wife – this caution, this not-asking, this wariness – is not new. They close the nursery door and leave it closed, and when Rosemary sometimes takes an hour to come to bed, then opens their bedroom door, red-eyed, George only looks up from his book and smiles in a way that he hopes tells her that she is understood. She starts to reach for him, in the night, again, and from this George takes that they are healing.

Rosemary has always been a conscientious, tireless teacher; and she has a knack not only with children but with parents and with other teachers too. George is also good with his pupils, especially the ones that feel doomed by the very idea of maths, or who have reached secondary school convinced of their own stupidity. He endears himself to parents with his unfailing faith in their children. But when it comes to the staffroom he doesn't join in. The other staff are wary of him, fearing that he will carry gossip to Rosemary, who had been made Deputy Head not long after her return to work after the loss of the last baby, at the age of thirty-eight. And George would rather do a crossword than try to contribute to a conversation about a football match he has no interest in or a TV programme he has no intention of watching. He gets on well enough with his colleagues; and when he and Rosemary bring in vegetables from their garden (there are only so many courgettes even they can manage) he enjoys being the centre of conversations. But he mainly keeps to himself.

Then Rosemary gets her first headship, and oh, George

is so very proud of her. She will be working at a small secondary school in Ripon; they buy a second car, second-hand, and for the first time in their life together they go to work separately. It's strange. It isn't terrible. Sometimes George listens to Radio 3 on his drive to school. They have new things, new people to talk about.

New people. George is not always a fan of them.

Rosemary, George notices, talks a lot about Glenn, her deputy head. He's a geography teacher and, by the sound of it, the socks-and-sandals sort. He has plans for something called an eco-garden where the children could plan and participate in gardening while thinking about sustainability.

'Gardens are inherently sustainable, though,' George says, more crossly than he means to. 'Collect rainwater in a butt, and use it to water plants. Make compost from garden waste, and dig it back in to feed the soil. Eat the food. Preserve the seeds. Propagate. Keep growing.'

'Don't be like that,' Rosemary says. So he keeps quiet.

When Rosemary comes home full of ideas that Glenn has for this and that, George makes a point of not reacting – or at least, of not reacting badly. How interesting, he says about spinach beds, or, we should try growing asparagus by putting in a trench. Glenn even has tips on using cloches, something George has done without issue for as long as he has had a garden. But he tries to be glad that Rosemary seems excited about life again. And he tries not to be jealous that Rosemary is finding her life away from him. He is not entirely successful.

She is too tired, or too busy, to help in the garden at the weekends; George labours alone. He thinks of how freely Rosemary talks about Glenn.

Surely if there is the slightest inappropriateness in their late-afternoon working, she would feel that she couldn't talk to her beloved husband about it.

And Glenn has a family of his own.

Which is more than Amber does.

Amber is a student teacher doing work experience at George's school. The first thing George notices, when they are introduced, is that there is nothing amber about her. She has pale skin, black hair, grey eyes; she wears navy-blue or grey dresses, and sometimes a silvery scarf that makes her look even more tired. George has what he assumes are paternal feelings towards her. (He really does think this, for quite a long time.) She seems lost. She has excellent lesson plans and she is very well up on educational theory. She has a first-class honours degree in Maths from Goldsmiths and is determined to teach, even though George is pretty sure she could be designing operating systems for nuclear submarines or projecting global economic growth for the Treasury.

But Amber wants to be a teacher.

Unfortunately, Amber seems to be, if not exactly terrified of children, at least surprised by them and their behaviour when in a bored, end-of-the-day tired pack. She brings her meticulously prepared lesson plans into the classroom and begins with a wavering confidence. But it never lasts. Usually things go wrong within the first three minutes, especially if the fourth or fifth forms start in at her with questions. (Miss, do you think you're old enough to be a teacher? Miss, have you got a boyfriend? Miss, why do you never wear make-up? Miss, what's your favourite number? Is it sixty-nine?) And Amber stands at the front of the classroom, lost and silent. A red blotch creeps up one side of her neck and steals across her face. Her pupils talk among themselves, even on the day George sits in so he can give her some feedback.

'I don't understand,' she says to him afterwards. 'If they would just give it a try . . .'

George shakes his head. 'You have to trick them into trying,' he says.

She shakes her head in return. 'I really don't understand.'

'I know.' He sits down next to her, and pats her shoulder, in a supportive way. 'Right. Let's see what we can do.'

Amber grows in confidence, but she seems to get her confidence directly from George: by osmosis, perhaps. She sits next to him in the staffroom. She writes down lists of questions when she is going over her day in the evening, brings them in the next morning, and goes through them with George, one by one, before the bell for first lesson rings. He refers some of the questions to Charles, their head of department, but Charles says, 'There's nothing about teaching Maths that George can't tell you.' George doesn't know whether he's pleased or not. Or at least, he's not looking closely enough to see.

Amber likes cryptic crosswords and she watches *Newsnight*. She worries about the state of the world. There is an abstract side to her that George is drawn to; the opposite of his practical Rosemary. When he thinks this his stomach closes in on itself as though it's trying to dissolve the shame he feels.

Despite her wan first impression, Amber is pretty. Beautiful, even, in the right light. George admits this to himself, boldly, as though by doing so he declares himself immune. (He is used to the shame, now; hardly even knows it's there.)

He mentions Amber to Rosemary, in the vaguest terms. Amber, the student teacher, he calls her, and he talks about her once a week at most. Rosemary replies with stories of their student teacher who doesn't know his arse from his elbow, which wouldn't matter so much if only he wasn't teaching biology. She laughs at her joke, but George doesn't. Rosemary says 'backside' and not 'arse'. It sounds like a joke someone else has made. No prizes for guessing who.

George doesn't worry about thinking about Amber, though, because he's sure of how happily married he is. And Amber is only at the school for the term of her teaching practice. When she leaves, she hugs George, and gives him a thank-you card. It contains such correct sentiments – 'I appreciate all you've done for me, and I hope one day I'll be as good a teacher as you are' – that he takes it home and shows Rosemary. 'She's been lucky to have you to support her,' she says, and she smiles in a way that makes George think that his wife really does appreciate him, and he's a fool to imagine anything different.

Glenn continues to be a feature of Rosemary's conversation. He is full of excellent advice; the kind of advice that George would never dare to offer his own Head. Or, indeed, Rosemary. George mentions this, one Friday, emboldened by his end-of-the-week beer and the fact that it is 9.30 p.m. and they are still on a blow-by-blow account of Glenn's radical rethink of parents' evenings. (Or Parent-Teacher Conferences, as he will call them, to suggest equality of inputs and a sense of outcomes being expected.) An

159

expression of flickering panic and hurt crosses Rosemary's face and makes him wish he had kept his mouth shut. She makes a point of not discussing school unless answering George's questions, after that. He is not sure whether he's won or lost this argument, and puts Glenn, and Amber, from his mind.

Then Amber applies for a permanent job at George's school. Charles asks George about it, with a wink: I thought I'd better clear it with you, old boy.

George, relaxed following a weekend trip to Whitby with Rosemary, after they had agreed that their aged parents could manage without them for a day, is taken off-guard. It might be the mention of Amber's name or the assumption Charles is making; but before he knows it, he asks, 'What? Why would you think that?' with the sharpness usually reserved for a pupil on their last warning for copied homework.

Charles claps him on the shoulder, and leans in. 'Come on. We all have eyes, George. And nobody blames you, with Rosemary doing so well, and doubtless being so busy—'

George turns away before he can hear any more.

Amber is offered, and accepts, the job.

That weekend, George double-digs the garden.

Amber stays at the school for a year and then moves on. George is flawlessly polite and helpful to her at all times. He no longer does a crossword at lunchtime, reading a book instead. He and Rosemary have money to spare by then. They have two good salaries, they pay into pensions, and they have no family to provide for. They buy two or three books at a time rather than agonising over their next choice and reading aloud to each other. Sometimes, George sits

160

in his car in the morning and watches Amber walk across the car park, her dark head down, books held to her body, wearing a new blue-and-white check coat that really suits her, although he will never tell her so. When she leaves this time, there is no card.

34

Rosemary, Now

'I don't think we ever read this, did we?' George had asked when the book arrived. Rosemary looked over at her husband, who has opened the parcel from Lost For Words and was holding up a copy of *The Age of Innocence* by Edith Wharton.

Now they are almost at the end of it, though when she first realised what it was she had wished it away from them.

She had certainly read it; she remembers it, vividly, as something recommended to her by the Head of English when she took her first job as a headmistress. She had begun reading it out of a sense of duty and politics – Glenn had warned her that the Head of English had applied for the headship herself – but soon found herself drawn in. It had been Rosemary's first Edith Wharton novel, though not her last. She'd been amazed, at the time, at how fresh, how modern, a novel that won the Pulitzer Prize in 1921 could be. But perhaps she hadn't mentioned it to George.

Come on, Rosemary, she says to herself. You might forget

the odd name these days, but you know exactly why you're not discussing this with George.

'I read it when I got my first headship,' she says.

'Ah.' George's face is still.

He remembers, then. Of course he does. He remembers everything. She has a flurry of panic and hurt: what will happen when he isn't here? How much of her will vanish, when she has no one to turn to to ask, 'What was the name of . . .' or 'Do you remember . . .?'

Rosemary hadn't had to feign her enthusiasm for the book to the Head of English: in fact, it had prompted her to suggest a separate section in the library for prize-winning novels, and then support the English teacher's counter-offer that the school should also be facilitating a reading and discussion group, perhaps involving other schools, and an essay prize. At the time, she had been working late and feeling lonely: George could not, or would not, talk about their lost children, and when she came into their bedroom late at night after sitting in their never-used nursery, he would smile and nod as though where she had been could not be acknowledged in words. He had even taken the socks and tiny vests from the drawers. He hadn't wanted to talk about it, and she hadn't had the strength to force him to. She hadn't really wanted to talk about it, either, but she had felt that they should. Maybe she was wrong. Now, she just remembers the visceral loneliness of her empty arms.

Ever since the hospital visit, Rosemary has watched her husband avoid any talk about the weeks and months of his gentle dying to come. And she has realised that the way he acted then was not something she should have taken personally. This is his way. She knows it. During the losses themselves, George was solicitous, caring, kind; there was nothing he wouldn't do for her.

She remembers watching him, digging the garden, every weekend, even when she didn't think it needed digging at all. She'd caught up on her paperwork and thought of Glenn, who spent his weekends, as he put it, 'ferrying his girls hither and yon'. He was married with three daughters. He never had a bad word to say about any of them. Some of the teachers complained about their wives' and children's needs and wants as though paying for dancing classes and Wendy houses, football lessons and trips to the cinema, was some kind of burden or penance. Never Glenn. He treasured his family, as Rosemary and George would have treasured theirs.

The paperback copy of *The Age of Innocence* that arrived from Lost For Words is a Penguin classic edition, with the cover showing a slender woman – slender to the point of absurdity, really, with a tiny, corseted-in waist – drawing back an arrow in preparation for shooting it from a bow. She's surrounded by other women in Edwardian dress; there's a strong sense of a house-party. It's the sort of cover that the long-ago Head of English would have asked her pupils to discuss. Is it a suitable cover for this novel? We assume they are firing at a target, but what is the broader implication? Would Edith Wharton have liked this cover for her work? Rosemary has always tried to keep in touch with her old members of staff. She can't quite bring this teacher's name to mind, though she remembers her tortoiseshell glasses, her bitten fingernails. She had died of a stroke when she was barely fifty.

Revisiting the novel has soothed Rosemary's heart. Newland Archer, Wharton's hero, did the right thing only when he was forced to; but Rosemary did the right thing all along. Not an inappropriate word passed her lips, or Glenn's. She knew what people whispered, and she knew what her heart was whispering. But she loved George. She never stopped loving him. Not even when she thought he might have been falling for that student teacher.

They have read to the part where Newland and his wife are throwing a farewell party for the Duchess. It feels overwhelming: the tension, the emotion, and also just the thought of so many people in a room. All of that shared air. Rosemary puts down the book and slides her palm into George's.

'I always loved you,' she says.

'I know,' he replies. He sounds tired, he looks wan, but the pressure of his hand on hers is the same as it has always been.

The air this afternoon is warm and still, the view over the sea clear and perfect. There's the sound of a car coming up the hill. Cars seem so noisy, now. In the taxi on the way back from the hospital yesterday Rosemary had felt overwhelmed by the sound of the engine, and of the radio, and of the driver, talking over the top of it, his voice raised over the music and muffled by the mask he wore, so it was as though Rosemary was being buffeted. She had looked out of the window, spotting the sea between the gaps in the houses, and then she had had what she could only describe as a premonition, so strong it seemed to still her heart between beats. What if George goes to sleep tonight, and decides, somewhere deep in his body, not to wake up? What if the thought of the indignities to come is enough to stop his diaphragm from drawing air into his lungs?

Yet here they are, today. She had woken twice in the night, and put her hand to his chest, the way she used to put her hand to her belly and will strength into her children.

35

Kelly

Kelly feels ridiculous for the way she rushes home from work. She's not a child on the way to a birthday party: she's an adult, in a committed relationship with another adult, and she imagines that such an adult would take the time to enjoy the fresh air, maybe think some philosophical thoughts about how spring bleeds into summer.

Nonetheless, since Craig moved in, Kelly walks briskly along the riverside path, thinking about the funniest and best parts of her day, the way she'll make Craig laugh, the way he'll listen. How the evening will fly by: a drink, a bath, one of them will cook or maybe they will get a takeaway; talking, reading with her feet in Craig's lap while he watches TV. Bed, not too late, and sex that's no less thrilling than it used to be. Better, even, because they know they'll go to sleep together and wake up together. Kelly can barely remember what her life used to be, without Craig so very present in it. And she has no need to. This moving-in is a permanent change. They have both said they're sure.

Today is Saturday, and Kelly has no need to pick through her day and decide what to tell Craig about.

When she arrives home, he's cleaned the kitchen and the bathroom and done the washing. She's not a fan of the way he bunches things on radiators to dry – especially when they aren't on, and if you're not careful everything dries creased and smelling of damp. But the windows are open, the flat smells of cleanness, and Craig hugs her, tight, and tells her he's missed her.

'How was your day?' he asks. They've settled on what have become their respective ends of the sofa. He's rubbing her feet, something he's good at: he has the knack of the perfect pressure, somewhere between a stroke and a knead.

Kelly laughs, and shakes her head. 'You know Loveday got someone to work Saturdays? Well, she started today.'

Craig laughs. 'I can tell from your face that we're going to have an ongoing source of anecdotes.'

'Well, yeah. Because this kid hates me.'

'They cannot possibly hate you. You're the best person there is.'

'Well, correct. But she does. It's like she looked at me and just – decided. Kelly is not my friend. All I said was, "Hey. You must be Madison. I'm Kelly. We usually start with cinnamon buns."'

'Madison?' Craig asks.

'Yup. That's her name. Apparently she came to the door for some books for her mum. Loveday must have felt sorry for her.' Kelly wiggles her toes, to get Craig to start massaging her feet again. He does, but too hard.

'So what did she say?'

'Nothing. I mean, literally nothing. To me. She asked

168

Loveday questions all day, so it's not like she's shy. But whenever she came anywhere near me she looked at her feet and pretended I wasn't there. Weird, huh?'

Craig nods, then shakes his head, which Kelly interprets as an I-agree-it's-strange-how-could-anyone-dislike-you move. 'Is she coming back?'

Kelly shrugs. 'I guess so. She got all the parcels wrapped and Loveday seems to like her.'

'Could you tell Loveday to get rid of her?'

Suddenly Kelly wants a bath, a cold beer, and not to have to think about a kid who's decided to take her teenage angst out on her. 'I wouldn't do that. If she wants to ignore me she's welcome.'

Craig nods. 'You're probably right. But—'

'But what?' Kelly stands, stretches. She wonders what ailments booksellers get. She sometimes feels as though she's wearing out her neck and shoulders faster than the rest of her body.

Craig shakes his head. 'Nothing. I'll run you a bath and you can forget all about her.'

36

Consider the author.

Living or dead, they have all done the same thing: laid down word after word, making a story.

They have many ways of doing it. Some create a story as though they are knitting a scarf. One stitch is made from the last. Quietly, slowly, through work and patience, a book – a scarf – grows.

Some authors create their stories in a frenzy of activity, short and sharp and frantic, as though they and their idea are lovers reunited. Some treat their work with caution, and do not so much write as listen, sometimes for years, for whispers and words to set down.

Some authors begin with a blueprint they have laboured over; others are chasing a thought or a feeling down on to the page; others yet write while hoping to excise the thing that squats in their belly and makes them separate to everyone else, however hard they try to fit in.

There are authors who write for a ravenous, waiting public, and authors who put down word after word with no expectation that their work will ever be seen by someone else.

The result is the same. There is a book in your hand. Behind it – maybe centuries behind it – stands an author. When you read their first sentence, you are completing their work.

Not all authors care about readers. Some of them write for the good of their own souls, and some of them, for all of their vivid imaginings, could never see their work being published.

But for others, many others, your gaze on the page of words they have written is the manifestation of a dream.

Thank you.

37

Zoe

It's raining again, but the three-quarters-of-a-family goes for a walk anyway. Zoe straps Ellie to her chest, and persuades Tommy to let her put the handle on the back of his bike so he can ride it. Tommy is in wellies and an all-in-one waterproof suit over his shorts and T-shirt. She has a cover for Ellie, too. She forgets her own hat. The park is quiet, for once. Zoe thinks of all the mums she knows whose houses have playrooms, or two living rooms, or a kitchen big enough to host a coffee morning. Of course they aren't desperate to get out. Tommy gets off his bike and jumps in puddles, and Ellie squalls, then sleeps. When they get home, Zoe decides, they'll have hot chocolate, and she'll put a film on for Tommy. She will take a bath with the door open. That's assuming Will has been in touch again. If he hasn't, she'll sit in her wet clothes and keep refreshing her phone and try not to catastrophise.

She is absolutely not going to start catastrophising. She promised.

But she will allow herself to worry. And to fear.

*　　*　　*

They stay out until Zoe's scalp is cold with rain and her eyes sting from the constant water running into them. Her showerproof coat isn't showerproof enough; the skin on her arms and shoulders feels clammy. You haven't got a fever, she tells herself crossly, you just need a decent coat. Or for the weather to get drier.

By the time they get home there's still nothing from Will. He isn't online, and Zoe imagines his dreaming face, one corner of his mouth twitching, his forehead smooth. Illness – any illness – always makes him sleep.

It's only 4 p.m., but she gets Tommy out of his dampish clothes and straight into pyjamas: no one is going to care if he doesn't have a bath tonight. Zoe forgot to stop for milk so there's no hot chocolate; but she hadn't offered it, so it doesn't matter. Ellie has a feed and Tommy gets the farm set out, spreading animals far and wide throughout the flat, pushing a tractor between them. Ellie's eyes open at the end of her feed, and she stretches her arms and legs and yawns – oh, tiny, tiny hands. Zoe isn't given to sentiment but she is afraid, suddenly, of all that Ellie, already, has missed out on. Grandparents; her father's arms; being passed from here to there as family and friends come to meet her. She hasn't even had the undivided attention that Tommy got, in the weeks after he was born, when Zoe would feed him and then lie him down next to her and watch him, for hours and hours, as though he was the best film she had ever seen in her life. There's none of that for Ellie. Feed, burp, put her down or strap her on while Zoe does other things. And that's before you count Covid. Zoe is afraid that her milk must be full of anxiety. She imagines it tastes of hand sanitiser. Poor little Ellie. What a world for her to be born into. Zoe turns away from the thought of it. She can barely contain her love, her worry, as it is.

The doorbell rings. It's an almost-forgotten sound. No one comes round any more, of course they don't, and the postman rings Julia's bell if there's a parcel for any of the three flats, because he knows Zoe's busy with the kids, and Jay upstairs has gone back to their parents' for the duration. Zoe props the flat door open so she can hear Tommy, and pads downstairs in her bare, still-damp feet, holding Ellie close. It can't be bad news, she tells herself, no one would have time to come and see me. They would just ring. She touches her pocket. Her phone is there.

When she opens the door, there's a parcel on the step, and a woman with a bike with a basket on the front and panniers on the back is standing at the kerb, a safe distance away.

'Zoe?' the woman asks.

'That's me.' Zoe realises that she had been – stupidly, pointlessly, irrationally – hoping it was Will, or someone with news of Will.

The woman nods at the parcel. 'Sorry to bring you downstairs. I wasn't sure how long the parcel would stay dry, on the step.' For all there's a canopy over the door, it's not going to keep the brown paper wrapping dry for long.

Zoe looks from the parcel to the woman on the bike, who has rain running into her eyes despite – maybe because of – her hood. Some days just want you to get wet.

'I'm sorry,' she says, 'I don't think I—'

'It's from the bookshop. Lost For Words. You emailed us.'

'Oh!' That long, rambling email, all that self-pity. And that was before Will was ill. 'I'm sorry about that.'

174

The cyclist shakes her head, sending drops horizontally through the determined vertical downpour, 'Please. No need to be sorry. It's hard for everyone.' The woman smiles as she looks at the parcel at Zoe's feet. 'I hope you enjoy them.'

Zoe considers the logistics of bending down and trying to pick the package up, while holding Ellie, and decides against it. Instead she nudges it over the step, into the dry, with her foot. She'll call Tommy down to get it in a minute.

'Thank you,' she says. 'I'd forgotten.'

The woman on the bike nods and then says, 'It's none of my business, but—'

Oh god, thinks Zoe, oh god. Do not let my only human interaction today be with someone who tells me that I need to get into a routine.

'Don't worry too much about bravery,' the woman says, glancing at her hands on the handlebars of her bike before looking back. 'I don't think any of us should be even trying to be brave. We just need to keep going.'

It could be a criticism – it would be, from her mother, or Will's – but Zoe looks into the stranger's eyes and knows that she's trying to help.

'Thank you,' she says.

'You're welcome,' the woman answers. She straightens up the bike, puts a foot to the pedal, and says, 'I'm Loveday. I hope you all like the books. Call us or email us if you need more. I can easily drop things off.'

'Thanks,' Zoe repeats, and then, in a blurt, 'my husband's a paramedic. He's got Covid.'

Loveday puts her foot back on the ground, 'Oh god. I'm sorry. Are you okay? Do you need anything?'

'He's not living with us.' Oh, Zoe is out of the habit of talking to adults. 'I mean, he's been living with a mate. So we don't get it and he can go to work.'

'God. I'm sorry,' Loveday says again. 'That's—' she stops.

'I know.' Zoe stores away the feeling of being not-alone that she gets from the expression on Loveday's face, the fact that she knows there is nothing she can say to make Zoe feel better.

Then Tommy's voice trickles down the stairs – 'Mummm-eeee? Are you still just gone to answer the door?'

'Hey,' she calls over her shoulder, 'come and see what's arrived for us!'

'He doesn't know, about his father,' she adds to Loveday.

The woman nods. 'I'm sorry. I don't really know what to say. My mum had it. She's getting better. If that helps.'

'Thank you for saying we don't have to be brave,' Zoe says, and she goes inside and walks up the stairs behind Tommy. How awful that she'd thought that was what her son needed. As though bravery could save any of them.

She realises too late that she should have quarantined the books, but Tommy is already opening the parcel. And then she thinks of Will, feverish and weak, cleaning Barney's bathroom after he's touched the toilet flush, the taps, the plug.

Will.

Zoe checks her phone. Nothing.

She bans herself from thinking about Will, and puts Ellie into her bouncy chair. She still hasn't got around to changing, so she takes off her sodden jeans and sits next to Tommy on the floor, in her knickers and only-damp T-shirt. It's the first time she's been able to sit so easily, she notices, since the birth; the feeling that the stitches won't hold and she'll split in two has receded. She still sits on a cushion, though. The paunch of her stomach flops forward and she strokes it the way she did when Ellie was still growing inside her.

There are five books. Three are for Tommy: *Billy and the Dragon* by Nadia Shireen, *The Book About Moomin, Mymble and Little My* by Tove Jansson, and *Frog and the Wide World* by Max Velthuijs. There's one for Ellie, a soft, black-and-white book with pages that rattle and squeak. And one that might be meant for Zoe, or maybe she could read it aloud to Tommy: *Anne of Green Gables* by L. M. Montgomery. She thinks she had this herself, when she was a kid.

Tommy squeals over his books. Zoe takes a deep breath, pushes the world away, and starts to read to her amazing little boy, who does not need to be brave, but only to be himself.

Tommy is asleep by eight, and Ellie's internal clock must be malfunctioning because she grizzles from seven until eight and then drifts off to sleep while Zoe sits with Tommy in the darkness. It's then that her phone rings. It's on the lowest-volume setting, but is still loud enough to make Tommy's eyelids flutter before slumber holds him again. Ellie snuffles, wriggles against her mother's shoulder, and settles.

'Will' flashes up on the screen.

'Hold on,' she whispers, 'I'm just going to put Ellie down.'

Zoe takes the phone into the living room, pushes the door to, and says, 'I've been worried about you, sweetheart. Have you been asleep all day?'

'Zoe? It's Barney.'

Oh god oh god. Zoe's throat goes cold and she has to force her voice past it. 'What's happened?'

'Don't panic, Zoe, but when I got back off shift an hour ago I could hear him coughing. I kept my PPE on and had a look at him. He's got a high fever—'

'How high?' She isn't a child. Sheltering her isn't going to help her, not now.

'Thirty-nine and rising, and his blood oxygen level was eighty-three.'

'That's bad, isn't it?' Will has drilled into her that if any of them are even slightly ill, they need to use the oximeter, and if it drops below 93 they need to call for help.

'It's bad. I got him straight into hospital and –' Zoe hears the hesitation in Barney's voice, and gets there a minute before he says the words, so she is already crooning, no, no, under her breath, 'I'm sorry, Zoe, we're going to have to get him on a vent. There's no other way.'

There has to be a mistake. 'I spoke to him this morning.'

'So did I.' She hears fear in Barney's voice. 'It gets some people like this.'

Zoe forces a breath into herself. 'I need to see him.'

'I'm going to FaceTime you from the ICU in a minute. Hold on. I'm going back in.' Barney hangs up. Zoe stands, staring at her phone, thinking of Will, his voice this morning, the way he told her not to worry. He was right. Worrying wouldn't have made him better. Maybe instead of agreeing what was the best way to keep the kids safe, they should have talked about the best way to keep their family together. He could have packed in being a paramedic and got a job as a delivery driver, or gone to work in a warehouse. They would have managed. They would

178

have been together. Christ, they could have moved in with his parents. Bloody Will and his bloody save-the-world philosophy.

Which is one of the reasons she loves him.

When the screen lights up with a FaceTime request, she fumbles to accept it, and then there's Barney's face, masked and behind a visor. 'Hey,' he says, 'I'm going to hold the iPad for Will, are you ready?'

'Yes,' Zoe says, but she knows from the distress in Barney's eyes that she probably isn't. She doesn't care. She needs to see Will.

'Hey,' Will says. His hair is wet with sweat. The skin beneath his eyes is white, the rest of his face an unnatural, coloured-in red.

A sob escapes her. She cannot stop it. 'Hey,' she manages.

Will starts to cough. She can see that it hurts him; sees, too, that he's scared. Her worry doubles, trebles. This is what exponential means. 'We're all going to be okay,' she says, 'don't worry. Just get well.'

He makes the smallest of nods, and then she sees him struggling to move; there's a soothing voice in the background, but Zoe knows what he's trying to do: to kiss his fingers to her. She kisses hers to him, and he closes his eyes. And then – too soon, oh, too soon, because Zoe knows how precious it is to watch a loved one sleep – Barney's face fills the screen. 'They're looking after him,' he says.

Zoe nods. She can't speak. She wants to ask, are they doing it now? Are they sedating him, getting the tubes ready to go down his throat? But the words won't come.

Barney looks as though he's reading her mind. 'The ward will keep you updated,' he says, 'and I'll look in whenever

179

I can. He'll be okay, Zoe. Hang in. You need to be brave for the kids.'

Zoe ends the call, puts down the phone, puts her head in her hands, and sobs. Her breasts are leaking milk and, three weeks after the birth, she's still bleeding. Every penny of their income is spoken for, she hasn't seen her mother in five months, and most of her adult conversation has been with Will, beloved Will, who might – think it – might never talk to her again.

Brave.

Zoe has no idea what that looks like.

She knows she ought to call Will's parents, but instead, she sits on the floor and starts to turn the pages of *Anne of Green Gables*.

38

Loveday

Saturday afternoons in the bookshop never used to be quiet. They used to be a haven for the bored and the lonely, the pocket-money hoarders and the curious, the researchers and the weekend I-deserve-a-treat folk. Loveday would look at her watch at noon, and then somehow it would be 4.30 p.m., and the time had been filled with orders and requests, and plenty of sales, and the desk was covered in scribbled notes and unfinished cups of tea. Even when Lost For Words was deep in the pre-pandemic doldrums, Saturday afternoons could be relied on for busyness and buzz and income. Loveday would resign herself to an afternoon of non-stop helpfulness, and when she got home, Nathan would run her a bath and tell her that she had done a good job. She would close her eyes and sink into the warm water, and later they would watch a film that she would never stay awake until the end of.

On Sunday, she would imagine all of the people she and Kelly had served the day before, now curled up on sofas with their new books, sitting in cafes ordering another cup

181

of tea to buy them half an hour of reading time, peeling potatoes in a hurry because they would rather be reading.

But in the pandemic world, it's as though people have decided that going out in the afternoon is frivolous, and a Saturday afternoon most of all. Mornings are busy-ish, with people collecting orders, and the cobbled street outside full of people walking their dogs or looking wistfully at closed restaurants. Richard next door has usually sold out of sandwiches, cakes and biscuits by noon: he thinks that despite the interest in baking, people are desperate to eat something they haven't had to make for themselves. Loveday suspects he is right.

This Saturday, Madison's second in the shop, seems quieter than usual outside, but there are plenty of book prescriptions to fill. Madison is in charge of packing and adding address labels, and printing off new prescriptions as they come in; Kelly and Loveday, either separately or in consultation, do their best to find books to fulfil the needs of their customers. Loveday still cannot believe how well it's going. She imagines that Archie would be proud of her, or tries to. But she knows he would have done better; done more.

Madison is quick to learn and keen to do a good job. She chats to Loveday, without seeming to notice or care that Loveday doesn't chat back; though Loveday answers Madison's questions about how the bookshop operates with patience and something approaching contentment. She explains that their stock comes partly from books that are sold to them by members of the public, clearing out; some come from house clearances; some from auctions. She tells Madison that there's no way of knowing, really, what's going to sell and what isn't, but the longer you do it the better you get at it. And that reminds Loveday of how much she knows – how much Archie taught her, yes, but also how much of her expertise is her own, worked for and worth something.

Madison seems wary of Nathan, who is clattering around in the yard again. Maybe, Loveday thinks, she is worried about getting roped in to some of Nathan's plans. He's talking about building furniture out of pallets, which sounds exhausting. But it seems to be making him happy. Vanessa has taken a job as a supermarket delivery driver, and so a lot of Nathan's schemes and pastimes have gone on hold.

Madison and Kelly, though, haven't hit it off. Madison sighs, turns her back, or begins a conversation with Loveday whenever Kelly appears. Kelly, last Monday, had told Loveday that she could cope with a disgruntled teenager taking her angst out on her, and not to worry about it. Since Craig moved in, Kelly is all the more unflappable; Loveday recognises contentment when she sees it, although Kelly wears it differently to the way she herself does. Loveday has taken Kelly at her word, for now, and tries to keep Madison out of Kelly's way. She well remembers that being a teenager is tough, and that Madison might not be entirely in control of her own reactions.

When it gets to three thirty, everything is done for the day. The shop is tidy, the packing-station cleared, a sack of parcels ready to be collected on Monday. Kelly has even washed up their mugs.

'Have you had time to do any reading?' Loveday asks Madison as she shuts down the laptop. She's giving her books to take home and, once Madison had established that they were in addition to, and not instead of, money, she had accepted them quite happily.

'I thought the one about the kid in the corn field was boring. I liked the one about all the awful rich men and the women in categories. I wasn't sure about the ending. I don't know why writers can't just tell you what happened.'

Good for *The Handmaid's Tale*, then, but so much for *The Catcher in the Rye*. Nathan is a big fan of Holden Caulfield, and is keen for them to get a new tattoo: 'Make sure you marry someone who laughs at the same things you do.' Loveday isn't sure she laughs enough to justify it. 'What about your mum's books?'

Madison shrugs, 'She says there's too much sex in one of them and too many fancy names for carriages and dresses in the other one.'

'Right,' Loveday says. 'In that case, go and get *Circle of Friends* by Maeve Binchy for her. I bet she'll like that. And if you liked *The Handmaid's Tale* I think you'll like *Never Let Me Go*. That's Kazuo Ishiguro.'

'Okay,' Madison says, her voice drifting behind her as she goes off to search, 'but I'm quite into the one with all the sex and horses that my mum didn't like.'

'I think we've earned an early finish,' Loveday says when Madison returns with the books. She doesn't feel equal to thinking about what Madison might be learning by reading Jilly Cooper. She told Nathan she would have a think about what she wanted to put in the space at the back, now jet-washed and cleared of detritus, but she can do that just as well in the bath. There isn't an inch of this shop-world that she doesn't know. But changing anything makes her think of Archie, imagine him looking over her shoulder, and it's not that he would ever stop her from making any changes. It's more that she needs to be a little bit elsewhere so that she can think without a bow-wave of missing her old mentor knocking her sideways.

'Will you still pay me?' Madison asks.

'I'll still pay you,' Loveday says. Madison was supposed to be here until four.

Kelly, who has just come downstairs, rolls her eyes, but Loveday pretends not to notice. As far as relationships between her team are concerned, she's only here for the text, not the subtext. And Madison is clearly worried about money. Maybe her wage is contributing to the household. A lot of people are having a hard time. Loveday isn't going to make it harder by docking half an hour of Madison's wages. And if she's wrong, and Madison is spending her money on trainers and whatever she puts on her hair that smells like flowers and bubblegum, so much the better.

She goes to the packing table and straightens a parcel. It's the latest one for Rosemary and George: it contains *I Capture the Castle* by Dodie Smith, *Atonement* by Ian McEwan and *The Secret Life of Bees* by Sue Monk Kidd. She's not sure why she chose them, except that no one could ever dislike the first, the second is compelling, and the third makes her feel warm just thinking about it. And, now she comes to think of it, there's something about the slow pace of life in all of the novels, of everything needing to be in its own time, that she thinks will appeal to Rosemary and George.

The thought of Whitby is suddenly more than she can bear. It's a beautiful day. 'I might deliver this myself,' she says. It was raining this morning so she brought the car in. It's a lot easier to park in York than it used to be. She can be in Whitby by 5 p.m. An hour and a half of driving – it took three goes to pass her test, but now she likes it – and not talking to anyone. Bliss. And sometimes, when she drives on her own, she imagines Archie next to her. She would see him if she only turned her head. She never turns her head.

'You're going to Whitby?' Kelly says.

'I thought I might.' Loveday – perhaps prompted by the thought of Archie – does the right thing: 'Do you want to come? For the ride?'

'If you could drop me at my dad's—' Kelly's father lives on the outskirts of Whitby, but has been shielding, and Loveday knows she hasn't seen him for months.

'Madison, we can drop you off at home if you like,' Loveday says.

'Sure.' Madison's expression wavers. It's just a flicker, but enough to tell Loveday all isn't well with her. She thinks of Madison's father, gone, her mother, watching *Bridgerton* and giving up on Jilly Cooper and Georgette Heyer.

'Or you can come?' Loveday says, 'If your mum says it's okay. We'll keep the car windows open.'

'I'll text her.'

They're in the car when Loveday thinks of how she promised her mother she wouldn't go back to Whitby without her. So they swing by home to collect Sarah-Jane, and then they finally get on the road to the coast. Sarah-Jane and Kelly sit in the back, Madison, who gets car-sick, in the front.

Loveday expects Madison to chat all the way – her assumption seems to be that the people around her will be interested in hearing about her mates, her music, and her dickhead dad – but she sits quietly with her eyes closed. Maybe the car-sickness is better that way. In the back seat,

Kelly and Sarah-Jane talk about long Covid, about Craig – Loveday is always astonished by how interested her mother is in other people's love lives, given how badly her own great romance turned out – and about Kelly's father. 'You should come and meet him,' Kelly says, 'if you don't mind sitting in the garden.'

'I was going to wait in the car,' Sarah-Jane says. 'I've nearly finished my book.' Loveday's mother gets nervous around new people. But when they arrive at Kelly's dad's, a neat semi-detached house on a 1950s estate, Kelly says, 'He's got a hammock in the garden, if you'd be more comfortable reading there.' And Sarah-Jane, much to her daughter's surprise, gets out of the car, takes her copy of *Bitter Greens* by Kate Forsyth, and waves Loveday and Madison off.

39

Paul

Dear Lost For Words,

My dad Frank was a really clever bloke. Always reading. For as far back as I can remember.

I never really read books. I'd always rather knock around the doors with my mates, and I left school as soon as I could. Worked on building sites for a bit, and then as a delivery driver's mate, and ended up with my own taxi. It's a good life. I think my dad was proud of me.

My dad died of Covid. It felt like he was one of the first, though that's probably not right. More like he was the first one I really noticed. It was early, on, though. February. It hit me hard. And of course, I wasn't working, apart from the odd job running people to their hospital appointments and suchlike. I had a lot of time on my hands. The wife works in a chemist so she's rushed off her feet. The kids can't get home, and they're busy with their own families. I was the one hanging around like one o'clock half struck.

So I boxed up my dad's library. He had shelves and

shelves of books, hundreds of them. I brought them all home with me, and I'm reading them. Every single one.

Like I say, my dad was a clever bloke. And he liked history, especially the Second World War and on from there, and he liked politics, especially anything about the trades unions and the Labour party and socialism and all that. I knew quite a lot about it, I suppose, from talking to him and watching documentaries and the history channel, but I had no idea how it all links up. How one thing leads to another, you know? How detailed it all is, when you look at it properly, the way books make you.

I've got enough books here to last me years. Most of it's factual, like I say, but there's a few novels by John le Carré in there. The novels really help. They bring it all alive, somehow. And things stick better. So I wondered, after I saw about your book advice in the paper, whether you could think of some more novels I could read? I can't concentrate on some of the heavier stuff in the evenings. And once I've watched the news, I don't want any more reality.

Yours sincerely,

Paul Pritchard

Dear Paul,

What a lovely thing for you to do to honour your father. I'm so sorry he died. I can't imagine. I haven't seen my dad since lockdown started and that's been really hard. I can't imagine knowing I would never see him again.

I love le Carré's novels. Funnily enough it was my dad who got me into them, too. I was stressing about my A-Levels and reading a lot of classics and he said, why not give your brain a little holiday somewhere else? I read le Carré every night before bed after that, and spent the summer waiting for my exam results reading everything he'd ever written. I used to envy the kids who knocked around the streets with their mates.

There's a list of books you might like below. I can post out the ones you think you might enjoy.

Stay well,

Kelly

Union Jack by Val McDermid. Murder at a Trades Union conference.

A Very British Coup by Chris Mullin. One of my dad's favourites, about a socialist prime minister trying to wrangle his party (it really is fiction).

House of Cards by Michael Dobbs. You might have seen the TV versions but the book is always better (I would say that, though!)

All the Light We Cannot See by Anthony Doerr. This is set in World War II, and follows a German boy and a French girl through the conflict. It made me feel as though I was there. I don't know much of the detail of World War II, but I'm sure that as you do this will be even better.

Transcription by Kate Atkinson. The story of a woman who starts her career as a transcriptionist (is that the word?!) at MI5, and gets entangled with spies and Nazis. It's both funny and absorbing.

Sea of Poppies by Amitav Ghosh. This is set in the early 1800s, in the run-up to the First Opium War, and – please, just read it. It's so good! Obviously, it falls outside your father's areas of interest, but it's all about the strange ways events and people connect and influence each other.

40

Casey

Dear lost for words
I'm not coping, and

Casey knew she didn't need a visit to a counsellor to tell her what the dreams were about. And she knew she wasn't the only one suffering. She could see it in the faces of her colleagues, blurred behind visors. Sometimes, her staff told her, through the masks that muffled their voices, that they didn't know how much more they could take. And Casey, her throat hurting with the effort of always talking through a barrier, told them: I know. I feel the same way. Let's just get through today.

It wasn't a deliberate strategy, even though, in the time before the virus, Casey had been on management courses and role-played empathy and learned about 'yes, and' rather than 'yes, but' as a way of building rapport with people you might not agree with. Casey agreed with what her colleagues said because it was true. She didn't know how much longer she could keep going either. But there was no other option.

So she dreamed and she tried and she did her best. And every day everything felt worse.

Casey tried to tell her parents enough to keep them safe, without scaring them: to remove the temptation to do a lot of popping in to check on their neighbours and friends from church. 'Please,' she said, 'please, remember that just because they are more vulnerable than you it doesn't make you immune. Don't go into anyone's house. Talk to them from their garden.' She didn't tell them how many people had died on her ward that day. What it was like to hold up an iPad for a family at home so they could stutter out goodbyes to an almost-gone parent, sister, child. How she always had a counter in her head, telling her how many ventilators she had available, how many ICU beds, and how a cold, clinical part of her brain was constantly recalculating the order of the queue of potential patients who were not quite bad enough to go on a ventilator yet, but might be, within hours. She didn't tell her parents that, because she didn't want to think about it once she left work. Which didn't feel like work any more. It felt, when she was there, like the only real thing. And when she wasn't there, it seemed like something worse than a fever-dream, so unimaginably strange that it couldn't be true. And then she stepped into the ICU again, for her next shift.

41

Loveday

Whitby has never been so quiet. There are no tour-
ists, no gatherings of friends on the pier, barely any
traffic. Loveday parks on the street outside George and
Rosemary's house. It's a terraced Victorian cottage, the
front door opening on to the street, the kitchen windowsill
a row of propagating plants, new roots straggling in jam
jars of cloudy water.

Now that she's here, she feels as though she's intruding.
They didn't even call. And they can't go in. She can't make
two elderly people stand in the street and talk to her. She
should have thought this through.

Before Loveday can suggest they do something else,
Madison, who has come back to life now they're out of the
car, walks up to the door and knocks.

It takes a long time for Rosemary to answer the door. She's
taller than Loveday expects, and stern-looking. Madison
slides her phone into her pocket the moment she sees her,
as though it might be confiscated, and Loveday feels herself
straighten. But as soon as Rosemary understands who they

are, she smiles, and makes a little 'ooo' sound, as though they are an unexpected birthday cake.

There's an alley at the end of the terrace that takes Loveday and Madison to the garden, so they don't have to go through the house after all. They pass two overgrown strips of lawn with lonely-looking outdoor furniture, before they reach the gate at the end of George and Rosemary's garden. It's a summer heaven of smells and colours, and by the time they enter, Rosemary has joined George on a wooden bench that has seen better days.

'These are our friends from the bookshop in York, George. Loveday and – Madison, yes?'

'Yes.' Loveday notices that Madison's customary belligerence has vanished when faced with Rosemary and George. She thinks they must have been the good sort of teachers: the ones who let you sit in their classroom at lunchtime on the pretext of doing homework, when they know that you are really there because you don't want to go outside and be picked on.

George looks troubled. 'I hope we didn't forget you were coming. We've had a lot going on.'

'No, no,' Loveday feels ridiculous, now she's here. Selfish. What right has she to sit in someone else's garden, when she has a garden of her own? When the Post Office could have delivered the parcel with a lot less rigmarole, and no disruption to Rosemary and George's afternoon? 'We've been in the shop all day, and we saw your parcel, and it's been so long since we've seen the sea.'

'Well,' Rosemary says, 'we're glad you came.' She looks at the basket at her feet, which contains a thermos. 'I don't suppose I'm allowed to offer you tea, or anything.'

'We're fine,' Loveday says. Suddenly her skin is itching with the thought of all the people who have walked past the shop today, stood at the door. Breathing, talking, touching the doorframe, reaching for packages, tapping their cards an inch from Loveday's fingertips. Sanitiser that smells of synthetic lemons and face masks made of cotton no longer feel like enough in the presence of George and Rosemary.

'We've had no company since it all began,' Rosemary says. 'You forget.'

'We didn't see a lot of people before,' George adds, as though to correct Loveday and Madison's unspoken assumption of a life of bridge parties and barbecues. 'But we used to chat to the neighbours, and see the odd old friend.'

Loveday makes a mental note that, if they come again – when they do – they'll do a better job. She'll let them know they're on their way, for one thing, and check that it's convenient. She'll get her mother to bake something, and they'll bring more than books that the couple have already paid for. Every interaction is precious, now.

'I work at the shop on Saturdays,' Madison volunteers into the quiet of the afternoon. It's as though everyone has forgotten how to have a conversation. They all keep looking at each other, smiling, as though they're guests at a wedding who are yet to be introduced. 'I'm in charge of finding books for you.'

Rosemary's original letter is pinned up on the notice-board by the packing table, and any books that Loveday, Kelly and Madison think might be suitable for them are put in a pile underneath. Madison collects with more enthusiasm than expertise; but everyone starts somewhere. Loveday has filtered out *Twilight* ('Loads of people at school have read it and they reckon it's really good') and *The Magic Cottage* by James Herbert ('It can't be horror. It's called *The Magic Cottage*.')

'Well, you're doing a grand job,' Rosemary says. 'Isn't she, George? We've loved everything.'

'She is that, Rosie.' George shifts on the bench, as though he's in pain, and his wife's expression flinches with an answering worry.

'I never used to read much, but then Loveday gave me some things to try,' Madison says. 'I like the ones where everything's awful. Have you heard of Margaret Atwood? She wrote a book called *The Handmaid's Tale*. It's been on TV but I think the book's better.'

Rosemary smiles. 'The book usually is.'

Loveday says, 'Your garden is beautiful.' She rarely has the pleasure of feeling that she's said exactly the right thing, but this is one of those moments.

George nods, and Rosemary says, 'It's been our labour of love.'

'I can see that.' Sitting in this garden is like reading a good book. The smells and the sounds all match, and George and Rosemary look as though they have grown there themselves. Everything makes sense. Nothing exists outside the bounds. Loveday closes her eyes and thinks of Lost For Words, of Nathan. And she knows what Archie would do with the yard at the back.

'We used to have a reading refuge upstairs at the shop,' she says, 'but of course, we can't have people in there, and we're not sure when we will be allowed to use it again. So we're going to set up a sort of – well, a sanctuary at the back of the shop, outside.'

197

'Well,' George says, 'that's a grand idea.'

'A reading garden,' Rosemary says.

'Yes, exactly! It was my partner's idea, really,' Loveday says. 'But now I'm wondering, if I got some pots, could you tell me the sort of things we could grow?'

It's as though she's found the right button to press. Twice in one conversation. Because George smiles, and sits up straighter; and Rosemary looks at Loveday with a face full of gratitude. Loveday doesn't really understand what she's done, but she's obviously done something. Half an hour later, as the sun drops and the shadows start to creep, she's full of ideas and possibilities. George has asked her a lot of questions about light and space, and which way the garden-to-be is facing, and taken her round the flower beds and vegetable patches. Rosemary and Madison sat on the farthest ends of the bench and talked about – well, Loveday didn't listen. They both looked happy, though.

'I can't thank you enough,' Loveday says, as they stand at the gate, ready to go back along the alley to the car. It's time to collect Kelly and Sarah-Jane, but she would have stayed there for ever.

'I went to sleep in the hammock,' Sarah-Jane says. 'Isn't that disgraceful? But Neil made me feel absolutely fine about it.' She yawns as she fastens her seat belt. 'He had to go. He says he's sorry he couldn't have a word. He's Zoom Quizmaster tonight.'

'Zoom,' Madison says, and rolls her eyes. Loveday agrees, but she doesn't say so.

When Kelly gets in, Loveday glances in the mirror and sees that she's crying. 'Are you okay?' she asks, and then feels stupid. Of course she isn't. Who cries because they are okay? Even happy-crying means you're terrified that the thing you have, right now, can't last.

'It was so good to see him,' she says, 'and so hard not to hug him.'

Sarah-Jane's voice comes quietly from the back seat. 'It's emotional, seeing people you haven't seen for a while.' Loveday knows she's thinking of the years that they were separated, and she can only nod her agreement. She really doesn't want to cry. Not here. Not when she's in loco parentis, and she has to drive home, and Kelly is the one who is rightly upset, while Loveday can turn around in her seat and touch her mother's hand, just like that.

'I'm starving,' Madison says, with a yawn.

'I know the fish and chip shops are shut, but there might be a van at the harbour,' Loveday says. Food is what they need. And she'll tell Nathan and Vanessa that they ate on the seafront, and that, plus having things to say about a garden, will give her points in their peculiar outdoors-is-good life-measuring system.

There is a van.

Madison, Loveday, Sarah-Jane and Kelly sit in a row on a low wall and watch the water. The light is making the surface shimmer a colour that veers between navy and silver-grey. The chips are just slightly too hot, the vinegar acrid in Loveday's nose, the salt sharp. She eats too fast and she doesn't care. She senses that the others are doing the same. Gulls stroll over but, sensing that there are not going to be any spoils to be had, wander off again.

Kelly stands up, brushes herself off, and collects their paper trays and wooden forks, which she puts in the bin.

Walking back, she stretches her arms above her head – it looks for a moment as though she's going to do a cartwheel – shakes out her hair, and says, 'That was so good. All of it. Thank you, Loveday.'

Considering that her original plan was an escape from everyone, Loveday doesn't think it's right to accept praise. 'We should have planned it better. We could have brought Craig. Has he met your dad?'

'No. I think they'd like each other. But we weren't that serious before the pandemic, so –' she shrugs. 'There'll be time.'

'Are you serious now?' Madison asks.

'Well, we've moved in together. And we love each other. So – yes.'

'Everything's weird in a pandemic, though.' Madison looks serious under the weight of her fifteen years of accumulated wisdom. 'I wouldn't trust a lad who moved in just like that.'

Sarah-Jane smiles, a little sadly. 'You never know what you'll do, Madison.' Loveday moves closer to her mother, so their shoulders touch.

Kelly says, not exactly to Madison, but definitely directed her way, 'Well, I've told him, about Loveday and Nathan's tattoos. He was reading *To Kill a Mockingbird* – we're doing no-screen evenings – and he read out the thing about,' she gestures, as if to say, I'm not going to get this right but you'll know what I mean, 'if love was labelled poison we would drink it anyway. So I said, that should be our tattoo.'

'I don't know why old people are so into tattoos.'

'I'm thirty, Madison. Craig's thirty-seven. We're hardly ancient.'

Madison kicks at the ground. 'Just because he gets a tattoo it doesn't mean he likes you that much. My mum said I had to be home for half-eight. Can we go?'

42

Trixie

To begin with, Trixie and Caz do well. They watch the same TV programmes at the same times, and eat the same snacks and drink the same wine. It's cute, to begin with. But not beyond the first month. The novelty of phone sex and solo dildos wears off too. Trix, who has absolutely nothing to do, compiles all of the films-to-see-before-you-die lists into one spreadsheet and shares it with Caz. They work through them in a pattern: one film that neither of them has seen, one that Caz hasn't seen, one that Trix hasn't seen, and then the pattern repeated. That keeps them going for about six weeks, at three films a week; but then Trix confesses that she's sick of seeing Excellent Films and Caz counter-admits that she keeps going to sleep before the end, and having to Google the plot the next morning. Then they both start to play a game where their avatars have a farm, but they forget to feed the chickens, and they can never agree what to buy with their coins.

When they've stopped doing well, they do okay. Trix gets to know everything there is to know about Caz's working life, and can soon calculate a time zone without trying. Caz is pretty good at feigning interest in Trix's attempts at macramé, as Trix holds up tangles of string and tries to explain where she thinks she's gone wrong.

Then they stop doing okay, and start to do badly. It's not their fault, they text each other after another snappy conversation. It's just that there's nothing to say. Nothing to do. No anecdotes. Caz says she cannot bear to spend any more time looking at a screen now she's doing it all day at home. Trix tries to stay motivated but being furloughed feels like being paid for doing nothing, and so, increasingly, she does nothing. When they talk there's a mismatch of energy, of experience. Caz is tired and wrung out, and Trix has been waiting all day to hear her girlfriend's voice.

'If only we could see each other,' they say, over and over. 'If only we could touch.'

'What if we did,' Caz says, one night, as Trix cries out of sheer loneliness. 'What if we both drove and we met in the middle.' Trix can tell from Caz's face that she's looking at Google Maps. 'Somewhere north of Birmingham? Tamworth?'

'There'll be nothing open,' Trix says, but she stops crying. 'What will we do?'

Caz grins. Properly. It's an expression Trix hasn't seen in too long. 'We'll feel each other up in the car. We'll eat sandwiches. We'll pee behind a hedge.'

So they had.

The feeling of touch – of being touched – was overwhelming. Trix, who had scrubbed and scrubbed at her skin in the bath, as though being alone had made a crust, burst into tears when Caz laid her palm against her cheek.

203

She had imagined they would be ravenous for each other, but they curled into the back seat of Caz's new car – it still smelled of air-freshener and rubber and plastic – and Trix put her head on Caz's lap and they dozed. They shared their sandwiches, and then they ate the cake that Trix had made, and Caz joked about crumbs on the back seat, and they were happy.

And when Trix got home, everything felt worse.

She couldn't sleep.

She missed Caz more.

And she could find less to talk to her about.

Then she was made redundant. The days got longer, and she realised that the hope of going back to work had filled a lot of her time. She had only ever worked in one place. She felt bereft.

But.

The redundancy money and the freedom meant that she could move to Cardiff.

She messaged Caz.

Caz didn't respond, though the two blue ticks, which showed the message had been received and opened, appeared almost immediately.

She called that evening. Well, she Zoomed, which Trix should have known was a bad sign. They talked on speakerphone, mostly; Caz got headaches from too many Zoom calls.

'You know I have so much love for you, Trix,' she said, 'but you moving here doesn't feel the right thing for us.'

'What is the right thing for us?' Trix doesn't say, what the fuck is 'I have so much love for you' supposed to mean? She had been looking at jobs in Cardiff all afternoon. Sure, there wasn't a lot now, but once restaurants opened up again she could find work in a heartbeat. There were shortages of staff everywhere, and she had eight years' experience, and an unblemished record. The area manager, who had seemed more upset about her redundancy than Trix herself was, had promised her a reference so shiny she would be able to see her face in it.

Caz looked to the side. 'I like this version of us.'

Trix heard herself snort. 'Hooking up in empty car parks? Please. I think we deserve better than that.'

'When this is over—'

'When this is over you'll still be in Cardiff and I'll still be in York.'

'We were making it work, Trix.'

It seemed inarguable. They had been happy until the pandemic. And then came the lockdown. And a lot of couples had become unhappy. The strain was many-faceted and strange. Trix had not got the career she had hoped for, but once she made peace with restaurant life, she had been happy. And it had never occurred to her that she would ever be unable to take a train, or that she might have a day off where she drove out of the city but there was nowhere to go. She had never thought that she would spend money on having bubble tea delivered, or go for months without seeing her grandmother. Everything in the world was off-kilter, hard in places it had not been hard before. No wonder this relationship was struggling. (Was the fact that Caz didn't want Trix to move to Cardiff a sign of struggle? Or was Trix overthinking? She has never had as much time on her hands as she does now.)

'Yes,' she says. 'We were making it work.' She knows

that she is making her voice deliberately dull, flat; that she is doing it so Caz will comfort her and tell her all the ways that she, Trix, is adored. She never would have behaved that way before. She would have said, look, I feel shit about this. Or, it seems as if you don't really care about me. She wouldn't have tried to pass-ag her girlfriend of nearly four years into some sort of performance of love.

'I've got to go. I'm shattered,' Caz says. Zoom light is not always kind, for sure, but the skin around her eyes is dark and her face looks flat. Trix asks her if she's drinking enough water, but Caz has already ended the call.

There's nothing wrong, Trix tells herself. Nothing specific to us.

She texts Caz, another speech-bubble to add to their months and months of lockdown conversation: I'm sorry. I'm tired too. I miss you and I want to be with you.

Caz doesn't reply.

Trix lies awake, and somewhere in the deeper silence of the darkness, she has an idea. She closes her eyes and sleeps dreamlessly until almost 10 a.m. When she has got up and had breakfast, showered and washed and dried her hair – hair that reaches halfway down her back, now, the longest it's been since she was ten years old – she checks to see that her idea is still sound, and it is.

She almost calls instead of messaging, but she knows it's a busy morning of Zoom meetings with Shanghai for Caz.

TRIX:
I could move to Cardiff anyway. Nothing to do with you. It's such a great city. I could do with a change. x

Two blue ticks, immediately, but three hours until there's a reply. Still, it's a working day for Caz. Trix hoovers the living room, properly, pulling out the sofa from the wall.

The message comes at five.

CAZ:
I think that would be weird.

No kiss, Trix notes. No question mark. A statement.

TRIX:
Why? x

CAZ:
Would you move to Cardiff if I wasn't here?

TRIX:
But you are there, Caz.

Then, silence.

The evening passes. Trix watches a film from the spreadsheet – *The Cook, the Thief, His Wife, and Her Lover* – that neither of them has seen. She doesn't much like it.

Just as Trix goes to bed, only just before midnight, her phone lights up with a message.

CAZ:
It's pressure, Trix.

After that, nothing was quite the same.

43

Bella

Dear Lost For Words,

I can't really put into words what I need from a book right now. I suppose if I boiled it right down, I would say, I'm scared. But I could Google that. I would probably get *Feel the Fear and Do It Anyway*, which is a terrific book, but I don't want to be helped in a self-help sort of a way. I want fellow-feeling. Camaraderie in the form of a novel. I think a bookseller is probably better at the algorithm than a website, at least for now . . .!!

I'm a forty-five-year-old actress, singer and voiceover artist. I've lived in York for most of my life, when I haven't been away with work. I've never made the big time (oh my broken dreams!!) but I've done pretty well. My seventeen-year-old self, forcing her parents and grandparents to listen to her practise audition pieces, wouldn't agree, but I'd like to think I'm wiser than her. Definitely older!!

I haven't really done much TV. My agent once let slip that a casting director said I had 'the wrong sort of face for a screen', bloody cheek!! But I've done a lot of theatre tours, over the years, starting with being Dorcas (one of the brides) in *Seven Brides for Seven Brothers* in 1998, when I was understudy for the leading lady. Who had the constitution of a horse, unfortunately!! Always the bridesmaid, never the bride, if you see what I mean!!

I'm generally touring for quite a lot of the year, and the rest of the time I've worked in my local pub. They like me because I know the ropes, and I'm more reliable than the youngsters. For the last fifteen years, my life has been: go on tour, do a good job, come home, sleep for a week, ring Jack at the pub, go back to work, where they act like I've never been away. Do the occasional bit of voiceover work (I got down to the last two for those M&S ads!!). I like the life. Or I did!

My worst fear is being on my own. That is to say, I live alone, always have, you can't sustain a relationship with a life like mine!! But I was never at home! I'd be working away, or catching up with people I'd missed. You make a lot of friends when you're on the road, so there was always someone visiting, or someone to visit.

So you can imagine that lockdown was quite a shock to my system!

I really had a horrible time at first. I was miserable. All day was Zoom, Zoom, Zoom, with one thing and another, but it wasn't the same as seeing people in the flesh. I don't really cook, either, or I didn't!! I ate a lot of tinned soup and toast. Then I said to myself, Arabella, you don't want to come out the other side of this looking like an absolute hag! Pull your finger out and learn to cook. I've got quite a repertoire now. I can even make a half decent hollandaise!

I did what I've always done when I'm down. I kept myself busy. It's the only way. I had a good old clear-out of the spare room, sorted out my wardrobe, even bought a shredder and shredded all of my old tax returns!! (I had them going back twenty years!) And I sorted out my kitchen cupboards. I found a tin of beans that went out of date in 2008! All that's left to do now is a sort-out of my old correspondence and I'm not sure I'm up to that yet!

Then one day I realised that I'd gone for three days without talking to a single soul. Not in person on my runs, not on Zoom, not a single phone call. And the funny thing was, I didn't mind a bit! Now, when you take into account the fact that before this wretched Covid arrived, I hadn't spent so much as a day without seeing someone else for the best part of a decade – well, I was quite surprised!

Ever since then, I've spent less and less time talking to other people. The novelty of all those Zoom virtual drinks seems to have worn off, but if I do get an invite, I just say it clashes with something else – people always believe you! I've been doing my voice exercises, of course. You can't afford to let your instrument get rusty!

I'm not sure where my time goes. Well, some of it in unnecessarily long emails! You see, once upon a time I would have just called you up, or taken a walk to the shop. Now I can't stomach the idea. My old friend Archie would think I was ridiculous!

I sometimes listen to an opera in the afternoon. And there are films for evenings. But I somehow feel I don't have time for the outside world any more. I truly cannot imagine putting on my face and going out and meeting people, which for someone like me is unthinkable. My whole livelihood depends on sparkling for the public. And believe me, serving behind a bar is just as much a performance as the London Palladium!!

Now, to the rub. Jack, my dear friend at the pub, left me a message. He's talking about being able to reopen soon, and he's spent the summer building some sort of glorified tent for people to be 'outside' in. He wants me to go back. And of course, I messaged back and said yes, but then I thought, Bella, how on earth are you going to do it? When you can't so much as pick up the phone?!

I know the doctor could probably give me some nice little pills to fix everything. But they always want you to give up smoking, don't they, and they are ever so tedious about blood pressure. Some of us are just highly strung!!

Love and kisses,
Bella xxx

Dear Bella,
I don't know if you remember me, but I remember you. I'm Loveday – I worked with Archie for ten years, and he left the business to me, after the fire. I remember how he loved it when you came in. He'd be even more cheerful than usual for days afterwards. He used to say you were a kindred spirit.

I'm not much of an extrovert myself but I do recognise the anxiety you describe. The thought of there no longer being safe distance between people makes me anxious, too. We went to see some friends – at a safe distance, and outdoors – and I was really nervous about it.

There's a list of some ideas, below. Just everyday books about everyday things, which I think might be reassuring. I can drop them off to you if you like, and we can say a distant hello on your doorstep.

Loveday

211

Where'd You Go, Bernadette by Maria Semple. An agora-phobic woman vanishes, and her daughter tracks her down. This made me laugh, a lot, and also made me think about how we become constrained by our surroundings, almost by accident. I spent a long time in my own life not really going further than the bookshop and my flat. Life got bigger after I met Nathan. I've been to stay with his family, and we used to go to a lot of poetry gigs – and I quite liked it. (Not all of the time.) Now I go between the bookshop and home, apart from doing deliveries, and I wonder if I might go further afield one day, when all this is over. Maybe a camper van holiday. It felt more possible after reading this novel.

The Blind Assassin by Margaret Atwood. I think you might like this for its complexity and drama.

The Tenant of Wildfell Hall by Anne Brontë. A woman moves to a remote manor-house and seems happy to become a recluse. Some argue that this is the first feminist novel. It's my favourite of all the Brontë novels – it deals with hard things (alcoholism, violence, reputation) so well. Though I also wish everyone would just leave the heroine alone.

Nella Last's War: The Second World War Diaries of 'Housewife, 49' by Nella Last. You may have seen the TV film dramatisation of this – I remember Archie raved about it, and he said he knew Clifford Last, the sculptor, Nella's son. Nella Last wrote a diary for the Mass Observation project, starting in 1939 and going on until she died in the 1960s. I think it was around 12 million words in total. Nathan's mum gave this to me as it's her favourite book. I read it to be polite, to be honest, and I was going to do about fifty pages to get the gist and leave it. But I've never read anything quite like it. It's very everyday and at the same time completely absorbing, and it made me think about how much I take for granted.

The Tale of Murasaki by Liza Dalby. This is another books-within-books one, and I think you'll appreciate the way it takes art seriously. It's a novel about Murasaki Shikibu (a real person), a really good read, and I think you will want to talk about it, too. (I always get the conversation on to books if I'm not sure what to say.)

'The Yellow Wallpaper' by Charlotte Perkins Gilman. Not the most cheering of stories, but definitely worth a read. It's about a woman who's shut in a room with (very ugly) yellow wallpaper, and can't escape it. It makes me want to run for the nearest exit every time.

And finally, *Flowers for Mrs Harris* by Paul Gallico. It's about a London cleaning-lady who saves up to buy a Dior dress. I think you'll love it. (I really can't think of anyone who wouldn't.)

Dear Loveday,
Of course I remember you! Archie's little waif and stray!!
I was so sorry to miss his funeral, but I was on tour in Australia for most of that year (can you imagine! That used to be normal!). The last time I saw Archie we had the most glorious dinner with a couple of old pals in Florence. I was rehearsing, our pals were trying to get a restaurant off the ground (they never did), and Archie popped in on his way to somewhere or other! Sicily, perhaps? There was no point

in trying to keep track of Archie!! He had us all laughing, as ever, and I had no idea it would be the last time I would see him. It's a good way to remember him. I think we drank a lot of limoncello that evening!!

It was very clever of you to think of this book pharmacy idea! All of the books you suggest sound marvellous. I've read *The Blind Assassin*, mostly in a terrible old bus rattling round Scotland in a touring production of the Scottish Play, but one doesn't complain, especially if one is playing Lady M herself!

Bring the books whenever suits you – I am always here!

Love and kisses,

Bella xxx

44

Kelly

CRAIG:
You forgot your lunch!

KELLY:
Oh, damn!

CRAIG:
I could drop it off?

KELLY:
That would be great.

CRAIG:
So long as Madison won't be there . . .

KELLY:
I think it's only me she dislikes.

CRAIG:
Better safe than sorry ;-) See you later x

When Kelly looks up at the knock on the shop door, and sees it's Craig, her heart gives a happy hiccup which is nothing to do with her lunch arriving.

She's been reading *The F*ck It Diet* by Caroline Dooner on her breaks, and really wants to get to the place where she doesn't look in the mirror and judge herself, or fail to fasten her jeans and feel as though she has failed as a human being. She isn't there yet. Her mother, like so many of her generation, had adopted Weight Watchers in lieu of a religion, obsessed with points and treats and the idea that some foods just couldn't be had, and Kelly still cannot completely shake off the idea that Thin Is Good.

'Thank you,' she says. 'Do you want to come through to the yard? Well, the reading garden? We can share it.'

Craig smiles, but looks uncertain. 'Am I allowed?'

'I'm the only one here.'

Nathan and Loveday have taken all of the rubbish to the tip, after the brickwork and paving have been jet-washed in an enthusiastic if amateurish manner; there's a stack of pallets waiting to be magicked into furniture. Kelly brings a couple of the folding chairs they used to use for Book Group and Storytime out into the sun. Strange to think how often people used to sit next to strangers, without a worry in the world.

'When you told me about this,' Craig says, 'I imagined it was smaller.'

Kelly looks around. 'I suppose it looked smaller. It used to be full of stuff. Loveday and Nathan reckon five people can sit out here, with distancing in place, maybe a dozen when the restrictions are lifted.'

'And – read?'

'That's the idea. Or sleep. Or talk. Whatever they need, really. Basically what we used to have upstairs.'

Craig nods. Kelly holds out her sandwiches, and he takes one. 'Are people going to feel safe outside?'

'Maybe not as safe as they would inside,' Kelly says. She tries to imagine being as scared as some of the women they have helped must be. 'But safer than where they've come from.'

Craig is pretty terrible at sandwiches. He uses butter from the fridge, and it tears holes in the loaf. He thinks cheese is enough of a filling. No pickle, no tomato, nothing moist. But after months of making meals on her own, Kelly delights in a sub-par sandwich she didn't prepare.

'What would you give me?' Craig asks. 'Books, I mean?'

'What's your ailment, sir?'

Craig laughs, and then looks serious. 'I'm in love with someone and I think I might have got in over my head. I'm scared she'll change her mind about me.'

'Be right back,' Kelly says, with a smile that feels like sunburst.

She has a glass of water on her way through the kitchen, and then walks around the shelves. She picks up *Love in the Time of Cholera* by Gabriel García Márquez, *The Prophet* by Kahlil Gibran, *Bel Canto* by Ann Patchett, and *Euphoria* by Lily King.

'Here you go,' she says. 'One's about loving someone for your whole life, one's the wisest book I know, one's about being ambushed, and one's about falling in love in bizarre circumstances.'

But Craig is asleep, his head against the wall, chin tipped back so his face is in the sun. Kelly thinks she can see what he was like when he was a little boy, in the smoothness of his forehead and the plumpness of his cheeks. When she gets to meet his family, when they are allowed out in the world again, she'll definitely ask to see baby photos.

Kelly puts the books next to him. 'I'm out of my depth too,' she says.

45

Jennifer

Dear Lost For Words,

My name is Jennifer Kingdom and I think I owe you my life. Your reading refuge gave me a safe place to be and when I needed to escape, Sarah-Jane got me and my little boy out of danger. I don't think we would have survived being locked down with my husband.

I'm getting better. My boy and I are living with my sister. I have a broken collarbone and a cracked rib which are still healing, but my nose wasn't broken and neither was my eye socket. They feel sore sometimes but I think that's when I think about being hit. It's like my bones remember.

I've started divorce proceedings and we have a restraining order. At the moment, David doesn't have access to Milo. If he wants it he has to prove he's not a danger to him, and to show that he's trying to change his violent behaviour. My police liaison officer says that even if he does get access to Milo it will all be managed and supervised. I hate the thought of it, though.

Sorry. Too much information.

Thank you for all you did.

Now that we're getting a bit more settled, I thought it would be nice to have some of our old favourite books around us. I'm sure David has destroyed everything he thought I valued. And I don't really want anything he's touched.

With love and endless gratitude,

Jennifer and Milo

Jennifer's requests:

Wide Sargasso Sea by Jean Rhys

The Secret History by Donna Tartt

Tess of the D'Urbervilles by Thomas Hardy

Beloved by Toni Morrison

The Mill on the Floss by George Eliot

Milo's requests, for bedtime reading:

Where the Wild Things Are by Maurice Sendak

If You Give a Mouse a Cookie by Laura Numeroff

Madeline by Ludwig Bemelmans

Moomin and the Wishing Star by Tove Jansson

46

I would say, imagine the reader, but you don't need to imagine yourself; you know how this works, this astonishing-ordinary transaction. Words plus spaces on paper, plus light bouncing on to eyes, plus brain, equal a place that can feel more real than the real world.

Now imagine every reader's vision of the world they are reading. Some things are fixed in place by the author: Emily Brontë's moors in *Wuthering Heights*, E. M. Forster's Florence in *A Room with a View*, Zoë Heller's London in *Notes on a Scandal*. Some are more ... abstract. Your imagined clock-striking-thirteen is almost certainly not mine. The cup you'd drink tea from in 221B Baker Street has a different pattern around the rim to mine: yours is a royal blue scalloped line, perhaps, while mine is made up of yellow roses interspersed with ivy leaves.

Does this matter?

No, it most certainly – most gloriously – does not.

Reader, the sound your Mrs March makes with her mouth just before she launches into 'Onward Christian

Soldiers' is entirely correct. The way you envision Hobbiton is the right one, no matter how different it is from the film. The woman who lived in London in the 1950s has a different relationship with *Small Island* by Andrea Levy than the woman who lives there now, or the teenager who has yet to travel outside Yorkshire.

In short: you, dear reader, are correct. You are always correct.

Not only in what you imagine, but in what you feel. You are allowed to not-love the novel the rest of the world is raving about; you are allowed to cordially loathe your sister's favourite author. Reading is not a test. Whether or not you love a book is not a matter for debate; and not something you can be persuaded into.

Books are the magical everyday that is all your own.

Read on, and enjoy.

47

Jonno

Dear Lost For Words,

Nothing makes me laugh any more. Comedy used to be my life. I used to go to comedy clubs all the time. I did open mic sometimes. I wasn't very good but, as my dad always says, no one is good at anything to start with. And I liked it. Loved it.

I don't work in comedy (depending on what you think of the insurance industry, ha ha) but I thought my job was okay. Now I realise that I just endured it to pay for the good stuff. I took my annual leave for the Edinburgh Festival and – well, you get the idea.

There's quite a lot of stand-up shows and panel shows on TV so I thought I'd be okay in the pandemic. But all of a sudden nothing seems funny. It's like I've heard all of the jokes there are in the world.

I don't really read, apart from biographies of comedians, and you can probably assume I've got all of those. So could you recommend some books? They don't have to be funny. In fact at this point it might be better if they're not. I don't know whether I've spent too much time on comedy and sickened myself of it, or whether the pandemic makes everything unfunny. It could be both.

Thanks,

Jonno

Dear Jonno,

Thanks for getting in touch. For what it's worth, I think a lot of people are discovering that their day jobs are worse than they realised, now it's all they have to do. (Not me, of course, I work in a bookshop. ;-)) And I think it's possible we've all overdone the things that used to make us feel special, too. You know how three days after Christmas, all you want to eat is an orange and a bowl of porridge? I think we're all a bit like that right now.

I've listed some books below. If you let me know which you'd like to try, you can arrange to collect them from us in York city centre or we can post them out to you.

I'm afraid I couldn't resist putting some funny novels in there. I hope you'll forgive me.

Very best,

Kelly

Lost For Words

The Colour of Magic by Terry Pratchett. If you haven't come across Pratchett, and you like him, then you're set, because this is the first in a long, and funny, fantasy series.

The Sisters Brothers by Patrick deWitt. This is a western about two brothers who are nasty pieces of work – but when you see them on their own, they are very different.

My Year of Rest and Relaxation by Ottessa Moshfegh. Dark, dry and weirdly compelling.

Me Talk Pretty One Day by David Sedaris. A book of essays about Sedaris's upbringing in North Carolina and move to Normandy. It's witty and well-observed.

My Sister, the Serial Killer by Oyinkan Braithwaite. I read this when it first came out and it gave me a strange feeling of contentment. I know that sounds odd. It did make me laugh, but more than that it made me think. And we all have a lot of thinking time to fill, right?!

Mr Fox by Helen Oyeyemi. Impossible to explain, and guaranteed to make you think. It's like reading a puzzle, and a novel about the nature of inspiration might be something you'll enjoy.

48

Loveday

Loveday and Nathan arrive at Lost For Words early the following Saturday.

There's a letter on the mat, addressed in Rosemary's neat hand. Inside is a list of plants she and George think would work well, with asterisks against the ones she and George can give them cuttings to propagate. Loveday is not ungrateful, but the thought of keeping tiny plants alive feels like another job too many. (Oh, it's very simple, her mother had said, before reeling off a list of steps that Loveday lost the will to listen to.) Plus, if they are going to call it a reading garden, it needs to be a garden. And to Loveday's mind, a garden is not a row of repurposed yoghurt pots on a windowsill, no matter how fast her mother and George claim they will grow.

Standing in the space, though, they feel a long way from plants. It's clean and clear. It's drab and grey. Nathan stands with his arm slung over Loveday's shoulder. 'What do you think?' he says.

Loveday sighs. 'I think, if someone could just write a garden into a book for me to copy, it would be much easier.'

Nathan laughs. 'Come on. It's not that hard. Close your eyes.' He's much perkier since the book prescriptions took off, and he and Vanessa have bought a second-hand tandem and are planning to do it up and ride around the streets juggling and fire-breathing. Or something. Loveday definitely listened, but she's so tired, and everything makes her think of Archie. Nathan has taken over the social media – Kelly's too busy – and he can just do it, in the same way that he can walk into a room full of strangers and be instantly comfortable.

Loveday closes her eyes.

'Tell me about a reading garden from a book.'

'There isn't a reading garden in a—'

'I'm going to kiss you,' Nathan says. He knows she doesn't like surprises. Then he says, 'If you had read a book about a reading garden. What would it be like?'

'Warm. Comfortable. Good smells. No one knows you're there. Leaves that move in the wind. A stone wall.' She opens her eyes.

'Right,' Nathan says. 'That was easy. I'll get on with it.'

'We can't afford to spend a lot of money,' Loveday says. Nathan's confidence that something good will come along is as strong as her certainty that it's just a question of time before everything goes wrong.

'Don't worry.' He raps the pile of pallets, then winces and examines his knuckles. Loveday laughs, catches his hand, and kisses it. Why can't everything be as easy as Nathan? 'This is just furniture waiting to happen. And we need to think about heat without screwing the planet, which can also make it cheap. Hot water bottles and blankets?'

Loveday nods. They have a whole shelf full of Archie's

various tartan blankets in the airing cupboard. It would be fitting to have them here.

'Talking of smells,' Loveday says. The aroma of warm cinnamon is coming from next door. It's nine thirty. Time to have a coffee before things get busy.

When Loveday returns, Madison has just arrived. She usually shows up before her threatened start time of noon. Loveday never comments. Madison doesn't like tea or coffee – she seems to live on energy drinks and bananas – but she takes a bun and says thank you.

'It was good at Whitby,' she says.

'Yes.' Loveday has wondered about saying something about Madison's rudeness to Kelly. But Kelly hasn't mentioned it, and they've worked together all week. Least said, soonest mended.

'The old lady was nice,' Madison continues. 'She said she used to be a headmistress. But it didn't feel like talking to a teacher.'

'What did you talk about?'

'Books, mostly.' Madison shrugs. Her cinnamon bun has, somehow, vanished, and she wipes her hands on her jeans then stuffs them into her hoodie pockets. 'She said it doesn't matter what you read as long as you read. She told me to try,' Madison closes her eyes, 'something about a caged bird.'

Loveday smiles. 'Maya Angelou.'

Madison looks amazed for a second, then her face settles back into its usual adolescent neutrality. 'Yeah. I asked her what she thought about the book pharmacy and she said it's good because sometimes you don't know what's good for you. And you need somebody else to tell you.'

Loveday nods. 'That's exactly it.'

'She asked me to get her a book,' Madison continues.

'Which book?'

'*The Secret Garden*? By somebody with three names. I thought I would remember but I can't.' Suddenly she's not a cocky teenager but a child who's lost a favourite toy.

'Frances Hodgson Burnett.'

'Are you sure?'

'Yes.' Loveday pushes up the sleeve of her jumper. On the inside of her forearm are the tattooed words 'somehow she did not feel lonely at all'. 'This is from *The Secret Garden*. We've got a few copies, I think.'

'Where?'

'Classics.'

Madison disappears and comes back, shaking her head.

'They're under B not H,' Loveday says.

'I know. Well, I looked in H first. But Rosemary said it had to be a special one. She said George loved it when he was a boy and it needed to be the one his mother used to read for him. It's got a girl with a red coat on the front. And a robin. We haven't got any of them there.'

'Well, we'll have a look online later, when things quieten down,' Loveday says.

'I'll go and see what Kelly wants me to do,' Madison says. The way she says 'Kelly' is heavy with darkness. Loveday cannot imagine why anyone would dislike Kelly. Sarah-Jane, after last Saturday, said that perhaps Madison just needs to dislike someone.

And then Nathan comes through from the back of the shop, pale-faced. 'Loveday,' he says, 'look.'

He passes her his phone. There's a story from the *York Gazette*. 'PARAMEDIC DIES OF COVID', runs the headline.

Below is a photograph of a man Loveday doesn't recognise. The story continues, 'Will Chambers leaves a wife, a son, and a baby daughter he barely knew, as he chose to flat-share with a paramedic friend for the duration of the pandemic, to protect his young family.'

And then there's a photo of Zoe and her two children. They are on the doorstep where Loveday left their books.

She nods to Nathan, her spine cold and her voice heavy. 'That's them.'

'I thought it must be.' He holds her, hard, and she sags against him, listens to his breath and tries to match her own to it.

'I told her she didn't have to be brave.' Loveday's words feel thick in her mouth.

Nathan exhales into her hair. Loveday knows he understands. Before she can say: never leave me, the first customer of the day arrives.

49

Anonymous

Are you people serious? There's a virus running rife around the world and you think books are going to fix it? There are going to be mass graves and global destruction as people fight over the last scraps of food. The world as we know it is going to break down and we're all going to die, sooner or later. And you think books can fix it? Wake up. Get a life. Do something useful instead of dicking around with your liberal bollocks.

Hello,
You haven't signed your letter so I can't use your name.
We're not proposing that books can cure disease or bring people back to life. Of course we're not.

Though one of my own liberal beliefs is that if the people making the decisions were well-read and intellectually open, we might be able to have better conversations about what needs to happen.

All we are doing here is what is in our power. We can help people who are lonely, or afraid, or bored, or at a loss. We can fill their time a little bit.

Before the pandemic, Lost For Words was all about safety and comfort and help. We're still trying to do that, in the only way we know how.

Books aren't for you. That's fine. But please, leave us alone to do what is in our power to make the days less frightening for others.

Best wishes,

Kelly

50

Rosemary

In the garden, on the bench overlooking the sea, Rosemary hands George his tea, and then says, 'Have you ever thought it was strange, that we outgrew our first house, and grew into something smaller?'

He looks at her. She knows that, even after all of this time, he's wary of how much he can say about those years of trying to have a family, and then the bleak time afterwards when they pretended they were just the same.

Nowadays, when women can't conceive, or if they miscarry, the fathers are treated as though they suffer a loss, too. It wasn't like that, then. George cared for Rosemary and she curled herself around the space in her body and she wept and she mourned and she ached. And she can't remember ever thinking about George, except that he did not ache the way she did. He had not been there when the bloody masses that could have been children wrenched themselves from her body.

He smiles and says, 'We got a lot more sky. And the North Sea.'

Rosemary nods. There's no point in reopening old wounds now. She can't make George less lonely, then. She can't undo those evenings when she worked late with Glenn – not that anything ever happened between them, but it could have.

She thinks she has made up for those times since. And she will certainly make up for them now. For however long he has, she'll make sure he is comfortable and happy, that he doesn't regret a moment that they've spent together. There will be all the time in the world for her to fall apart when he's gone.

The sensible thing to do would be to give some of their fully grown plants to Loveday and the shop, of course. She won't be able to manage all of this garden on her own. But for as long as George is here, she wants their garden to be complete around him.

George has picked up the copy of *I Capture the Castle* by Dodie Smith that was in the parcel Loveday and Madison brought. 'We're nearly at the end. Shall I read?'

Rosemary puts the thought from her mind, very definitely, and tries to remember where they were up to, in the trials of the Mortmain sisters. Cassandra and Rose. She and George would have called a daughter Rose, she is sure.

'Read away,' she says. She supposes she had no right to feel slighted when George chose not to discuss the past. She was impossible to talk to, about any of it, for so many years, and she knows it. Just because she feels the urgency now, doesn't mean that George should respond to it. Especially when he is in his own pain: something she can't share. She has not known, until now, what it is to watch her loved one suffer and not be able to help. George is never ill. Was never ill. Until he was.

He nods, and opens the book; starts to read. During the first sentence his voice sounds unsure, wavering, but he soon finds his rhythm. Rosemary closes her eyes and puts her mug to her lips; not drinking, just feeling the warmth on her skin.

He reads on until the end. And then he closes the book, takes her hand, and says, 'I've always liked that ending.'

'Don't you wish it was more definite?' Rosemary is somewhat against books that fade out rather than stopping properly.

'It seems definite enough to me,' George says, and he squeezes her fingers; smiles.

And Rosemary understands. He's telling her that when things end, the things unsaid are not necessarily things unresolved. And that if there was a fracture in a relationship then the relationship simply would not hold. He's telling her that they are all right, and they always have been.

51

George, 1987

George and Rosemary like to spend every other Saturday in Whitby. They get up early, park up high, near the abbey, then walk down the 199 steps from St Mary's Church to the main part of town. Then they meander along the street, looking in shop windows at jet jewellery and trinkets for holidaymakers, all the time breathing deep, inhaling the sea, exhaling their working week.

They head to the harbour for what George calls a fish-and-chip-brunch – they tend not to have breakfast before they leave, and are ravenous by eleven thirty – and then, they sit on a bench on the promenade. 'We're just like old people,' Rosemary says, and George squeezes her hand and says, 'It's just the ticket, isn't it.' She laughs. They've always said they are old souls.

This Saturday, the weather is especially good – bright sun, barely any wind – and they sit for a long time, watching gulls peck and children run. There was a time when George thought Rosemary would never be able to look at a small child without radiating pain and longing into the air around her. But it seems she has found something like acceptance.

They will both be forty-five this year, and their centenary, as they call it, fifty plus fifty, is suddenly on the horizon. (Rosemary, on their honeymoon, had made George promise that they would both live to be a hundred, and die in their sleep on the same night. The idea of even being fifty had seemed preposterous to them both then.) Maybe that's what prompts George to say, 'What if we lived here?'

'Here?' Rosemary looks around her.

'Well, not specifically on this bench, but in Whitby, yes.'

Rosemary is on her feet in a second. 'There's an estate agent, we passed it on the way along.'

The houses in the window all seem to be perfect-looking, new-estate, mock-Tudor this and that. George looks sideways at Rosemary, and behind the quiet blankness of her face sees that the idea of a move is also the answer to whatever this is that they are in. Not unhappiness. Maybe just the normal sort of nearly-fifty ennui. But because they are not spending their evenings helping with reading and their weekends going to other children's parties (this is as far as George's imagination stretches, when he hypothetically parented their would-have-been-seven-year-old), they have more time to notice it.

Although his 'what if we lived here' was a sort of idle wondering, he realises, in this moment, that if a move will make Rosemary happier – if he could be happier himself – then now is the time. He opens the door. 'George?' Rosemary says behind him, and George says, 'there's no harm in asking,' and, without needing to look, he senses her following him.

The office holds only one tired-looking woman, who gives

off a strong feeling of 'is it five o'clock yet'. Undeterred, George sits down at the desk in front of her, Rosemary sits beside him, and when the woman says, 'Can I help you?' George smiles his most charming smile, the one he uses on the parents who come in spoiling for a fight because their child has got a low mark in their mock exam. He says, 'Yes. We want to move to Whitby. We don't want a new house. We'd like a big garden.'

She looks at them, judging, and seems to decide that they aren't timewasters. 'Anything else?'

'A view of the sea,' Rosemary says. 'And all of the usual things, of course. Bedroom. Kitchen. Living room.'

'Inside loo,' George supplies, with a smile.

Unexpectedly, the woman laughs. 'We have got something, though it needs a bit of doing up,' she says, then, looking stricken, 'I mean, updating. It's empty, so I could take you at four, when Mr Bennett's back in the office.'

Rosemary and George have coffee and chocolate cake in a cafe as they wait for four o'clock to come around. They look at the floor plan of the house for sale and try to remember how big their own house is. What does four-by-three metres look like, when it's a living room? Is that huge, or impossibly tiny, once you think about all the things a living room needs to contain? Even though there are no real clues – they don't know the address and they don't recognise the house from the photograph – George and Rosemary speculate as to where the place could be, to have a sea view. 'Do you remember,' Rosemary says, 'the sea view from our honeymoon?' They laugh, and she squeezes George's knee, under the table. He catches her hand and squeezes it back. Rosemary tends to behave, in public, as though she is being monitored at all times by the more hostile members of the Parent–Teacher Association, and/or the fiercest people in her late father's congregation. Public displays of affection are, therefore, rare. George has never minded. He understands what it is to have your life made a misery by pupils seeing you do something considered laughable. He has always got off fairly lightly – Mathy Athey is an easy nickname – until he was pictured in the local paper with his prizewinning carrots and parsnips, since when he has been known as Square Root. He thinks it's quite funny, but he also appreciates the value of keeping your head down. And he's a well-liked maths teacher in a well-thought-of school. Rosemary is battling on all fronts as an unknown head in a failing comprehensive.

But there she is, smiling and squeezing his hand.

The cottage is part of a terrace. The front door opens from the street straight into a small, dark hallway. The kitchen is through a door to the right. The lino is curling up at the edges; the units are grubby green melamine. George reaches for Rosemary's hand. She has a determined look. George thinks of all the months and years they put into making their first house a home. He isn't sure he has the energy to do it again.

The kitchen runs the length of the cottage – the window at the front, where the sink is, looks out on to the street, and the one at the back is overgrown with ivy. George sighs. Ivy can play havoc with brickwork.

'It's been empty for a couple of years,' the woman from the estate agent says, as Rosemary opens cupboards and closes them again. George doesn't. The kitchen will have to come out, so he doesn't care about cupboard space.

'Why?' Rosemary asks. It's a nice street, in a good position – not too far out of town, a bit of a steep hill, but there's no way to live in Whitby without encountering a steep hill somewhere in your day.

The woman shrugs. 'The woman who lived here died. The family couldn't decide what to do. There was talk of doing it up for a holiday cottage but they decided against. Come through,' she adds, perhaps feeling they have spent enough time in the grim kitchen. She ushers them into the living room, which is brighter and better. Yes, there is an old, dirty carpet, and the walls are covered in gloss-painted woodchip that will take a lot of getting off. But there is no furniture, so they can feel the size of the space.

And it's light.

And there are patio doors leading out to the garden.

The garden, of course, is overgrown: a broken fence, brambles and ivy, and what might have been a lawn is now an unkempt meadow. But it is long and straight and wide enough for beds at either side of a path. The soil will be sandy, of course, but if George digs in enough compost and uses plenty of mulch, then he can probably grow anything he wants to. There's space for a greenhouse. He turns and looks back at the cottage. Yes, it's covered in ivy, but there's a friendly cast to the brickwork, somehow. His heart starts to expand.

'Rosie –' he says, but she isn't listening. Or rather, she can't hear. She has made her way through the undergrowth to the bottom of the garden, where there is a fence, a path, and then a view across the rooftops of the town to the sea. George walks down and stands behind her, putting his hands on her waist. She is crying. 'We could live here,' she says. 'It would be just right for the two of us.'

'Yes,' he says. Thinks: this can be the place where we are always, and only, ourselves. In this house, they will declare that they are enough.

No, that isn't quite right. First, they will remember they are enough. Then they will declare it, through the happiness of their living, the beauty of their garden.

'We could put a little paved area here,' George says, scuffing the earth at his feet. 'We'll need to level it. But we could have a bench, and look out over the sea.' He rests his chin on his wife's shoulder, and feels her smile.

They sell their house to a family with a toddler and a bump, who are looking to move out of their top-floor flat before the new baby arrives. ('Imagine! All those stairs!' Rosemary says to George, and he says, 'Yes!' but neither of them is imagining it, not really.)

And before the year is over, George and Rosemary Athey are living in Whitby, in a cottage overlooking the sea.

And they are happy.

52

Casey

Dear lost for words,
There's so much to do, and it feels as though it's never going
to end, and I just can't

And then Casey stopped sleeping at all. She got into bed,
and she listened to music, and she pretended to herself that
it was the same. That rest was almost as good as sleep. That
closing her eyes and breathing in the calm of the darkness
was a kind of meditation, a quicker-than-sleep recharge. She
told herself that perhaps she had slept. But she knew, when
she got out of bed after eight or ten hours, to eat, and to
get ready to go back to work, that she had neither slept nor
rested. The muscles of her lower back and shoulders ached,
her dry hands rasped along her clothes, and her night-time
brain had fought itself, between trying to think of nothing,
and trying to remember the names, the faces, of all of the
dead she had seen.

53

Adjoa

Seven texts this morning. Adjoa feels her belly drop. She must stop looking at her phone before she's got properly into the day.

Seven texts usually means that somewhere in the world something bad enough to merit headlines has happened to a person of colour. It means that before Adjoa has had time to read the news story, to absorb it – or even to decide whether she needed it, today, or whether she might wait until tomorrow – she needs to reassure her friends that she is okay with it. Not that she can be. But that's the way it's framed, always.

Yup. Look.

From her colleague-work-buddy Tom: Ads. Can't imagine how this must feel. Here if you want to talk.

From Ruthie, her friend from uni: So, so horrible. Thinking of you.

And on the street WhatsApp group – and it had been Adjoa's idea to set this up, at the beginning of the pandemic, so she only has herself to blame – someone has posted a

243

link to the news story with the comment, This is terrible, will be interested in Adjoa's ideas on what we can do.

Adjoa puts down her phone before she can reply Dismantle the American justice system and rebuild from the ground up, based on a different set of criteria than white men needing protection from 'their slaves'. She goes to take a shower. She remembers the week when five different people asked her whether she washed her legs, because they'd read on the internet that Black women did and white women didn't.

So it's another day when Adjoa's well-meaning friends are Checking In.

It will start with oh god, did you see what happened? It's so awful. Hope you're okay. And within three texts it will be, Do you think they ... or I don't understand why ... or didn't the police ... Or surely ... And Adjoa will spend another day teaching her informal, and unending, series of seminars on 'How Racism Works'. With, for those who are looking for extra credit, side modules: 'Privilege Isn't Having Stuff, That's Why You Can't See It'; 'It Is Not the Job of Your Black Friend to Educate You'; and 'Just Because You Have Only Just Noticed Racism That Doesn't Mean It's New'.

Since the murder of George Floyd, it's all been worse. Well, better, Adjoa knows, in that at least these things are being discussed. Her friends and colleagues are well-meaning to a person, not a deliberately racist bone in their bodies. But Adjoa knows that doesn't stop their fingers itching to touch her hair, or to confide, when drunk, that her skin is so beautiful that it mesmerises them, as though she is nothing but her otherness. She knows that if she challenged them on this, they would say: but you said my haircut suited me, or, you told me the colour of this dress brought out the colour of my eyes, so how is that different? To pull people up on every damn thing is not only exhausting but also makes her 'sensitive' and 'touchy'. Smile, Black friend, smile.

They don't mean it. She knows they don't mean it. That only makes it worse.

And there have been some unexpected apologies, too. One of Adjoa's old school friends messaged her via Facebook to say she was sorry for the jokes about her hair at school, saying she realises now that it wasn't appropriate and she is making sure her own children do better. Her line manager has been in touch to say she will be clamping down on any and all inappropriate 'banter' she sees in future, rather than letting it pass because she assumes Adjoa doesn't mind or thinks it's funny. Her neighbour, who makes a point of making eye contact when they see each other in the street, rather than looking at his feet.

Adjoa is the only Black woman – the only Black person – in a team of six, at work. She's fairly sure she didn't think about it when she used to go to the office. But six boxes on the Zoom screen, and it's very clear that she's the odd one out. Well, Duncan is the only man, but Duncan is three years from retirement and has clearly never spent a moment of his white male life wondering about the space he takes up, literally or metaphorically. He begins every call with 'Hello, ladies,' even though every single time he does so Lara immediately types either '"hello" will suffice, Duncan' or 'outdated language alert' in the chat box. Lara is their graduate trainee and Adjoa likes her a lot. There's something in the way she operates that makes Adjoa think she has had a hard-scrabble kind of life, has earned every damn thing. Also, Lara has never expressed much interest in Adjoa as a Black woman, and her only comment on global news is that 'the world is all shit'. Which Adjoa has a certain respect for.

Adjoa calls her mother.

Catherine is a white woman from rural Yorkshire who married Kwadjo, a Ghanaian man, in 1985, so there's not a lot she hasn't experienced in terms of the genteel kind of racism that so many British people think is okay. She had only once been spat at – on the way back from their honeymoon, getting off the train at Leeds central station. The first thing Catherine had thought, she told Adjoa, years afterwards, was that if Kwadjo went after the bloke who did it then he would be the one who would be considered to have started it, and a criminal record plus the colour of his skin would be the end for his ambition to become a doctor. So she had clung to his arm as he radiated hurt on her behalf. She had understood, then, why it was that he so rarely held her hand in public. It was to protect her.

The spitting was, somehow, not as awful as the muttering, the side-eyeing, the words shouted after Catherine when they were out together. It wasn't every time – if they stuck to the student streets, the jazz clubs, the down-at-heel places where it was normal to be Black, or in a mixed-race relationship, they felt fine. They knew other couples who were more than one colour. And when they were alone, Kwadjo studying and Catherine writing newsletter copy and advertising slogans for an agency where she found freelance work, they were themselves.

Kwadjo took a job in general practice in a small town in the Yorkshire Dales. It wasn't easy to settle in. Catherine was isolated as Kwadjo worked long hours and established himself. He was soon known as Joe. Sometimes he came home with stories of successes, the reason he went into general practice in the first place: the undiagnosed type 2 diabetes that had made a woman convinced she had cancer because she was so tired; the man who had never spoken to anyone about his depression before. But at least twice a week there were other stories. The man who sat silently with his wife throughout her consultation because he was 'protective'. Kwadjo had been concerned about possible domestic violence, but it had transpired that the husband did not feel compelled to attend his wife's appointments with any other members of the medical practice. The woman who opened the door to the consulting room, looked at Kwadjo, and walked out again without a word. She had complained at the desk that she should have been warned that Dr Addo was – The receptionist telling him about it paused with embarrassment, and Kwadjo had said, it's okay. Catherine fumed about these kinds of things on her husband's behalf. 'He was the one who had to make her feel better,' she told Adjoa, when Adjoa was a teenager and they had many, many conversations about all the ways the world was going to be a lot harder for her than it was for the white contemporaries that made up the majority of her school classmates.

'Hey, Mum,' Adjoa says when Catherine answers.

'Adjoa!' Her mother is always, always delighted to hear from her. 'Everything good? Your father and I were just saying we wished you had come home.'

'I'm fine, honestly,' Adjoa says. And she is, since she and

her boyfriend Nick decided to move in together. They are both only children, so it took them a while to make up their minds. Partly because they felt equally responsible for their parents and wondered if they ought to move in with them; and partly because they were both used to their own space. But it's been six weeks and they're doing well. Nick goes out to work, at a school that's open for the children of key workers, so that helps. 'Nick too. Is Dad there?'

'Dad's at the surgery. Aren't you working today?'

It's 10 a.m. Catherine, who has never worked in an office, is convinced that every job starts at nine and ends at five. 'I am, but my first call's not for half an hour. And I've got some time banked. I just felt like a slow start.'

She hears her mother exhale. 'George Floyd?'

'And Breonna Taylor. And the rest.'

'I know, honey. I know.' Her mother is probably the only white person Adjoa could bear to hear this from. Her mother does know. 'Your dad and I are the same.'

'And is everyone asking him about it?'

'Of course.' Her mother laughs. 'Because a GP from Yorkshire who's the only Black man in the village is the closest thing there is to an authority on American institutional racism. Heaven forbid anyone should find out anything for themselves.'

'Thanks, Mum.' Adjoa feels better just listening to the laughter. She might be nearly forty but right now she misses her mother as though the missing is a toothache. She can imagine the smell of her parents' house, lavender and bread and coffee; the kitchen, dark with a small window, a set of shelves with jars and jars and jars of this and that, all in rows. Her father in the doorway: 'I am HOME!' and her mother squealing as though this is the best and most surprising thing that has ever happened to her.

'Find yourself a nice thing to do today,' Catherine says.

Adjoa does as she is told, like all good children.

She cannot help but think of herself as a good child, because her father told her that she was, every day of her childhood. She supposes it could have been a burden – Nick has had therapy to try to untangle what he is from the person his parents are determined he should be – but Adjoa liked being her father's good girl, and she always will. When she failed her driving test, she was a good girl for trying; when she got into trouble for fighting at school, she was a good girl for standing up for herself, even if she had chosen the wrong way to go about it. Her mother was more likely to have harsher words, but none that ever really stung, and when Dad told her she was a good girl, Mum always smiled and shook her head, as if to say, these people I love. These people.

Nice things to do are few and far between. Adjoa has long since stopped thinking of a bubble-bath as a nice thing, more of a daily necessity, and she and Nick make a point of having evenings they enjoy, because otherwise, what's the point of anything? So Adjoa has to think quite hard before she comes up with the idea. As soon as she finishes work, she goes out to collect a cook-at-home meal from a restaurant that they would normally only ever go to on a birthday. 'Full instructions', declares the website, alongside many five-star reviews.

Adjoa takes her bath and then clears the papers from their dining table, which has become her desk for when she

249

has meetings. The rest of the time, she works from bed, or on the sofa.

She lights candles. She finds their napkins, at the back of what Nick calls the Everything Else drawer in the kitchen. She lays out the ingredients.

'What's this?' Nick asks when he gets home, just after six.

'My mum told me to do something nice,' Adjoa says, 'so we are having a Michelin-star at-home dining experience.'

'When does the Michelin-star chef arrive?' Nick asks, looking down the list of instructions, and all the tiny packets of things.

'I forgot to order them,' Adjoa says. 'What does a sauté pan look like?'

'I think if you have to ask we haven't got one.'

The wild mushroom tarts are tasty but a bit dry; Adjoa finds the coulis that was supposed to go with them when she goes to get the sauce for their steaks out of the fridge. She forgot to leave the oven on to warm up the dauphinoise potatoes so they eat the steaks first and invent the 'potato course'. That reminds Adjoa that she also forgot about the sorbet, so they have that as pre-pudding. Pudding they don't bother to assemble, but eat the meringue, cream, and fruit compote from the containers it came in.

The wine is excellent. The food is, too, or maybe it's just the fact that they laugh so much as they try to make it look like the pictures on the instructions.

Afterwards, they ignore the carnage in their tiny kitchen, and flop on the sofa. Nick pops corn in the microwave when Adjoa admits that she knows she's eaten a meal but somehow . . . it seems as though she hasn't.

'I haven't heard you laugh this much in months,' Nick says, kissing the top of her head.

'Global pandemic, sweetie.'

'Well, yes, but it must be tiring, being everybody's go-to Black person.'

She lets herself sink into him. 'It is. It really is.'

That weekend, Adjoa switches her phone off on Friday night, and leaves it switched off until Monday morning. They don't watch the news. Nick goes out for a paper as usual on Saturday morning, but she sticks to the supplements. She reads about container gardening, virtual comedy festivals, and store-cupboard cookery. They watch *Howl's Moving Castle* and play Scrabble, which Nick wins in a best-of-five tournament. Adjoa doesn't mind him winning; she would always rather play 'masque' for satisfaction than 'Qi' on a triple-word score for 33. As they put the board away, Nick looks at her and says, 'You're mentally claiming the moral victory, aren't you?' Adjoa laughs at the pleasure of being so thoroughly understood.

When she switches on her phone on Monday morning, most of her messages are well-meaning you ok hun type things, or links to videos of police brutality. She can feel the muscles in her shoulders knotting as she scrolls.

And then she remembers the cutting from the local free paper that she kept because her mother is always interested in anything to do with bookshops. Adjoa had meant to post it but it's on the fridge, still, with the out-of-date takeaway offers and a postcard from Nick's parents that they sent from their holiday in Portugal last summer.

Holiday. Adjoa cannot remember when holidays were

normal. Her world has become part isolation, part representative of All the Black People.

Maybe she needs a book prescription.

Dear Lost For Words,
I have mixed race heritage (my father is Ghanaian and my mother white British) and I identify as Black. I've always been a bit unusual in Yorkshire. It's been manageable, I suppose, because I don't know what it is to be part of the majority. But lately I'm everyone's go-to Black person/race consultant/ defence against the accusation of being a racist, and I'm SO VERY TIRED.

Whenever I read a book with Black people in it, the point of them always seems to be Black, or it's a novel about slavery or oppression, and that's important, it really is, but I would like to see myself represented in the pages of a book and for there to be joy, rather than ISSUES. Or I would like to read books that feel true and real but are not about Black people suffering. I want to be offered books the way you would offer a white woman books, assuming you don't feel the need to reflect them.

Thank you.
Adjoa

252

54

Here is a question that no one should ask:

What's your favourite book?

And, if you are ever asked it, you are 100 percent within your rights to refuse to answer.

Reasonable questions about books are:

What's your favourite book to read when you are sad?

What's your favourite book for comfort?

What's the book that's guaranteed to make you laugh?

Which book has stayed with you the longest?

Which book kept you awake at night?

Which book do you wish more people knew about?

Which book changed the way you think about the world?

You could choose to answer one of those instead.

55

Adjoa

Dear Adjoa,

Thank you for getting in touch.

This is not the same thing at all, I know, but my boss here is not a fan of the way care leavers are portrayed in fiction. They are always troubled, or afraid, or the causes of trouble, she says. I hadn't noticed until she pointed it out but that's the point, isn't it?

I've put a list of books below – if you let me know which are of interest I'll parcel them up ready for collection. Some of them might seem screamingly obvious so please forgive me if you've read them. Something I'm learning more and more through this is that one person's classic is another's great new discovery. Last week I spoke to someone who wanted to try something new and she is now reading Marian Keyes for the first time. (In case you haven't read her, she's very funny and cheering, but can make you cry a heartbeat later. My favourite is *Sushi for Beginners*.)

Stay well,

Kelly

Homegoing by Yaa Gyasi. I have an awful feeling this book has been given to you several times, and/or been discussed with you by every well-meaning white person you know, but I'm including it just in case, because I absolutely love it. It follows eight generations of a family, beginning with two sisters separated in the 1800s in Ghana.

Girl, Woman, Other by Bernadine Evaristo. I really, truly couldn't put this down. I can't comment on whether it's the right thing for you right now, of course, but it's been described as a choral love song to modern Black womanhood in Britain, and I thought that might appeal.

Days Without End by Sebastian Barry. This follows two young men, one an Irish immigrant, who become soldiers in the Native American and Civil Wars in America. It's one of the most moving things I've ever read. It has themes of identity and belonging but most of all it's just – human.

Educated by Tara Westover. This is a memoir about a young woman brought up in an American religious sect who fights to get an education. I'm not sure why I thought of this for you except that it made me feel full of hope, somehow.

The Confessions of Frannie Langton. The author, Sara Collins, describes this as 'a gothic romance about someone who happens to have been a slave'. I'm not sure where this fits in your criteria but I read it in twenty-four hours and I still think about it.

The Language of Flowers by Vanessa Diffenbaugh. I loved this. It's an American novel about a young woman who uses the language and meaning of flowers to create meaningful arrangements and bouquets. There's a companion non-fiction volume about the Victorian language of flowers, by the same author.

The Bees by Laline Paull. Set in a beehive, and about bees. Actual bees. It's very hard to explain why it's compelling, but it is.

Dear Kelly,
You're right, I have seven copies of *Homegoing*. Or had. My mum bought hardbacks for me and my dad for Christmas, when it first came out. The rest I gave away to people who said they knew nothing about Ghana.
I'll take all of the others. Thanks.
Adjoa

Dear Adjoa,
They'll be ready whenever you are.

I've been thinking about your original email and whether there's a way we can do something, here, to – well, to pre-empt concerned white people expecting their non-white friends to do the heavy lifting on this. I was talking to my boyfriend about it (only in the most general terms) and he is internet first for everything, so he said, put a section on the front page of the website called 'Questions about BLM?' but I think 'Black Lives Matter – Educate Yourself' is better. My boss says telling people to educate themselves immediately get their backs up, so we still haven't

256

decided. We'll have a section in the shop, too, visible from the doorway, so people might be prompted to ask when they're waiting.

56

Simone

Dear Lost For Words,

I am sick to the back teeth of being on this godforsaken island. My partner and I can't stop watching news and talking about how awful everything is. The only people we speak to are our neighbours and – well, let's just say we aren't exactly in the same wheelhouse, politics-wise. Help! What could I read to get me away from here, at least in my head?

Simone

Dear Simone,

I'm not sure that this helps, but you and your partner are definitely not alone in feeling that way. Obviously there are lots of books set in other places, but in a case like yours I'd prescribe novels in translation. Here are some of our favourites.

Take good care,
Kelly

Lust, Caution by Eileen Chang. This is set in mid-twentieth-century Shanghai, and it's short and shocking and entirely absorbing.

Homer's *Odyssey*, translated by Emily Wilson. Not only is this a joyful and vivid translation, but it's, literally, quite the journey . . .

Before the Coffee Gets Cold by Toshikazu Kawaguchi, translated by Geoffrey Trousselot, is set in a coffee shop in Tokyo, where it's possible to go back in time. I read it before the pandemic began and I can't stop thinking about it.

Out Stealing Horses by Per Petterson. Set in Norway, during and after the Second World War. Probably not the most cheerful book you've ever met but I think it's worth it.

57

Bella

Dear Loveday,

Thank you so very much for popping in! Well, popping out-side! And it wasn't actually much of a pop, was it? I hope I didn't keep you for too long. Your reading garden sounds like a marvellous thing.

I know that to you I'm just another customer, but any time you want to talk, I'm here. I could talk about my dear friend Archie until the cows come home!

I'm reading the Anne Brontë and I can't help but think it would make a marvellous play – all that handsome dissolution and drama, and such a strong female lead!! (Too young for me to play, unfortunately!) And it has made me think about how I can't stay cooped up for ever, you clever thing.

I've told Jack at the pub I'm feeling a bit wobbly, and he said, everything is wobbling, and he expects it will be very quiet. He says we can ease ourselves back in. I hope he's right!

In the meantime I am going to tackle that box of letters! Wish me luck!!

Love and kisses,

Bella xx

Dear Bella,

It was very good to see you. There aren't many people in my day-to-day life who remember Archie the way you do. My family understand what he was to me, and they loved him. Archie was a – a sort of lovely add-on for so many people. A bonus chapter. He was the plot driver that kept me alive, though I didn't realise it at the time. I don't think people ever do. But Archie was the person who made my life possible, and much as I love the stories people have about him, it was good to talk about him properly with you.

I really hope you like the rest of the books. Helen Graham from *Tenant* is one of my favourite characters. I have a tattoo of a line from the book – 'No one can be happy in eternal solitude'. It took me a long time to learn that.

Loveday x

Dear Loveday,

You must absolutely feel you can come and talk about Archie any time at all. The behind-the-scenes Archie, when the curtain came down. You know what I mean!

I agree about Helen Graham. Gilbert Markham, on the other hand . . .

Love and kisses,

Bella xx

58

Adjoa

The bookshop staff seem like good people. It feels as though no one there is going to want to touch her hair, though the pandemic has been a win in that regard at least. Her braids are loosening; she wonders how long it will be before she can get to the small, speciality hairdresser she goes to. No doubt she'll be in the queue with every other Black woman in York. Maybe her father will do it, when she can see him. Adjoa does not remember this, but when she was small and her family visited Ghana, her father asked one of the aunties to teach him to braid her hair, the Ghanaian way. The way her mother tells it, the aunties had assumed that Catherine hadn't wanted to learn, but it was more that Kwadjo had wanted to share in this heritage. It was many years before Adjoa understood the real reason that she didn't go to the same hairdresser as her friends.

Adjoa leaves Nick in bed. They'd had a late night, watching films then having sex, then, unexpectedly as neither of them could sleep, watching another film. She sets off for Lost For Words. It's a warm day, not especially summery, but it is still

August, and so she passes a man wearing shorts and flip-flops, then another in an unzipped puffa jacket and jeans. She can tell the children who have been allowed to dress themselves, wearing reckless combinations of superhero costumes, pyjamas, and wellies; she smiles at the mother of the girl who is wearing a bright yellow cloak. Some adults look as though they have barely been outside, grey-skinned and walking as though they have forgotten what shoes are. Adjoa wonders how many of them have lost someone. Or are going to. She has to stop at the thought; she stands in a doorway and pulls out her phone, because that way no one will ask her if she is okay. There's nothing on her phone except a fresh text from a colleague – OMG Ads I can't believe what is happening in America!!! There are so many ways Adjoa could reply to this. What particular racist outrage are you referring to? Think yourself lucky that it's a surprise, maybe. Or Have you also texted your white friends? Or My name is not Ads. She doesn't reply at all. But she texts her Dad, just a little heart, so he knows she is thinking of him.

Adjoa has never visited this bookshop before. It's been a while since she's been in any bookshop, actually, pandemic notwithstanding – she doesn't read a lot, and Amazon is just so easy. But when she turns into the street she recognises Lost For Words: of course, this was the place that nearly burned down a few years ago. There's already a customer standing in the doorway at the makeshift counter, so she stands back and looks in the window: a pile of books on a table, a kid wrapping parcels and sticking labels on them, and beyond, shelves and shelves and shelves of books, the sort of shelves that confuse your brain because you lose your sense of perspective. It looks so tidy, so clean, and at the same time, so welcoming. There's a sign in the window about a book group. Would Adjoa like to be in a book group? She's always assumed she would hate it – just the idea of someone telling her what to read makes her feel as though she's back at school, her teacher pretending he cannot understand her accent when she reads aloud, even though she was precisely as Yorkshire as the rest of the kids. But Kelly has, in effect, told Adjoa what to read, and it feels both comforting and exciting. As though someone is looking out for her for a change. As though she has one less thing to carry.

The man ahead of her peels away from the doorway, smiles at her, hugs a parcel of books to his chest, and heads in the other direction. Adjoa steps into the space he's left. The woman on the other side of the table is smiling a welcome, her brown hair loose around her shoulders. Adjoa wonders whether anyone ever asks to touch it.

Before Adjoa can say anything the woman says, 'Adjoa, right? I'm Kelly. I've got your books.'

'Thanks.'

They are in a brown paper bag; Adjoa wonders whether it will hold. But presumably these guys know what they're doing.

'It's really nice to meet you,' Kelly says. 'I don't know if you can see from here, but that cleared bookcase over there is where we're putting the new section.'

'You should have some books for kids as well,' Adjoa says.

'I was wondering about that,' Kelly says. 'There's a lot of great books around for kids and young adults.'

'That's good.'

Adjoa almost doesn't say anything else. Dad always says,

you don't have to fight every battle. Adjoa was thirty before she realised he was right; her life felt easier after that. She stopped taking antidepressants and she found a job she liked enough to make it worth thirty-five hours of her life every week. She met Nick. When they moved in together they made not so much a life as a nest. She loves it.

But some battles – the ones you might win – are worth fighting. Adjoa taps her card to the reader, puts her purse away, and asks, 'Why did you assume I was Adjoa?'

265

59

Kelly

'Could you take over for a bit, Loveday?' Kelly calls through to the back of the shop when Adjoa leaves. Loveday and Nathan have been building furniture and, from the sounds coming from the yard today, it's not as easy as the internet makes it look. Nathan was out there alone for the morning and early afternoon; once business slowed down, Loveday went out to help, but she told Kelly to call her if she needed her. Madison is upstairs, counting how many copies of their most in-demand books they have in stock: the pandemic means that no one is bringing their old books to sell, and the book prescription pages on the website have been hugely successful. After what Madison said in Whitby, Kelly is damned if she's going to ask her for help. Craig had been sympathetic when Kelly told him about it, but reminded her that teenagers were tricky, and it might be a good idea to cut Madison some slack. Kelly had agreed, because he was right; but still, she doesn't see why she has to be the one that Madison takes her angst out on. It's easy enough for Craig to be understanding of Madison when he doesn't have to see her every week. Kelly had hoped Loveday would say something, but apparently they are all just going to pretend it didn't happen. Hey ho.

Then again, maybe she has somehow done to Madison what she has inadvertently done to Adjoa: made an assumption, caused pain by thoughtlessness. Here she is, making lists of books about white privilege, and she assumes that a Black woman at the door is the Black woman who placed an order. She closes her eyes against her tears. If she tells Craig about this he'll reassure her, but she really doesn't deserve reassurance. She needs to learn.

Still, she wishes it was time to go home.

Loveday comes through from the reading-garden-to-be. She's wearing old sweatpants, a T-shirt that must be Nathan's as it's practically down to her knees, and anyway Kelly can't imagine her boss at an Imagine Dragons gig. Kelly thinks of her and Craig, so comfortable together and yet she is still sleeping in the best of her pyjamas, which are nothing fancy but at least match. Craig didn't bring a lot of clothes with him, but often goes to check on his place on the Saturdays when she's at work; he brings more of his things then, but has not yet appeared with a pair of ratty old tracksuit bottoms or socks with a hole in the toe. Maybe he's inherently smart, Kelly sometimes thinks, glumly, as she once again decides against her old-favourite jeans which she stopped wearing in public after her dad offered to buy her some new ones, but she lived in on days when she wasn't going to leave her flat. In which case Craig should accept that she's inherently not smart at all. But Madison's words have made her doubt him. And so she is still putting mascara on, before breakfast, and feeling pathetic about it.

'Is everything okay?' Loveday asks.

'Yes,' Kelly says, and gestures at the door, 'I just – I made an assumption. I need a break.'

'Take your time.' One of the things that's great about Loveday is that she doesn't make you talk about everything. 'What can I do?'

'We had a call this morning about a recipe book with dolma in it, for a woman called Lorraine. The note's on the desk. I was going to start with the Middle Eastern cookery books but I haven't had a chance to look yet.'

60

Loveday

Loveday is quite happy to get away from the pallets. The people who do this kind of thing, she realised by 11 a.m., are not the people who first look at the array of tools in their inherited garden shed, and wonder why there need to be so very many different kinds of saw. But Nathan was undeterred and is still, she would say, sixty percent undeterred, four hours and zero completed items of furniture later. She wishes she hadn't made such a thing of sticking to a budget for the reading garden. Then she could have got on the internet – the shopping part, not the make-do-and-mend part – and solved this in fifteen minutes.

'Hey,' he says, coming through from the yard. 'I'm going to need some more nails. Maybe another couple of pallets. I'll be back in a bit.'

'See you later.'

She goes to the cookery section and finds three books that have recipes for dolma: one by Claudia Roden, who even Loveday has heard of, and two more recent, more lavish books. She takes them to the desk, with the intention

269

of calling Lorraine, but finds herself turning the pages, wondering whether she could manage some of these dishes next time it's her turn to cook. Everyone seems to be getting sick of her sausages and mash, even though Loveday would happily eat the same meal for ever.

Lorraine doesn't answer, so Loveday leaves a message.

Almost all of the parcels for collection that day have gone. On Monday they'll start on the weekend requests that have come in by email: book prescriptions seem to be needed by more and more people, and Loveday is glad. Glad to help people; glad that she's found a way to make the shop succeed. Of the parcels remaining, there's one for a woman who said she wasn't sure whether she would come today or on Monday, one that has been hanging around for a couple of weeks, and one for someone called Jennifer. The name rings a bell, but Loveday can't quite place it. Madison has the laptop upstairs, so she can't look it up. In the absence of anything else to do, Loveday gets on her hands and knees, crawls underneath the packing table, and starts to pick up the mess from under there: the shiny backing from a sheet of labels, the inner tube from a roll of packing tape, pleasing-in-the-hand offcuts of bubble-wrap and crisp brown paper.

'Hello?' The trouble with the shop door being propped open is that there's no bell to warn you to get up off the floor.

'Just a minute,' Loveday calls. She stands up, and thinks of dusting off her knees, but given the all-over state she's in there's really no point. A man is leaning on the doorframe, half-smiling.

'Was there anything good down there?'

Loveday laughs. It's the kind of thing Archie would have said, before segueing into a story about the time he found one of Princess Margaret's least favourite earrings caught in a tiger-skin rug. 'Not today. How can I help?'

The man is wearing a suit and tie, which is not exactly usual for a Saturday afternoon bookshop customer, but each to their own. Maybe he's come from work.

'I said I'd look in,' he says. 'My wife ordered some books for collection. She was taking our son to a birthday party this afternoon and was going to come and collect them on her way home. But I said, look, Jenny, Milo will have cake in his hair and you'll have the beginning of a headache, so why not let me do it?'

Loveday nods. And decides she doesn't like this man after all. She couldn't say why. She's gone from finding him funny to something feeling – off. 'Just a minute, I'll take a look,' she says. 'What's your wife's name?'

'Jenny. Jenny Peterson. Though she sometimes uses her maiden name. Which would make her Jenny Kingdom.' He holds Loveday's gaze just a moment too long, then laughs, 'I just go along with her. You women.'

Loveday goes through the remaining packages waiting for collection. One of them is addressed to Ms Jennifer Kingdom. Of course. She's the woman who wrote to them to thank them for helping her get away from her husband. Loveday's blood seems to pool in her stomach, and her face forces itself into a smile. She slides the parcel back into the box under the desk, and says, 'It's not here. I'll just check to see if we've processed it. It's been busy this week. And I think we might have had to order something in for her.'

The folder on the packing table contains all of their book prescriptions. Nathan sometimes takes tasteful, identifying-details-blurred-out photos for Instagram, and has suggested

271

they print out their most popular Insta posts and make a window display. Loveday prefers their rainbows.

She turns the pages in the folder slowly, as though she is looking, and her mind goes through the options. The simplest: to claim the parcel isn't ready, to let him walk away, to contact Jennifer and let her know he's been here.

What would her mother do? Loveday closes her eyes. Her mother would say, keep yourself safe. You always keep yourself safe first. And then you make sure you're not endangering anyone else.

The man is tapping at his teeth with a fingernail, a click-click-click that matches Loveday's pulse.

'Could she have collected it already?' Loveday asks.

'Surely you should know that?'

Loveday shrugs, a 'you're right' gesture – keep yourself safe – and says, 'This will teach me, for having the morning off.'

He laughs. 'If you want something done right do it yourself.'

Loveday straightens up to face him. 'I don't have it. I'm sorry. It's possible that your wife has already collected it. Maybe on the way to the party? Could you call her to check?'

'Oh.' He makes a puzzled face that would be entirely convincing if Loveday hadn't remembered Jennifer's letter so clearly.

'Oh,' he says again. He doesn't move. Loveday hopes for another customer, but the street has reached its mid-afternoon state of quietness. So she makes herself smile, and she turns away.

When the man slams his fist down on the table, she jumps, even though she had been half-braced for something.

272

A husband who has gone through whatever calculations this man has, in order to try to find his wife, is not likely to be fobbed off easily. Maybe he remembered his wife mentioning Lost for Words, or he had seen their name on a bank statement from before Jennifer got away. This is a long shot for him. He must be desperate. 'Don't walk away from me,' he says. 'We haven't finished.'

Loveday hears feet on the stairs – Madison – and the kitchen door open and close – Kelly. She turns, straightens. 'I don't have your wife's books,' she says.

'Has she collected them already?'

Kelly steps next to Loveday, and then a little in front of her. 'That information is covered by the Bookseller's Oath,' she says. 'Sorry.'

Just for a moment, the man drops his smirk, and his face is almost a snarl. 'Nobody likes a smartarse,' he says.

Kelly stands still and says nothing, waiting, though Loveday isn't sure what for. Maybe she's hoping that if they don't react he'll just go away. It seems like the safest strategy. Then Loveday hears Madison, behind her, make a sort of whimpering sound. 'Could you go and fetch Nathan, Madison?' she asks, without moving her gaze from the man in the doorway. Nathan won't be there, but Madison doesn't know that. And she'll be out of the way, and this man might not like the idea of someone called Nathan coming to join the potential fray.

'Bitches,' the man says, his word a spit, and he turns and walks down the street, away from the shop.

'You bet,' Kelly says, once he's out of earshot, and Loveday sees that her colleague's hands are shaking. She moves the table away from the doorway, closes the door, and flips the sign to 'closed'. She slides the bolt into place, just in case.

Later, at home, after they have eaten, Loveday relates it all to Sarah-Jane. Nathan is soaking his pallet-wrangling aches away in a bath, and Vanessa is doing an online origami workshop. 'I was so close to handing it over, Mum,' she says. 'And then, he would have known where she was. All that good work you did to make her safe and I almost put her back in danger.'

Sarah-Jane nods, 'Men like that are clever. They're manipulative. They know how to make you do what they want you to do.'

It's at times like this, Loveday knows, that they both think of her father, her mother's husband, who was killed as her mother defended herself from his temper, his jealousy, his inability to process the disappointments in his life except by venting them on his wife. They don't talk about him. Most of Loveday's memories of him are good: he was, for the most part, a doting and generous father, and although, looking back, she sees how he made her mother anxious, then fearful, and then downright afraid, she cannot help but remember him with some love. Love that she keeps to herself, although she knows her mother would not begrudge her it.

After a moment, Loveday says, 'I felt bad that Madison was there.'

'You protected her,' Sarah-Jane says.

'I know. But they come to work in a bookshop, Mum.'

'A bookshop that has a reading refuge. They know what you're about.'

Loveday isn't sure that Madison is: she only arrived after lockdown began.

Sarah-Jane goes back to stroking Loveday's head. Loveday will never get weary of this, as long as she lives. For so many years, this was the only touch she wanted, and she couldn't have it. She imagines the feeling of her mother's hand running across her hair is how it feels if you're a book, being read. After a moment her mother says, 'It just goes to show, though. Women need refuge. I need to go back to volunteering.'

'But Mum, you're still not well.'

'I'm tired,' Sarah-Jane says, 'but, Loveday, I'm tired when I sit on the sofa all day, so I may as well get tired being useful. And the women we work with are going through worse.'

'I know, but—' Loveday almost says, *but I have not had you long enough to risk losing you. But we don't know enough about this wretched virus to assume that you're safe, just because you didn't get worse and worse and die within three weeks.* 'But I don't want you to make yourself worse. Why don't you come and help Nathan and me sort out the reading garden? It feels as though we're just making more mess at the moment. We need a foreman. And we need someone who can tell us how to make it feel safe.'

She can't stop thinking of the fact that Jennifer got to know them because she could come into the shop; she doesn't want to imagine the women trapped at home, afraid, not even a bookshop to go to. The news is full of statistics about the increase in domestic violence during the pandemic, and every time she hears about it on the radio, Loveday feels a little sicker. And she thinks of Zoe, with her toddler and her baby, and no husband now to ever come home. How she imagined that books would help her. She pushes the thought down, down. Because if Loveday doesn't believe that books can help, can heal, then she doesn't really know what she is doing with her life.

Sarah-Jane doesn't reply, and her hand has gone heavy on Loveday's head. Her mother falls asleep at the drop of a hat, these days. Loveday's book, *A Long Way From Verona* by Jane Gardam, is within reach on the floor, so she starts to read about Jessica Vye navigating her way through adolescence, and wonders if Madison would enjoy it, or if it would be too close to the bone. The weight of her mother's hand gets heavier, and then slides down the side of her head and comes to rest on her shoulder.

61

Jennifer

Dear Jennifer,

We're happy that we have all of the books you requested, and we hope they will help you start to feel at home in your new life. There's an extra something for Milo, too – *The Story of the Little Mole Who Knew It Was None of His Business* has been a firm favourite at the Lost For Words Storytime since Kelly set it up when she started working here. All those parents and children sitting squished together on a carpet . . . it was so normal then. We hope your new normal is a happy one.

Something happened here at the bookshop this weekend that we thought you should know about. A man came to the shop, claiming to be your husband, and looking to collect your books for you. We didn't say that we knew you. We didn't give him the books, or the address, and we haven't kept your address here – we've taken your original letter off the premises, on Sarah-Jane's advice, so you know that even if he did come back, get in, and try to look for it, there's nothing to find. We've deleted your address from our shop

277

database also. But we thought you should know he had been here – we don't want to upset you, but we thought it best to tell you. We can confirm what happened to the police if it will help your case.

Please, look after yourself, and stay safe. Sarah-Jane sends her love and says to tell you that she is sorting out some books to top up the library at the shelter. Everyone seems to be reading more. Let us know if you and Milo would like more books.

Loveday, Kelly and Madison at Lost For Words

278

62

Casey

Dear lost for words,
There's so much to do, and it feels as though it's never going
to end, and I just can't sleep, or turn off. I don't want

Casey begins walking to work. It isn't far to the hospital, it's
quiet and the breeze feels clean against her face. She claims
to her parents that she needs the fresh air. When her father
offers to pick her up at the end of her shift, she shouts at
him, furious and unkind; she can't stop herself. All these
months of trying to get her parents to understand how
they need to be careful and here is her father, offering to
collect her from the hospital when she's spent anything up
to twelve hours on a Covid unit. He doesn't offer again. He
waves away her apology; but she can see she has hurt him.
She doesn't tell him that she doesn't trust herself behind the
wheel of her car any more. She doesn't think about how,
if she isn't safe to drive, then she isn't safe to do any of the
small but necessary tasks she does at the hospital. Because
they need every nurse they can find.

63

Jamie

Dear Lost For Words,
Some of my colleagues were talking about how good you
were at finding books for them and their families. I wonder
if you can help me.

I'm a supermarket manager.

Obviously, over the last few months it's been quite – full
on. I run a large store – I have more than 200 staff and we
serve a big area. There have been a lot of challenges (we're
not supposed to say problems) but I feel as though we (the
store team) have managed really well. My colleagues are
amazing and I try hard to support them. And for some of our
customers, we're the only people they get to talk to – they're
living alone and we're a lifeline, in more ways than one.

I'm not complaining about any of it. I feel lucky to – well,
to serve, I suppose, although they usually say that about
the military, don't they? I love being at work, and being
useful. Some of my staff have had people close to them
die of Covid, quite often alone, and I haven't had anything
like that happen to me. And not so much of a sniffle, either.

Really, I'm lucky. No health worries. No money worries. I'm being useful.

But when I get home I have a problem.

At work I'm fine. I know I'm doing the best I can.

When I get home, I have something to eat, I might watch some TV (not the news, I feel as though I get enough of that through talking to people during the day), and when I'm so tired I can't keep my eyes open I go to bed. I sleep for maybe an hour. And then I'm wide awake. I start thinking of all the people who come into the store, the customers who pull their masks down when they cough and the ones who don't seem to have a clue about what two metres of distance look like. I think about my staff, coming in to work on buses with people who might be ill. A lot of my colleagues are in tough situations financially, and I'm afraid some of them might not declare symptoms or self-isolate because they need to work overtime to keep things afloat. A lot of our delivery drivers are new, and some of them look tired, or as though they're not sure what they're doing, and sometimes when they drive away I wish I'd stopped them and got them to take a break.

Basically, when I go to bed, I start to convince myself that there's a massive outbreak of Covid about to happen in York, and it will be on me. I've been awake until 4 a.m. every morning for the last three months. My alarm goes off at six most days.

In the morning, I'm a bit better. I have a shower, I remind myself that if we were a hotspot someone would have come to close us down, and I get on with my day.

I've been thinking that if I'm going to be awake for three or four hours every night, it might be better to read. I know

281

some people swear by podcasts, but I listen to talking all day and I just can't do it all night too.

Can you help?

I haven't had much time for reading since my uni days, and then it was mostly sociology and psychology textbooks. But now the thought of a book feels like something I need.

Thank you,

Jamie

Dear Jamie,

First of all, thank you for keeping the supermarket running. Those first few weeks, when the shelves were empty, were really weird. There are four of us in our household, and we'd make a meal plan and a shopping list, and it wasn't until we got to a supermarket that we realised it wasn't going to be that straightforward for a while. Not that we thought we would starve, but it really made us appreciate how much we took for granted. Scrambled eggs used to be what we ate when we couldn't be bothered to cook, or were too tired for anything more interesting. Now every time we eat it we talk about when we couldn't get eggs. My mum thinks we should get some chickens but I can't help worrying that they're a lot more complicated than they look.

I've attached a list of books, below, and if you tell me which you think might suit you, I'll send them to you, at home or work – whatever's best.

Although I'm running a book pharmacy here I'm not actually a medical professional, so please take what I'm about to say in the spirit of advice. Do you think you could be suffering from anxiety? I used to. Five years ago, my oldest friend died, and our shop burned down, and I met my mother again after we'd been separated for a really long time. The days were okay. There was so much to do. But when I went to bed I would do exactly what you're doing. I could sleep for an hour or two but then I lay there all night thinking about whether I was doing things the way my friend would have done them, and whether my mother and I could really make things okay between us. I genuinely couldn't have worked harder on the shop, or tried harder with my mum, but that didn't seem to matter, during the night. I thought it was normal, for someone who was grieving. And then one night my boyfriend woke up and realised I was awake, and I broke down and told him everything.

He said that everything would be fine, and there would be something wrong with me if I wasn't finding these things hard. And he persuaded me to go to the doctor. I took medication for a while. I'm not saying I was instantly better, but I was able to cope more easily, and once the edge was taken off the anxiety, I could sleep. And once I could sleep, everything got easier.

I suppose what I'm saying is: books are excellent, and I'm sure these ones will help. But it could be there are some other things you could do too.

Loveday

PS The world is a horrible place right now. It would be crazy not to feel that.

Books to read in the middle of the night:
None of This is Real by Miranda Mellis. This is a short story collection, so it's a good way back into fiction. The title story is about anxiety.

Nightwalk by Chris Yates. It seems you haven't seen a lot of the outdoors lately, so I thought you might enjoy this. It's a book about nature, as seen at night. (I prefer nature in books rather than outdoors and this is a really good read.)

Wild by Cheryl Strayed. This is a memoir about a young woman in a dark place, who takes a very, very long walk along the Pacific Crest Trail. My colleague Kelly recommended it to me. I really liked the book, and the author.

The Night Circus by Erin Morgenstern. Magical realism isn't for everyone, but you might like this. All the important things happen at night, and it's pretty long, which can help. When I'm tired or down, I don't want to have to start a new book too often. I'd rather have a long one that's going to last me for a while.

The Kite Runner by Khaled Hosseini. A novel about surviving and taking responsibility. It's partly about being in the right/wrong place at the right/wrong time, which seems to be what life is all about at the moment.

64

Loveday

The following Saturday, Madison arrives just after Loveday, Nathan and Sarah-Jane. She takes the list of books to locate. Loveday has realised she mustn't make assumptions about what Madison knows, so she prints out the list of book suggestions and writes the section next to them. Being made to feel stupid about books is not the way to help a kid fall in love with reading.

Giving her books seems to be working, though. Madison liked *Jane Eyre*, though she has opinions about men who keep wives in attics and women who forgive them for it. She's read the first of the Earthsea books by Ursula Le Guin and asked for the second, 'but not straight away, it's a lot of wizards and I'm not one of those people who only does wizards and nothing else.' So while the wizards wear off, Loveday has given her *Fingersmith* by Sarah Waters. The first line – 'My name, in those days, was Susan Trinder' – was the last tattoo Loveday got before the pandemic made the very idea of one human coming close to another human with ink and buzzing needle unthinkable. She watched those first horrifying days of news with a healing itch on her left shoulder blade. The TV spooled out images of deserted streets in Wuhan, people wearing masks in long airport queues, reporters discussing the possibility of life closing down in straight-to-camera pieces, their voices smooth but the look in their eyes close to panic. And Loveday balled her fists so she couldn't scratch the place where her skin was healing. When she sees the news now, the ghost of that itch is there.

Madison has nothing to say when she arrives at work, though. It's so unlike her to be mute that Loveday asks her what's wrong. She shrugs and says, 'Bit tired,' and doesn't look Loveday in the face.

Loveday leaves her to it. The books are all picked and packed by early afternoon: the advantage of having someone who is not a habitual reader working at Lost For Words, Loveday has discovered, is that they don't stop and read the back of every volume they pull off the shelves. Nathan and Sarah-Jane have been and gone, Loveday's mother having walked around the space, talked about gates that keep others out rather than making you feel locked in, and then sat down, suddenly, on a pile of pallets in the approximate shape of a chair. 'We've had enough for one day, then,' Nathan had said, and Sarah-Jane had laughed, and Loveday had wished, once again, that she had his ability to make everyone around him feel comfortable. Loveday had bought cinnamon buns first thing; she makes tea, and she and Madison sit upstairs. Kelly is downstairs with the laptop, catching up on the prescription requests that have come in via their social media.

Madison takes a bun downstairs for Kelly, and Loveday

hears her ask Kelly if she needs anything else. This is a major step forward in Madison/Kelly relations, and Loveday isn't sure whether to put it down to the mellowing power of reading or the bonding brought about by facing down that awful man last week.

When Madison returns, Loveday tells her, 'I've got something to talk to you about. *The Secret Garden.*'

Rosemary had been very specific about the edition she wanted to give to George: a cover with a girl with curly blond hair, in a red coat and hat, bending over to put a key in a hidden lock, with a robin watching from a branch above. It had been easy enough to find. It was a 1911 edition, which Loveday and Madison had thought made sense, as it was a book that had belonged to his mother when she was a child. The problem was the price, which was upwards of £400, and that was for a copy that looked likely to fall apart as soon as George looked at it, let alone turned the pages.

'I've found a facsimile copy.' Loveday sees the blank look on Madison's face. 'It's when publishers reproduce an old cover of a famous book. Basically so that people who remember that edition, maybe from when they were kids, can buy it again.'

Madison nods. 'Did you order it?'

'Not yet. It's a lot cheaper than the original ones, but it's still quite rare. It was published in the 1980s, in hardback, and there probably weren't many of them printed. It's in good condition and it's £60. I wondered if Rosemary had given you any idea of her budget?'

Madison shrugs. 'No. Can't we just – give it to them? The shop seems to be doing really well.'

Oh, for a fifteen-year-old's perspective on the world. 'I

should be able to get a trade discount from the dealer, and I won't charge anything extra, so we won't make a profit, which is fine this time. But it will still be fifty pounds, I would think. We can't spend that without checking with Rosemary.'

This seems to satisfy Madison. 'What's so special about this book, anyway?'

'We've got a copy downstairs,' Loveday says. 'You can take it today, if you like.'

Madison nods. 'That book you gave me last week. It's – thick. And I haven't felt like reading this week. My mum keeps crying. I think she thought my dad would have moved back by now, but he just comes round to get things.'

'That's tough,' Loveday says.

'Yeah,' Madison says, and she heads off in search of *The Secret Garden*.

65

Which is the first book you remember?

Imagine a three-year-old, beloved and indulged by her grandparents, and already obsessed by words on paper.

Imagine a book, longer than it is high, easy to hold and carry, creating a landscape when opened. *Jim and Mary and the Rocking Horse* by Sue O'Brian. The child couldn't say her 'r's – she was only three – so she asked for Jim and Maly and the rocking horse. (Family legend does not record whether she could pronounce the 'r' in 'rocking'.)

'Lead it again, Grandma.'

And Grandma did. *Jim and Mary and the Rocking Horse* was about a long metal horse in a playground, that came to life for Jim and Mary.

The child was warm and comfortable on her grandmother's lap, and the fact that she knew what would happen to Jim and Mary on every page made the story better.

The words became recognisable. The letters made sense: they associated themselves with sounds, with objects, with each other to make new sounds.

Perhaps your first memory of a book, of being read to, also comes with a sense of warmth, of comfort. Bedtime, after-bath-time, tired-from-playgroup time.

If you didn't have books at home, or someone to read to you, perhaps you remember being squished on a carpet with your classmates, while a teacher read a story that could turn out to be anything: caterpillars, tigers, a determined girl on a mission.

Or a library, with favourite books of the librarian faced-out and easy to reach.

I'm glad you remember.

Because this is how readers begin.

Writers, sometimes, too.

66

Kelly

Now that Kelly has been to visit her father once, the thought of seeing him again won't leave her alone. Zoom is not enough, now that she's drunk tea in his garden, out of the mug he always gives her; it's green, with roses on it, and was a secret-Santa gift from a university colleague who clearly didn't know her very well. She left it behind when she moved out because she hated it. But she almost wept when her father brought it into the garden for her, last time. She'd noticed that he'd given Sarah-Jane the bone-china mug with no chips in it, and put it next to her where she slept in the hammock. Her father is a good man.

Craig is going for a long run today, which will be followed by a long soak in the bath. She loves that they know so much about each other's preferences and needs. He's even starting to annoy her, now and then, although she will never be someone who complains about their partner to their friends. Craig has too many good qualities to deserve that. She enjoys that little twitch of annoyance. He doesn't put his toothbrush away; he leaves electricals on standby rather than switching them off at the wall. He burps. A lot. None of which she minds at all, because also: he listens to her talking about work, and books, and the people who need them. He's even interested in Madison. He does the washing and he thinks about dinner, even though he's working too. He loves her. He needs her. He tells her that she's beautiful and, ever since he caught her bunching up her belly and looking at herself in the mirror, he's made a point of running his hand over her midriff and telling her how wonderful she is. He tells her, too, how much he loves her, how important she is to him. He seems almost scared that she doesn't believe him.

If Craig is running-then-soaking, then Kelly is going to go to Whitby, see her dad, and be home in time to get a takeaway and maybe watch a film. Craig had asked if she wants him to come. He could run tomorrow, he said, and it's a lot of driving for her to do on top of a day at work. But Kelly surprised herself by saying no, she'd be fine. Of course she wants to introduce Craig to her father. But not yet. There's something about the lockdown isolation they live in that she isn't ready to disturb.

Lost For Words is as happy a place as it's possible for it to be, that Saturday. It's not as simple as the sunshine, though that helps. The thought of a winter of restrictions, dark mornings and cold afternoons and nowhere to go, makes Kelly's heart shrink with dread. But everything feels . . . steady, today. Nathan and Sarah-Jane are busy in the garden. Loveday and Madison are finding the books Kelly asks them for. Loveday is quiet, but in the way that it was usual for her to be quiet, before the pandemic, Kelly thinks.

Or it could be that she's still taking that paramedic's death hard. Kelly has noticed how the pandemic seems to hit her in different ways at different times. Some mornings, it feels like an act of purest recklessness just to leave the house, and listening to the news gives her a whole-body convulsion of sickness and fear. The infection rates and the numbers of the dead are suffocating, blinding: she cannot get her breath, cannot see further than her own shaking hands as she dresses. On other days, like this one, she can be aware of all the horror that's happening around the world at the hands of this virus, but feel as though she has a small corner where she can work and do good. She thinks of Adjoa. Not just do good: do better.

There's another good thing about this particular Saturday. Madison is something approaching friendly. She even makes tea for them all, and includes Kelly, rather than 'forgetting' about her, which is what has happened before. Kelly has always done her best not to mind the way Madison behaves towards her, but it's hard to remember that you're the adult when a kid behaves as hurtfully as Madison did that day at Whitby. Kelly goes through the emails to check for anything she's missed, the social media for messages or comments that Nathan has flagged as needing bookseller expertise. She prints off the new book prescription requests, so that she can start to think about them, and talk to Loveday about them.

Although Kelly jumps every time there's the sound of someone at the door, there's no sign of Jennifer's husband. After they wrote to Jennifer, the police called and took details of David's visit, and asked Loveday and Kelly to confirm his identity.

Loveday and Nathan have installed a Wi-Fi doorbell,

with plug-in extension units upstairs and at the back of the shop, underneath the makeshift counter in the doorway, to act as a panic button. If it's pressed, they will all go to the front of the shop immediately. This has made Kelly feel safer, although she's not sure, objectively, that three booksellers in a defensive formation would be a lot more use than one against someone truly determined to do them harm.

'Do you need me to do anything?' Madison asks. 'It's all tidy. Loveday says I can go early but—' She shrugs. As far as Kelly's aware, it's just Madison and her mum at home. Fifteen-year-old Kelly would have given several teeth for that; but she also remembers what it was like, just her and her dad, rattling round a house made vast by grief when her mother died. Being the only child of an only parent can be a lot.

Kelly shakes her head. 'No, I'm pretty much done, myself. I'm going to go to Whitby to see my dad, I think.'

'Right.'

Kelly thinks of Adjoa, and decides against making assumptions. Maybe Madison doesn't dislike her. Maybe she's just having a tough time. 'Do you want to come? If you haven't got plans.'

Madison snort-laughs, 'Plans? What are plans?'

'You're right. I don't know what got into me.'

'I could go and see Rosemary and George,' Madison says, looking at Kelly in a way that suggests Kelly might refuse. 'I need to ask Rosemary about something. Loveday asked me to.'

'So long as it's okay with your mum.'

* * *

Kelly and Madison don't talk a lot, on the way to Whitby. Kelly gives Madison her phone to put some music on. Madison spends a long time scrolling through Spotify – Kelly presumes that her menu of post-Britpop playlists, indie rock, and podcasts about feminism and history don't appeal – and eventually puts on a Taylor Swift playlist. Between the pandemic, and the things she and Craig talk about (fitness, the best way to get to London, York pubs they used to go to in their teens), Kelly is realising that she's getting older. Thirty may not be old, but she can't conjure the ambition she thinks she once had, before the pandemic, before Craig. She's less enthusiastic about finishing her PhD. She's wondering about having a baby. If she's going to, she really should do it before too long. She doesn't want to be an old mother. She wants a kid to have a mother who'll be around for a reasonable amount of the kid's life. And a sibling to share the load, too, when Kelly gets old. Not that she sees her father as a load. But it would have been good to have a sister or brother to share her worries with over the last few months.

Next to her Madison is looking out of the car window, her head turned away from Kelly.

'Everything okay?' Kelly asks.

There's a pause, and then Madison says, 'Loveday's car is nicer than this one.'

Kelly smiles to herself. It sounds as though everything is just fine.

67

George, 2005

Retirement becomes a more and more regularly discussed topic between George and Rosemary, and not only because it's getting closer. One Thursday evening towards the end of the autumn term, while they sit on the sofa, George rubbing Rosemary's feet, she says, 'George, I think I've had enough.'

He almost makes a joke about only just getting started on her feet but there are tears in her eyes. 'I know, love,' he says. She's been Head at her current school for almost a decade, and not an easy one. Every time she got the school the way she wanted it – 'up to scratch', as she put it – something changed. A strike, or a wrong-headed new curriculum from the powers that be, leading to a strike; teachers on long-term sick leave, or leaving the profession altogether; a shortage of teachers meaning that Rosemary interviewed graduates hoping that they would choose her, rather than debating whether to choose them. George noticed how his wife complained more. Pupils were getting louder, their parents more demanding. Poverty was biting at the heels of many of Rosemary's pupils' families.

Rosemary shakes her head. 'Some of the things I heard about at the staff meeting this morning remind me of my parents' stories.' George knows what she means. Rosemary's parents had begun their married life in the East End of London immediately after the war, when Rosemary's mother would hand out twists of tea at the end of the service, and women would tuck them into their handbags without making eye contact, as though such charity was shame. 'There's a family who are making insoles for their children's shoes out of carpet offcuts, because they can't afford to get them soled. There are so many kids who don't have a hot meal unless they are at school. And I'm supposed to care about their exam results.'

George shakes his head. He cannot bear to think of children going hungry, their parents going hungrier. 'I know, love.'

George's role as Head of Maths has started to pall, too. He has always loved his job. But his job, increasingly, is that of administrator, troubleshooter, and meeting-attender. Apart from his A-Level group, he only really gets to teach classes when another teacher is sick, although that is increasingly often, as stress takes its toll. A year ago a new Head joined George's school, with no background in education, something he seemed proud of, and a stated aim of running the school as efficiently as a business. And George just cannot see the point. He wants to support the Head – he has always been loyal, job-focussed, and has never got involved in the politics or the social climbing of the staffroom. But there is no business analogy – and the new Head has many – that George has been able to 'get on board with'. His classes aren't conveyer belts. His pupils aren't products. His department's exam results, excellent though they always are, aren't the bottom line, as the Head would have it. Grades aren't the only thing that matter. George cares about his pupils as individuals. He always has. He wants their learning to be meaningful and useful. If someone who expects to fail – who has no confidence, no incentive – can get a D grade rather than an F, George is delighted. But his job is supposed to be to get the pupils' predicted Ds to Cs and Bs to As. There is no value, as far as the school's ratings are concerned, in getting Es to Ds or Cs to Bs. After a year of clashes, George has stopped trying to make his case to the Head, but he has no intention of changing his teaching practices.

Rosemary nudges him with her toes. 'Penny for your thoughts?' she asks.

'I was just thinking,' George takes a breath. 'It might be time for us to leave teaching.'

Rosemary sighs, and George closes his eyes. Perhaps he's judged it wrongly. But she says, 'I suppose we have to give it to the end of the year? Not just not go in tomorrow?' And she laughs; laughs again, when she sees George's surprised face.

'I suppose we ought to see the year out,' he says with a smile, and within him he feels something that has been tight around his lungs let go. 'But we can start planning now.'

68

Rosemary, Now

George is sleeping on the sofa when there is a knock at the front door. Rosemary, who might have been dozing herself in her reading chair, if that was the sort of thing she did in the late afternoons, takes a moment to place the young woman standing there. Masks make things difficult.

'I'm Madison,' the visitor says, 'from the bookshop.'

'Oh! Come in, come in,' and Madison does, and they are standing in the kitchen before they look at each other and realise what they've done. 'Force of habit,' Rosemary says. 'Why don't you go through there and out into the garden that way, and I'll follow you down with some drinks. Tea? Coffee? Something cold?'

'I'm all right, thanks,' Madison says. She has a peaky look to her, Rosemary thinks. It's the face of a child who is carrying too many worries.

'In that case, lead the way.'

Rosemary listens to Madison's earnest explanations of old editions and facsimiles, and then she nods. 'Yes,' she says, 'yes. Please order it for me. I'll give you a cheque before you go.' She cannot think of a better use for fifty pounds. The thought that this will be the last gift she gives her husband leaps at her, crushes her heart and lungs. She notices Madison looking at her, anxiously, and swallows down her tears. 'It's his birthday soon. This will make his day.'

Madison nods, 'I had my birthday in lockdown. It was sh—' Rosemary makes sure not to laugh, as Madison almost swears, but loses her nerve, 'it was a bit rubbish. All my presents came from Amazon and my mum just left them in the boxes for me to open because she said going out to get wrapping paper wasn't an essential journey. And she made me a cake, but she's no good at baking, and she hasn't got the proper things you need. Cake tins and eggs and all that.'

'It was nice of her to try,' Rosemary says. She's always been one for shop-bought. She spent her childhood watching her mother bake because the Church Ladies would not be impressed if she didn't, and that had cured her of any desire to turn out cakes and biscuits when she could buy them from a shop. She'd rather be reading, or gardening. So that's what she does.

Madison shrugs, and then she says, 'I read that book as well.'

'*The Secret Garden*? What did you think?'

'Well,' and Rosemary sees that Madison is almost bursting with the need to talk. If Rosemary was Madison's teacher, she'd be thinking: I've done it. I've got through. 'Well. I know it's from the past, and everything, and stuff was different, but I thought it was racist, the way they talk about servants in India? I mean, quite often when things are called "classics" that's what it means. Racist. Or sexist. Loveday gave me something about a man who locks his wife in the attic because you couldn't get a divorce then and apparently millions of people have read it.'

Rosemary nods. 'The world has changed a lot, even in my time, and mostly for the better. You liked *The Secret Garden*, though?'

'Yes. But they are really awful to that girl Mary. Telling her she's ugly and too thin. I mean, that's just as bad as fat-shaming. Ignoring her. And the boy. They just tell him he's ill and shut him in a room. Of course he's going to be ill. Anyone would be.'

Rosemary waits. She senses there's more. 'The kids are actually better than the adults. The kids are pretty nice to each other. The adults are too busy with their own problems to care.'

Rosemary smiles. 'So you didn't think much of it?'

'That's the thing.' Madison sighs. 'I really did. I sort of loved it. I felt like I shouldn't. I wanted to read it again, straight away.'

'Which parts did you like?'

'I like the way Mary doesn't know anything, and she learns without noticing. I like that everything gets better. It makes me think that—' Madison gestures, a sweep of her arm, and drops her head, and Rosemary understands what she isn't saying: this book makes me think that things being better is possible.

'Yes,' Rosemary says. She and George have had their time with their garden; she'll always be grateful, though she cannot imagine how she will manage it without him. If she had the option to lock the gate, leave it to run riot, then she would probably take it.

'I like', Madison says, 'the way all of the kids understand more about what's going on than the adults.'

Rosemary, to her surprise, laughs. 'I was a teacher,' she says, 'and I know for a fact that that is true.'

Madison stops fiddling with the cuffs of her hoodie, and looks out across the sea. Rosemary strains to hear any sound from George, but all's quiet. She hopes he's resting. His nights seem more and more disturbed.

And then Madison says, 'If the kids at your school knew things. Would you want them to tell you?'

'Always,' Rosemary says, without hesitation. She bites back what she almost says, young people of your age are not as grown-up as you think, because she knows it won't help. Instead, after a moment where it seems Madison isn't going to say anything else, 'I think any adult will say the same. Young people have good instincts.'

'Yeah.' Madison gets to her feet with an ease that Rosemary cannot remember ever having. 'We do.' She looks around the garden. 'Plants are nice,' she says. 'I've never really noticed before. But yours are . . . it sounds stupid, but they seem happy.'

'We've been here for a long time,' Rosemary says. 'Gardens can't be rushed.'

'It's just a lot of growing, really, I suppose,' Madison says.

'It is.' Rosemary closes her eyes and thinks of all the children she has ever taught. What space would they fill? A hundred school halls? A thousand school buses? Rosemary doesn't kid herself that she had a huge influence on all of them. But some of them, she did. She was good. She was capable. She made a positive difference.

'You're the ones who grew it, though,' Madison says.

302

Apparently unconscious of the damage she's causing, she pulls a leaf from the silver birch tree and examines it. Rosemary hides her smile. In the quiet, she thinks of George, sleeping.

She and George made this garden.

It could be that she's equal to what's ahead. She doesn't want to be – she wants to lie down and die, when George does – but that's not the point. She must do what they've always done. Adapt. Make a new place when they outgrow the old.

Madison drops the leaf, suddenly aware, it seems, that she's destroying the thing she's admiring. 'Will it be weird? Giving plants to the bookshop?'

'It will still be our garden,' Rosemary says. She's aware that she's not quite answering the question. 'But we won't be able to manage it for ever.'

One of the best things about the young, Rosemary has always thought, is how they accept the old as being old. If she'd told Loveday she didn't think she could manage, Loveday would have offered to help or been encouraging. Neither of which are what Rosemary needs. She needs to know that, when she's on her own, she won't be over-whelmed with everything she can no longer do.

69

Max and Kate

Dear Lost For Words,
Could you suggest some books for our young teenagers to read? Now we can't get to the library (we're shielding) we're missing out on a lot of good advice. We're especially keen on books with strong female role models and/or novels where gender isn't an issue. This may be too much information but we wouldn't be surprised if one of our kids was transgender and we want them to have at least some sense of a world that embraces them and/or a world where gender is insignificant. We're not really looking for transgender characters specifically. Just a sense of a world where it's okay to be different.

Thank you,

Max and Kate

Dear Max and Kate,
We're happy to help with this. And, though you didn't ask for my opinion or my judgement, I really think your kids are lucky to have you. They might not realise it now but they will.

There are some suggestions below – let us know which

304

you like the look of/haven't read and we can arrange to send them out to you.

Some of these are books for adults, but I'd say they were pretty accessible to teens, and anyway the two of you might enjoy them.

Very best,

Loveday

The Left Hand of Darkness by Ursula K. Le Guin. This has themes of sex, gender and androgyny, but more importantly, it's an absolutely involving story.

The 'Graceling Realm' novels by Kristin Cashore. This series is set in a world where some people are born with Graces – unique talents. The characters are vivid and kickass, and the relationships feel so authentic. I wish I'd read it as a teenager.

The Long Way to a Small, Angry Planet by Becky Chambers. A sort of soap opera in space. Everyone I've recommended this to loves it.

Simon vs. the Homo Sapiens Agenda by Becky Albertalli. A sixteen-year-old tries to traverse the worlds of school, friendship, and coming out.

We Were Liars by E. Lockhart. Twisty and gripping. You'll have to swear not to give away the ending until you've all read it!

70

Kelly

Madison is waiting to be picked up at the place they had chips last time, as agreed. The chip van isn't there, though, and when Kelly asks her if she'd like to try and get something to eat somewhere else, Madison looks at her and says, 'We should just go home.'

'Then let's do that.'

But when they get in the car, just as Kelly presses the ignition, Madison says, 'It's bad to tell someone a bad thing when they're driving, right?'

'Right.' Kelly turns towards Madison, who is looking at her hands, which are clasped in her lap, in an oddly prim way. Madison tends to favour the slouch. 'I've often felt as though there was something you want to say to me. Would this be a good time?'

Madison nods, and a tear breaks loose from the rim of her eyelid and makes its way down her face. 'You know Craig? Your boyfriend?'

'Yes?' Kelly looks straight ahead. She can feel the pulse in her throat. Her hands are on the wheel, gripping, still.

Madison starts to cry. 'I looked at photos on your phone. Even though I was sure. I wanted to be really sure. It was when I was supposed to be choosing music.'

'I don't know what you mean.' But Kelly does. Or at least, she knows something bad is coming. The knowledge is making its cold-footed way up her spine.

Beside her, she hears Madison inhale. 'He's my dad. Me and my mum didn't know he had a girlfriend until he left us to live with you.'

'But that's—'

Out of the corner of her eye, Kelly can see that Madison is sitting very still. Of course. She's waiting. She's given this thing – this knowledge – to Kelly, and now she doesn't know what's going to happen.

Neither does Kelly.

She closes her eyes.

Oh god oh god. Not this.

Kelly feels – and oh, she will feel the shame of it later – the way she felt on the day she knew her mother's death would be soon. That it would be this day, or the next; that there was no point in hoping any more.

The feeling is a combination of falling, of flailing, of panic; and at the same time of resignation, of fathoms-deep sadness already even though she knows the full impact of events hasn't hit her yet.

She sucks in a deep breath.

It must be a mistake.

And it can't be.

'Madison. I didn't know.'

'I didn't think you did.' Madison's voice is wobbly, full of tearful relief. Even through her own approaching pain,

Kelly can imagine what a weight must have lifted from her. Although she doesn't need to imagine. She's carrying the weight herself, now.

'I mean,' Kelly is having trouble arranging words into a sentence, in the same way that her heart is struggling to put her feelings in order. Distress, denial, panic, love, all are fighting it out within her. 'I mean, I didn't know he had a wife and a daughter at all. Not just that I didn't know it was you.'

'Really?' Madison turns in her seat to look at Kelly. 'I thought – even if you didn't know it was me—'

'No.'

That's when Madison bursts into noisy, furious tears. 'So he pretends we don't exist?'

It's worse than that, Kelly thinks. He's tried to persuade me not to take you seriously; to keep away from you. She doesn't say so. She swallows down tears and, when Madison is calmer, asks, as gently as she can, 'Shall we go?'

The journey back to York is quiet. Madison sits in silence and Kelly drives in silence. A couple of times, she feels as though she ought to say something, but she's afraid that if she opens her mouth she'll either start crying, or say something really unhelpful. It's fifty-fifty 'Why did you have to tell me this?' or 'Why didn't you tell me this before?' When she drops Madison off, at the end of her road, which is not at all as far out of York as Craig has had her believe, they both mutter, 'Sorry,' to each other, at the same time. Kelly thinks, as Madison walks away, that she should have told her that she has nothing to apologise for. It's really not Madison's fault that her dad – her dad, Kelly's boyfriend – has done this.

When Kelly gets home, she parks and then sits in the car until she works out what to say to Craig. That's her plan, anyway. She has kept a lid on everything so she could drive from Whitby back to York.

Now, disbelief, the beginnings of a bigger hurt, crash through her again.

Craig didn't mention so much as an ex-wife, let alone an actual wife, or a daughter who was part of his life.

Well, there's his story about a pregnancy, a relationship that moved too fast, a kid – unnamed – that he doesn't see any more. And which he had led Kelly to believe was way, way back in his relationship history. Plus, he definitely didn't mention that he doesn't see the kid any more because he walked out on her and her mother to move in with Kelly, two months ago.

Somewhere in Kelly is a simple wish that Madison had kept her mouth shut. Or had never come to Lost For Words. A part of her, too, whispers that none of this is Madison's fault. More, that you don't blame women for what men do. You don't blame children for what their fathers do.

Kelly's hands shake. Her neck feels as though it's wrapped in something that's shrinking and the back of her eyes burn. She might be sick. She thinks of angry people in films, who push their car horns again and again and again as a way of expressing their fury. It had always seemed a bit theatrical to Kelly. Now she gets it. It's not about alerting the world. It's about making a noise that's louder than your own pain.

She might have sat in the car for ever, if Craig hadn't looked out of the window, seen her, come out into the street and opened her car door, with a theatrical bow. 'My sweet lady. Welcome home.'

He's looking at her like butter wouldn't . . .

He's looking at her, nice as . . .

No, Kelly is truly lost for words.

She almost shuts the car door again, and locks herself in. Maybe in the darkness it will all make more sense. Maybe her brain will be able to take all of the things Craig has said, and done, and put them into a pattern where all of this is a horrible misunderstanding, a weird coincidence.

But then he says, 'What's wrong? Kelly?' and there's just the slightest flicker in his eyes that tells her he knows he's been found out. And Madison checked the photos on her phone. Also: believe women. Especially the ones who are very obviously in pain.

'I don't really want to discuss this in the street,' she says. A minute ago, she would have said she didn't want to discuss it at all. And that would have been closer to the truth. But she is where she is.

They go inside, in silence.

Kelly sits at the dining table: the one that has become Craig's desk, although he makes a point of tidying his papers away at the weekend. He sits too. His face is pale. Kelly remembers something she read – maybe it was in an Ian Rankin novel – about how you can tell if someone is guilty of a crime because when you arrest them and put them in a cell they are calm. They know it's over. They might deny everything when they're confronted, but when the door is locked and they are alone, they sit and wait. It's the innocent who pace and rage in a holding cell, who cry and protest regardless of whether anyone is watching or listening.

And now Craig's knee is jiggling against the table leg, making it wobble. He does it when he's under stress. It drives Kelly crazy. Her heart snags. They know each other well enough to have things that drive each other crazy. He hates that she leaves her half-drunk cups of tea everywhere; he's started to leave them on the draining board, so she can see how many there are, over a weekend. It's kind-of playful, but the last time she'd seen the pile of mugs, she'd thought: this is the thing we'll disagree about for the rest of our lives. And she'd felt both warm and sad. Little did she know. She knows she'll be sad, later. But now, deliberately, she invites her rage to burn. It's the only way she's going to get through.

'I've been thinking,' she says, 'about the advice you gave me. To keep away from Madison. I thought you were trying to protect me. But you weren't, were you?'

He shakes his head. 'What you have to understand, Kelly—' he says.

'What I have to understand,' she says, channelling Elizabeth Bennet from *Pride and Prejudice*, 'is up to me. And what I understood, today, when a broken-hearted teenager finally told me the truth about the man I love . . .' She thinks about correcting it to 'loved', cannot, quite, yet. The fact is, she's being truthful, and oh, she loves him. It fuels her fury and her hurt. 'What I understood is that you've lied to me from the very beginning. You never, ever said you were married. Or even that you'd been married. You never mentioned a daughter. When you moved in you didn't say you'd left your wife that morning. That morning, Craig.'

She puts her head in her hands. He puts his fingertips on her forearms, their touch language for 'I want to hold your hands.' She shudders him away.

'When I met you,' he says, and she doesn't look at him, stops the impulse to cover her ears with her hands. 'When

311

we met, I admit it, I was looking for – a bit of fun. It said so. On my dating profile.'

'It did. Right under where you'd ticked "Single".'

Craig takes a breath, 'Under single. I didn't want things to be complicated.'

'And how's that going?'

Craig looks at his hands. 'My marriage had been as good as over for a long time. I knew Jo had had a thing with a guy from work. She more or less told me. We hadn't had sex in – in months – but it wasn't just that. We didn't seem to like each other any more.'

He pauses. Kelly knows him well enough to know that he's hoping for her to say something. To make it easy. She pushes her feet against the legs of her chair, thinks of Madison's half-brave, half-hurt face. 'Boo hoo.'

'We didn't have anything in common. And Madison – Madison's not easy.' He half-laughs. It's an invitation.

Oh, Kelly is not going to let this go. 'Are you about to blame a child for the fact that you made a dating profile and didn't mention that you were married? That you moved in with me without telling me about your family?'

'Of course not. I'm trying to explain. Kelly, I – I was lonely. I was looking for a bit of – fun. I didn't think things would end up like – this. I didn't think I'd meet someone like you. Let alone fall in love with you like this.'

'Why date? Why not just – hook up?'

'Because I didn't want hook-ups. I wanted something—' He shakes his head. 'I don't know what I wanted. But once I met you it was irrelevant. Because then I just wanted you. Before the pandemic, I was thinking about leaving Jo. We'd even talked about it. A bit.'

'Would she corroborate that?'

'Well, she'd say we'd argued about it.' Craig shrugs. 'If I hadn't fallen for you—'

Oh, she's not having this. 'So now it's my fault? I've heard you blame three women, so far, for the fact that you lied to me and kept on lying. Your wife, your daughter, and your – whatever I am. Idiot girlfriend. Ex-girlfriend who saw the light.'

Kelly looks up, to see Craig holding his hands aloft in a 'please don't shoot me' gesture. She's crying. It can't be helped. Her tears feel hot on her face and her belly seems to hold a cold, hard rock.

'I'm not saying I was right. I just – I love you, Kelly, and I went a bit mad, I think, in the lockdown. Jo and I were barely speaking and Madison didn't come out of her room if she could help it. I kept thinking, this is my life.' Kelly doesn't look but she knows that he's crying too, now. 'Every day, all those people dying, and all those people mourning them, and I thought, if I died, I would regret not being with you.'

Kelly looks away and exhales, a long, slow breath that she imagines dissolving into the atmosphere around her. Good people make bad choices. She has never doubted that Craig loves her. She thinks she's right about that. She thinks of her thesis. All those average men, all those brilliant women who stood behind or to the side of them. A separate part of her brain says, at least you can finish your PhD now. Then you could go anywhere, do anything.

'If I could do it all again,' Craig says, 'I would do it differently. Properly. I would face up to the fact that my marriage was over. I would move out. And then I would

313

meet you. And on our first date I would tell you about Jo. And Madison.'

Kelly looks at Craig. She believes him. She really does. But. Her tears have stopped falling. They've gathered in a soft, wet ball at the back of her throat.

'Please, Kelly.'

'Please what?' she gets out. Oh, how she loves that face. And did she really not know? Did she really never suspect? The fact that she never went to his place, his sketched-in dating history with nothing significant, really, since his early twenties? His dedication to his career meaning he had never really committed to a relationship, when there was no real sign in him of loving his job?

'Please. Let me try. I'll – I'll move out of here, and move out of—' Kelly realises he catches himself just before he says 'home'. 'Out of Jo's, and I'll find a flat, if you don't want me here. I could get a six- month lease. I'll get a divorce. I mean – I'll do that at the same time as I move out. I'll start tomorrow. I was going to do it anyway.'

She almost relents.

Then Kelly remembers the books that Loveday gave her. Each of them featuring a woman in a world stacked against her; a woman keeping faith with herself, no matter what the world said.

'Actually, Craig. Get a divorce if you want. I think you probably owe that to your wife. And next time you start dating, be upfront.' She feels a rush of love – yes, love – for Madison, watching her mother struggle at home, her father suddenly and inexcusably absent; going to the only place she could think of that her father might be. And then spending weeks listening to Kelly talk about Craig.

'I don't want to date. I want to be with you. I was scared.'

'I can see that. But you've behaved shittily to me and unforgivably to your wife and daughter and I'm done with you.'

Craig starts to really cry. He wipes his nose on his fingers. She can't look.

Kelly closes her eyes, opens them, gets up, and steps past him. She goes into the bedroom – her bedroom, again, not theirs any more – and empties the contents of his drawers and wardrobe-space on to the floor, then pushes the whole pile out of the door so he can get it from the landing. Craig has followed her, and is looking from his clothes on the floor to her face, as though he cannot believe that she has taken what seems to her to be the only possible step.

'I want you to go,' she says. 'I don't want you to come back. If you do I'll report you.' She's not sure who she can report him to, or what for, but he's in no position to argue the toss.

'I love you,' he says.

She swallows down something that's more like nausea than love. 'If you leave anything at all behind I'm going to bin it.'

'Kelly. I love you.'

'I don't care,' she says. 'I'm going into the bedroom and I'm not coming out until you've gone. Leave your key on the dining table. Take everything because you're not coming back.'

'But—'

She does care, of course. But she thinks she's allowed one lie here. And there'll be time to think about love when he's gone.

Kelly takes off her shoes, and gets into bed. She has no intention of undressing while Craig is in her home. This morning, she wandered around in her knickers, drinking tea and trying to remember what still fitted her so she didn't have to talk herself out of cinnamon buns at work, while Craig lay in bed with his hands behind his head and watched her. And he told her she was beautiful. And she laughed and said 'thank you' and told him he was handsome. She had curtsied, which they agreed made no sense, as a gesture, if you were wearing only your knickers.

Tonight, she's as likely to undress in the street as she is with Craig still in the flat.

She pulls up the duvet, and picks up her copy of bell hooks' *All About Love* from her bedside table. But she can't concentrate. Of course she can't. She's too upset: and she doesn't want to cry until he's gone. Then there's the fact that she knows all she wants to about love, for now. She has a gutful of it.

And she's hot. So hot.

71

Casey

Dear lost for words,
There's so much to do, and it feels as though it's never going
to end, and I just can't sleep, or turn off. I don't want any
book in particular. I just want

Casey had thought, at the beginning, that when her friend
Will, the paramedic, died, nothing could be worse. He had
sent pictures of the new baby to the WhatsApp group. He
had moved out of home to keep his family safe. The three
days after he died were the worst working days of Casey's
life, up to that point. None of her colleagues could look at
each other without bursting into tears. One of the student
nurses screamed at someone in the corridor who wasn't
wearing a mask. None of them could, would, believe that
Will was gone.

But now, she has lost count of the dead. She looks back
on the time when she had feelings to spare as something
she can barely understand. When she thinks about Will
now, it's as though her heart is all used up. When she calls

relatives to tell them that their loved one has died, or to arrange for them – one of them – to come in to say goodbye, she feels a sort of abstracted compassion. She knows that it's difficult. She does it well, with kindness and attention. But her feelings are somewhere else. Perhaps in the same place as her sleep.

She watches her colleagues. Some of them lose weight, some gain it; some crop their hair, some let it grow. None of them could stay the same any more, it seemed. The quiet room that was set up for them at the beginning of the pandemic is rarely used, now, because they are always quiet. Silence is everywhere. There's nothing to say, apart from the exchange of information that they need to do their jobs. Conversation might come back with good news: something coherent about a drop in cases. Or a vaccine.

Eventually, Casey gives in. She takes the offer of a prescription for sleeping pills, and she deletes the half-written email to the bookshop from her phone.

72

Loveday

On Monday, the summer air is hot and dry, and Sarah-Jane is up and in her gardening clothes, before Loveday and Nathan leave for the shop. 'I need to get everything watered before the sun comes up,' she says.

'Take it easy,' Loveday says, although what she means is, *I'm so happy to see you feeling so much better.* She hugs Sarah-Jane, her head on her mother's shoulder, and feels like a child, but in the best way. Sarah-Jane is going back to volunteer at the women's shelter tomorrow. Just for a couple of hours; not to do anything strenuous. But it makes Loveday happy, to see such a clear sign of recovery. Since the news of Will's death she has clung to every sign of hope. She's taken more books to Zoe, left them on the step, rung the bell and ridden away, because she cannot think of what to say to a woman who has lost her husband, to Covid.

As she unlocks the front door of the shop, something makes her pause. She almost sniffs the air. Nathan stops behind her, puts his hand to her waist: 'Okay?'

'I think so,' Loveday says, because there is quite enough

to do in the world by dealing with what you can see, without worrying about what you can't. She reaches for the hand sanitiser, something that has become a reflex; but this morning, it's protection. She couldn't say from what. There's just something that she doesn't like, in the air. It's funny, and also not at all funny, how the sixth sense she developed during her parents' violent marriage will never leave her.

'I'm going to get a second coat of paint on that brickwork.'

Loveday loves that, since Nathan started on this project, a wall has become 'brickwork'. 'Sounds like a plan,' she says. Then, because it's always easier to speak your feelings when someone isn't looking directly at you, she adds, 'I know I wasn't enthusiastic about the garden to start with. I was wrong. It's really important.'

Nathan turns back towards her. 'You had a lot on your mind,' he says, 'without some deranged poet turning up with half-baked ideas because he had nothing else to do.'

'Even so.' Loveday swallows, hard; she doesn't think she'll cry, but it's best to be sure. 'That's the thing, isn't it? Everyone so busy with making things work that we forgot – I forgot – what was really important.'

He looks at her; the kind of eye contact she can bear, warm and understanding. 'I don't think you did. You had a lot of important things to think about, at once. That's not the same.' He steps towards her, kisses her forehead. 'Coffee in a bit?'

'Coffee in a bit.' Loveday switches on the laptop. Book prescription requests are still coming in, at a rate of anything between a dozen and forty a day. Books to help me cope, books to teach me to crochet, books that look like new to give as gifts. Books I vaguely remember from my childhood.

320

Large-print books I can send to my father's care home. When they can have people in the shop again, which may not be for a while, Loveday is thinking they might have a counter that's exclusively a book pharmacy. Vanessa might paint a sign for her; she seems to be able to turn her hand to anything artistic. She did an excellent job of the 'Black Lives Matter – read more here' sign to go above the bookcase at the front of the shop, which is getting a pleasing amount of interest when they've posted about it on social media. It's strange, to think that people might be here again, rather than barricaded out by a trestle table across the door. Loveday checks her heart: yes, she will be glad when she can welcome people back. Even if people can be a bit much sometimes.

Kelly has a document for book prescriptions which makes it easier to find recommendations, rather than reinvent the wheel every time a new request comes in. It makes sense: a lot of people are lonely, a lot of people are reaching back to their childhood favourites for comfort and hope, a lot of people are looking for escapism. One book can speak to a lot of people.

But Loveday has never really bothered with the spreadsheet. She thinks that if someone has been brave enough to write their heart out in an email to a bookshop, then she should respond with undivided attention. Unless she's stuck, of course. Crime requests make her queasy, and she has very little to offer when it comes to kids' books. That's when she thanks her past self for having the foresight to employ Kelly in the first place.

'Loveday.'

It's not often Nathan looks, or sounds, rattled. It's not

often his already-pale face is even more devoid of colour. But he's standing in front of Loveday and agitation is jangling in the air around him.

'What? What's happened?' She stands; looks him over for signs of blood or hurt. Nothing.

'Someone's broken in at the back. They've—'

'No.' But she knew. She knew something bad had happened, as soon as she walked through the door.

'Yes.'

She follows him out to the back of the shop, where the outdoor reading refuge is almost ready.

Or it was, yesterday; the pots waiting for their plants, the pallet furniture, much laboured-over, now with the promise of not looking terrible when covered in blankets.

She reaches for Nathan's hand. She's not sure which of them is holding the other.

It can't be.

It can't be.

It is.

Everything is broken.

The trellis is splintered, the pallet furniture tipped and toppled, smashed to pieces. Trellis lies on top of wooden slats, and the pots are upside-down, the terracotta ones shattered, the wooden ones splintered. The blanket-box, filled with Archie's tartan rugs, has been pulled over, the hinge on the lid smashed; blankets spill out, reds and greens and creams and oranges. Loveday, not able to grasp what she is seeing, but understanding what she can do, goes to pick the blankets up. She can take them home. She can wash them.

As she stoops, Nathan holds out a hand. 'Don't touch them. Can't you smell it?'

'Smell what?' As Loveday says it, she realises. 'Oh god. Why would someone—'

'Malice,' Nathan says. His voice is half-and-half rage and tears.

Loveday nods. Urinating on blankets points to more than simple vandalism.

And now, she wants to shout, to rage. To break something herself. To turn her face to the wall and wail.

She breathes deliberately, slowly, deeply. It gives her a flashback, to performing poetry, to finding steadiness in a place where she was exposed and afraid.

Loveday reaches for Nathan's hand.

Her throat fills with sadness. Yesterday, this space was full of . . . space. Clean air. The idea, the possibility, of peace. Of safety. It smelled of wood shavings, waiting soil and drying paint. Now it's fractured and full of rubbish and has the stink of a car-park stairwell. It looks worse – smells worse – than it did before Nathan went to work on it. And there was no hope for it then. Now it's not neglected. It's spoiled. It's deliberately broken.

Loveday can't cry, if Nathan doesn't. He did the work. He made this happen. Now he's shaking his head, rubbing his forehead, as if everything is actually fine and he is somehow seeing it wrong, processing it incorrectly.

She knows how solid the furniture was, how heavy the pots. Whoever has wreaked this havoc has been determined to spoil everything.

'How have they done it?' Loveday asks.

Not that it matters. The damage is done. But it's the question that her brain has decided to think about. It acts like a barrier to hold the other questions back.

Nathan shrugs, 'Something with a blade. An axe? I don't know. I've never hacked something up like this.'

No, Loveday thinks. You make things. We make things, together.

'It's—' she says. Then tries again. 'So much work.' She means: how much work has been undone. How much more work there is to come, to put it right.

'Loveday—' Nathan says.

'I know.' She knows what he means, because she can feel it coming. A swell of something worse than the defeat of looking at this destruction. It's the fact that someone came here to destroy. To hurt. Someone they don't know – or, more likely, someone they do – wanted to break this safe place to pieces. She moves closer to Nathan; puts her arms round his waist; clings. He puts his arms around her shoulders and clings back.

'We can fix this,' he says, but his voice is dull and tired. 'I'll get a van and we'll go to the tip, later on.'

'Yeah.' The last thing Loveday wants to do is load a van. The second-last thing is go to the tip.

'At least we hadn't got around to collecting the plants from George and Rosemary.'

'I suppose.' Loveday isn't really up for a bright side.

Nathan is nudging the splintered pieces of trellis with his foot. They're in an odd sort of pile. Loveday's guts curl in on themselves, she tastes bile. 'Oh god. Nathan. Do you think they were planning to start a fire?'

Nathan comes close, holds her shoulders. 'They were making a space so they could spray-paint the walls,' he says, 'that's all.'

Loveday had barely taken that damage in. Nathan's

324

scrubbed-clean brickwork and patched and painted cement, scribbled over with dark paint.

She can't bear it.

For Nathan. For Archie. For her.

She can't stop thinking: this was going to be a safe space. And it's destroyed.

Nathan has his head on one side, looking at the spray-paint. 'It doesn't look as though they've tried to write anything. I don't know if that's better or worse.'

Loveday laughs. 'Better,' she says.

Nathan stands up straight, sighs. 'I suppose so. Do you want to call the police, or shall I?'

And then there's a rap on the front door.

A man and a woman, masked and suited, introduce themselves as being from the council.

'We've had a report of non-compliance with Covid regulations,' says one. 'We're here to help and advise.' They put business cards on to the desk. Loveday wants to ask, don't you have anything better to do? But she doesn't. You don't antagonise the person with the power.

'I noticed neither of you were wearing masks when you came to the door,' the other adds.

'We're partners,' Nathan says. 'As in, we live together.'

'No one else is coming into the shop today,' Loveday adds. 'It's my manager's day off. And we put masks on and sanitised our hands before we let you in. We know the rules. And we don't usually let customers in at all.'

'And what's your cleaning regimen?'

'When we have other staff in we stick to social distancing and we each work in one zone. We clean every evening.'

'Other staff?'

'Our manager. When she's here we work in separate areas of the shop. And we have someone who helps out on a Saturday.' Loveday thinks about the coffee breaks, upstairs, how maybe sitting a long way away from each other isn't good enough. They mustn't be lax.

The shorter of the two inspectors says, 'If we find you to be non-compliant we can close down your business until we're satisfied that you've understood, and will adhere to, the rules in future. We can also impose a fine.'

'Who reported us?'

'We can't say, I'm afraid.'

'But—'

'We're bound by confidentiality, Ms Cardew.'

'It's just,' Loveday says, and she hates that her voice sounds full of tears, but there it is, 'our reading garden was vandalised last night and it seems someone is out to get us.'

'We can give details of the informant to the police. Though it's possible the tip-off was anonymous. The important thing is that we help and advise you as necessary.'

Loveday breathes as deeply as she can in a futile attempt to find some calmness. Her heart is behaving the way it does when she's allowed Nathan to persuade her to go for a run. Her fingers twitch the way they used to when her parents were fighting, and she was up in her childhood bedroom, scared, turning the pages of a book faster and faster, gobbling up words as though they would fill her up enough to make her safe and happy.

As she inhales, she detects the smell of cinnamon buns

from next door. A mouthful of sweetness is exactly what she needs, but she doubts that offering to do a coffee-run will go down well. 'What do you need from us?' she asks. Her voice hardly shakes at all, this time.

73

Kelly

Covid hits Kelly fast, and hard. The first twenty-four hours pass in a kaleidoscope of headache and heartbreak: she sleeps, she wakes, she reaches for Craig, she remembers. She feels thirsty, but cannot imagine how she could ever get as far as the kitchen or the bathroom. She feels sick, but she doesn't have the energy to even think about being sick, so she lies on her back with her eyes closed, one hand on her stomach and one across her eyes, and she breathes. Not too deep, because deep breaths make her cough, and when she starts coughing she cannot make it stop. So this is it, she thinks, this is it. Over and over. She doesn't know what she means by 'it'. Or maybe, she means everything by it. This is Covid. This is betrayal. This is loneliness. This is the end. This is horrible. This is impossible. This is my life. This is too much. This is too little. This is being alone. This is dying. This is what's happening to the whole world.

She lulls herself into something that is neither sleep nor rest, but is a sort-of quiet. It's night, and then it's day, and then it's night again. She needs a drink. Her throat hurts with coughing and her eyes burn.

When she gets back to bed she notices that her phone, on the bedside table, is glowing. She can't even think about it. She goes back to sleep. If it's sleep. She's not sure. It's more like being crushed under a great flat stone. Everything hurts. Her throat, her head, her chest. Her lungs burn.

74

Rosemary, 2005

Rosemary is not, precisely, worried about retiring. But she's not not worried about it, either. She knows that the person she is at work isn't always a person that she likes. Headmistress-Rosemary wears what George calls Margaret Thatcher suits, and he thinks it's a joke, but it isn't. She knew, when she was promoted (and got the tough schools, because you can't promote a woman above her male peers without making sure it's going to be hard for her), that she was going to need armour. And Thatcher, who Rosemary had no time for otherwise, knew how to dress like a woman you wouldn't want to cross.

When Rosemary puts on her armour, she is a Head through and through. She listens; she's fair; but when she has made a decision, it stays made. When she needs to talk tough, she can do it. When she needs to take off her jacket and be reassuring, she can do that too.

But she always takes off her jacket as soon as she comes home to George. It's usually a relief, but she wonders: what if headmistress-Rosemary needs an outlet? What if I can't leave her behind? What if I start to get cross with George because he doesn't do things the way I would do them?

They have decided to retire, though, and their successors are in place, and there is nothing they can do but go through with it.

'Do you worry?' she asks him one evening, a week before term ends.

'Worry about what?' He has brought home a box full of thank-you letters from pupils and parents over his career, and programmes from the plays he'd coaxed and pummelled into being every year, and every year sworn he would not put himself through again.

Rosemary shakes her head. It's going to sound silly when she says it out loud, but she says it anyway. 'We did our courting in a staffroom. Our whole lives have been at school.' She can't articulate it, exactly, but she knows he will know what she means. Their lives together have been punctuated by their long summer breaks and their Christmas plays, their exam seasons and their Sunday afternoons at the dining table, making sure everything was in order for their teaching week ahead. Parents' Evenings were the only time they had takeaway, eating chips with their fingers from the wrappers, both too hungry and too tired for cutlery and patience.

George smiles. 'And now the rest of our lives will be in our garden,' he says. And Rosemary feels something drop away from her. Of course, he is right.

The next day, when she gets dressed, she leaves her jacket on the hanger.

When she gets home, George has arrived first, and is pruning their beloved apple tree. They planted it during their first spring in the cottage, and now it's as tall as he is. 'Look,' he says, when she comes to stand next to him, 'do you remember when we put this in? We had to stake it. Look at it now.'

And Rosemary stops worrying.

75

Kelly

The next thing Kelly knows, there's a buzzing in her head, loud and unstopping. A banging at her ears. The sound of her name, over and over.

She gets to the door. She doesn't know how long it takes her. When she opens it she finds a bag on the step; Loveday and Nathan, standing a good distance back. Loveday says, 'Oh! Thank goodness!'

And Nathan says, 'We were about to call the police.'

Kelly props herself against the door of the hallway, but still she can't stand. She does a slow slide to sitting and closes her eyes. Loveday's voice washes over her. She hears mention of Madison, of Craig, of her father. Your dad is well, he says not to worry about him, she hears, and a doctor is going to call you and we'll check in tomorrow and call if you need anything. She attempts a nod, which almost makes her throw up, and then she pulls the bag into the flat and pushes the door closed. She curls up in the hallway and when she wakes again it's dark once more.

The dreams are the worst. Or the coughing. Or the

tiredness. Or the combination of all three. Anyway, the first time she opens her eyes and doesn't wish she hadn't, three days have passed. In her hallway are the bags Loveday left on the doorstep. Just the sight of what's in them – bananas, yoghurts, cereal, milk, chocolate – make her stomach turn. She wonders whether, if she gets in the bath, she'll be able to get out again, and decides it's not worth the risk.

By the time Loveday comes the next day, Kelly has managed to look at her phone long enough to read the texts from Craig, which started almost as soon as he left. He's sorry; he doesn't know what to do; he's going home, not because he wants to, because he has nowhere else.

It's 2 a.m. the day after he left when the Covid text arrives. Kelly. Temperature and coughing.

A day later, Hope you're okay.

A day after that: Madison and Jo aren't speaking to me but they are leaving food at the bedroom door.

And then, over the next few days, a flurry of messages: he hopes she's okay, he's feeling a bit better, he knows she won't believe it but he does truly love her. He misses her.

Then, a change in tone: Kelly. I know you're angry. I understand you don't want to hear from me. But Madison says no one has heard from you and you're not answering the door. Could you at least let me know you're not dead?

Kelly almost replies, but then she realises that the message is three days old and he will know by now, via Loveday and Madison, that she's okay. She deletes his texts and blocks his number. She might be up to a bath, tomorrow.

76

George

George knows it's August, but somehow the garden is as cold
as late November. Perhaps it's being ill, or the aftermath
of Covid, that does it. Whichever. It doesn't matter. The
important thing is this: George has never had cause to doubt
what his body is telling him, before. But he doubts it now.

The sun is shining, so he can't be cold.

He's eaten, so he can't be hungry.

He's taken painkillers, so he shouldn't hurt.

And yet.

What he needs is Rosemary, with her basket, a flask and
a blanket and some fancy biscuits that she imagines he
thinks are a treat. Rosemary is a good woman. Over the
years of their togetherness they have worked out a routine
for everything. When they're in the garden, they do some
bits together, and then he tidies up while she makes the tea.
Lately the tea breaks have got longer, and whereas once the
late afternoons would be time for a little more work – a check
on the compost, or inspecting the undersides of leaves for
troublesome larvae of one sort or another – now they are

time for reading. If either of them drops off to sleep, the other leaves them, unless it's getting chilly.

Not being able to get warm was one of the things the doctors said might happen. It seems odd to him, but there you go. Everything's gone odd. Days of the week. Mealtimes. Nothing makes sense. He thought they'd just got some milk but when he went to make a cup of tea it smelled peculiar. Though they say Covid plays havoc with your sense of smell. It could be it's that.

'Rosemary?' His voice is so feeble he can barely hear it himself. No wonder she isn't coming.

George knows that as his disease strengthens and feeds, grows and conquers, there will be more days like this. Still, he's suffered worse. Of course he has. His bones ache, now, and his head; and he can't concentrate like he used to. But, as Rosemary says, who is like they used to be? None of us are.

When George thinks about the most important parts of his life, they are Rosemary, and their garden. Not that teaching didn't matter. But once they retired – and he knows she was worried about that, but he knew she never needed to be – it was as though their careers had never been.

Sometimes he wonders when he and Rosemary decided to become teachers. People often talk about teaching being a vocation and they're not wrong, in the sense that no one would go into it for the money. And it isn't an easy life, despite the appearance of endless holidays. But when he looks back he cannot really pinpoint the moment. His own father was an engineer, working long hours on the factory floor of a textile manufacturing company, his feet always cold and his fingers and arms nicked and cut, as though he was keeping count of his working days on his flesh. His mother stayed at home, and wanted nothing more than for George to work somewhere warm and safe. He had helped out with photocopying and post-sorting in an office during university holidays, and had disliked the mandatory blokeishness of the atmosphere. The thought of a life of day-in-day-out talking about sport and 'joking around', which seemed barely discernible from bullying and unkindness to George, held no appeal at all. Then he was volunteered by his mother to help his boisterous cousins with their maths, and getting them to first listen, then engage, was a thousand times more satisfying than any other work he'd ever done. So he became a teacher. With as little thought as that, really.

Rosemary's choices were not the same as his. The ideal, as far as her parents were concerned, would have been to marry a vicar or become a nun. (She used to say this jokingly – and stopped saying it at all once her parents died – but George knew that it was, essentially, true.) Failing those, her next tiers of choices were: nurse, teacher, secretary. And only until she was married and started to raise a family of her own. (Something else Rosemary used to say: 1960, 1860, it's all the same to my parents.) 'I like my sleep,' she told George during one of their first conversations in that long-ago staffroom, 'so I was never going to make it in nursing. And being a secretary is . . . I'm sure it's fine, but it's really not for me.' Even then, George had been hard pressed to see Rosemary, who could silence a room of pupils with the smallest twitch of her precisely-drawn-on eyebrow, spending more than an afternoon taking dictation.

He supposes, sitting there in the cooling afternoon – it's going to be time for supper, never mind tea, before long – that they did find something in teaching. They wouldn't have kept on the way they both did, otherwise. They knew plenty of teachers who coasted; who did what they needed to, and went no further. George and Rosemary were never those people.

'George!' The face is familiar. Rosemary is better at names than he is. She will know. Then a tall man follows.

'You must be George,' he says. 'I'm Nathan. From the bookshop. Loveday's partner.'

'Hello,' George says. Ah yes, Loveday.

He looks, and sees there's a book next to him. They must have been reading it. He's too tired to properly remember.

Loveday has seen it too. 'How are you getting on with *Atonement*?'

George makes a noncommittal face. He can't really bring anything about it to mind. Something to do with a war, maybe. Or a play. A fountain.

'It isn't for everyone,' Nathan says, 'though Loveday has a tattoo from it. It's to do with the life of stories.'

Suddenly, George is too tired. 'Are you here to take the plants?'

'Yes,' Loveday says. 'We were so pleased when we got Rosemary's message about you giving them to us. I'm sorry it's taken so long, but Kelly's been off with Covid, and we wanted to be certain we weren't bringing it with us. We both tested negative yesterday. I left a message on your answering machine.'

George nods. He thinks about telling them it really doesn't matter, he and Rosemary have had the virus. But he can't find the energy.

'We can come back.' The tall man looks as though he might be pitying him. George could tell him that one day,

338

he too will be old and tired and sad. But he doesn't bother. Just as well. Who would trudge on knowing what was to come? Who would teach? Who would plant? Who would love? Who would care?

Rosemary always says, pain distorts everything.

'Is Rosemary here?' Loveday asks.

'No, she isn't,' George says, then adds, 'We ran out of all sorts when we were poorly.'

'We can go to the shop.'

'No need.' If Rosemary was here she would know how to be pleased to see them, and then he could follow her lead. They would like talking about them when they'd gone. How good they are, the young.

'How's that young one?' he asks.

'Madison? She's doing okay,' Loveday says. 'Her dad has Covid so she's staying away for now. Better safe than sorry.'

George thinks of the father he would have been. A dad that even teenagers would be proud of. A bit of a fuddy-duddy, but nothing too much trouble for his children.

'Yes.' He can't explain – wouldn't try – what it was like to try to drag in breath after breath, when every breath was nothing like enough. To watch Rosemary doing the same. There was a night when he thought they were both done for.

He puts his hand to his lower back, where the pain is worst. Maybe it would have been better if they had gone. At least it would all be over and done with, and he wouldn't be sitting here, giving his garden away because Rosemary thinks they can't manage it. That's what she says, anyway. She means, because she won't manage it when he's gone.

'Rosemary tied labels on the plants you were to take,' George says. He remembers her sitting next to him, writing while he closed his eyes. The occasional question: do you think it matters that their garden is north-facing, for the lilac? How often should I tell them to water the hosta, or should I just say give all of them a good drenching once a week, you know what pots are like. 'There are pots in the greenhouse.'

'We brought pots to transport them in,' Nathan says, 'plastic ones. We've got some terracotta ones at the shop, ready, from our friend Archie's garden.'

'I filled the bottoms with gravel, then soil,' Loveday adds.

'Good, good.' George knows that he cares about this, somewhere, but there's too much pain to find the place right now.

When they've gone, he closes his eyes, and the next thing he knows, there's Rosemary's voice. She isn't reading *Atonement*, but the other one that came in the parcel. The one about bees, and patience.

77

Madison and Kelly

MADISON:
Hey. How r u doing?

KELLY:
I had a bath for the first time in a week. So, good?

MADISON:
I was worried about u

KELLY:
I got your messages. I just haven't had the energy to text anyone back.

MADISON:
And my dad?

KELLY:
Only to tell him I didn't want to hear from him. I really didn't know, Madison.

MADISON:
I know

KELLY:
Good. I'm sorry. I hope you're okay.

MADISON.
Yeah. Loveday's dead busy and I don't want to bother her but do
you know any good books to read if your dad's an arse? And for
my mum? She's stopped crying but she's proper mad

KELLY:
Let me think about that! I have post-bath exhaustion (I actually do,
I've never felt so tired in my life) so I'm going to sleep now. More
later. Xxxx

KELLY:
Right. Ask Loveday for these for you:
I Capture the Castle by Dodie Smith (This is one of the ones we
chose for Rosemary and George)
How to Build a Girl by Caitlin Moran
The Knife of Never Letting Go by Patrick Ness

And these for your mum.
Everything I Never Told You by Celeste Ng
Room by Emma Donoghue
Yes Please by Amy Poelher
Take care, and I'll see you soon.
K x

78

Bella

Loveday, darling,

Those wretched people. I never understand why people break things. It is almost impossible not to take these things personally, I know. (Reviews, darling!!) But what happened to your reading garden was everything to do with the person who wrecked it.

My return to the pub was, if I say so myself, a triumph!! I thought myself the heroine of *The Yellow Wallpaper*, half-mad and prowling, and all of the customers as figments of my imagination!! It was like the early days in a rehearsal room, when we are all imagining ourselves to be our own breath, or telling tales of our darkest thoughts. And very soon, I forgot all about the pandemic, and being afraid, and your helpful books (sorry!!) and it was as though I was stepping into an old role that I remembered in my muscles and my bones!

Except, because no one has been allowed out much, everyone is much more kind and polite than they used to be to a barmaid who has seen better days!! Tips were good too!

I know not everyone is feeling sociable, but if you and

your poet would like to come for a drink, I will guarantee you excellent service and tip you off about the best things coming out of the kitchen!! Just give me some warning so I can reserve you a nice quiet booth.

Love and kisses,

Bella xx

Dear Bella,

I'm so glad to hear this. And equally, you are welcome here any time.

We're repairing.

Loveday x

Dear Loveday,

Thank you. I might well pop in for some more books!! I have the reading bug now!

There's something I have been wanting to say to you but I haven't been sure how. Where is a playwright when you need one?!

Archie thought the world of you, darling, and he was right. Doubt yourself if you must, but remember, also, to look back and see how far you have come. You are capable of anything and everything you want to achieve. Archie knew that, and now I can see what he meant. So – onward! And remember, you are allowed to ask for help.

Love and kisses,

Bella x

79

Loveday

Kelly comes back to work on the following Thursday; that way, she can work two days, and take the whole weekend off. Loveday doesn't feel up to having Kelly and Madison in the same space on Saturday, and she's fairly sure she's not the only one.

Kelly has lost weight and – well, the only word Loveday can think of to describe it is 'sheen'. She looks exhausted. She can't seem to be still: she disinfects her hands every time she looks at them. It seems her way of navigating her heartbreak is going to be to finish her PhD and dedicate herself to her job, and Loveday knows how that feels as a way of coping. Whatever gets you through.

Loveday brings cinnamon buns and hot chocolate. Kelly almost cries. 'I actually dreamed about these,' she says. 'Do you think you can marry a bun?'

'Marrying Richard Morris would make more sense. Or keeping him prisoner in a baking dungeon.'

'Oh god, Loveday.' Kelly shakes her head, and scoops icing up on her finger. 'I've been such an idiot.'

'You got taken in,' Loveday says.

'I don't think he was bad,' Kelly says. 'Just unhappy. And stupid.'

Loveday agrees with the part that she can best get on board with. 'Really stupid.'

Kelly's shoulders slump. 'I couldn't think about anything for the first week, and the second week, I couldn't move a muscle so all I did was think.' She contemplates her bun, and then her hot chocolate. 'And it's so bloody obvious from here. I mean, why didn't I question it? I never went to his place. I didn't meet any of his family – his parents, I mean. His sister. I just believed everything. Like a—'

'Like a good human who believes the best in people,' Loveday says. What has happened to Kelly would, once, have been yet more evidence to Loveday that you should always believe the worst, and so be prepared, and be safe. But then it turned out that she had the best of people all around her, and she didn't know. Archie. Nathan. And then, her mother, returning to her life when they were both ready.

'Exactly,' Kelly says, glumly. 'Is Madison – do you think she's going to be all right?'

'I think she's better now it's all in the open.'

'Poor kid. I can't believe how I went on and on about Craig in front of her.'

'That wasn't your fault.' Sarah-Jane has a lot to say about women blaming themselves, and it's made Loveday even more aware when people around her do it. She can't do a lot for Kelly, but she can give her this. 'You mustn't blame yourself, Kelly.'

Kelly shrugs. And then she asks the question that Loveday has been dreading. 'So, what have I missed?'

80

Kelly

Kelly stands in the reading garden. It's not much of a garden any more. And definitely not the space Loveday and Nathan had envisioned. In fact, it's pretty much back to square one.

'Someone smashed it up, one night. Spray-painted the wall and – well, it was a mess. So,' Kelly feels Loveday slump, next to her, 'we're starting again.'

There have been times when Kelly has had less than enthusiastic feelings about the reading garden. As in, it's all very well saving hypothetical people, but what about her, drowning in social media comments to keep on top of, racking her brains for book recommendations for people she doesn't really know about. And these are feelings she has talked to Craig about.

Oh god.

'You don't think – do you think Craig did this?'

Loveday sighs. 'No. We think it was Jennifer's husband. The police have been, but there's no CCTV.' She looks at Kelly, a look that Kelly knows means there is more to come. 'It looks as though he reported us for Covid breaches too.'

'Shit.'

'I know.'

'Oh, god, Loveday, I'm sorry.' And she's crying. Again. She's not sure why. Because, just for a second, she thought the man she loved so much had done this? Because she's too tired? Because she insisted she was well enough to come to work, and now she thinks she isn't, but she's committed because she's here? Because, while the world is destroying itself, someone thought to wreak some additional vengeance on a bookshop, of all places?

'Hey.' Loveday lays her hand on Kelly's back, between her shoulder blades, and Kelly thinks, touch, and she cries harder.

'I'm okay,' she gets out.

Loveday guides her to an odd-looking seat. 'Be careful,' she says. 'Nathan built this out of the biggest bits of the wrecked stuff and there might be some splinters he missed.'

Kelly sits herself, cautiously. 'A splinter in my backside would be just the thing.'

Loveday squats in front of her. 'We've got someone coming to fit some proper gates next week, to make sure everything's really secure. It can't happen again.'

Kelly knows a brave face when she sees one. 'But Loveday, this is awful.'

'I know,' Loveday says.

'I mean, it's awful for you. All this work. And all of your – your intentions. This wasn't for you, was it? It was for the women who used to use the space upstairs.'

'And my mum,' Loveday says, and for a minute Kelly thinks Loveday is going to cry too. But she doesn't. She closes her eyes, puts her palms on her knees, takes a breath in, and stands up. 'I've got some things to do upstairs. Take your time.'

'I will,' Kelly says. She might be recovered, but the idea of rushing is unimaginable. 'Loveday?'

'Yes?'

'Thank you.'

'What for?'

Kelly almost says, because if I didn't have this job, didn't have you, then I don't know what my life would be. But she thinks Loveday might hear that as pressure and not thanks. 'For putting *Station Eleven* in with my groceries,' she says. 'I read it in a day. I've never read anything like it. When I finished it I knew I was going to be okay.'

The old Loveday, the pre-pandemic, pre-garden-vandalisation, pre-Covid inspection one flickers briefly into being before Kelly's eyes: the mention of a book makes Loveday utterly herself. 'I felt exactly the same when I read it,' she says, and she leaves Kelly sitting in the pale mid-morning sunlight.

81

Jay

Dear Lost For Words,
Do you have books that will scare me, but with imaginary stuff? As in, not global viruses or rising seas. I want a bit of pure, escapist terror. Something I can close a book on.
    Cheers,
    Jay

Dear Jay,
BOO!
    That's an interesting thought. Hypothetical fear to drive away the real fear. I like it.
    I'm not much of a one for horror, or generally being afraid, but when I thought about it I have read a fair few creepy books of one sort or another. I've also included some more directly terrifying suggestions from my colleague Kelly. Let me know which you'd like, and we'll go from there.
    Loveday

Dracula by Bram Stoker. I'm a fan of this, though I only read it to begin with because I grew up in Whitby. You might think you know the story, but the original novel is really something.

Rebecca by Daphne du Maurier. Creepy rather than terrifying, but it will definitely distract you from the world as it is at the moment.

The Truth About the Harry Quebert Affair by Joël Dicker. Not horror either, but definitely creepy and twisty.

Mexican Gothic by Silvia Morena-Garcia. Clever, spooky and moody with a couple of really weird and scary bits . . .

Kelly's picks:
The Haunting of Hill House by Shirley Jackson. Apparently the best ghost story ever.

'*The Call Of Cthulhu*' and Other Weird Stories by H. P. Lovecraft. Horror writers aspire to be 'Lovecraftian', so that tells you a lot.

Pet Sematary by Stephen King. According to Kelly, a B-movie horror in book form. Apparently this is a good thing.

Coraline by Neil Gaiman. Don't be put off by the fact that this is ostensibly a children's book. It's really scary.

The Shining Girls by Lauren Beukes. Not horror, but crime, with a mind-bending quality that will definitely distract you from the here and now.

82

Loveday

Dear Lost For Words,
Which books should I read when I feel I've let someone
down? When I feel as though I'm pretending my feelings
rather than feeling them, because if I let myself feel anything
at all then I'll be lost? I want to cling to my mother and cry
and beg her to be the way she was before she got Covid. I
want to stay in bed with Nathan and pretend we have nothing
to do but sleep, have sex, eat fried egg sandwiches, read
poetry to each other, and decide about new tattoos. I want
to tell him that I'm scared I'm not strong enough. I want to be
useful to him when he wants to tell me how he feels, rather
than feeling paralysed because even after all this time I still
don't really know how to do this stuff.

Most of all I feel as though I've let Archie down. When
he was alive I knew he was my friend: it was only when he
died I discovered how much he trusted me. I never have to
worry about having somewhere to live again. I have my own
home and I'm safe and so is my mother, and it's all down
to Archie. And I can't help feeling he would have . . . risen

to all of this, somehow. Much better than I have. He'd have opened the house to the homeless, or made the shop into a temporary vaccine centre/food bank, or given books away for free and tapped one of his famous, rich friends for the money. He would have known what to do. And I don't, so I've fumbled on. I've got Madison into reading, but I know she wouldn't have knocked on the door if she hadn't been trying to find out what her father was up to.

And now someone has vandalised the shop and I am small and frightened again. They have reported us and I am angry and upset again. My feelings are filling me up, and I can't let them out, because I don't know what will fill the space they leave. I haven't felt this powerless since I was a child.

I've tried asking myself what Archie would do, but all I can imagine is him holding a glass of port and laughing so hard he can't finish the story he's telling.

I think there's a book to help with everything, but I cannot find the book for this.

From

Loveday

She doesn't send it, of course. With Kelly barely well enough to get through a day, and full of heartbreak and fury, and her mother weak as water but soldiering on, and Madison way too young to take on any more than she is already bearing, Loveday knows she can't weaken.

Even Nathan is quiet, since the vandalism. They hold each other, they touch, they smile, just like before. He gets up early and goes for a run and she rubs the knots out of his shoulders when they go to bed at night. But he hasn't pulled a chocolate coin from behind her ear for months now, even though he knows it always makes her laugh.

Loveday is good at bearing things. It's just as well.

Except, the attack on the shop takes her back to the last time someone tried to hurt it. To hurt her. Objectively, coming in to find the garden trashed is nothing like being trapped in a burning bookshop. Emotionally, Loveday fills with panic whenever she sees the beloved place. She cannot lose Lost For Words again.

83

Loveday

The following Saturday, Loveday watches Madison take the copy of *The Secret Garden* from the envelope, and turn it over in her hands. She flicks the pages as though they are a deck of cards: Loveday tries to keep her wince internal. Madison nods and says, 'That's what Rosemary wanted.'

'You did well,' Loveday says. 'She's going to be really pleased.'

'We should take it for her. It's a present for George's birthday. If we send it he might open it and spoil the surprise. She isn't getting him anything else.'

Loveday bites back: there isn't time, or, if it's addressed to her he shouldn't open it, or, that is the least important thing right now. She's just tired. And Madison doesn't seem to have a lot of people who have time for her. 'We'll look at going one afternoon. We can't do it today.'

'Sure,' Madison says. 'What am I doing today?'

'Packing books, if that's okay,' Loveday says. 'Nathan is repainting and I'm sorting out orders.'

'Sure,' Madison says, and then she adds, 'Thanks, Loveday.'

'What for?'

Madison shrugs. 'I wasn't really nice to Kelly. When you offered me a job I shouldn't have said yes. I didn't want it, you know? I just wanted to see what she was like.'

'Do you want the job now?'

The expression on Madison's face flickers: panic, determination, happiness. 'I really do. I promise. It's much nicer here than at home.'

At moments like this, Loveday thinks of how much easier her life might have been if she'd actually talked to Archie when he asked her about how things were in her own life. What would Archie do? 'Things still tough?'

'Yes.' Madison rolls her eyes, but Loveday can't be fooled into thinking it's all a big joke. She waits. 'I thought it was bad when my dad was isolating in my room and I was sharing with Mum. But now he's out again, they just argue. Or sulk. He's supposed to be working but he keeps cancelling his meetings because he says there's no point in anything. I'm scared he'll lose his job. And then it will all be worse.'

'It sounds awful,' Loveday says. She's learned from her mother that all she needs to do, when she's talking to someone who is having a tough time, is to agree.

'Yeah. It is,' Madison says. Then she asks, her face half turned away, 'Has Kelly said anything?'

'No,' then Loveday realises what Madison is asking, 'but I know for a fact that she wouldn't take Craig back.'

'Do you?'

Loveday isn't fooled for a second by Madison's casual tone. 'I do. She was very badly treated by your dad, Madison. I don't think she'll want anything to do with him.'

'Right.' Madison looks as though she might have more to say, but after a moment she picks up the list of books to find and sets off among the shelves without another word.

84

Helen

Dear Lost For Words,

I'm not sure this counts as a problem, exactly, but can you recommend some books about really average people? I'm absolutely sick of reading about people with amazing lives/people who amazing things happen to. I think it's because they're everywhere, all of a sudden. I mean, not just in books. In real life. I can't remember the last time I brushed my hair, and yet everyone I know is taking advantage of lockdown in ways I can't even imagine having the energy for. My nineteen-year-old youngest sister has got millions of followers on TikTok who watch her make vegetables into the shapes of other vegetables. No, me neither. My younger brother is doing a virtual climb of Mount Fuji by going up and down his stairs hundreds of times a day. Even my mother, who's sixty next year, has started writing a novel. I started clearing out my spare room when lockdown started and gave up halfway through. I do cook dinner from scratch for my husband and me every day, and then he washes up, and then he gets on his exercise bike. He's cycled thousands of miles since the pandemic began, as he would tell you if you spoke to him for more than twenty-three seconds.

So. Please send me books that make me feel that it's okay to be me. (And to stop me from cooking my husband in a pie.) I suppose I could do something amazing if I wanted to. But I really don't. I want to get through my work for the day and then cook some pasta and watch TV.

Cheers,

Helen

Dear Helen,

I have to confess I looked at TikTok and decided I'm too old. Good for your sister, though. And good for you, for avoiding the desire to Achieve. It seems to me that going above and beyond feels like way too much to be expecting at the moment. (I make an exception for people like my father's neighbours, who have kept him fed and been fantastic over-the-fence friends to him, for the months I haven't been able to go.) I think maybe doing a lot is some people's way of coping. I have to confess, doing very little is mine.

I've had a think – thank you, by the way, I'm going to put a 'Not feeling up to much? Neither did these characters' section on the website. There's a list below. Let me know which books you'd like, and whether you'd like them delivered or to collect them, and we'll go from there.

Stay well,

Kelly

The Stone Diaries by Carol Shields. Follows one woman through her, objectively, not very interesting life. But the sort of read you don't forget. It's ten years since I read this and I still think of it.

Stoner by John Williams is entirely different, but has the same vibe. It's the telling of a whole, unremarkable life, but it's compelling too.

Pachinko by Min Jin Lee. Three generations of a Korean family living everyday, and often difficult, lives. It gripped me, and I really related to it, even though I have nothing at all in common with the lives of the characters.

Such A Fun Age by Kiley Reid. A young Black woman who works as a nanny for a white family is accused of abducting the child she cares for, and then her life gets complicated.

Excellent Women by Barbara Pym. An older novel but such a beautiful read, about the kind of women who get utterly overlooked by the world. If you haven't read Barbara Pym before, beware – this novel was my gateway drug to everything she ever wrote. Which would give you a Lockdown Achievement . . .!

Midnight Chicken by Ella Risbridger. Not a novel, but a cookery book – the recipes are great (I've made the Paris cookies and the fish finger sandwiches, and they are both delicious) but more than that, it's a beautiful story of love, loss and healing, told through food.

I Am, I Am, I Am by Maggie O'Farrell. This is non-fiction, and it's excellent. The sub-title is *Seventeen Brushes With Death* and, counter-intuitively, I think it's perfect pandemic reading. (It doesn't feature any pandemics.)

85

Loveday

What would Archie do?

Well, Archie wouldn't be in this situation, for a start. He'd have managed everything much better. No one would want to trash Archie's reading garden. They'd be lining up to provide beanbags and bookcases and some sort of peculiar yurt. He'd rustle up a couple of Poets Laureate to do readings and then, when the fuss was over, he'd make sure that anyone who needed help, would get help.

Loveday goes to sleep, wretched, again. Nathan curls his body around hers and says, 'I'm here.' She nods and closes her eyes. And the answer comes. The least wanted answer, but the right one. Archie would talk to people.

Nathan has gone for a run when she wakes. Kelly is opening the shop today so she has time. Sarah-Jane is already up, pottering in the kitchen, weighing out ingredients.

'What are you making?'

Sarah-Jane's face lights up every single time she sees Loveday. It makes Loveday feel like a child, again; it makes her remember when everything was easy, when she was small and her parents were happy. 'Brownies,' she says. 'They always vanish.'

'Weird, that.' Loveday puts the kettle on. She takes a breath, and says it. 'Mum, can we talk?'

'Of course, my darling.'

Loveday takes mugs off the draining-board. Her mother isn't a fan of the dishwasher, and washes up slowly, meditatively, in a way that makes Loveday feel calmer when she watches. She pours water into the teapot to warm it. 'I feel as though I'm failing,' she says.

Sarah-Jane pauses before she asks, 'Failing at what?'

Loveday shrugs. 'Everything. The bookshop. The refuge. I keep thinking of how we could have put Jennifer at risk, if we'd handed over those books. And how many other Jennifers there are out there who we haven't been able to help during the pandemic. People like we were, when I was little. And I keep thinking,' her certainty that she could talk about this without crying vanishes as though it has never been, 'I keep thinking that Archie would know what to do.'

'Oh, Loveday.' Sarah-Jane opens her arms and Loveday lets herself be hugged. She rests her head along her mother's shoulder. Sarah-Jane loves anything that smells of flowers, and uses shower-gel, moisturiser, shampoo and perfume with heedless joy. 'I think you would be so much happier if you stopped trying to be Archie and started letting yourself be you.'

'But nobody wants me.' And before her mother can object, as Loveday knows she will, she adds, 'At the bookshop, I mean. I was never the person people wanted. Or needed. When they came in.' She gulps at her breath. 'They wanted Archie. He was like a – a – he sheltered everyone, and they miss him. I'm not enough to shelter anyone.'

'People need more than shelter,' Sarah-Jane says, stroking her daughter's hair. 'Think about that, Loveday.'

When Nathan gets back from his run, Loveday has got out of the bath her mother ran for her. He kisses her head before pulling off his T-shirt. 'You smell like a garden. Don't tell me what I smell like.'

She laughs. 'Okay.' Then, before she changes her mind, 'I need to talk to you about something.'

'Sure,' he says, but she reads the seriousness on his face. It's one of the truths of their relationship that she never asks to talk. Talking about feelings is something Loveday has accepted as a necessary part of being a functioning adult, but it still makes her feel . . . squirmy.

Nathan lies down on their bed beside her. He smells of warm air and fresh sweat and she breathes deep. This is what love is. 'I'm listening,' he says.

She flops back next to him, looks at the ceiling. 'I just – Nathan, I don't know what I'm doing. Except I know that I'm doing a bad job. If Archie was here he would know exactly what to do but I haven't a clue. One minute I feel as though I'm doing the right things but the next I think, why bother? And what if—' the words are out before she realises what she's going to say, 'what if books aren't the answer? I mean, I know they can't fix everything. They almost got Jennifer Kingdom into really serious trouble, and if I'd handed over that parcel I would never have forgiven myself.' She has to stop, to make herself breathe. 'But what if the Book Pharmacy is just a stupid waste of time?'

She doesn't cry, this time.

She feels as though she's writing a mathematical problem on a blackboard. Lost For Words minus Archie plus pandemic = slump. Slump plus book pharmacy = survival. Survival and striving (Loveday) is less than exuberance and compassion (Archie). QED.

Nathan is quiet, for what feels like a long time. The air around their bodies cools, and despite the warmth of the mid-morning air, Loveday feels goosebumps rise on the skin on the top of her arms. Then he reaches for her hand and holds it, hard. 'Loveday. I know you miss Archie. We all do. But you miss him so much that there are things you don't see. But I see them. If I tell you, will you listen?'

'Yes.' A part of her already wants to cover her ears.

'Good. First, Archie was a one-off, but so are you. You were a team. How long would the bookshop have lasted without you? You opened it every day and he rocked up when he was ready. You valued the books that came in while he chatted to everyone and anyone. You put the bills in a pile where he couldn't miss them and you made sure he dealt with them. And you held the fort when he went off on a jaunt.' He pauses, and squeezes her hand. 'Yes?'

'I suppose. But anyone could have done my bit.'

'That's irrelevant. You're the one who did it, Loveday.' He leans up on one arm, puts his finger in the middle of her forehead, strokes in a straight line down the bridge of her nose, across her lips, over her chin, down the skin on her throat. 'If I could change one thing about you I would have you know how – impressive you are.'

Loveday sighs. It's not the first time he's said this, or something like it. It's a nice thought, she supposes, but she doesn't see it, herself. It would be like saying she would have him be less tall. 'I don't know what to do,' she says. If she's going to have a talk, then she needs something real to come out of it.

Nathan is on his own track. 'I still think about the fire, you know,' he says. 'I think of you being trapped in there and how I wouldn't have blamed you and Archie if you'd given up the bookshop and done something else. I mean, if he'd – if he hadn't died.'

'Lost For Words was my home for all those years I didn't have a home.' And this is why you shouldn't talk. It brings up too many things that it does no good at all to think about. Books talk about hearts as though they are good things but Loveday's more often feels as though it is trying to choke her.

Nathan nods. 'And it's fine to be upset that someone attacked your home. It doesn't make you weak. It makes you – Loveday, it makes you normal. Human.'

'I know. But – I don't like it.'

'Of course you don't.' He pulls her close. His sweat has dried to a pungent saltiness. 'We are having a horrible time. Individually and collectively. The fact that you're feeling it doesn't make you weak. None of us has died.'

Loveday nods, although she doesn't mean it. 'Archie never seemed weak.'

'But Loveday, you don't seem weak to most people. Archie was probably making it up as he went along just as much as you are.'

Loveday nods against his chest – tickle of chest-hair, cold skin. She knows he's right. 'So what would Archie do next?'

Nathan pulls her in. 'He would make sure everyone was

okay. And he would supervise us sorting out the garden without ever actually touching a tool or a plant himself. But what would Archie do isn't really the question, is it?'

86

Trixie

If lockdown relationships are hard, and long-distance lock-down relationships are harder, then lockdown break-ups are hardest of all. The first crying jag takes for ever, because crying alone feels plaintive, performative, and Trix can't seem to sustain it even though she is full of tears. So she sleeps. And pokes food round plates, and then bowls, when she runs out of plates. She leaves voice messages, until Caz asks her not to. So she stops. Trix knows that when Caz realises how much she misses Trix, one of the things she will remember is how respectful Trix is.

After ten days without going out, Trix decides to go and buy some oat milk, and some food that isn't in a tin. She sits on the stairs and sorts out the pile of papers, post and leaflets that have accumulated behind the front door. Bills for Izzy, that Caz is authorised to open, although all of their payments are automated; a couple of postcards for Philippe; phone bills for Trix. Bridal catalogues for a couple who moved out at least four years ago. And a great pile of free newspapers.

Something on the front page of the local free sheet catches Trix's eye. LOCAL BOOKSHOP PRESCRIBES READING FOR ALL OF LIFE'S PROBLEMS. Huh.

But then Trix remembers that if she hasn't been out of the house for more than a week, and if she's (respectfully) stopped calling Caz five days ago, then she hasn't used her voice for five days. She hasn't spoken to another soul. She hasn't even sung along with anything.

She calls twice before she manages to wait for the phone to be answered.

'Lost For Words. Kelly speaking.'

'Hello,' Trix says. Her voice sounds discoloured. Like water from a rusty tap.

'Hi,' Kelly says, 'take your time.'

It's the kindness that undoes her. Trix starts to cry. Again.

'Is that – is that Jennifer?' Kelly asks.

'No,' she manages, 'it's – it's Trix.'

'Trix, I'm here in the shop on my own. I'm going to put the phone on speaker, and I'm going to do some admin, and when you're ready to talk, I'm going to stop what I'm doing and talk back.'

It's only a couple of minutes, but it feels longer, until Trix begins. 'My heart is broken,' she says. 'What book can fix me?'

Something she doesn't expect comes back down the line: a sympathetic sob. 'Mine too,' Kelly says. 'It's the worst, isn't it?'

'It actually is,' Trix says, and she doesn't bother with the 'global pandemic notwithstanding' caveat. 'I'm sorry.'

'Thank you.' Kelly sniffs. 'I can put a few books together for you.'

87

Loveday

When Loveday and Nathan arrive at Lost For Words that afternoon, all ready to clear and paint and meet the man who's going to fit the gates, Kelly is at the desk. Loveday nods to Nathan, and sits down not-quite-next to Kelly. 'How are you?'

Kelly looks up. 'I'm okay.'

'You don't look okay.' Nathan's tip for talking to people is 'say what you see' and it's surprisingly useful.

Kelly laughs. 'No shit, Sherlock.'

'I want to help,' Loveday says. 'I'm not sure how.' Nathan's second tip: be honest.

And now Kelly crumples. 'It's just all – Loveday, I thought he was the one, and I thought my life was going to be – different. I thought we'd settle down together, like a real couple, and I one hundred percent trusted him and I just feel stupid. Stupid stupid stupid. And the stupidest thing of all is that I miss him. I thought I wouldn't, by now. I thought once I was back at work he wouldn't matter.'

'None of that sounds stupid.'

'And that poor kid,' Kelly says. 'Imagine being Madison.'

'Madison will be fine,' Loveday says. This she knows. She already sees Madison as part of the Lost For Words family she's slowly realising that she's making. Loveday will care for Madison the way that Archie cared for her. 'How are you feeling? Physically?'

'I'm okay,' Kelly says. 'I'm tired. But that's good. At least when I go to bed I sleep.' And then she starts to cry. Well, weep. Well, leak tears, as though she doesn't have the energy to cry properly.

Loveday takes a deep breath. What would Archie do? Something perfect, no doubt. He would make Kelly laugh, or perform some sort of mind-trick on her to make her forget she ever cared about Craig, or he would have Craig run out of town.

She remembers what Nathan said. What would Loveday do?

She'd get on with the day.

So that's what she does.

She and Kelly are working at opposite sides of the shop, in silence. Loveday usually likes silence, but this is different. Her ears are permanently pricked for noises at the back of the shop. And she is painfully aware of how much unwanted silence there must be in Kelly's life now.

Kelly sighs, in a way that suggests she might bring her guts up with it. 'It's crazy, isn't it? One minute you're thinking about having someone's babies, the next you're wondering if they might be breaking up a load of furniture and pissing on them.'

'Yes,' Loveday says, 'it is.'

Kelly half-laughs. 'It's a bit of an achievement, isn't it?

Something happening to you that actually feels crazy, this year.'

'I suppose,' Loveday says. 'Did you really think Craig had done it? We assumed it was Jennifer's husband.'

After a moment, Kelly says, 'No. Craig wouldn't do something like that. It would have been good if he had. I could properly hate him.'

'It must be hard.'

'It is. I spend all day talking to myself about how I'm better off without him, and by the end of the night I've convinced myself. Then I wake up in the morning and I wish he was with me.'

'Yes,' Loveday says, which doesn't seem quite right, somehow, but it's the best she can do.

88

Trixie

On the day the parcel arrives, Trix has had a good hot shower and washed her hair and put it in two plaits, and is wearing a pair of jeans rather than one of the three pairs of leggings she's had on rotation for months. Going through her wardrobe for something that is not one of her on-repeat band T-shirts, she finds a shirt of Caz's, and that almost undoes her. But she takes a deep breath, folds Caz's shirt away and puts on her own favourite checked shirt from the days when she used to spend free afternoons roaming National Trust houses.

The parcel contains six books. She hasn't read any of them. She spreads them out on the table. None of them tell her much. Then she sees the note.

Dear Trix,
I'm sorry you're having such a tough time. I'm really glad you called and I hope these books help towards healing, if only by filling your days. I don't think time heals, but things that take up time are useful. I've got the tidiest kitchen cupboards you have ever seen.

To help you decide which of these to read first:

The Priceof Salt by Patricia Highsmith is about Carol and Therese and their love story. I think it's a great book, especially when you need some hope.

Instead of a Letter by Diana Athill is a memoir about how she was ghosted (though it wasn't called that then) by her air force pilot fiancé in the 1940s. It's another world, but it's so recognisable.

Conversations With Friends by Sally Rooney is a novel about two former lovers trying to be friends as their world is changing.

All About Love by bell hooks. This made me think about love in completely new ways.

The Song of Achilles by Madeline Miller is a retelling of a Greek myth. It's about love and fury, war and friendship, the power of the broken heart.

Jane Eyre by Charlotte Brontë. I don't know why, but I thought of this novel as we were talking, so I'm going to go with my instinct and include it.

Also, and please feel free to ignore this if it isn't for you, I wondered if you knew much about cookery books? And if you did, whether you could put together a list of recommendations for our website? We'd pay you, of course. Give me a ring if you'd like to talk it through.

Trix starts with the Sally Rooney, on the basis that she's seen it around. There was a time, before the restaurant closed, when every eating-alone diner who wasn't on their phone seemed to be reading Sally Rooney. Trix isn't sure that it makes her feel better, exactly, but she goes for a whole hour without checking her phone. Maybe that's a beginning, of sorts.

89

Rosemary, 2005

On the day Rosemary and George come back from their respective school farewells, they are quiet. Rosemary's goodbye bouquet is ostentatiously huge and nothing she would have chosen herself: the perfume of the lilies makes her think of her father's church in the days after a funeral, and the roses, hothouse-forced, have no scent at all. Still, the John Lewis vouchers will come in handy – maybe some new towels, or bedlinen.

George shows her the watch he's been given, and says, 'The funny thing is, I don't need to care what time it is, any more.' He's delighted by a scrapbook filled with notes from his colleagues and ex-colleagues, pupils and ex-pupils.

They sink on to the bench, tired and a little tearful. Rosemary says, 'What now?'

Just for a moment, she wonders if it's too late to rescind a retirement, or if she's too old to be a supply teacher.

George, of course, reads her mind. He takes her hand. 'Well, we'll get that greenhouse properly sorted, for a start. And then we can think about a caravan.' He squeezes her fingers, not too hard. 'Trust me. We've done the right thing.'

'Yes. Greenhouse. Caravan.' She says it as though she's reciting a to-do list. She's good with lists, and she likes them.

And so they set themselves to the new work of retirement.

Their greenhouse crops are the best they have ever had. The garden seems to bloom brighter, this summer, and the smell of salt in the air makes them as hungry as children; they listen for the ice-cream van in the late afternoons and Rosemary goes for screwballs and oysters for them, which they eat on their bench overlooking the sea. They take some trips up and down the country, with long weekends in bed-and-breakfasts in Melrose and Stratford-upon-Avon, and although they look at caravans, the fact is, they like home too much to ever want to spend more than a few days away from it.

When September comes, Rosemary shakes off the should-be-going-to-school feeling and donates all her formal work suits to charity. 'Every day is a holiday or a weekend now,' she tells George, 'because all of my weekend and holiday clothes are my everyday clothes now.' George's work wardrobe had been three pairs of smart trousers and a variety of shirts that he now wears in the garden with the sleeves rolled up, instead; but in a gesture of solidarity he puts all of his ties, apart from the ones Rosemary had bought him, in the charity shop bag too.

'Are you happy?' Rosemary asks, one late-September afternoon as they watch the light fade.

'Of course,' George says. 'Are you?'

'Yes,' she says. And it's true. But it's a different sort of happiness, now; no longer the tired-out sense of achievement from sorting out a tricky staff situation or quelling a febrile assembly, but a gentle sense of quiet rightness. She definitely likes it. She just needs to get used to it.

90

Loveday

Saturday again, and Kelly comes to work, even though Loveday has told her that she doesn't need to. This is very much along the lines of What Loveday Would Do. But when Kelly arrives, Loveday decides to take the lead.

'I'm glad you're here,' she says, 'and I'll keep Madison busy with me. But you don't have to stay if you're not up to it.'

Kelly looks at Loveday for a second before she speaks. 'Up to it physically or emotionally?'

'Exactly,' Loveday says, and they smile at each other.

'Thanks, Loveday.'

'I'll do anything I can to support you,' Loveday says, and she means it. She's said the same to Madison, and meant it. Kelly and Madison are in a bad situation not of their own making; Loveday can't fix the hurt but she can minimise it. She can make Lost For Words safe for them the way Archie made it safe for her.

Archie would probably have taken them both out for lunch, and drunk a bottle of Madeira by himself, and told the two of them stories until they were both laughing so hard that they'd forget that there was ever a difficulty. But that isn't Loveday's way.

Today Nathan and Sarah-Jane are at the back, Sarah-Jane supervising Nathan's efforts, the garden almost back to its old self. After the pressure-washing, Loveday had helped him with the painting, and they had talked about choosing a quote for the wall the way they talk about choosing tattoos. The gates have been fitted: wooden, high, but a beautiful varnished almost-gold that creates a sense of safety rather than making the space feel locked in.

There is no point in Loveday asking herself what Archie would do about re-furnishing the space. Because the answer is that he would have a friend who was renovating their orchard and had some old-but-beautiful furniture they would no longer be using, or he would just happen to come across some abandoned ironwork chairs in the street. Loveday does things her own way. That is to say, the new way she has found, which is based on being a bold and confident version of herself.

So she looks at the bank balance and instead of thinking she should save everything in case it all gets worse, she decides to spend something because it will all get better. Their weather-proof rattan chairs arrive within days, and they are comfortable and welcoming and they match, and Loveday cannot for the life of her imagine why she didn't do this sooner. Safety doesn't have to be ramshackle. People in trouble are not second-class citizens. Just because they are grateful for anywhere safe to sit, doesn't mean that anything will do for them to sit on.

When Madison arrives, the first thing she does is ask

Loveday if she can go and talk to Kelly. Kelly is upstairs, sorting out the paperwork that Loveday has not entirely stayed on top of during Kelly's absence. 'I'll check,' Loveday says.

But Kelly calls down, 'Of course.' So Loveday goes to get hot drinks for them all, to go with the brownies her mum sent in with her.

91

Kelly

When Madison comes up the stairs and into view, Kelly's first thought is that she must have had Covid too. She's so pale. 'Are you okay?' she asks.

Madison shrugs. 'Not really.'

'Did you read the books?' It's not the question she really wants to ask, but she can't mention Craig unless – until – Madison does. And she's not sure she can keep it together if they talk about him. Why did she never see that Madison has her father's blunt chin, his pale brown hair?

'Yeah. They gave me something to do.'

Kelly smiles. 'Sometimes that's what you need.' She's racing through her studies, now. When she first started working on it again, it wasn't for the sake of the work, but to have something to do to stop her thinking about Craig. But then she had fallen in love with her research once more. All of those women, clever and prolific in a world that did not care for clever women or value their output. Dorothy, Dora and Mary Wordsworth. Zelda Fitzgerald. Véra Nabokov. She wants to spend as much time with them as she can.

'Yeah.' Madison looks as though she's going to go back downstairs, but then, after a deep breath, says, 'Dad knows he was an idiot. He keeps telling Mum. And she keeps telling him he's right. They argued a lot to start with but they're not doing it so much now. I think they might just be tired.'

Kelly makes her voice as gentle as she can. 'It's none of my business any more, Madison. It never was. I didn't know.'

'I know. I think they're going to get divorced.'

'It's hard to come back from something like this. For any relationship.' Kelly sounds wiser than she feels. She wants to shake Craig's head from his shoulders. Stupid, stupid man, making three women miserable when, if he'd been honest, he might have – well, there's no point in speculating. But Kelly spent her second week of Covid speculating, so all of the possibilities are in her head anyway. He could have talked to his wife, tried again, been happy with her, left Kelly to keep dating and maybe get to be happy with someone else. He could have talked to his wife, tried again, then they could have split up. And then he and Kelly could have met, and been happy. And of course he could have said he was married and unhappy. Kelly would have told him to get lost, naturally, but if he had there might have been a possibility for later. But not after all these months of lying.

'But,' Madison says, 'everyone makes mistakes. That's what you people are always saying. Make mistakes and learn from them. Say sorry and move on.'

'You people?'

'Adults,' Madison says, glumly. 'Well, teachers. Parents. You and Loveday and Nathan. You're all always saying stuff like that to teenagers. But you don't do it yourselves.'

Kelly hears herself laugh. 'You're not wrong,' she says. 'Do as I say not as I do.'

'Exactly.' Madison pauses. 'I wouldn't mind.'

'Wouldn't mind what?'

'If my parents split up. If you and Dad got together.'

'Oh, Madison.' If it wasn't for the wretched rules, Kelly would hug Madison so tight right now. 'It wouldn't happen. He wasn't honest with me.'

Madison nods. 'Would you be friends?'

'I don't know. I don't think so.'

Madison nods again, as though disappointment is exactly what she expected. And Kelly, who checked all the advice about how long she was infectious before coming back to work, thinks, sod it, and she opens her arms, and lets Madison sob against her shoulder.

92

Back to that awful question:

Should you have a favourite book?

I suppose I should know. I studied books and I love books and I read books and I write books. When I still believed in Santa (and he may very well be real where you are in the world, so please don't let me worry you) I sent him lists of books. Books are very much my jam. (If jam was books.)

Here is what I know.

Sometimes, a book will sing to you. Sing to your soul, your pain, your being.

Sometimes a book will know you, inside out, and it's as though the pages have some sort of magical quality and the words are appearing on them just a little bit quicker than you are reading, because they are so very connected to your own heart and your own story that that's the most logical explanation for what's happening.

Sometimes a book that you once gave up on takes on a new quality when you re-read it; when you get past the part you were stuck on, when you have the brain space or heart room to experience the words for what they can be.

All of these books can be your favourites.

So can the books that make you laugh out loud on a train, making other people look at you and smile behind their masks. And the ones that make you think that you might fall in love again, one day. The one that your grandmother loved and you didn't really think that much of, but now that she's gone and you're older you feel the pull of her presence when you read it. The one you read on your first solo holiday, that kept you company as you learned how to eat alone at a table and appreciate the experience.

Books don't care how many favourites you have.

Favourite books love being in the company of other favourite books.

Choose. Don't choose. Have one favourite, or a hundred.

Reader, whatever you do, you are right.

You must be. It says so, here, in a book.

93

Loveday

Loveday is about to close for the day when she sees a man standing on the other side of the street, texting, a newspaper under his arm, glancing at the shop. Before she can really think about what she's seeing, Madison comes down the stairs and stands beside her. 'My dad wants to talk to you,' she says. 'Can he come in?'

'No,' Loveday says, 'but he can come closer.'

Craig approaches like an injured dog. Loveday isn't one for violence but if she was she would want to kick him. Madison is distraught, Kelly is in pieces, heaven only knows what his poor wife is going through. And all because he couldn't be honest: with himself, with his wife, with Kelly.

'Madison,' Craig says, and then, with less confidence, 'Loveday?'

'Yes,' Loveday and Madison say in unison. Craig looks ready to run. But he doesn't. He looks at Loveday.

'Madison tells me that there's been some damage to the shop.'

'Yes.'

Craig nods. 'It wasn't me.'

Loveday hears footfall on the stairs behind her; she waits, to see if Kelly will join them. Craig looks over her head, blanches, and says, 'Kelly.'

'Craig.'

Kelly obviously isn't going to come any closer. Craig, it seems, isn't going to stop looking at her. Loveday suspects that he really does love her – he has that broken air that only comes from utter heartbreak – but he's made his bed.

'You were saying that you didn't destroy the garden. I didn't think you did.'

'No.' Craig looks back at Loveday, and then at Madison, 'I was in isolation when it happened. And weak as water. I couldn't have left the house.'

Madison, her voice flat, says, 'He's telling the truth. Me and Mum had to take him meals. He was quite ill.'

Craig almost laughs, 'You can say that again. I've never felt worse in my life.'

'Well, boo-hoo,' Kelly says.

'I'm not asking for sympathy. I just wanted to tell Loveday – in person – that I didn't do the damage.'

'A phone call would have done,' Loveday says. She's about to shut the door, when Craig coughs. It's an I'm-about-to-make-a-speech cough, rather than the kind that starts and doesn't stop.

'But I did report you for Covid breaches,' he says. 'I'm sorry.'

'Dad!' Madison barks, at the same time as Kelly says, 'You absolute bastard.'

Loveday waits.

'I was,' he says, then stands up straighter. 'I was – that night you threw me out, Kelly—'

'After finding out you were married and didn't tell me?'

Craig hesitates, and Loveday thinks: if you decide to defend yourself, there's no hope for you. But Craig looks at his feet, then at Kelly, then back at Loveday. 'Kelly's right. I've no excuse. I could say, I was ill, I was hurt, I wasn't thinking straight. But I've no excuse. It was petty and I'm sorry. I was sitting in the car, trying to brace myself to go and talk to Jo, and I was thinking about sitting in the garden with Kelly. And the next thing I knew I was filling in a form on the government website.'

Loveday knows she ought to be angry but she can't quite muster up the energy. Just another moment where someone else's inability to cope is bumping up against her own life. 'Kelly invited you to sit in the garden when there was no one else here and you used that against us?'

Madison shakes her head. 'Dad.'

'I know,' Craig says.

'Well,' Loveday says, 'you're right. It was a petty thing to do. But I appreciate your apology.'

She nods, and then they are standing looking at each other, three women in various states of anger and disappointment, and a hangdog man.

'Well,' he says, and he turns away. There's a meniscus of feeling between Loveday, Kelly and Madison, holding them all back from saying anything else to him. Let him walk away, and feel the weight of their silence pushing at him.

He turns back.

'I meant to say. I'm really sorry about your friend.'

It's not clear which of them he's talking to. 'Which friend?'

Loveday asks, because Kelly and Madison are clearly both signed up to a 'say as little to Craig as possible' policy.

Craig holds out the newspaper. BELOVED HEADMISTRESS TAKEN BY COVID, reads the headline.

'No,' Loveday says. She takes the paper from Craig and scans the article, feeling Madison and Kelly's eyes on her. She reads aloud. Her voice fills with tears.

'Rosemary Athey is a name that will be familiar to many people who were educated in the York area. She was a well-known and well-loved teacher and headmistress with a career of more than forty years, a pillar of local school communities, and a tireless advocate for education throughout her career.

'Rosemary (or "Mrs Athey", as many of us would call her, through force of long habit) died in York Hospital after a short illness caused by Covid-19. She is believed to have spent less than forty-eight hours in hospital. Because of her age she may have been considered too vulnerable to go on to a ventilator.

'Sister Casey Ripley, who cared for Mrs Athey, could not comment on the case directly, but said, "It is always sad when one of our patients succumbs to Covid, and it's very hard that the rules mean that their loved ones may not be able to be with them. Please, everyone, take the rules seriously. Wear a mask, wash your hands, keep your distance."

'A nurse, Carol Johnson, who was taught by Mrs Athey – who was married to fellow long-serving Yorkshire teacher George Athey – said, "She was a wonderful woman. Always kind and fair-minded. A lot of people have a lot to thank her for."

'George Athey, who is believed to have suffered from

a milder form of the virus that did not require hospitalisation, was not available for comment. The couple had no family.'

Madison and Kelly are both crying by the time Loveday reaches the end of the article. Craig says, 'I assumed you'd have known.'

'No,' Loveday says, 'we had no idea.'

'Do you think she was in hospital when we went to see George and collect the plants? She wasn't there.' Loveday hates the thought of it but she has to say it. She, Kelly, Madison and Nathan have moved to the reading garden; the pavement felt too public for their grief. Craig had followed them through the shop and no one thought to stop him. Madison is stroking the leaves of the hosta; she is dry-eyed, now, but Kelly is still crying.

Nathan takes Loveday's hand. 'She might have been. She might have died by then.'

'We should have known,' Loveday says. She looks at Nathan; wants so much for him to say, there was no way to tell, or, there was nothing we could have done.

But all he does is wipe his eyes and say, 'I know.'

What would Loveday do?

Well, she wouldn't leave an old man to grieve alone.

'I'll go.'

Nathan nods. 'I'll drive you,' he says.

'It was just the two of them,' Kelly says. She seems to be talking to herself.

And now it's just George, Loveday thinks. George, who clearly isn't in the best of health.

'I'll close up here,' Kelly says.

'Can you manage? I mean, are you well enough?'

'I'll be fine.'

'I'll stay too,' Madison says, then puts her face in her hands, overcome with tears again. Craig holds his arms open, but it's Kelly who Madison, sobbing, launches herself at. Craig, after a moment's hesitation, puts his hand on Madison's back, rubbing. Then Kelly is crying too, and Craig, his face wearing a cautious sympathy, says, 'Kelly. I'm sorry.'

He puts an arm out to her. She ignores it, but she stays close.

Madison takes a deep breath, sniffs her tears back, and looks at Loveday. 'Take the book for him,' she says.

94

Loveday

George is in the garden when they arrive. Of course he is. He's not working, though. He has a spade; he's leaning on it, looking out over the sea, and he is still. So still. As Loveday makes her way along the path she wonders if it's possible that he can have died, too, that the spade is somehow supporting his cold body in place. But then he turns towards her, as she opens the gate at the bottom of the garden.

'George,' she says. 'It's Loveday. From Lost For Words.'

'Oh.' He seems to make some small effort at recognition, 'Hello.'

'George.' Loveday stands a conservative two metres away, and puts her free hand, to her surprise, to her heart. 'I'm so sorry about Rosemary.'

'Not as sorry as me.' He starts to cry; produces a handkerchief from his pocket and blows his nose.

Loveday tells herself, as firmly as she can, not to cry. She isn't here to be comforted by a man who's lost his life partner in the worst possible way. She's here to help him, if she can. To let him know that he has friends in the world.

She clutches the package containing the book to her, and she stands, opposite him.

Archie would put his hand on his chest, above his heart. She's done that. And then he would share his best memory of Rosemary.

But Loveday's brain won't do that. It's too soon to think of Rosemary, alive – and she cannot bear to think of her gone. All she can do is think of questions.

'When Nathan and I came for the plants. Had she died then?'

He nods.

'Oh, George. I wish you'd said.'

'After you'd gone, I could hear her. Clear as anything. Reading to me. And then, George Athey, you didn't even offer them a cup of tea. And you're not going to get through all of those biscuits on your own before they go soft, are you?'

'I'm so sorry, George.'

He nods again. 'She was frightened of being on her own. She thought she couldn't have done it. That's why she wanted to give you the plants.'

Loveday thinks of the Atheys' beautiful plants, safe, now, in the reading garden.

'We thought I was going first,' he says. 'I'm glad she hasn't had to do this. It's bleak, when you've spent your life with someone, and she's gone.'

George is looking out to sea. Loveday does the same. 'Are you – how did you manage? The funeral and everything? We would have helped.'

'There were plenty of people,' George says. 'I rang the first funeral director on the list and it was someone I had taught. She and her husband arranged everything. They said we could have a memorial when people can come together but I haven't the heart for it. If I'm here.'

'What do you need now?'

Loveday knows what the answer will be, and she's right.

'Me? Nothing.' His tone says, nothing except Rosemary.

'Is someone shopping for you? Would you like—' Loveday stops herself. He said he didn't want anything. She takes a breath and swallows her tears; it seems she can taste the salt running down her throat.

They stand. The sea is grey, today. 'I used to live in Whitby, when I was a girl.'

George smiles. 'You were lucky, then.'

Loveday isn't going to argue. She wasn't lucky then. She's sure as hell lucky now. She thinks of Nathan, in the car, listening to the radio, watching the world pass by, waiting for her, so he can drive her home.

'I came because I saw the news in the paper, about Rosemary, and I wanted to say you're part of our bookshop family. It's not much, I know. But we won't forget about you.'

'I don't know what I am, without Rosemary. She was . . .' He gestures, just a small movement of his free hand, but enough to convey: there are no words to ever express the depth and meaning of what my wife meant to me, every day of our lives.

And Loveday has one of those rare moments, where she knows exactly what to say, with her own words, not someone else's, from a book. 'She was what she was because you are what you are,' Loveday says.

And George looks at her and says, 'Yes.'

*   *   *

Loveday can't persuade George inside, but he does give her permission to go and make some tea. She finds the wherewithal for a sandwich, too, and carries it out, carefully, on a tray. Rosemary's basket is by the door, but Loveday can't imagine using it.

George is sitting on the bench.

'Is there a blanket?' Loveday asks.

'I'm not cold,' George says, and she can see he's telling the truth. The air will chill soon, but for now the sun is hanging in. And the sea is hypnotic. Loveday puts a mug of tea into George's hands, and watches as he drinks in silence.

'She liked you. All of you.' George puts the empty mug down next to him.

'She asked us to arrange a gift for you,' Loveday says. 'Before she caught Covid. I think it was for your birthday.'

George nods. 'That was yesterday,' he says. 'I shouldn't be getting older if she isn't.'

'Here,' Loveday says. She wishes now that she'd wrapped the copy of *The Secret Garden*, rather than handing it over in a paper bag. But perhaps birthday wrapping would be too much.

He takes it out of the bag, turns it over in his hands. He looks at the cover, the spine, the back cover. Back to the picture on the front again.

And look. He's smiling. Loveday (well, Rosemary) has made him smile.

'She asked you to get this?'

'Yes,' Loveday says. 'She was very specific about it being this edition. She said it was the one you had when you were a boy.'

'It is.' He's turning the pages. His fingers are clumsy at first, but they soon find a rhythm.

'I'm glad.' Loveday lets herself cry, just a little, quietly. George isn't looking at her. She may as well not be there; it's the best possible feeling she could have right now.

'Have you read this?' George asks.

'I have,' Loveday says, 'a long time ago. I thought I was Mary.'

George laughs. 'I thought I was Dickon.'

'You are,' Loveday says, looking around. 'See what you've done here.'

George waves a hand. 'Just patience.'

Patience and love, Loveday thinks, but she doesn't say so. He seems fragile enough.

'My Rosie arranged this with you?'

'She did.'

George smiles. 'The time was I imagined I'd read it to my children. But you never know what's going to happen, do you?' He puts the book on his lap, and presses it there, tightly, with both hands.

'You don't,' Loveday says. She thinks: except, in a book you've read before. And maybe, if you've made it yourself, in a garden.

95

Kelly

Kelly thought she would find Lost For Words being open to the public again stressful. But once she and Loveday had worked out how it could all be managed, with limited numbers and a one-way system, and bookings for the reading garden, she had started to look forward to it. Now, a week after the restrictions were lifted, she's completely happy in this cautious new world. Or she would be, if she wasn't so tired. She's not used to so much interaction, and it's draining her energy in a way she wouldn't have thought possible before the pandemic.

She wouldn't dream of complaining, though. The gentleness of readers is perfect when held against her slowly healing heart. She didn't realise how much she'd missed conversations about books, and the weather, and what a pain it is to get parked in York. And the recommendations! She and Loveday have been so busy prescribing books to others that they've forgotten the thrill of a customer coming in, picking up a book, and saying, 'Oh! Have you read this? You must.' Readers are the only people who Kelly will allow to tell her what to do.

Madison comes down the stairs. 'Do you think Loveday will give me a job when I leave school?' she asks. 'It's brilliant when people don't know what book they want and you can find it.' She laughs. She's been doing more of that lately. She's a good kid, Kelly thinks. Craig and his wife must have done something right.

'You've had a good day, then?'

'Yeah,' Madison says. Then, shuffling her feet, she brandishes her phone at Kelly. 'There's this old film I want to see but my mates don't. I think it used to be a book? *Wuthering Heights*. I don't mind going on my own but I thought you might want to come? It's tomorrow afternoon.'

Kelly is going to see her dad tomorrow, but he won't mind if she leaves straight after lunch. Especially as he's invited Sarah-Jane too. He can give her a lift back later, if he wants to. Time with her father is so much easier to come by now. 'You're on.'

Just then, the door opens, and a woman pushing a buggy comes in. She looks tired. A toddler bounces in behind: 'I would like a book about elephants!' he declares to the shop and everyone in it.

'Fact or fiction?' Madison asks.

The child says, firmly, 'I would like a storybook please,' before looking back at his mother.

'You can go with the lady, Tommy,' she says, and the child follows Madison. Then, to Kelly, 'Loveday brought us books during the lockdown and we were so grateful. I hadn't read a book for such a long time. Now it's all I do. Apart from look after the kids.'

There's something in the way that the woman speaks that stops Kelly from making a comment about it being a good life. Instead, she asks if there's anything else the woman needs, and goes to find books 5 and 6 in the *Anne of Green Gables* series.

When she returns, Madison has brought Tommy back, and he is sitting on the floor with his book. His mother is wiping her eyes.

'Is everything all right?' People do get overwhelmed, from being out in the world.

'Yes. No,' the woman says, then, glancing at her son to see that he's not paying any attention to her, 'My husband died. Of Covid. Sometimes it just – I miss him with my whole heart.'

'Of course you do,' Kelly says. She wasn't much of a hugger before Covid but now she wants to embrace everyone. Instead, she finds that she puts her hands together, presses her fingers to her lips, as though she's praying.

'Yes,' the woman says, and Kelly realises: this must be Zoe, that Loveday talks about. She almost calls for Loveday, but she stops herself. This woman hasn't come here to be the centre of attention. She hasn't asked for Loveday. She wanted books for her and her kid.

After the little family has left, Madison fetches her jacket. 'My dad's picking me up,' she says, with an apologetic half-smile in Kelly's direction. 'He's taking me to see his new flat.'

'Have a good time,' Kelly says, and she means it. She wishes Craig no ill, now. But she's not even thinking about romance until she's got her doctorate, has had at least one article published, and got through the piles of newly acquired books waiting to be sorted upstairs. That's at least two years of celibacy, which sounds about right.

In the reading garden, Loveday and Nathan are sitting

on the bench. When George called and asked them to collect it, a month after Rosemary's death, Loveday had wanted to refuse. But Sarah-Jane had pointed out that George would be going into a hospice whether she took the bench or not, and so she and Nathan had gone to fetch it. George had come out on the street to wave them off. 'Don't worry about me,' he'd said to Loveday. 'I'm ready. Rosemary wasn't, but I am.' Loveday had cried half the way back to York, and that night, after hours of quietness, she had said to Nathan, 'I will never be ready to lose you.'

'No,' Nathan had said. 'I'll never be ready to lose you either.'

Since then, they have been closer than ever. Loveday has stopped pretending she is wholly separate. Nathan has stopped pretending he is always happy. They talk about the future, sometimes.

Now the bench is sanded smooth, re-stained, and repaired; Sarah-Jane made some cushions, and Nathan and Loveday have got into the habit of spending a few minutes of the day here. It might be Loveday's favourite place.

'Oh,' Nathan says, 'Bella came by. She's invited us to dinner.'

'I'm game if you are.'

Nathan laughs. 'I'm never turning down an invitation again. And I bet she can cook. If she can't, it will be an anecdote.'

Loveday laughs back. 'I think we might have had our best day,' she says. 'I mean, takings-wise. I want more days. Even better than this one.' When did this happen to me? she wonders. When did I start to look forward? When did I begin to . . . to expect? To hope? It would be strange, she thinks, if a pandemic has done this to her. But life is always strange, in her experience.

'I'm proud of you,' Nathan says. 'What you've made here. It's so much more than a bookshop.'

Loveday shakes her head, then rests her head against his shoulder. 'Nothing is more than a bookshop.'

And she closes her eyes and wonders how many people there are, right now, turning the pages of a book that she and Archie, Kelly and Madison and Loveday and Sarah-Jane, have put into their hands.

96

Jennifer is reading to Milo, who is warm and soft after his bath. She has started to walk barefoot around their flat; she no longer feels that she has to be ready to run, to get out, to find safety, at any moment. She has safety, here. And she has a new book, *Agnes Grey* by Anne Brontë, to read later. She went into Lost For Words on Wednesday, when Milo was at nursery, and she bought it. It felt beautifully everyday. Even if she is still looking over her shoulder, just in case.

Jamie has an assistant manager who works the Saturday night shift, so Jamie is driving home. He'll go for a run and then he'll finish the last few pages of *Wild*. It's his favourite of the books so far. He's wondering if he should try to tackle an epic walk like that.

Adjoa has started passing books on to her mum, who reads much faster than she does, so there's a pleasing urgency to her reading time. She puts down any book where she sees white-saviouring or black-best-friending.

Bella has an audition to play Amanda Wingfield in a tour of Tennessee Williams' *The Glass Menagerie*. She thinks she's too young for the part, but she's going to give it a go. Nothing ventured, nothing gained!! She doesn't have a lot of time for reading now her social life is up and running again, but she's determined to keep in touch with Loveday and Nathan, who have proved to be excellent dinner guests. Nathan's business with the chocolate coins never stops being funny.

Casey is thinking of retraining as a palliative care nurse. She has found a charity shop on her walk to work; she sometimes goes and picks up a book. She's reading *Gone With the Wind* by Margaret Mitchell, and a few pages when she gets into bed seems to help her sleep.

Hozan and Zhilwan have their house to themselves again, although, once a month at least, both of the children come for the day and bring their families. Being back at the university means Hozan misses most of the *EastEnders* conversation between Zhilwan and Lorraine, but he usually sees Claire and Arthur at the weekends. They are sometimes invited over for supper. Lorraine's dolma was not the best he's ever eaten, but the fact that she made it almost brought him to tears. Loveday has found Hozan a book he doesn't have on Kurdish politics, and another on South American bridges.

97

Loveday

Loveday and Kelly leave through the reading garden. Even now, in late September, it's well used until the last minute of the day. Loveday locks the gate behind them. The wood is warm under her hand. It's been another good day at Lost For Words. Kelly and Loveday took it in turns at the pharmacy counter. Trixie, who is learning the ropes more quickly than Loveday would have thought possible, worked with Madison on the till, and the two of them advised and sold and helped readers to find what they were looking for. It's hard to believe that this time last year Loveday was afraid that the business would fail, and then convinced that the pandemic would finish it. Business is as good as it has ever been, and Loveday is proud: of the shop, and of the work she, Kelly, Madison, Nathan and now Trixie have put in to make it a success, when Lost For Words could so easily have slipped away. The pandemic isn't over, but between the vaccine and their no-mask-no-entry rule, Loveday feels, they are over the worst.

It's quiet in the car as Loveday drives them along the road

across the moors that will take them to Whitby. Saturdays in the shop are so busy that they're both shattered and talked-out by the end of the day. The time was when Loveday would rather have headed straight for home. But life is different now.

'It's a shame Madison couldn't come tonight,' Kelly says. 'Good that she's seeing Craig, though.'

Loveday says, 'Yes,' though what she means is, *I have no idea how you are so good at dealing with all this*. Kelly's suspected long Covid – tiredness, sickness, everything tasting strange – was actually an unsuspected baby. Now four months pregnant, she seems happy about it; and Madison is picking out names from her favourite books for her half-sibling. (This week she has suggested Scout, after *To Kill a Mockingbird*, or Stanley, for the boy in Louis Sachar's *Holes*.) Loveday often hears Kelly and Madison laughing together. She isn't sure what they are doing to make a relationship, but it seems to be working.

Loveday and Kelly are on their way to see Kelly's father, Neil, and Sarah-Jane, who is spending more and more time with him. She says she's too old for a boyfriend, but that definitely seems to be what Neil is. Nathan and Vanessa drove over earlier in the day; Vanessa has come back for a long weekend between jobs, now the world is getting back to normal. There's going to be supper, and a film; although they've had a few of these get-togethers now, and they always say there'll be a film, and then they sit around the table until midnight, just talking and being together.

And Loveday cannot wait to spend time with them all. Her family has grown, during this time when the world

406

shrank; and, instead of feeling lost and scared in a world she can no longer touch the edges of, being part of a big and happy family is a pleasure and a joy.

On a par with reading a book.

The Books

The Professor and Lorraine: Books for a Neighbourly Support Bubble

Michael Bond, *Paddington Bear*

June Brown, *From the Year Dot*

Claudia Roden, *A Book of Middle Eastern Food*

Mo: Books for a Person Who Misses Small, Inconsequential Conversations

Fredrik Backman, *A Man Called Ove*

Christina Baker Kline, *A Piece of the World*

Grégoire Delacourt, *The List of my Desires*

George Eliot, *Middlemarch*

Mark Twain, *The Adventures of Tom Sawyer*

Bryony: Books for a Sleepless Crime Fan

Wilkie Collins, *The Woman in White*

Helen Dunmore, *Birdcage Walk*

Gillian Flynn, *Gone Girl*

C. J. Sansom, *Dissolution*
Muriel Spark, *The Prime of Miss Jean Brodie*
Josephine Tey, *The Daughter of Time*

Madison's Mum: Tall Hats, Big Dresses and Horses (And Some for When You're Furious)
Maeve Binchy, *Circle of Friends*
Jilly Cooper, *Riders*
Emma Donoghue, *Room*
Georgette Heyer, *The Grand Sophy*
Celeste Ng, *Everything I Never Told You*
Amy Poelher, *Yes Please*

Madison: Not Too Many Wizards
Maya Angelou, *I Know Why The Caged Bird Sings*
Margaret Atwood, *The Handmaid's Tale*
Charlotte Brontë, *Jane Eyre*
Kazuo Ishiguro, *Never Let Me Go*
Ursula K. Le Guin, *A Wizard of Earthsea*
Caitlin Moran, *How to Build a Girl*
Patrick Ness, *The Knife of Never Letting Go*
Alice Oseman, *Solitaire*
J. D. Salinger, *The Catcher in the Rye*
Dodie Smith, *I Capture the Castle*
Sarah Waters, *Fingersmith*

Zoe: Books to Absorb Children – and Their Mother
Tove Jansson, *The Book About Moomin, Mymble and Little My*
L. M. Montgomery, *Anne of Green Gables*
Nadia Shireen, *Billy and the Dragon*
Max Velthuijs, *Frog and the Wide World*

Paul Pritchard: Books For Someone Who Wants Fiction To Bring Ideas To Life

Kate Atkinson, *Transcription*

Michael Dobbs, *House of Cards*

Anthony Doerr, *All the Light We Cannot See*

Amitav Ghosh, *Sea of Poppies*

Val McDermid, *Union Jack*

Chris Mullin, *A Very British Coup*

Bella: Everyday Books About Everyday Things

Margaret Atwood, *The Blind Assassin*

Anne Brontë, *The Tenant of Wildfell Hall*

Liza Dalby, *The Tale of Murasaki*

Paul Gallico, *Flowers for Mrs Harris*

Nella Last, *Nella Last's War: The Second World War Diaries of 'Housewife, 49'*

Charlotte Perkins Gilman, 'The Yellow Wallpaper'

Maria Semple, *Where'd You Go, Bernadette*

Craig: Books for Someone In Love And Out Of His Depth

Gabriel García Márquez, *Love in the Time of Cholera*

Kahlil Gibran, *The Prophet*

Lily King, *Euphoria*

Ann Patchett, *Bel Canto*

Jennifer: Old Favourites

George Eliot, *The Mill on the Floss*

Thomas Hardy, *Tess of the D'Urbervilles*

Toni Morrison, *Beloved*

Jean Rhys, *Wide Sargasso Sea*

Donna Tartt, *The Secret History*

Milo: Bedtime Reading
Ludwig Bemelmans, *Madeline*
Werner Holzwarth, *The Story of the Little Mole Who Knew It Was None of His Business*
Tove Jansson, *Moomin and the Wishing Star*
Laura Numeroff, *If You Give a Mouse a Cookie*
Maurice Sendak, *Where the Wild Things Are*

Jonno: Books for Someone To Whom Nothing Seems Funny
Oyinkan Braithwaite, *My Sister, the Serial Killer*
Patrick deWitt, *The Sisters Brothers*
Ottessa Moshfegh, *My Year of Rest and Relaxation*
Helen Oyeyemi, *Mr Fox*
Terry Pratchett, *The Colour of Magic*
David Sedaris, *Me Talk Pretty One Day*

Adjoa: Books That Represent Difference With Joy
Sebastian Barry, *Days Without End*
Sara Collins, *The Confessions of Frannie Langton*
Vanessa Diffenbaugh, *The Language of Flowers*
Bernadine Evaristo, *Girl, Woman, Other*
Yaa Gyasi, *Homegoing*
Laline Paull, *The Bees*
Tara Westover, *Educated*

Simone: Books to Get You Away From Here
Eileen Chang, *Lust, Caution*
Homer's *Odyssey* (translated by Emily Wilson)
Toshikazu Kawaguchi, *Before the Coffee Gets Cold* (translated by Geoffrey Trousselot)
Per Petterson, *Out Stealing Horses*

Jamie: Books to Read in the Middle of the Night
Khaled Hosseini, *The Kite Runner*
Miranda Mellis, *None of This is Real*
Erin Morgenstern, *The Night Circus*
Cheryl Strayed, *Wild*
Chris Yates, *Nightwalk*

Max and Kate: Books That Embrace Worlds of Equality and Equity
Becky Albertalli, *Simon vs. the Homo Sapiens Agenda*
Kristin Cashore, the 'Graceling Realm' novels
Becky Chambers, *The Long Way to a Small, Angry Planet*
Ursula K. Le Guin, *The Left Hand of Darkness*
E. Lockhart, *We Were Liars*

Jay: Pure, Escapist Terror
Lauren Beukes, *The Shining Girls*
Joël Dicker, *The Truth About the Harry Quebert Affair*
Neil Gaiman, *Coraline*
Shirley Jackson, *The Haunting of Hill House*
Stephen King, *Pet Sematary*
H. P. Lovecraft, *'The Call Of Cthulhu' and Other Weird Stories*
Daphne du Maurier, *Rebecca*
Silvia Morena-Garcia, *Mexican Gothic*
Bram Stoker, *Dracula*

Helen: Books That Make Me Feel That It's Okay to Be Me
Min Jin Lee, *Pachinko*
Maggie O'Farrell, *I Am, I Am, I Am*
Barbara Pym, *Excellent Women*
Kiley Reid, *Such A Fun Age*

413

Ella Risbridger, *Midnight Chicken*
Carol Shields, *The Stone Diaries*
John Williams, *Stoner*

Trix: Books to Fix Heartbreak

Diana Athill, *Instead of a Letter*
Charlotte Brontë, *Jane Eyre*
Patricia Highsmith, *The Price of Salt*
bell hooks, *All About Love*
Madeline Miller, *The Song of Achilles*
Sally Rooney, *Conversations With Friends*

George and Rosemary: Books for a Lifetime

Jane Austen, *Persuasion*
Frances Hodgson Burnett, *The Secret Garden*
Lewis Carroll, *Alice in Wonderland* (original illustrations by
    John Tenniel; newer by Helen Oxenbury)
Ian McEwan, *Atonement*
Sue Monk Kidd, *The Secret Life of Bees*
Dodie Smith, *I Capture the Castle*
Edith Wharton, *The Age of Innocence*

And Some More Books You Might Find of Use

Jane Austen, *Mansfield Park*
Elizabeth Barrett Browning
Judy Blume, *Are You There, God? It's Me, Margaret*
Clare Chambers, *Small Pleasures*
Roald Dahl, *Matilda*
Caroline Dooner, *The F*ck It Diet*
Kate Forsyth, *Bitter Greens*
Jane Gardam, *A Long Way from Verona*

James Herriot, *All Creatures Great and Small*
Andrew Kaufman, *All My Friends Are Superheroes*
Marian Keyes, *Sushi for Beginners*
Harper Lee, *To Kill a Mockingbird*
Carson McCullers, *The Heart Is A Lonely Hunter*
Alice Munro, *Dear Life*
Sylvia Plath, *The Bell Jar*
Louis Sachar, *Holes*
Emily St. John Mandel, *Station Eleven*

Questions for Book-sharers

1. *"I don't think any of us should be even trying to be brave. We just need to keep going."*

Many of the characters in *Found in a Bookshop* do act with courage – pandemic-related or not. Whose bravery stands out the most to you?

2. *Found in a Bookshop* features some of the same characters as Stephanie Butland's earlier novel, *Lost For Words*. Did you read *Found in a Bookshop* as a standalone novel, or after reading *Lost For Words*? Do you think it makes a difference?

3. *"George is quiet to begin with, because he cannot balance small talk with the overwhelming feeling of rightness that comes over him when Rosemary is there."*

George and Rosemary's is a lifelong love story, but it's one firmly rooted in everyday life: the joys of gardening, tea-drinking and peaceful routines. Is love like this is rare, or ordinary? What makes an authentic 'love story', in your opinion?

4. Many of the characters in *Found in a Bookshop* look to books as an escape. What kind of books, films or TV lift you up and bring you joy? Are books that distract you from current affairs worth any less than books with an important message?

5. "*Because no one has been allowed out much, everyone is much more kind and polite than they used to be to a barmaid who has seen better days!!*"

Found in a Bookshop is a story about the people behind the counter, or stocking the shelves – the people we might often take for granted. Has the novel made you more likely now to ask for recommendations from booksellers?

6. "'*But,*' Madison says, '*everyone makes mistakes. That's what you people are always saying. Make mistakes and learn from them. Say sorry and move on.*'"

Do you think Kelly made the right decision for her relationship? Which character did you relate to most, in terms of the conclusions they came to at the end of the novel?

7. "*Once, they had bought books one at a time, and read aloud so they would experience the pleasure of the pages, the first time, together. She's not sure when they stopped. When they got too busy, she supposes. Or when owning a book became less of a luxury.*"

Have you ever read a book or a poem aloud to someone, or had one read aloud to you? What could be the pleasures of sharing a book in this way – and the less-pleasurable aspects?

Acknowledgements

First and foremost, I'd like to thank booksellers, book bloggers, readers, reviewers, bookshop-browsers, librarians, library users, book groups, book Twitter, book Instagram, and everyone who knows that books can help. You are the people who know what books can do, and I'm happy to be one of your number. I'm also grateful to you for the way you recognised Loveday, who I first wrote about in *Lost For Words*, and took her to your hearts.

Oli Munson has been my agent for more than a decade. He's always championed and supported me and my writing – and has been absolutely heroic during the planning and writing of this novel. Thank you, Oli. You know.

I've had the privilege to work with two exceptional editors on this novel. Thank you, Eli Dryden (who had the original idea) and Marion Donaldson, for your insight, patience, intelligence, and encouragement. I've learned so much from working with you both.

The novel in your hand (or on your screen) needs input, professionalism and excellence from a lot of people in the publishing world. Thank you, Harmony Leung, Rosanna Hildyard, Flora McMichael, Sarah Bance, Kate Truman, Sophie Ellis, Chris Keith-Wright, Rebecca Bader, Isabelle Wilson, Zoe Giles, Rhys Callaghan.

Thank you CoT: Carys Bray, Sarah Franklin, Shelley Harris. I don't know what I'd do without you.

Beta readers really help to shape a novel, as well as saving me from my own ignorance. Thank you Alan Butland, Susan Young, Sharon Davis, and Sazan M Mandalawi. Thanks too to the Garsdale crew of Spring 2022, who were my first audience and were (and remain) super-supportive and helpful.

In order to write this novel I've spent a lot of time reading about the pandemic. I'm grateful to everyone who has been brave and public-spirited enough to share their stories, on social media, in online and print journalism, and in books. I see you. Thank you.

My research included these books, all of which are accounts of pandemic medicine:

Intensive Care: A GP, a Community & a Pandemic – Gavin Francis
A Nurse's Story: My Life in A&E During the Covid Crisis – Louise Curtis with Sarah Johnson
Duty of Care – Dr Dominic Pimenta
Breathtaking – Rachel Clarke
Catch Your Breath – Ed Patrick

Paul Pritchard – thank you for telling me about your father.

Richard Morris – thank you for inspiring me to try making an opera cake!

And finally, thank you to the people who love me and make it possible for me to live this life: my dear friends, my husband Alan, my children Ned and Joy, my dad, and beloved Auntie Susan.